Praise for Faith O'Shea

Faith O'Shea is a contemporary women's literature writer who loves writing about romance, magic, conviction, and loyalty, with strong women and the friendships they build. She has created many series of stories to make us laugh, cry and feel empowered and writes in a voice that speaks to women of all ages. Faith believed there were subjects and life that needed to be written about. ~ Loyce M.

I truly love the Everyday Goddess series. The strong, leading women characters, in this day and age, are inspiring to me and keep me coming back for more! The books are light, fun, extremely relatable and I can't put them down! ~ Kathryn B.

I just finished the Fire and Ice series. It had romance, strong friendships between the women characters and complex stories that were clearly very well researched. Loved all of them and looking forward to the goddess series next! ~ Gail N.

Books by Faith O'Shea

The Greenliner Series
Four baseball players, one team on the rise

Thrown for a Curve
League of Her Own
Clutch Hit
Out in Left Field

The Scalera Family Series
Five boisterous Italian siblings, five ways to find love

Cold Sweat
Edge of Forever
Thin Blue Line
Coming Home to You
Finding Joy

The Fire and Ice Series
One law firm, six partners, friends to the end

Consumed by Fire
Skoli on Ice
Heart on Fire
Heart of Ice
Tendril of Ice
Rekindling the Fire

The Everyday Goddesses Series
One extraordinary café and a circle of magical friends

Magic Bean Café
Once There Was a Tree
Tipping the Scales

FIRE AND ICE

One law firm, six partners, friends to the end

Consumed by Love

Nell Warren has just won a Supreme Court victory but it comes at a cost in the form of Congressman Jack Adams. They've got a past, and he wants to resurrect it, but she's not sure. There's a problem still lingering in the shadows. Will he be able to convince her, he's in it for good this time?

Skoli on Ice

Camille Bissonnette's expertise is asylum, and she's done some work, for the FBI. When they drop Maksim Skolikovsky in her lap, she's not sure if he's a spy, a journalist or someone more dangerous. The Russian trusts no one, for good reason. Will she be able to prove she's his fighter, or will he cut her loose, in fear for his life?

Heart on Fire

Emilia Spenser-Ronan deals with families in crisis, and her best friend, Nick Katsaros's is a mess right now. He calls her his lifesaver, but she's feeling like a two-pound whirly sucker. She drops him flat, just as he's seeing her in a new light. Will the college besties find their way back to each other?

Heart of ICE

Jelani Ramirez has been looking for love in all the wrong places, but there's no way Alec Cleland is in the right one. He's a member of ICE, part of Homeland Security, and she's sure he has a heart to match. Will it take more than his smile to melt away her misgivings?

Tendrils of Ice

Arianna Woodley, original partner of Woodley and Fisher, has spent her life nurturing the firm since her divorce but when her ex-husband, Evan Cox, makes a run for governor, she throws her hat in the ring. When time spent together begins to heal the fractures in her heart, he asks if she's willing to go back and change the ending. Can she trust him enough to try?

Rekindling the Fire

Mia Fisher's life is unraveling and she's ready to leave it all behind, and that includes her husband Nate, an FBI analyst. He's inattentive, work-driven and useless when it comes to keeping the home-fires burning. When he realizes she's serious, he commits to doing whatever it takes to keep her in his life. Will he be able to keep his promise?

Consumed by Fire

Fire & Ice Series
Book 1

FAITH O'SHEA

Cover Design by Jaycee DeLorenzo at Sweet 'N' Spicy Designs
Formatted by Woven Red Author Services, www.wovenRed.ca

Consumed by Fire/Sue Campbell writing as Faith O'Shea-1st Edition
ISBN ebook: 978-0-99-96806-0-5
ISBN print book: 978-0-99-96806-1-2

To My Readers

Over the last year there have been many changes in life, government, and politics. Immigrants are being deported in record numbers, Dreamers are being forced to stop dreaming, first amendment rights are being assaulted, and extremism is expanding its base. It has created anxiety for many and I am one of the many.

The four stories that make up the series *Fire and Ice* touch on some of the issues being confronted today by undocumented residents and citizens alike. The heroines are strong women, lawyers who have decided to make a difference, each with their own area of expertise. Nell, Camille, Emilia and Jelani are partners, friends and comprise the support system needed to fight in the trenches. They come from different cultures, different economic backgrounds, different parentage, and each of them live with a wound that makes them human.

Consumed by Fire is the story of Nell and Jack. My imagination began churning a story line after a trip I made to the Franklin Roosevelt homestead. I've always loved Eleanor's strength and character, so I purchased one of her biographies. During the reading, the seeds were planted: a child deprived became a female warrior and a man pampered and spoiled found his own voice.

I hope something resonates with you and this couple, and you enjoy their journey back to one another.

Please feel free to contact me at my website www.faithoshea.com and follow me on Facebook and Twitter.

CHAPTER ONE

Nell Warren sat at her desk, still picking at the salad her assistant had brought her hours ago, anxiously awaiting the decision. It should have been posted online this morning and she'd already logged in five times, in between client appointments and phone calls.

Nothing.

Impatient for an outcome, she glanced at the antique clock sitting on her credenza, the time ticking away much too slowly and gave it another try.

As soon as the face page of the website appeared on screen, her heart began to race and her fingertips tingled. Pausing for just a moment, she clicked onto the opinion page and held her breath as her eyes scanned the document.

Unable to believe what she was reading, she began again, scanning the paragraphs in astonishment. She'd hoped…but never really believed…

"My God. You won. Nell, you won!"

Jelani was running down the hall, her voice raised a thousand decibels above normal. She careened into the door on her way into Nell's office.

Announcing so the world could hear what they'd all thought impossible to achieve.

Arianna Woodley and Mia Fisher came bolting out of their offices, Emilia Spencer-Ronan and Camille Bissonnette following, clients left behind as the lawyers congregated in a cluster of squeals, smiles and high fives.

Once a lonely little girl with no one to share things with, Nell had felt invisible most of her life. She'd come a long way. She was now surrounded by friends who would celebrate her success and this win just as they would have grieved with her if she'd lost. They were her sisters. All newly minted attorneys when they joined Woodley and Fisher within a year of each other, they came from differing backgrounds, cultures and continents. The firm had been in its infancy, Mia and Arianna the foundation as founding partners, and they had all worked tirelessly to make it one of the best in the city. It didn't start out as a haven for women and their rights, but it had become the dominant force dealing with immigration, rape, inequity in the workplace, sexual harassment, domestic violence, and discrimination.

She looked at each face with an expression of disbelief. Words slowly tumbled from her mouth in an almost whispered breath.

"I won!"

Lawyers, assistants, and aides were peering out of doorways, all of them knowing the time and dedication Nell had put into this. It was not only a victory for her individually but for the office as well. Woodley and Fisher had an impeccable reputation, in no small part because of the woman being congratulated. This would only add to it.

"I can get Ramona out of detention. She's free. I can't believe it."

Jelani hugged Nell, bouncing her up and down in excitement.

When she released her, she asked more seriously, "What was the vote?"

"Five to three."

Mia, standing by the window of the corner office, her arms crossed casually against her chest, asked, "Who wrote the opinion?"

"The Chief Justice."

"Who was the deciding vote?"

Nell's voice held a tinge of awe. "The Chief Justice."

"This is huge."

Coming out of her stupor, Nell smiled and said frantically, "I've set precedent. Maybe this will open the door, even if it's just a crack."

Arianna was standing across from her, a bemused smile on her face. She'd accompanied her as second chair, her first appearance in the Court chamber after twenty-five years as an attorney, spending most of that time in the District Attorney's office.

"It seems I wasn't the only one impressed with your performance."

Then as if it registered again, Arianna came around and hugged Nell. "You've won a Supreme Court case!"

Nell's assistant popped her head in, a broad smile on her face. "Congrats, boss. You have a call on line two. It's someone from the congressional office on immigration. And someone from *The Globe* on line one."

Most of the faces in the office registered surprise, especially Nell's.

The bigwigs in Washington had been paying attention and main stream media wanted an interview.

Arianna's face showed her concern.

"I have a feeling the powers that be are going to try to draft you for more important work. Winning a case of this magnitude will give you the opportunity to work on a much larger scale than out of an office in downtown Boston."

Her expression gave away her sinking heart and she moaned, "I'm not letting you go anywhere."

She turned to Nell's administrative assistant.

"You'd better cancel all her afternoon appointments. I think it's going to get busy around here."

Nell shut her cell off, the pings coming one after another, planning to sort through them later.

After announcing she'd take the call from Washington first, Nell asked Hani to see if she could re-arrange her schedule rather than cancel all her appointments. This was important but so were the clients who'd carved time out of their day to see her.

"Just give me some time to take these calls. Afterwards, screen the rest and send in only the most important."

"Sure thing. And Nell, kudos. You deserve this."

"I couldn't have done it without you." Glancing at Emilia, she added, "Or you."

The two women smiled at the acknowledgment and Hani backed out of the space.

Sitting back down at her desk, her partners filtering out to give her some privacy, Nell took a moment before picking up the land line.

"This is Nell Warren."

"Nell, this is Zelda Nilsson. I'm a congresswoman on the Judiciary subcommittee for Immigration and Border Control. I just read the opinion and wanted to congratulate you. This is a major coup for our side."

"Thank you, Congresswoman Nilsson. I appreciate you taking the time to call me."

Zelda's reputation was legendary. Anyone interested in the direction of the country knew of it.

She'd been in Congress for decades, was one of the voices that spoke out for the less advantaged, and was a leader in the march for immigration reform.

"I read the transcript of the oral argument the day you gave it and found it a compelling one. After it came out, you were put on the short list of lawyers we wanted to join the congressional committees on immigration. I've been following the case closely, and when the slip opinion came out today, I was very pleased. You've certainly made a name for yourself. And please, call me Zelda, at least in private."

"I'm just relieved that my client will finally be released and returned to her family."

Ramona had spent two years in the deportation center, her children without a mother. A Haitian immigrant who'd fled the endemic poverty and political instability over twenty years ago and settled in Dorchester, she was given a temporary work authorization which had expired, and was told to prepare and arrange for deportation. It was an all-too-familiar story, and Nell had heard it over and over throughout the years. Undocumented residents who lived, worked, married, and had children here were no safer than those who had just arrived. It was always the children who suffered.

"There are still far too many who won't have you to represent them. So many parents still left at risk without any real pathway to citizenship."

"I know. I'll be using this precedent for years to come."

It still confounded her that it would be her own precedent. And a thrill went through her.

"Which leads me to the other reason I called you, Nell."

"Which is?"

"Any hope we had about a regaining a majority is dead in the water which means the job I wanted to offer on the congressional staff would never be approved. With the new administration's rumblings about immigration, wall, borders, travel ban, we feel it imperative to line up specialists who can help us fight what they try to put in place. I would very much like for you to join our team as a consultant. Representative Conlin, the ranking member of the Constitution and Civil Justice subcommittee, wants to begin a discourse on constitutional law and First Amendment rights and how we can protect those most vulnerable. He'd like you to be a witness at some of the hearings we've got scheduled. He'll be calling you later today."

There was a pause that Nell didn't know whether to fill or not, until Zelda went on, telling her what she already knew.

"I'm expecting it to get highly contentious across the aisle. Jeannette Rankin will be writing policy and defining the legality of imposed restrictions. I'm sure you've heard of her."

Jeannette Rankin had thirty years of experience in immigration law and had won several groundbreaking cases over the course of her career. Today she was on the staff of the congressional committee that drafted the bills sent to the floor. Working with her would be a dream come true.

"Everyone's heard of her. And I'm certainly honored by the invitation but I'm not sure that I have that kind of time to spare. Or the patience. I don't play well with others when there's truth and justice at stake."

"I know what you mean. And I'm sorry to say I believe it's only going to get worse. It's more important than ever that we're vigilant, with the rights of so many at risk."

Currently, Zelda was the ranking member of Immigration and Border Security, but on the minority side. If the Democrats had regained control of the house, she would have been heading the immigration reform task-force, but it hadn't worked out as planned or predicted and everyone was scrambling to put their world back on its axis. Millions would be in limbo. Or on the other side of the proposed wall.

Working with Zelda would put her on the front line of the resistance, but she'd be on that front line no matter where she was. She preferred to wage the war from here.

"I'm not sure it's in my best interest."

"When you're called to public service, Nell, it's not your best interest that's important but the country's. I do hope you'll agree to at least come and talk to us. I want to pick your brain."

Nell knew she couldn't turn down an interview even though she'd never make the move, wouldn't even think about it.

"I will do that...Zelda. When would you like me to come to Washington?"

"As soon as possible. I am chomping at the bit to get our ducks in a row. We need to have certain parameters in place. We have no idea what the administration is up to. All we know is how divisive it's become."

Nell flipped through her day book, scanning her appointments, mentally juggling it in her head to see where she could carve out some time.

"I've got a full schedule that I'll have to re-arrange, but it looks like next Tuesday might work."

She let the pages slip through her fingers, sat back in her chair waiting for a response.

"We're on recess next week. I know I shouldn't ask you to shuffle things around, but could you come tomorrow?"

Nell's eyes went back to her day book. She had several appointments that she could probably move although she didn't like rescheduling. Her clients were important to her and she felt they deserved her time and attention.

"It couldn't wait until after your break?"

"Then we're in the opening session of the new Congress. There'll be so much to do, I'd prefer to get this done before hand."

Pausing, weighing her options, Nell finally agreed.

"I'll have my assistant book a flight down. Can I call you when I have things in order?"

"Absolutely. Call and speak to my personal assistant. She'll arrange everything from point of touchdown."

"I will. And thank you. It would be an honor to meet the people you mentioned."

It was a dream come true. These were the lawyers she modeled herself after.

"It's an honor you've earned with that win. I'll see you tomorrow."

As soon as she put down the receiver, Nell sat back, her mind racing, going back to the day she'd stepped into the hallowed halls of the Supreme Court chamber. For the first few moments she'd sat transfixed, taking in the opulent and historical surroundings. When the judges had filed in, taken their seats, she'd been unable to take her eyes off the solemn faces.

Then she was called to the lectern.

After several minutes of tension, the Chief Justice had called on her to begin.

Addressing the court as protocol demanded, dressed in her navy suit, the style more conservative than usual, she'd laid out her arguments, barely touching the notebook she'd brought with her. She'd cited volume and page as reference when asked, kept to the points of law that supported her argument, spoken in a clear and distinct voice, and answered every question put to her without hesitation, proving she knew her case from the inside out. It had been a heart-stopping procedure, but she'd remained calm and cool under the pressure. In total, it'd taken her only seven minutes to lay her case before the court but she had done it skillfully.

So skillfully that she had won.

As if in a daze, Nell wrapped her arms around herself, finally allowing the full effects of the victory to seep in.

Picking up the quill pen she'd been gifted with as a souvenir of her day in court, she fingered the cool steel and thought back to the day she'd received the note from the court with the scheduled date for argument. Amazed that it had been granted and put on the docket, she'd worked diligently on her client's behalf, memorizing the rules and procedures of the court, filing motions, briefs all correctly color-coded, reviewed any cases that would support her opinion, examined every facet of her case from every angle. The case had consumed her for more than two years and now it was over.

So many had warned her it couldn't be done, begged her to reconsider filing for a docket number. If she'd lost, it could have set the cause back in innumerable ways. But she had proceeded anyway, following her intuition, determined to do the best she could for her client, hoping it wouldn't come back to haunt her career.

Her first steps were taken at the local level, before she'd moved it to the state's highest court. She'd worked her way up the ladder until she'd exhausted every avenue but the Supreme Court. She'd had no recourse left but to file. Ramona Perez was an undocumented person, married to another undocumented but had two children born American citizens. She'd become an American in waiting, waiting for the right path to open so she could become naturalized. On that treadmill for fifteen years, she'd been picked up and detained. If deported, she'd be returned to Haiti, a place she hadn't called home for almost half her life. It would tear her away from her children, who might also lose their father to the same fate.

She believed that Ramona's children, Graziela, sixteen, and Geraldo, twelve, deserved the right to life, liberty and the pursuit of happiness. Didn't happiness include having your mother living with you?

It came down to what rights do American citizens have and at what age they could claim them? She'd spent hundreds of hours researching, documenting, analyzing, praying, threading the history of immigration into her presentation. The United States was still working within the framework of a bill passed in the 1960s, which had become antiquated and brittle. Groups of immigration lawyers had wanted her to wait before filing, hoping for a more liberal court down the road but Ramona didn't have the time. She needed a stay and the only way Nell could achieve that was to keep moving the cogs of the judicial machine. The lunacy of the current law was apparent in cases like this. Ramona and her husband, David, had stayed in the country too long and had become inadmissible for green card status, even though they had been hard-working, productive members of the city in which they lived. Nell had proposed an adjustment of status based on their children's welfare and rights as citizens.

The six months she'd spent in the newly opened Stanford Court clinic when she was attending law school had given her the foundation she needed to piece the components of the case together and her years defending women's rights had given her the experience arguing before a judge. Not that arguing a case before the most influential court in the land was in any way the same. Her briefs had to be succinct and well thought out, her documents well crafted, providing critical background information, sworn affidavits from family, friends, employers were pivotal, and she had a mere thirty minutes to present her side. The outcome would determine the fate of not only one woman and her family but also those who came after.

With her win, Ramona would be free, granted a green card, and would be allowed to pursue naturalization. With time spent in detention, she could file papers for citizenship immediately.

Her insides were still shimmying.

Just yesterday all her thoughts and energies were spent on her next case, the next client she'd help navigate the decrepit system in place for both legal and illegal immigrants. In twenty-four hours, her sphere of influence had expanded, and she was now being considered as a possible contributor to an issue that would have far-reaching consequences.

Maybe she should take all she had learned to Washington. It wouldn't be full time, merely a part-time project.

She was going to have to think long and hard about it.

CHAPTER TWO

Jelani poured herself another glass of champagne and refilled the paper cups of everyone else at the oval conference table. The partners had taken an early lunch and decided one bottle to toast the star of the hour was appropriate.

Arianna lifted her cup. "To one of the best decisions we made. Hiring this beautiful attorney to join our firm. Mia and I had no reservations what-so-ever but if we had known what she was going to do for our reputation, we would have brought her in as partner right away."

"Instead of making me slave for the first two years to get it?"

"You would have slaved anyway. You don't know how not to work."

Everyone at the table laughed because it was true. Nell stuffed life with all kinds of work, from litigation, defense, pro bono, research, and support to training. In the office by seven a.m., she was out no earlier than seven p.m. most nights. There were a few exceptions.

Regardless, her briefcase always went with her.

"You've taken our reputation to the next level with this win. I can only guess at how many calls are going to come in this week for representation."

Originally known for their achievements in women's rights cases, they had expanded their base to include the LGBT community and immigration. It looked like they were on a road paved of gold.

Nell looked at each member of the tight-knit group. These were her partners yes, but more importantly they were her friends, good friends and she loved them all. Loved fighting with them for just causes, for victims, for survivors.

Arianna Woodley was the oldest of the group. At forty-eight, she had put her life on the back burner to build the firm from an empty office to a beehive of activity. Unmarried, with no children, she'd created what other women could only dream of. Mia Fisher was with her from the beginning, putting her life savings into their start-up and never regretting the decision. She had taken a break here and there, marrying her college boyfriend and having two children that she doted on in her spare time, and she made sure she carved it out. With the support of all on board. There was no glass ceiling here and no expectation to choose between family and work. It was one of the reasons that the women who worked here were loyal and industrious.

Jelani Ramirez was Nell's best friend. Born a couple of years after her parents immigrated from the Dominican Republic, she was raised in a multiethnic city. Her parents had waited too long to file papers for naturalization and had suffered the consequences. Other members of her family had been just as negligent. She was a firsthand witness to the ill effects of deportation, and it had become her area of expertise, the Deferred Action for Childhood Arrivals taking up most of her caseload. Emilia Spencer-Ronan hailed from Australia but when her parents died in a car crash, she'd come to live with her aunt and uncle in a small town north of the city. She worked tirelessly on the cases having to do with immigrant family law, usually advocating for the children left behind, her focus on keeping families together. Camille Bissonnette, was from an old, revered family in Canada who'd immigrated to this country several generations back, her mother a former French national with a Russian heritage. She had the highest rate of success with their asylum cases, so all applications went to her desk. Her job was not only to prepare the document package but to protect the applicants rights and help them escape persecution.

The four women hired by the founding mothers were all in their early to mid-thirties. They'd joined the firm within a year of each other and had suffered through the first few years of sixty-hour weeks and no social lives to speak of. And had bonded closely.

Jelani sat with her feet tucked beneath her on the sofa that offered clients and their families a place to sit.

"Are you tempted to become one of their consultants?"

Nell was fiddling with the charm on her wrist.

"Tempted maybe but there's no way I'm spending most of my time in Washington. Not for a few years anyway."

"What if the President calls?"

Nell looked up at Jelani and admitted, "Actually, he already did. To congratulate me. He said it was a landmark case and might open some doors down the road."

Nell smiled as her partners talked over each other, each asking a different question about that conversation.

"He wanted to thank me for my contribution."

Arianna sat back down, across from Nell, and leaned towards her.

"Who else called?"

"Some of the members of the Immigration subcommittee. The minority members of Judicial."

Mia amended, "Yeah, why would the Republicans call to say anything nice to a flaming liberal who wants justice for her clients?"

Nell's smile turned into an expression of fake shock.

"Hey, I'm not a liberal, just a bleeding heart."

"And our resident feminist. All bad in their book."

"Did Gorgeous Eyes call? You are one of his constituents."

Arianna was referring to one of the congressman from Massachusetts. Everyone in the office had been attending his local fundraisers since he'd first run for office, although Nell had yet to join them.

Her eyes glanced up to meet Jelani's.

There were only a few people who knew things about her past she'd wanted to keep hidden, but maybe it was time to share with the rest of her...what would Chloe call it? Her peeps.

"No. And he probably won't."

Mia's lips turned down.

"I am thoroughly disappointed in our boy."

Arianna snickered at the description.

"Boy. He's no boy. He is all man."

The jokes were ribald at Jack Adams' expense. In his thirties, he was tall, good-looking, smart, charming and available.

Glancing around the room, Nell admitted, "We dated in college. As you might have noticed, it didn't end well."

The room became filled with stunned silence.

Arianna broke it.

"You're saying it's Gorgeous Eyes?"

Knowing she wouldn't get out of the room alive unless she spilled something more, Nell nodded.

"He's the one I lived with for a couple of months before I went to Stanford."

Mia asked, her eyebrows arched in surprise, "Why didn't we know this?"

"We came to an agreement that he'd have no part in my life. If I told anyone about it, he'd be back in it."

"My God, Nell. And here we've been trying to convince you to support his campaign for the last six years. I wouldn't have if I'd known he left you high and dry."

"I left him, so don't go down that road. He seems good at his job. And it keeps him out of the city most of the time."

"Nell, this is huge."

"Please. It's been over for a long time. Don't make a big deal about it."

The women sat looking at each other as if they didn't know what to say until Arianna asked the important question, her eyes mischievously sparkling.

"What's he like in bed?"

Nell's eyes flashed up. Images blurred: heat invaded.

"Excuse me? That one I'm not touching with a ten-foot pole."

"Okay, give him a grade if you won't give us details. Scale of one to ten."

She looked up at the expectant faces and gave them a smile.

"An eleven."

Arianna had always been infatuated with the man although Nell knew she'd never have moved on it. He was much too young for her and she liked them a bit more biker, lots of tattoos and muscle.

"That kind of sex doesn't come along too often."

"What was I supposed to do? Stay with him for the sex? I had a little more to think about than that. Just sayin.'"

Emilia asked, her forehead crinkled as if she was still wrapping her brain around this new information, "Is this why you don't date much?"

"I date."

Jelani barked out a laugh.

"No, I date. You step out every once in a while."

Nell asked, "What about Howie?"

"What about him? You see him, what, two times a month? And that's it."

"I don't have time to do more than that."

"Right. I bet if he was an eleven in bed, you might rethink your priorities."

Arianna's eyes were boring a hole in her forehead.

"Still waiting so let's have it."

Nell weighed her words, not really wanting to get into the sordid mess. "His mother was a little intrusive."

"You broke up with him because of his mother?"

Emilia frowned.

"What is he, a mama's boy?'

"Not Mr. Gorgeous Eyes?"

"Maybe, although I don't think I'd go that far. I didn't like her or how he dealt with her. She ran the show and she told him I wasn't right for him. Too liberal, too strident, too feminist. We both began to believe it."

And because he'd usually defended Eloise, she'd been left to defend and protect herself. Something she'd gotten good at over the years.

Emilia's expression gave away her confusion. "The guys an eleven. How could you just walk away?"

"You'd have to meet his mother to understand why."

Jelani showed her stripes when she said, "I have sharper claws. She'd be shredded if she came between me and my eleven."

Nell pushed her hair off her face ready to defend herself when Arianna informed, "He's not good enough for you."

Emilia, Camille and Jelani looked aghast at Arianna as she said it. She thought the sun shone up his ass.

"Those were my last words to him before I left. Told him his mother was perfect for him and I wished them a good life together. His mother was the one who wanted him in politics. When he threw his hat in the ring after Tomms retired, I figured he'd just given in to her demands and it wouldn't amount to much. I was wrong. He's good at it. She was right all along. Maybe about other things as well."

"Not about you. You'd be right for any man."

Nell sat chewing on her thumb nail.

"Not if the man needs someone to dote on him. That is not my particular strength."

Jelani added, "Or needs being needed. I went out with one of those. He wanted to *fix* everything, wanted to chew my food for me. It didn't last more than a few weeks before I got sick of it."

Mia said, "He's on a couple of those committees that will be holding the hearings. Will you be able to work with him?"

"It should just be a cursory involvement. The members will ask some questions, and they have limited time to do so. I may be on his hot seat for five or ten minutes. If there's a travel ban put in place as threatened, then they might want my opinion on how to counteract it, maybe request me to file injunction papers at the state level. Then it's just a day trip down with most of the work being down locally. I think I can suffer through it."

Emilia advised, "If he gives you a hard time, tell the wanker to shove it."

Em, having spent the first ten years of her life down under, still went with the slang of her childhood.

Camille laughed. "You're the real-life *cause célèbre*."

"If I believed I was a celebrity, maybe, because then it would mean I've bought in to my own hype. I don't."

"You never did. It's one of the things I love about you. You've never let your success come between friendships."

Nell sat back in her chair. This was where she belonged. It's where she was valued, respected, and loved, something that had been missing until she started working here.

"Thanks. Now why don't we all get back to work."

Arianna left, shaking her head, Mia behind her. Camille, Em and Jelani each gave her a fist pump before vacating the office, smiling and joking as they did so.

The media had started occupying the lobby, one reporter at a time until there was no room for clients, no peace for the lawyers.

Arianna stuck her head into her office.

"We better give them what they came for. A short interview and photo op should get them out of here. Then things can get back to normal. If there is any such thing now."

At five p.m., just in time for the evening news, Nell came out of her office to address the crowd and to open it up to a Q and A session.

⌒

"Hey, Jack you might want to see this. Channel Five. Your district."

John Emerson Adams, Jack to his friends and co-workers, turned on the TV in his office, still going over the notes the chair of the Department of Homeland Security had issued. He was glad to see the congressman was taking the hacking seriously and agreed with the report. They needed to investigate it to the full extent possible. Any outside interference in the election process was not acceptable. The comment that concerned him was that they would be working with the incoming administration on it. He wasn't sure that would help the cause. The new faces on the committee would be from the other side of the aisle. Holding the majority meant they'd have the numbers to shoot down any attempts by his party to dig in. He'd met all the newcomers during orientation, and many of the men and women being sworn in at the beginning of the year were aligned with the new president. He'd been surprised when the Speaker of the House handed him an assignment for the induction. They were on opposite sides of most issues and he was still one of the junior members of the Massachusetts contingent. The topic was a challenging one: how to be an effective congressman. There were so many things he would have liked to say but couldn't, like it didn't matter how hard you worked, if you were on the minority side you might not even be heard. That you'd spend most of your time at call centers raising money because Citizens United upped the ante, that all your committee meetings would be held at the same time and you'd be hard-pressed to stay on top of the topics for review. Even now, during a recess break, he was running between luncheons and meetings while he was holding court with some of his peers, studiously surveying some of the pitfalls that might be waiting for them once the new year began. With the incoming administration, they would be wide and varied.

His eyes glanced up to the screen, and he sat forward when he saw who was speaking at the microphone and used the remote to raise the volume.

He hadn't seen her in person in years.

An overwhelming sense of longing came over him.

She was dressed appropriately for a powerful entry into the world of media blitz. With her high-heels back on her feet, her five-eight frame now three inches taller, professionally attired in red suit, sheer white blouse, her black hair held back in Chinese sticks, she had quickly attained the celebrity status she wanted no part of. She looked good, but then she always had. Although she dressed more conservatively now, she still had her bangles around her wrist and he could almost hear the way they tinkled when she talked.

Her voice rang out in command as she answered the questions posed to her, showcasing her brilliance and the confidence he had once admired.

Satisfaction shone in her eyes.

What she'd accomplished didn't surprise him.

She had been the best he'd debated back in college, her at Yale, him at Harvard. They had clashed time and time again over the two years they were undergraduates and she'd beaten him every argument. When she'd appeared on stage for their first face-off, he thought she was a light-weight.

His cockiness had been misplaced.

He had walked over to where she stood as she was collecting her things from the podium and asked, "Do you always use your feminine wiles to win?"

She'd worn a girly dress, flawless make-up, her hair flowing down around her, her eyes amber and filled with passion.

With barely a glance in his direction, her voice clear and distinct, she said, "I guess if you're a sexist, you might feel that way. I trust the judges are not and count on my presentation to achieve my goal. But I guess you'd have to blame something for your rather shoddy performance."

She had left him standing there, his mouth agape, exiting the room with her peers.

The next time they met, she was dressed in a suit, hair back in a bun, her make-up minimal, the Bohemian beauty transformed.

And she had trounced him again, even given the fact he'd studied his opinion vigorously.

Enchanted with her mind, he had asked for her phone number and she'd reluctantly given it to him.

It had taken him two weeks to call her and another week until she had time, but he'd finally gotten her to dinner and begun the endless task of getting to know her. She was a dichotomy of brilliant and humble, an introvert who somehow managed to speak publicly in front of an audience, beautiful in a bohemian way, who both asked and answered questions in a manner that struck at the core of an issue. That she had gotten the Chief Justice to side with her on this issue was proof of her organizational mind, her ability to keep the dialogue to the salient points, and her way with words. Her manner and confidence might have worked in her favor as well.

He looked at the phone for a moment thinking maybe he'd call and tell her, but their past intruded as it always did. He'd promised to keep his distance. Instead, he pushed his chair back and leaned his foot on his desk.

Carla, his receptionist, came in and informed him he had a call, announcing who was on the phone. Not taking his eyes off the screen, he picked up the landline. Watching Nell was more compelling than any conversation, but he had to take this.

"Zelda. How are you?"

He lowered the volume on the remote but continued to watch.

"Did you hear?"

"Hear..."

"We got an opinion. It's unbelievable."

"I'm watching the press conference as we speak."

"Do you know her? She works out of Boston."

Pinching his bottom lip, he considered what to tell her.

"I met her in school."

"I thought you went to Harvard. I know she's Yale and Stanford."

He continued to keep it neutral.

"Clashed on our debate teams."

"How'd she do against you?"

"You got it backwards."

"I love it when a woman wins."

"I know you do."

"I've got her coming in tomorrow. I want her as a consultant."

Old feelings of both irritation and something softer came bubbling up.

"I'm not sure she'll accept the position."

"I'm not, either. I wanted her as soon as I read her brief but my intention to offer her a job here is a non-starter. My hope now is that she'll devote some time to us and the mess we're in."

"What did she say?"

"That there's no way she'll make DC her second home. She's done some good things where she is, and I can't say that I blame her. Working here is close to being unemployed. We get nothing done. Do you want to sit in?"

A knot began pulsing in his gut.

"Probably better for you if I don't."

"Why? More of a history than you've let on?"

Knowing he couldn't continue to stonewall, he admitted, "Ancient and in ruins but still relevant."

"Will you be able to work with her?"

He pictured her across from him while they studied for upcoming tests, went over cases to be analyzed in class, traded questions to ask to enhance class discussions. He had worked well with her for a time, his grades improving because she was able to get him to think more in depth about so many subjects.

Then she was gone. He was left to his own devices in law school and he didn't do nearly as well, bored with the subject material, the professors and the students. It was her love of the law that was the spark he needed to keep him interested. She was passionate about so many things- inequality, inequity, immigration, women's rights and it was hard not to fall in love with the doctrines and practices that governed political communities that they debated so vigorously.

It was hard not to fall in love with her, which was what he'd done.

It had been a mistake and there was no going back.

"Will my answer affect your decision?"

In blunt Zelda fashion, she said, "No, it won't. I need her more than I do you."

He almost laughed outright.

He had needed Nell, too. Could he handle being in the same town, working on the same issue?

He wasn't sure, but it seemed he might not have an option.

"Then why did you ask the question?"

"To measure what kind of resistance I might get from your direction."

"We get enough resistance from the other side. I'll watch my p's and q's. You won't get any trouble from me."

"Good. I want you there. You know her, might know a way to get her to agree."

He had barely scratched the surface. There were layers still unearthed.

"I'm not sure what I can bring to that table, other than some bad memories."

"How well did you know her?"

He paused. There was a concrete answer to the question in terms of physicality, a more nebulous one in terms of depth of understanding. For as much as he'd thought he knew her, and how she felt, he'd been wrong.

"We dated while we were in college, lived together one summer. She worked twelve-hour days for a legal aid clinic. I cooked her dinner. That was my contribution. Then things got in the way. She left for Stanford, and that was it."

"You didn't keep in touch?"

Regret rolled through him, hot as lava.

"No."

"What happened after she graduated?"

"She went to work for Tomms in DC"

"I remember that. She was here, what, two or three years?"

"Two. She moved back home, got a job with Woodley and Fisher and the rest is history."

There was another reason she might have moved back to Boston. He didn't want to look at it any more closely today than he had back then. She'd left right before he moved in as part of a newly elected Congress.

"She's done quite well for herself."

"She has. It isn't any surprise, between her work ethic and her mind she's incomparable."

"I can tell you respect her."

"In that, yes."

"I still think it's a good idea for you to be there. The interview starts at eleven a.m. If you can make it, I'd appreciate it."

"For you, anything."

"Thanks. Write up a list of questions and email them to my office. It'll help if we have an agenda."

"Will do."

"Gotta go. Talk to you later."

CHAPTER THREE

Jack was glad Zelda had given him a heads-up about tomorrow's meeting. It would prevent him from being blind-sided.

Leaning back in his chair, a pen in his mouth, he wondered what Nell would do when she found out he was on the committee. If he knew anything, he'd swear she'd research the hell out of the members and their agenda before she got here tomorrow.

He'd lucked out on his assignments. Newbies got what was given, not what they necessarily specialized in. He could have found himself in Agriculture, knowing less than nothing about those issues, but he'd come under the wing of two very influential members, Zelda being one of them. As a new congressman, he was assigned to Intelligence and Homeland Security, added Education and Workforce second term. When Zelda approached him to resign from the latter and join the Judiciary, he couldn't refuse. Judiciary was the oldest committee of the House and one of the most significant although one of the most polarized when it came to casting votes. The members of the majority had refused to hold hearings for the Supreme Court nominee, promising they would hold them off until the next president was elected. He wondered if the American people would be interested to know how many millions that stand-off had cost. With a president on their side, it was a whole new ball game. He'd originally hoped for a place on Armed Services, but Intelligence was an achievement and he wasn't disappointed. Charged with oversight of the US intelligence community, including the CIA and FBI, their plates were filling up with reports, memos, and accusations of foreign meddling. He'd traveled to many parts of the world to meet and show support for the operatives. He was going to have to juggle an agenda top-heavy with hearings and subcommittees.

He glanced back to the television. This time he bolted out of his chair, his feet taking him across the carpeted floor until he was standing only inches away. He wanted a closer view of the girl in the background. She was standing by the double glass doors of the attorney suite, tucked in a corner, as if attempting to stay in the background until the press conference was over.

Chloe Adele Warren.

Nell's daughter. Eleven years old, tall for her age, long black hair like her mother's. Was attending a school in Milton, which was where they lived, was on the field hockey team, had a part in the school play and took Spanish instead of French. She loved her friends, spent her spare time reading, going to the movies, and shopping.

She wore a backpack over her heavy jacket, the weather in Massachusetts a wintry mix today.

She was watching her mother intently, her lips pursed, her eyes wide. Was her look one of pride or embarrassment? What did girls think and feel at eleven?

When Nell finished the interview, she turned as if she knew her daughter was there, although he didn't see how. She'd had her back to her, facing the cameras, the whole time. Chloe moved forward when Nell beckoned and slid into an embrace as they walked off, down the hall to what he assumed was Nell's office.

He envied the connection. Chloe was proud of her mother. He could tell by the smile she bestowed on her.

He closed his eyes and squeezed them shut.

Nell's daughter.

And his, though only a handful of people knew it.

He'd given up the right to claim her when Nell had called to discuss the pregnancy. He'd been ready to fly out to California to join her when his mother had made a request. Eloise Adams would pay for his travel and his education if she knew for a fact Nell was carrying his child. All she'd asked for was a paternity test. Nell had declined both the request and his presence when he tried to reason with her. He didn't think it was a big deal, or that proof was an undue burden.

She'd informed him that if she had to prove anything to him, they didn't belong together. What had gone unsaid was if his mother was going to continue to call the shots, she wasn't interested in a life with him. After she told him to stay away from them, to pretend she'd never made the call, he'd abided by her wishes. He was struggling to find his way back then, unable to commit to the law, unable to commit to Nell and their child. He'd had nothing to offer them. His mother had been ready to cut him off, had told him in very clear terms that he'd be on his own. And he'd believed her. Years later, when he'd finally agreed to run for public office, he found his passion, felt invigorated. He hadn't started small like most politicians, at the local or state level. He went for a seat in the United States House of Representatives when one of the revered veterans of Congress retired. With a successful campaign in full swing, he'd contacted Nell about meeting his child. He'd known nothing about how the pregnancy had gone, little more than the gender and name of the child, and only because it was listed under children on her Linked In page. What he did know was he had a deep-rooted desire to be part of her life. Nell had convinced him it would be too big a distraction for a rookie politician who was running against a strong contender to bring the paternity issue to the table. His mother had agreed, and she was his fundraiser. He'd let them talk him out of it, Nell insisting on privacy for their daughter, not wanting her to become fodder for the election newspaper cycle, his mother agreeing with Nell for once in his life. The one promise he'd wrung out of Nell: he would be given updates on Chloe's life. And she'd been as good as her word. Getting to know Chloe from afar was making it more difficult to keep his distance. He didn't want to see her on a television screen or as a disguised spectator at one of her field hockey games. He wanted to meet her.

And he was going to push for that soon, with the full might of his position.

⌒

Chloe went right to the staff kitchen to grab a drink and a snack and then wandered back into her mother's office. She shrugged out of her coat and hung it on the back of a stuffed chair that sat opposite the desk.

"It's totally lit Mom. But the cameras? Really?"

"I know. I was hoping it would be over by the time you got here."

Chloe thought celebrity of any kind was "trash." She didn't watch celebrity television, didn't read rag tag magazines, and believed you had to earn respect, not be born with the right name. She was too serious about life at times, out-going with people she knew, things she enjoyed although it was a big surprise when she announced she had tried out for the school play and had gotten a part.

"Marah already texted me. She said you were dope."

She was one of her field hockey friends.

When Nell looked up from the file on her desk, Chloe had her phone in hand, her thumbs busy texting something back. She'd live on her phone if allowed, but Nell took it away for hours at a time, explaining the dangers on both a psychological and social level. Chloe went along for now but as she got older...? Nell cringed. She'd heard bad things about the evil teen years.

And the slang? She was on-line a lot trying to decipher what the hell the kids were talking about. She knew *lit* meant awesome in teen vernacular and *dope* meant seriously great. She'd take them both as a compliment.

"Homework?"

Not once looking up, Chloe continued to multi-task.

"I did some before rehearsal. All I have left is some science and math."

Nell smiled. She was glad she'd signed her up for the afternoon drama class. She'd been surprised when Chloe brought the packet home for her to look over, excited about the prospect of being in a play. The teacher, Ms. Suarez, was new to the school and was offering a ten-week session called Youth Acting Studio for middle-school students. The hand-made brochure described the purpose and objective. It spoke to connections, stories, and communication which would help promote creative thinking and discipline. Not that Chloe needed the latter. She was a good student and homework was always a prior-ity. What she liked about it, was it offered Chloe something constructive one afternoon a week. The first production was titled *American Idols: Women of History.*

"How's the play coming?"

"Good. I'm getting better at rap."

"I know."

Chloe had chosen to represent Eleanor Roosevelt, one of Nell's heroines, and the script was more rap lyrics and beat than actual script. Nell couldn't wait to see the finished project.

"I just have to call one more client and then we can get going. Chinese to-night?"

Chloe's nose scrunched up with her frown.

"Had it Saturday. Can we have something different?'

Jelani popped her head in.

"How about some home-cooked pork carnitas and rice with gandules?"

Chloe gave her attention over to some face-to-face interaction.

"Yes, please."

Nell's stomach did a pom-pom cheer. She wasn't looking forward to any more Chinese either. With an aversion to the stove, or rather, the inability to make any kind of food tasty, she rarely cooked, which meant pick-up or take-out was an almost daily ritual.

She gave her friend a warm smile.

"Do you always have to show me up?"

"Only in the kitchen, my friend. You show me up in every other way."

Her hand on the receiver, ready to pick it up and make the call so they could go home, Nell said, "I'm thinking about taking cooking lessons. I'm trying to fit it into my schedule. I'm failing."

Jelani rested her shoulder against the door jamb.

"Why don't you just hire a cook? You've got the money, and Chloe might enjoy more than one home-cooked meal a month."

That's how often they got an invite to Jelani's.

"There's an easy solution. Invite us over more often."

After stepping inside the plush office, Jelani sat at the edge of one of the chairs facing Nell's desk.

"They have this new service. It's called Fresh Serve or something. A box is delivered with step-by-step instructions and all the ingredients you need to enjoy the cooking experience. You might give that a try."

"There is nothing about the cooking experience I enjoy."

"I could give it a try, Mom. I might like to cook. Did my dad?"

There was a hopeful look on Chloe's face. It caused a small pit to form in Nell's stomach. It signaled the onset of distress and it came when Chloe mentioned her father in any way. She'd sworn she wasn't going to involve him in their lives. His mother held too much juice with him and it wasn't something Eloise was willing to share. When the old biddy had demanded she make her infant daughter take a paternity test, she'd gone off the rails. Told Jack that she didn't want him, didn't need him. And she hadn't called him again. Not when Chloe was born, not when she could have used some help, not when she could have used a shoulder to cry on. She'd had no idea how to raise a child and she'd been in way over her head. There were endless nights of no sleep, an infinite number of hours she had to study while comatose. For the first three months, until she'd gotten a grandmother type to watch Chloe, she'd wrap Chloe in a sling and bring her to class, feeding her during breaks, praying she'd stay quiet during lectures and court room simulations. Maybe that's why Chloe was so expressive today. She'd had to keep things in for so long.

This new, improved interest in her father was being compounded by Jack's more recent calls. He wanted to meet her, but he'd told her that a couple of times in the last eleven years. Did he mean it or was he paying lip service to the grand idea of fatherhood? She'd kept her promise to keep him up to date on what she was doing. He got a copy of her grades, knew the names of her friends, knew her favorite subjects and her favorite books. He knew that she had his ancestral grey eyes, flat feet, and a way with words.

Wasn't that enough?

"Did he, Mom?"

Did he have skill in the kitchen? Yes, he did. He was resident chef when they were together. He'd introduced her to some of her favorite meals.

Nell chewed on her pencil as she studied her daughter. She'd given away bits and pieces about Jack, answered questions when asked. As Chloe got older, the questions came more frequently, were more complex. She knew she was going to have to sit down with her at some point and explain things. But how would she explain her grandmother's cold heart? Or Jack's continual acquiescence to a woman he should have outgrown? The nagging fear that he'd abandon them had become reality.

"I guess we could give it a try. Your father kept me fed when we were together."

Now Nell had her daughter's full attention.

"He did?"

"Yeah, he wasn't working at the time. It was his contribution to the relationship."

"And you were probably working seventy hours a week."

"Not quite that many. I was working in a legal clinic at the time. It was the summer before I went to Stanford."

"Was that why you broke up?"

"Because I left for school?"

"No, because you're a workaholic?"

"I am not."

"Seriously, Mom? When you're here, you're working, when you're in court you're working, and when you're at home, you're working. Isn't that a perfect definition?"

Jelani made her way to the seat next to Chloe and dropped into it.

"You are getting close to insulting my best friend. And I can rescind my invite. Tread lightly." Jelani had stepped in when Nell had to go out of town, for a conference or a Supreme Court hearing and Chloe considered her more than just her mother's friend. She'd become family.

"Sorry."

"Please raise your right hand and repeat after me."

Jelani waited until Chloe's hand went up. It was a ritual they played often.

"I swear to tell the truth the whole truth and nothing but the truth."

Chloe repeated the phrase and then dropped her hand into her lap.

"Ready?"

Chloe solemnly nodded her head.

"Does your mother ever miss one of your field hockey matches?"

"No."

"Does she have dinner with you every night?"

"Yes."

"Does she pick up your friends for sleepovers and dinners out?"

"Yes."

"Do you go on shopping sprees, to get mani-pedis and is your closet filled with dozens of pairs of shoes?"

"Yes."

"Well, then, Chloe, I submit that you're not as abused as you're suggesting."

"I plead the Fifth."

"On the grounds you'd be incriminating yourself, if you answer that charge?"

"Just like you taught me."

Jelani got up, patting herself on the back as she did so and bragged, "I'm good."

As she headed out of the office she said, "Let me get my coat and we can go to my place for some food."

Nell had finished up with her call while Jelani was occupied with Chloe and was now salivating for the carnitas. If Jelani had chosen another field to excel in, she would have donned a chef's hat.

Projecting her voice down the hall, she said "Works for me."

Jack got back to his condo earlier than usual. He wanted to keep busy so his mind didn't continue to wander back to the woman he had dated when he was younger. Or the girl who resembled her so closely.

Staying at work would have given him better odds of that, so maybe it was the restlessness that drove him to take off. There was a lot of buzz going on regarding Nell's win, her interview tomorrow and the possibility she'd be in Washington periodically.

The image of her standing, talking to the press came back to haunt him.

There wasn't a shred of gypsy about her. She looked poised and composed.

Her mind was the first thing that had attracted him, and he hadn't met anyone like her since. Things had gone well at the beginning, when they were in school, sharing commute time to be with each other. It deteriorated once they were both back in Boston, living together. The arguments about his mother were endless and raged into all-out battles. Her hostility was met in spades by the other side. His mother railed against her, vehement in her opinion that she just wouldn't suit. She was too driven, too independent, too forceful

He'd felt like a ping-pong ball, that bounced back and forth between sides.

It took some time but he'd realized his mother was probably right.

They would never mesh.

Not because she didn't suit, but because he refused to spend his life at war.

Unable to get her out of his head, he paced the confines of the condo.

His mother had done it up big. On Pennsylvania Avenue, he enjoyed views of all major landmarks through walls of glass in the dramatic living room. There was a roof deck and pool, all kinds of amenities but it hadn't come cheap. He'd wanted to keep the cost down, but in this city, that was a huge feat. It meant going small, which his mother all but forbade. She had purchased the two-bedroom space right after the election, so pleased that he'd finally succumbed to his destiny.

After pouring himself a scotch, he dropped down into the chair and flicked on the TV. The news was over for now, thank goodness. He didn't want to see Nell on air again.

He groaned.

If it was this hard to see her through a filter, what was it going to be like tomorrow when he saw her in the flesh? Flesh that was soft, smooth and extremely touchable. As were her lips.

Her hair was silky, and he could almost feel the strands brushing his chest after their lovemaking.

Shifting to make himself comfortable, the thought of her bringing up more than images, he wasn't sure he could sit across a desk from her and not lean out to finger her cheek.

He'd thought they had a symbiotic relationship, and they were firebrands in the bedroom. For some reason, it wasn't enough to make them stick.

Chloe entangled them even further.

How had Nell managed back then? Law school was a bitch, and he'd had a hard, enough time with his coarse load as it was. To add a baby to the mix? It couldn't have been easy. After going back and forth after her initial call, her telling him he was going to be a father, him telling her he needed a test for proof, she'd given him hell and hung up on him. She'd never reached out again, so she must have managed.

Why had he told his mother? Why had he let her take the decision to move out of his hands?

If he thought about it honestly, it hadn't been difficult. He'd had nothing, couldn't afford the hefty tuition. He wasn't sure Eloise would have ever allowed him to join Nell in California, even if Nell had agreed to the test. His ancestors had been going to Harvard since it opened its doors in the 1600's and she never would have allowed him to be the exception. She'd found a way to make it happen, which meant she probably knew Nell better than he did. The result: he'd been denied the fruits of fatherhood. What couldn't be denied was that Chloe had his DNA. He had a child living in the world. Didn't they have a right to know each other?

He almost jumped when the buzzer sounded and scrambled up to see who was here.

The voice that echoed back was a welcome one.

"It's Ron."

Opening the door to await his arrival, he was relieved that he wouldn't have to be alone with his thoughts any longer.

Ron Rubini was his communications director. A friend since Harvard, Ron had been part of his first Congressional campaign run and had agreed to come to Washington with him when he'd somehow gotten elected. He handled all media relations, wrote his press releases, penned his speeches, and made sure his constituents were kept up to date with what he was working on at district, state and national levels. An economist by trade, Ron was also responsible for guiding his accountants, who kept track of donations and campaign funds. He trusted him to keep all dirty money from his coffers.

"It's good to see you. I can use the company."

"I thought you might."

Ron knew the history. They used to double-date when Nell came up to the Harvard campus to visit. He knew about the animosity between mother and girlfriend, the break-up, the pregnancy. He also knew that Jack had suspended his rights. When he'd found out that Nell had been invited to DC for an interview, he'd offered his condolences.

It seemed he was willing to offer his friendship as well.

"Want to join me?"

Jack lifted the tumbler, clinking the ice as he shook it.

"Sure. Why not."

After refilling his own glass, he poured another and handed it over.

Ron had taken a seat in one of the chairs, leaned back, and asked, his voice somber, "So, she's in tomorrow. Are you looking forward to seeing her?"

Jack jingled some loose change in his pocket, took a sip of the amber liquid.

"Yes and no."

"Yes because...?"

"I'm a masochist?"

"I knew that a long time ago. Admit it. You've missed her."

Looking up, his thoughts of her racing through his mind, he confessed, "Yes, I've missed her."

"Is it no for the same reason?"

"Pretty much."

"How much does Zelda know?"

After draining the glass, he put it down on the bar top and took a seat in the chair opposite his friend.

"She knows there's a history."

"Are you going to tell her the rest?"

"No. Not until I can get Nell to agree to outing it."

"You're leaving the decision to Nell or Zelda, or in other words, you're leaving it in someone else's hands. Again."

The assessment wasn't complimentary. He laughed in his defense.

"I cooperate with strong women. I've had practice and it's something I'm good at."

Ron's tone was sharp and pointed.

"We talking about Eloise or Zelda? I never saw you back down from Nell."

He let that arrow whiz by.

"I should back-door it, call Nell and tell her to cancel."

"Why don't you just tell Zelda you don't want to be there tomorrow?"

"And what reason do I give her? That we have a past seems kind of lame, don't you think? It's been twelve years, Ron."

"Doesn't look like you've moved on, to me."

Ron was right. He wouldn't be having this much of a problem with the upcoming interaction if he had.

His fingers began to jingle the coins again, his agitation showing.

"I'm sure Nell thinks I'm in Congress because of my mother."

Ron leaned forward, the tumbler of amber liquid held in both hands.

"And you know why. This would be a way to prove to her that you're not. You work hard, Jack. If she's in town, she'll see it."

Jack walked over to the window, took in the lights of the city.

"If my mother had lightened up on the political thing I would have run for something, a couple of years earlier."

Ron's lips twisted into a sardonic smile.

"Rebellion comes with a cost."

"You're telling me."

"So back to my original question. What are you going to do?"

He'd told Ron when he'd started emailing Nell a couple of months ago, so his friend knew he wanted to have a relationship with his daughter. They'd discussed what it could mean, in terms of a relationship with Nell. Not that it mattered. She didn't seem open to any change in dynamics.

"Nell has to accept the terms before there's anything for me to decide."

Ron took the last sip from the tumbler before putting it down on the coffee table.

"She looked good at the press conference."

"Nothing's changed there."

"More mature maybe."

"She was always mature, twenty going on forty-five. Poised, confident. People say I'm persuasive, but I have nothing on her."

"Since she got the Chief Justice to rule in her favor, I think you might be right."

"I'm proud of her. Crazy, I know. But she accomplished what so many said she couldn't."

"If she could have just won your mother over, we'd be having a different discussion."

Jack turned from the window but continued to stare into space. He'd hoped the two women would eventually reach a truce, but it had never happened. Nell was unwilling to co-operate on any level.

"Yeah, well, she gave me an ultimatum. I couldn't choose between them."

He noticed Ron's expression harden.

"It seems your mother did as well, so in a way, you did choose."

Jack's head snapped up. Ron had been telling him that for years. It was the first time he'd heard it. Before he could begin to process the new perspective, Ron added, "Nell really didn't have a chance, did she? Your mother needed you: she didn't. It didn't work in her favor."

"That simple, is it?"

"Probably not."

Jack's mind was trying to keep up with Ron's assessment. It wasn't flattering. Going back to a more comfortable place, he said, "My mother just wanted to make sure that Chloe was mine."

"And you sided with her. Didn't push back. You didn't need that test, did you?"

"No, not the test. I did need the money for school. I couldn't have gone out there with nothing. I planned on revisiting it once I got on my feet."

Ron got up, his hands on his hips, his voice taking on an irritated tone.

"Revisiting it? That makes it sound trivial. It wasn't. Your mother didn't just win that battle, she won the war. Your daughter's eleven, Jack, and you're still watching from the sidelines."

Literally. When he was home, he'd sneak out to attend her field hockey games. He'd had to bone up on the rules, positions, so he could follow the action. She was a mid-fielder, who he'd learned supported both offense and defense. And she was good. He'd only been to two, one in Groton, one in North Andover. He didn't want to risk running into Nell, so he'd chosen out-of-town rivalries. When she'd shown up, he'd had to pull his hat down and stay out of sight. It had led him to believe she attended them all. It spoke to her priorities as a mother. Chloe came before work.

He was almost surprised, given her lack of motherly attention when she was a girl, but he was glad Chloe was so well loved. He was sorry he didn't have a role. Wanted to change that but didn't know how.

"I can't just spring it all on her. I need to ease her into it. And I need Nell's permission."

He'd made a promise not to make his presence known. He'd kept it to this point. He wasn't sure how much longer he could.

"You don't think Eloise will make it easy, do you? She'd have to get out of the way to make room for someone else."

"What are you talking about?"

"Eloise still doesn't like Nell, for whatever reason. I'm still not sure what it is. If you think she's going to allow them into your life without a fight, you're naïve or stupid. The jury is still out on which one."

"Look, my mother was trying to protect me. There's no need anymore. This is about Nell. She's still cutting me out."

The irritation moved into anger.

"Nell didn't cut you out. She called you, told you, gave you a choice. *You* opted out. I'll never understand that one, Jack. I didn't then: I can't now."

Going on the defensive, he asked irritably, "What could I have done differently?"

Ron was glaring at him now. He'd never seen his friend get angry over this before.

"Moved, managed, been together."

"Weigh her down with my poverty?"

"She wouldn't have been weighed down by that. You would have been. God forbid an Adam's does without. Some of us had no alternative. I was on scholarship. I worked almost full-time just like Nell did. You trust fund kids have no fucking clue how to live in the real world. I love you bro, but you are the cover boy for privileged white male and don't even realize it. Or what you missed out on."

Ron placed the tumbler of ice on the credenza, shaking his head.

"Get your head out of your ass, and take a good look at what's going on."

Jack watched as Ron walked out the door without giving him a chance to rebut it. It was probably a good thing, because he wasn't sure he could.

CHAPTER FOUR

Nell shadowed Jelani's car into the driveway, then pulled alongside it and parked. She still couldn't believe this had been Jelani's pick out of all the places she looked at, before buying a couple of years ago. Born and raised in Lawrence, she'd lived there for the first few years after joining the law firm. When the money began to accumulate in her account, her accountant told her to diversify. She'd bought in the same town as Nell, falling in love with an old house that had been renovated from top to bottom. With over an acre of land, the trees offering a beautiful backyard setting for barbeques and lots of kids, a huge kitchen that spoke to her domestic side, it was the kind of house you chose with a family in mind. It's what she thought of as conservative suburbia. Jelani was anything but conservative. She thought she would go for something trendier, in a more, hip neighborhood. Go figure.

She followed Jelani up the back stairs and into the kitchen. As soon as they entered, Chloe made herself at home, dropping her bag on the dining room table, and leaving her coat hanging on the back of one of the chairs. Chloe felt as at home here as she did at their place. It helped that it was only five minutes from the school and twenty from work.

Jelani stripped off her suit coat on the way to her bedroom.

"I'm going to change because I can. Pour us some wine, Nellie and I'll be right out."

Nell narrowed her eyes, but the smile gave away the fact she wasn't upset. She never would have let anyone else call her that, but Jelani had since the day they met.

They'd been hired within a week of each other, the first two attorneys taken on by the newly minted law firm, incorporated by Arianna and Mia. Their offices were side by side, in a much smaller space than they enjoyed now, and they worked around the clock, as invested in the firm as its founders. Eating together was a daily event, sushi, pizza, Thai, as they went through files, picking each other's brains as they wandered through the maze of the legal process. Jelani, the expert on deportation spent many nights up late giving input on her prep for the Supreme Court case. They knew each other's secrets and had each other's backs.

After uncorking the wine, Nell took two glasses out of the cabinet, and poured just as Jelani came out, dressed down in leggings and jersey. She immediately got to work heating up the carnitas she'd programmed into her Crock Pot this morning.

"Set the table, will you, Chloe?"

"Sure. In a minute."

"Um, now, please. You've talked to your friends all day. It's my turn now."

"Keileh's grandmother is sick. Her mom might have to go to Iran to see her. I'm commiserating."

"Good friend."

Once they were sitting at the dining room table, now cleared of homework debris, they savored the food before picking up the conversation thread they'd dropped. Nell hadn't wanted to scare Chloe earlier but her immediate reaction when told about Samira was one of concern. "Did Keileh say what's wrong with her grandmother?"

"She has a bad heart and might have to have an operation. Her mother wants to bring her here but she's not sure it'll be possible."

"That's too bad. When is her mom leaving?"

"I'm not sure. Next month sometime."

"How long will she be gone?"

"I guess it depends on what they find."

She glanced up to Jelani. That would take them into the aftermath of the inauguration. Rumor had it a travel ban would be enacted within days. That's one of the reasons she was going down to Washington. Zelda was looking for attorneys who could help them brace for what was coming.

Wiping her mouth with a napkin, Chloe asked, "Am I sleeping over at her house on Saturday?"

"Yes. I talked to her mom this morning. She's going to make sure you work on your book project."

Nell had begrudgingly agreed to attend the Massachusetts Bar Association dinner, although she didn't know why she didn't fight it more strenuously. It was being held by the city's judicial branch of government and Jack Adams had agreed to attend. He'd skipped the event every year up until this one.

Was it an omen?

Jelani pushed her plate away, took a sip of her wine. She glanced over to Chloe before giving a shorthanded response.

"I was surprised you agreed to go."

Nell understood what Jelani was saying. It had to do with Jack's presence there. They didn't usually talk about him in front of Chloe.

"I tried to get out of it, but Arianna pretty much told me I had to go. She wants me out there discussing the win."

She wasn't great at networking. She'd rather be working on a brief than shaking hands, but it was a required part of the job, especially when you won a big case.

Chloe didn't look up from her phone when she asked, "Are you going with Howie?"

"I'm meeting him there."

Chloe asked, "Are you dating him?"

Jelani laughed. "Imagine that. She can't tell." Glancing over to Chloe, she said, "Your mother doesn't date."

Once the text was sent, she looked up, took a sip of water and asked, "Why not? Do you still love my Dad?"

Nell blanched. Why did it seem every word out of Chloe's mouth lately had to do with her father? It was hard enough living with the fact Chloe had his eyes. Every time she looked at her, she'd be reminded of what they'd had between them. It just hadn't been enough to keep them together.

"Love has nothing to do with it, Chloe. It didn't work out between us, but I got you and that made the whole thing worth it."

Nell got up and cleaned off the table, rinsed out the Crock Pot and stacked the plates in the dishwasher. It seemed Chloe wasn't going to let her turn her back on the topic.

"Why?"

Stalling for time, she asked, "Why what?"

"Why didn't it work out between you? Is it because you worked so much?"

There was a dose of pre-teen angst, or was it just plain old sarcasm? Tamping down her impatience she answered as moderately as she could, "I was in school back then, remember? I studied. So did he."

She didn't have to know they'd lived together one summer, and yes, she worked around the clock. It was the only thing she knew to do to keep the fear of him leaving her at bay. She was always on the edge of a cliff, never sure if Eloise would be able to shove her off completely.

Chloe was on her way to the refrigerator for the flan she knew was in there when she asked, "Is he smart?"

Nell dropped back in her seat while Chloe got spoons for everyone before reclaiming hers. Her daughter angled her head, her grey eyes repeating the question. Nell heaved a sigh.

"Yes, he's smart. I could not have been with someone who wasn't."

Chloe seemed to think about this while licking off the caramel goodness from the spoon.

"Did Grandma and Grandpa ever meet him?"

Resigning herself to another round of questions, she took a small bite of the flan before answering.

"No. They only came back once during the couple of years we were together, but they didn't stay long enough for me to set it up."

"You were together that long?"

"We were."

Chloe's spoon had stilled which meant her curiosity had taken control of her taste buds. Fiddling with the spoon, her eyes downcast, she asked, "You didn't plan on me though, did you?"

Closing her eyes, not wanting Chloe to think she wasn't wanted, she wished the whole conversation would go away.

"No, we didn't, sweetie, but you were made in love."

Her eyes flashed up to meet hers a look of relief on her face.

"You loved each other."

"We did."

"Did you want me?"

"More than anything in the world."

Chloe was the culmination of everything she'd loved about Jack, his eyes, his personality, his intelligence.

"Why didn't he?"

Nell lost her breath. Chloe had been coming to this question with everyone that came before. She didn't know why she wasn't prepared for it. But she wasn't.

Her mind scrambled for something to tell her, the look on the young face heartbreaking.

"He didn't, did he? And don't lie to me."

She reached out for Chloe's hand, but her daughter snatched it away. How to answer this? He'd been asking to meet her for years: it had just come too late.

"He did, Chloe. In his own way. But there were obstacles to it that he wasn't willing to overcome. He was young, and he felt he had nothing to offer us."

It was as close to the truth as she was going to get.

"And now? Are there still obstacles in the way? Did he ever call you, ask to meet me?"

"The obstacles are still there."

The main obstacle was, anyway. Eloise would never make it an easy meet and greet. And there was no way she was putting Chloe in the line of that fire. She didn't trust Jack enough to put her at risk. He'd chosen his mother over them both before and she had no doubt he could easily do it again.

"Did he ever call?"

"I'm not going to continue this conversation. I told you there were still too many things that get in the way. When you're older, you can make the decision to see him yourself. Until then, my rules."

"But I have a right to know who he is. To meet him if I want. It doesn't matter how old I am. I have that right."

Nell's anger was simmering. At Jack, his mother and now Chloe for getting the better of her. She could feel herself losing control.

"You have what I decide to give you. And right now, he's still off-limits."

"Maybe I'll hire an attorney from your law office. Oh, wait, you're the expert on civil rights. Can you give me a referral, so I can take you to court?"

The bitterness in Chloe's voice caused Nell more undue stress.

"Chloe, you're eleven."

"What does that mean? Graziela wasn't much older when you represented her. You fought for her to keep her mother. I'd be fighting to know my father."

Nell looked up at Jelani, asking for help, but had a sinking feeling Jelani was on the wrong side in this. They'd had discussions about it, one of the last times Jack reached out.

She was surprised when Jelani said quietly, "Chloe, your mother has done everything she can to make a good life for you. At times, even though you don't understand her reasoning, you're going to have to trust her to know what that is."

"Why are you on her side?"

"I'm not taking sides. I'm confident she knows more about this than I do and I have faith that she'll do the right thing."

"Whatever."

Brushing the tears that collected in her eyes, Chloe jumped up and fled the room.

Jelani broke the silence that had settled in.

"Nellie, you are going to have to confront this. This is not just a childhood request. She does have the right to know. And you are going to have to tell her soon."

"I know. I'm getting there. I just need a bit more time. Let me see how things are between us when I see him tomorrow. Maybe that will help me decide what to do."

While she shrugged back into her suit coat and heels, she called out to Chloe, who came out, phone in hand, probably texting about what a horrible mother she was. She wanted to scream.

Instead, she kept her calm.

"We better get home. It is a school night and we've stayed up way past our bedtimes."

Chloe gathered up her computer and backpack, put on her coat, and waited by the door.

Nell reminded Jelani, "Don't forget to pick Chloe up after school."

"Would I do that?"

"No, or I would have asked someone else. My return flight should have me home by six-thirty or seven, depending on traffic."

Jelani said to Chloe, "I'll pick up some ingredients for supper and I'll let you put it together."

The smile reached out and squeezed Nell's heart.

"Cool."

When they got home, Chloe went straight to her bedroom. Nell headed up to hers.

What the hell was she going to do? Chloe was soon going to blame her for her father being MIA. And the blame would be well-placed. If Chloe knew Jack had been calling off and on for years, was interested enough in her life that he'd requested pictures, updates, school reports, she'd be all over her. Things had gotten complicated since the beginning of the school year. Chloe was growing up and becoming more observant, more analytical in her thinking. It was as if Jack's absence had a bearing on her self-confidence, as if she couldn't quite define herself with all the missing pieces. She knew she had to fill in the blanks but didn't quite know how to go about it yet. There was so much at stake.

Including her own heart.

She'd be seeing Jack tomorrow. She hadn't seen him in the flesh for years, although she'd followed his career since he'd shown some proclivity for it. It hadn't taken long. He seemed to be out front on some hefty issues and the spokesman for his party when they needed a moderate voice. There were a couple from the state who were combative, openly hostile to the current environment. That she could understand. To be a moderate voice to her meant there was less passion.

Admit it. Also, less vitriol.

Which meant people listened. Not that it got them anywhere.

She'd seen clips of a press conference he attended, after the president had nominated someone for the Supreme Court. He was well spoken, lobbied for a hearing, a couple of great sound bites coming out of it. It hadn't done any good. The opposition was adamant in their opposition. The seat was still vacant but wouldn't be for long. She cringed thinking about some of the names on the short list of replacements. It was one of the reasons she was glad she'd gone ahead with the SCOTUS test case. It gave her one less vote to worry about.

It had been no surprise when he'd gotten assigned to Homeland Security. Lee Adams's death and the tragic terrorist attacks had been part of his initial campaign, and it catapulted him into the public spotlight on the issue of national security, screening, and border security on transportation matters. She wondered if he'd be voting against party when the ban was put in place. She knew his opinions on that and they didn't agree, although she couldn't blame him for his antagonism. She'd seen him on C-SPAN, one of the most vocal interlocuters when questioning the Transportation Security Administration, or TSA, for what he called gross mismanagement, during one hearing, blasting them for withholding information in another.

And more recently, he'd become a voice for the Intelligence Committee's search for the truth as far as the Russian hacking of the election. He was pushing for answers and some transparency. He was also raising the alarm on the other side's complacency.

He was a good congressman. Maybe it was in his genes.

Genes he'd passed down to Chloe at conception.

She'd come around full circle and still had no answers.

⤙

The lights of the city beckoned Jack to the window and he stood looking at the expanse of the capital. He had come to love this city, with its history and its drama. He didn't like what the government had become in the last two decades and he was always at odds with the partisanship that controlled both sides of the aisle. It used to be a place of consensus, policy constructed around what was best for the country and its citizens, not the radical principles of a few. It had gotten worse in the six years he'd been here instead of better, and he didn't know what was going to happen in the future. The voters this election cycle seemed to have increased their intake of Kool-Aid. The Republicans were still able to maneuver their base to vote against their own best interests. Killing child care tax credits, fighting deregulation, refusing to invest in community colleges or manufacturing communities had done nothing but pit the middle class against a government they felt had betrayed them. That the incoming president was promoting violence, racism, and ignorance didn't seem to matter. He'd become the spokesman for an angry electorate who wanted change. They all wanted change: they just weren't taking the same roads to get there. Gearing up for a conventional fight was probably a mistake because the man in question wasn't conventional. In his opinion, he was a disaster waiting to happen. He could only hope the chaos would work in their favor.

After flopping down on his sofa, he scanned his home. Opulence surrounded him, chrome and glass, modern but sterile, and he realized how distasteful it was to him. It was worth much more now than when purchased and he could sell it to provide money to Flint in a small relief effort, build a homeless shelter, fund a small country. But it wasn't his to sell.

The person who lived here wasn't who he wanted to be. Why had he let his mother convince him it was appropriate for his status?

Status.

He didn't even like the word. It implied he was better than everyone else, and that was far from the truth. Nell was a better person than he was. She always stayed true to who she was. Worked hard, lived well, used her talents to help others, didn't let anyone tell her what to do.

Or what not to.

Maybe it was hard wired in her genes.

Wasn't that what her parents were doing? Helping others? Yet they'd taken it to the extreme, leaving their daughter behind to fend for herself.

He peered into the past to the day she'd told him about her life after they left, why they'd relocated on another part of the globe.

It had been a shock.

She'd been seven-years-old when her parents decided they wanted to do some good in the world. Signing on to Doctors Without Borders, the need for surgeons a dire one, Dr. James Warren and his wife Merry had left for Ethiopia on their first assignment for what was supposed to be a year stint. Believing Nell was too young to go along, they'd dropped her off at her grandmother's, a house she'd never been to before, on their way to the airport. Nell had, had no inkling that her world was about to change until they pulled out of the drive-way, leaving her behind. Adele Warren's house had become her home base as her parents took on other assignments, to Egypt, then Thailand, and to other parts of the world he didn't know about. As far as he knew, they were still involved with the organization over twenty years later.

He'd once asked her how she felt when her parents left.

She had laughed, maybe a bit too tinny.

"Hysterical if I remember correctly. I begged them to take me with them. I didn't know my grandmother that well and I was afraid I'd never see them again."

"You did, didn't you? See them again?"

"A couple weeks at a time between missions. Maybe every couple of years."

"Did they ever take you with them?"

"No. They said it was too dangerous. I stopped asking when I was old enough not to care."

The sadness in her eyes told him a different story. That she'd cared, probably more than she should, more than she'd acknowledge.

As he glanced around at the ornate fixtures in his home, he thought it ironic that she had parents who gave too little attention, while his remaining one gave too much.

Had he shut Nell out as far and wide as her parents had, kept her on the periphery of his family circle?

Rubbing the back of his neck, he let Ron's words sink in. The remarks stung. Maybe because there was some truth beneath them, truth he didn't want to see.

Nell hadn't cut him out until he'd acquiesced. To his mother.

If he had forced the issue, chosen differently, how would his life have turned out?

Would he be in Congress? Would he be married? Would they have had more children, or would the relationship have floundered on its own?

If they had changed one thing, how many other outcomes would have been affected?

The one truth that hadn't changed: he missed her. Still.

Life without her was colorless: life without Chloe was...He didn't know a word for it. She'd never been in his life, not with the kind of affinity he knew could exist between father and child. He'd had it with his. They'd spoken the same language, had the same priority: public service. Working for the most influential think tank in the country, Lee had been engaged in political strategy and was a strong advocate for fact-based analysis. He had to be rolling in his grave at the inundation of fake news infiltrating social media. He could never have foreseen the impact of the "catfish" out there who spread so many lies and gave away so much misinformation. And how it had paved the way for someone like the incoming president to win an election.

Maybe he should have followed in his father's footsteps. They'd had discussions about it, but Lee had thought politics was a better fit for him. He had the temperament, the intelligence, the common sense to act against injustice and discrimination on a different stage.

You have the charm and the powers of persuasion I lack.

Cerebral rather than social, Lee had been an intellectual who thrived in an environment where ideas drove the agenda. He'd reported on his subject material in a clear, concise way, devoid of the emotion that might have colored his testimony. Sought after for lectures and panel work, he'd been on his way to California to lead a forum on how well cultural assimilation was working across the country, a project designed to help both citizens and local leaders.

The metrics had suggested that adaptations were needed to improve relations so that the people and ideas could be integrated more seamlessly into a new and ever-widening society. The program had been developed to measure the effects on absorption of differing ethnic groups, and whether there was progress being made on key issues such as social, environmental and economic concerns. It included both immigration and emigration status, those coming into the country and settling in the area and those moving in from other parts of the country. Lee wasn't the only member of the team to die on that plane. The institute lost several critical advocates and it had taken time to recover from the effects of the loss. Lee's death had left a gaping hole within the think tank. It had left a hole in him, as well. He'd begun to think Chloe might be able to fill it.

It's what had prompted the first call to Nell when Chloe was six. Nell was moving them back to Boston. He was running for Congress. She insisted it was not the best time for another change in Chloe's life. She was also concerned that Chloe would become embroiled in the campaign and not in a good way. As persuasive as she was, he'd had to agree, although reluctantly. But he wasn't giving up that easily. They'd negotiated back and forth over a couple of weeks and came to an agreement. He would continue stay in the shadows for the time being, but Nell would give him periodic updates on his daughter's life. If he wanted to check in, he'd do it through email, Nell's chosen mode of communication. And she always got back to him. She sent everything to him through his personal computer, and the only two people who had access, other than him, were Ron and Dave. Ron knew Nell: they both knew their story. It might have been a consolation prize but Nell more than kept her word.

The first pictures had arrived the week he moved down to D.C.

There were several stuffed in the envelope addressed to him in Nell's neat script.

Chloe's class picture, her in her jeans, boots, and sparkly pink shirt standing in the back row. Even then she was tall for her age. Nell had written on the back of it, letting him know who her best friend was. Keileh had moved up every grade with her, and from what Nell said, the friendship was as strong as ever. The next was one of Chloe in a tutu, with the words, WORLD CLASS BALLERINA on the back. It was accompanied by a smiley face. He'd since learned that the smiley face was to let him know it was not her calling. In another she was dressed, in a girly-girl dress and patent-leather T-straps for the christening of Mia's youngest kid.

Then, his favorite. A close-up. Her face shining, a mischievous twinkle in her eyes, and a devilish smile. He'd fallen in love immediately, and sat mesmerized, a feeling of pride washing over him at her mere existence. He'd framed that one and it was sitting on his bureau here in the city. No one had seen it, because he'd never invited anyone to share his bed here. It was too easy to be scammed, too easy to be victimized, too many eyes, too many wagging tongues. Hope had never come down. She'd never been invited.

There were a few more he'd framed over the years, things he'd saved, like report cards and evaluations.

When Nell had sent him the first copy of Chloe's report card, he'd checked out the school, wanting to make sure it was the best, and he'd found Nell had chosen well. It had the kind of diversity that Nell would have looked for, but the school's reputation was based on the academics and they were first-class. Her grades were always good. In second grade, she was top of her class in English, third grade found her voted student of the month, fourth grade she'd won a writing competition and read the piece out loud over the school loudspeaker system. Even at nine she had her mother's skills at crafting an opinion. She'd started gaining weight in the fifth grade, but he was told it was the age. Dave's wife, Ellen, gave him a year-by-year assessment of what was age appropriate and it helped him understand how Chloe was developing, where she was mentally, academically, and physically. When he'd seen her hiding in the corner at the press conference, she'd looked taller, which might mean her baby fat was melting away. She was going to be as beautiful a woman as her mother and he wanted to be there to protect her. In full body armor.

There had to be a way of convincing Nell to let him into their lives. Her apprehension was stalling things and he thought he might know why. If he was in Chloe's life, he'd be in hers as well.

He didn't consider that a stumbling block, almost relished the opportunity to get to know her again. Maybe it was just the history that was luring him back, not the reality. Maybe he'd find his heart had deceived him.

What would he do if she was everything he remembered? Would he be able to leave it in the past?

The answer was as elusive as sleep.

CHAPTER FIVE

Hurrying into the Longworth House Building, Nell checked the slip of paper again to see which room she was headed for. The morning had not gone as easily as she would have hoped. She'd had to wait for Chloe. Who'd changed three times before they could leave for school. She'd gotten to the airport with time to spare, but her flight had been delayed and she'd arrived in the capitol with thirty minutes to grab a cab and deliver herself to the appropriate room assigned for her interview.

The security check had stolen it from her.

Checking her watch, her breathing shallow, she had two minutes left before she was late. Picking up her pace, she glanced from right to left, until she stopped short in front of 1302.

She quickly glanced down to the number highlighted in bold print, which matched the one on the plaque to the left of the door. It was almost surreal seeing it in concrete form.

Representative
John Emerson Adams
Massachusetts
1302

He'd made it work, and done a good job in the process.

Zelda's assistant had texted letting her know the change in venue for the meeting. She was glad she had. Otherwise she would have blamed it on Jack, thinking he'd set her up to talk about Chloe again.

She took a deep breath. This was it. She'd tried to block out all thoughts and feelings, and she'd done a fairly good job until she saw his name etched on the rectangular panel. Then everything came rushing back, the fluttering wings of emotion more like a tornado than a gentle breeze. What would she feel when she saw him? Would the magnetic pull still be there? And if it was, what then?

Turning the door-knob, she slowly opened the wooden panel and entered the common area, agitated now as to what she'd find. The room was well furnished, the fittings almost regal. She took a moment to appreciate the historical significance before she was welcomed in with Zelda's firm hand shake.

"I am so happy you could join us."

Looking Zelda in the eye, she said, "I am more than honored by the invitation."

Zelda had the grace to explain the change in offices.

"I'm sorry about the subterfuge. I'm trying to keep this all under wraps. I don't exactly want the opposition to know what I'm up to. I thought Jack's office would be the safer bet. I'm sorry if you're uncomfortable with it."

It was the man himself who made this whole situation uncomfortable. Her partners at the law firm Woodley and Fisher called him Mr. Gorgeous Eyes for a reason. They were the blue-grey of a storm cloud, striking at will. Every conversation she'd had with him regarding Chloe had been done by email. She didn't dare meet him in person. She had a sinking feeling they could still work their magic on her. Her nerves were on alert. She was in his office, so she knew he was lingering somewhere close by. She tried to brace herself for the impact of his appearance, straightening her shoulders, she took a deep breath as people started filtering in.

Recognizing some of the big guns in the fight for immigration reform as Zelda motioned them into a room to the left, she tried to calm her nerves, waiting for the man himself to appear.

Did Zelda sense her nervousness? She could tell by her tone that the elder stateswoman was doing her best to make her feel welcome. There was a hint of humor when she said, "I hope you don't mind that we want to pick your brain. We'd love to know how you won that case. We also would love your presentation skills at work for us. Whether you like it or not, you've become a critical component in our fight. And if that travel ban goes into effect, we want you in the fight with us to overturn it."

Her eyes flicked warily as more people filtered in, before they came to rest on Zelda's.

"I can guarantee I'll be in that fight in Boston."

"There is an upcoming hearing on the USCIS failure to conduct background checks on immigrant applicants and I need to prepare a write-up for my presentation. If you were on staff, I would assign that task to you, but unfortunately, you are not. I've got my legislative assistant coming in and I'm hoping that you can give us some legal points to include in my opening statement. I want to include Deferred Action for Childhood Arrivals and how the applications will be processed. There's no promise this program will survive the new administration and it annoys me to no end."

Nell almost suggested Jelani would be the one to talk to on that issue. She was the partner who locked horns with the Homeland Security forces more than the rest of them but she decided against it. Nell licked her lips and said, "ICE has eased up arrests and we've seen a decrease in the deportations of children by Immigration Services but there is a four-year back-log. Those with valid claims are waiting too long for determination. I'm afraid for the ones still in line. Time may be running out for them."

Jack all but ran into the office, came to an abrupt stop when he saw her standing there. Time stood still along with him.

She didn't miss the huskiness in his voice when he said, "Hello, Nell. It's good to see you. Congratulations on your win."

She could only stare at the man in the doorway, all six-foot-four of him, slightly muscled, broad shoulders, chiseled jaw, close shave, smooth skin, lips so soft they felt like rose petals, his brown hair slightly curly and brushed off his face, making those eyes the focal point.

Her breath hitched but she kept the moan hidden and her voice modulated.

"Thank you."

She wondered if Zelda could feel the energy between them. It was like an engine had been turned on and the hum was vibrating at full throttle.

She had her answer when Zelda glanced at Jack, a speculative gleam in her eyes.

Thrusting his hands in his pockets, he looked over at her.

She patted her skirt, more to keep her hands from shaking. There was a simmering heat coursing through her and she did her best to push it out.

Zelda surprised her out of her agitation by admitting, "I asked Jack if he thought you might be willing to work here as a lobbyist. He told me in no uncertain terms that your answer would be no."

Tilting her head in Zelda's direction, she asked, "Why would you offer me that kind of job? I'm not experienced in politics: in fact I'm not good at it, can't play well with others at all, and I haven't worked in DC in a long time."

Capitol Hill was like a neighborhood where rival gangs were constantly at war, doing what they needed to, to win. She didn't have the patience or the ability to soothe egos, something necessary to avoid a bloody crossfire.

"You've accomplished what we've been waiting years to accomplish. It gives us a foothold on what, up until now, has been a slippery slope. You could be a critical component in out fight, but I understand your refusal to move down here. May I ask that you be available to us on a regular basis? If I can't have you here full-time, it would be good to know you're a phone call away."

"I do a lot of pro bono work out of Representative Adams field offices, so I would be open to that kind of a contribution."

A familiar face peeked out of another office. One she had gotten to know well during her years working for Tomms.

Moving toward her, Nell smiled. "It's great to see you, Tahlia. Does Jack know how lucky he is to have you?"

Tahlia embraced Nell in a warm hug. "I remind him daily but I'm not sure he listens."

"If I remember correctly, you have a way of getting through to people."

Squeezing her hands, Tahlia said, "Tomms always knew talent. You've done well for yourself since you left us."

"Anyone who had the benefit of working with him learned how to do things well."

Zelda began to hover, and Tahlia had learned to read the cues.

"It was good seeing you, Nell. And congratulations. I'm sure Tomms is very proud of you."

As soon as Tahlia retreated to her office, Jack led Nell into his small conference room. Some of the people in attendance were already seated around the oval table, while some were left standing around the perimeter.

As she scanned the room, Nell recognized several of the lawyers, Jeannette Rankin among them. Also in attendance were Tabit, Harper and Salazar, members of the Judiciary subcommittee and some members of the full Judiciary who had an interest in the hot topic.

Nell could have been intimidated with the distinguished audience but after facing the Supreme Court justices, and the historical prominence of that chamber, she put it all in perspective.

Zelda completed the introductions, although that was just a courtesy. Nell knew most of the faces here and had to take a breath. She needed her wits. Jack could do strange things to her nervous system and the synapses in her brain. That he was there, on the periphery, was an ever-present danger.

After some initial remarks, Jeannette began the Q and A with the one thing that had played a prominent role in the outcome.

"Why did you pick this case for the Supreme Court test?"

"It had all the quantifiers I was looking for. Ramona Perez had her green card, had even signed an intent to naturalize, but the laws, the expenses, the governing rules that changed every year got her caught up in so much red tape she was unable to move forward. Anyone who knows the history of immigration in this country knows that immigrants were once treated as future citizens. For decades, up until maybe 1952, every applicant for naturalization had to file an intent, years in advance of their oath. They were said to be in transition at this point and although they weren't granted any protection, they had given notice of their intention to grow their roots in this country. I hoped the groundwork they laid would provide context."

"How did you find them?"

"I met Ramona through a friend of mine. She was working for a landscape design company, had two children born in Boston. She was afraid of being deported. Didn't know what would happen to her children if she was. There are a lot of war stories out there, where children are left homeless, falling between the cracks, young citizens who should have their government's protection. Instead they are given a life sentence of poverty and welfare services they don't need. Ramona was anxious and willing to take her oath of allegiance as soon as it was legal for her to do so. She felt she was American, acted as if she were American, and wanted to be legally naturalized."

"The statistics of those children left behind are striking. What made you file from that angle?"

"I talked to her daughter. She was the one who put it into words for me and I thought, why not? Cases had been presented to protect the children of immigrants, more from a detention perspective than a citizen's. Immigration judges are prone to release minors, citing noncompliance with the Flores Settlement Agreement, which states that every child should be processed out as expeditiously as possible. We thought that a citizen's rights should carry the same kind of weight. It was Graziela who become my client. She was a perfect model of citizen child whose family was at risk of being broken apart. Within a month of filing with the state's supreme court, Ramona was picked up and detained. I had warned the Perezes it might happen with the exposure. No one in the family knew how it was going to go, but they were willing to take the risk if it meant winning in the long run. They're good people and should be welcomed with open arms instead of forced into the shadows. It's crazy out there right now. What happens depends on the judge, the arresting agents, the part of the country you live in, the weather, the way the wind blows. Now, with the incoming administration? Who knows what will happen."

She still couldn't believe she'd won the case and that it opened new avenues to fight on the front lines. They'd hoped that a new, more lenient administration could get the Dreamers Act and a new reform package passed, but the election hadn't gone the way they'd anticipated, or the way every news outlet had predicted. No one knew what was coming now that the newly elected president could keep his campaign promise of deporting millions.

"That's what we have to change. We have to have consistent laws, pre-ordained steps, a straight road to naturalization that works for everyone."

"I agree. We also need to figure out who stays and who goes. There should be more leeway given to citizens' parents, especially if they've lived good lives, paid taxes, worked, contributed to the community. Of course, we have to guard against those who willfully come into the country to have a child. There needs to be certain measures in place like length of residency, work status, and country of origin."

"How many cases have you handled?"

"Over the last five years, I've defended women immigrants in abusive relationships, sought asylum for dozens due to persecution of race, gender, and religion, and pursued pro bono cases for as many deportation stays, as I could."

She had a soft spot for children at risk of losing parents. It was a cataclysmic event in the life of a child. She should know. Her mother had left her when she was only seven. It had been debilitating and it had taken years to get over it. It hadn't been due to unfair legislation but her mother Merry Warren's free will. If there was a mother out there who wanted to stay with her child, Nell was going to fight like a tiger to make it possible.

"You've set the stage for more of these wins. It's an incredible achievement."

"I didn't seek out my clients to make a name for myself. I did it to give them a fair shot at the legal system."

"For justice's sake?"

"Is there justice today? I'm not sure. Illegals commit horrific crimes, aliens are deported and return without consequence on one side, families are being torn apart because of quotas, delays, and financial constraints on top of the fear mongering perpetrated by our elected officials, on the other. It can takes decades to become eligible for naturalization. Good people are being turned away, some returning to certain death because of who they are."

"You seem passionate about what you do."

"If you have a heart, you have passion. I want to make a difference, and this is the way I've chosen to do that."

Zelda sat back, rubbing her hands together as if she needed to get to work.

"I'm putting together a list of measures for my presentation at the USCIS hearing. I'd love your input and hope you can put something together, send it to my office. I'd also like to set up a couple more interviews before the inauguration. I want all our ducks in place the minute that oath is taken."

"I can look at my schedule, arrange that."

"She can also drop by one of my offices for a conference call if something comes up that needs your immediate attention."

Jack's voice washed over her, and her skin erupted in gooseflesh. It never failed.

She looked up to see him staring at her. Why had he offered that? She could as easily talk to Zelda from her own office with much less anxiety. Before she could suggest that, Zelda was already agreeing.

"I like that idea. Maybe she could carve some time out every Friday and we could consult then."

She clasped her hands tightly in her lap more to keep the annoyance from showing than nervous tension.

"Maybe you could ask me since I'm sitting here."

Zelda's head jerked up, a look of apology on her face.

"Sorry. I'm used to—"

"Controlling the agenda? I appreciate that, but you won't control mine."

She didn't like that they were moving pieces around their chessboard at will.

"Fridays would be a problem for you?"

"Not necessarily. I can't commit to a routine time. It would all depend on my case load and my clients. I could have my assistant let you know what would work that morning."

"You said you do pro bono out of Jack's offices. Could you check in with me when you're there? If I have any impending legislation, interview, hearing that I could use another opinion on, it would give me the opportunity to speak to you."

"Don't you leave on Thursday like everyone else?"

"I do but that doesn't mean I don't work weekends. Fridays aren't filled with congressional activities and if there's something pending that needs to be addressed I'd have more flexibility if I'm in one of my field offices."

Nell noticed Jack's attention focus back on her. He wouldn't have known she worked out of his offices. She arranged her sessions during the week, while he was here in D.C. She'd even been given a key to his office for early-morning meetings. It wasn't unusual for her to meet with the clients before sunrise, so they didn't miss any work.

Nell stood. She needed to get going. It took some time to shake all the hands that reached out, and she promised she'd make herself available for whatever the committee needed.

After saying her goodbyes, she headed for the door, and immediately sensed that Jack was at her side. She could feel his eyes touch her from thirty feet away.

Standing at the threshold, she waited to hear what he had to say.

CHAPTER SIX

Jack's hands were in his pants pockets. His expression might have mirrored her own.

She caught a whiff of his after-shave, the same one he'd worn when they were dating. The scent wrapped around her and tried dragging her back to a past she refused to repeat. His voice was low, in direct competition with the murmurings going on behind them, so she had to lean in to hear him. Something she should have tried harder to avoid.

"How long have you been doing that?"

She straightened, forcing herself out of his personal space.

"Working out of your office? A few years. Dave asked me to do some pro bono for one of your constituents. It kind of spiraled out of control from there."

She could hear the coins jingling in his pockets as he fingered them.

"Why didn't I know? Was it a state secret?"

"I asked them not to make it public. I didn't want your mother to find out. It would have ended a good relationship between me and your staff."

"You thought I would have told her?"

"I do. You always told her everything."

As she was ready to step out into the hallway, he put his hand on her arm, effectively stopping her. She made the mistake of looking back and fell into his eyes.

It was a moment before Jack could get words past the lump in his throat. She was a beautiful woman. Amber, doe eyes that burned, long black hair, her slender fingers always playing with the wispy bangs, full lips, and a mole that sat just above them on the left side. His mother called her a gypsy and maybe there was a bit of that heritage that had been passed down. He thought of her as bohemian, a free spirit who always followed her heart. Maybe the gypsy label fit better because of her passionate, fiery nature. She was like a maelstrom that couldn't be contained.

She was dressed more conservatively today, grey pin striped suit, pale grey shell, high heels that he swore made her more intimidating. Her black hair cascaded down her back, causing a surge in his electric meter.

Stifling the urge to lean in for a kiss, Jack cleared his throat.

"I know now and I'm around on Fridays."

Her eyes had a faraway look in them.

"There's always a downside."

"You could work for me here. I'm looking for a new legislative director."

The firm set of her jaw gave him his answer. He didn't need the words that accompanied it.

"You know what it entails, Jack. I'm not relocating, taking Chloe out of her routine, or putting her in boarding school. I know what that's like and it's not an option."

He knew that's what her parents had done soon after they left. Nell had sworn she'd never do the same thing to any of her children.

"Would living in DC be so bad? We could tell her. I'd be there to help."

"You're here three, maybe four days a week. And then there's all those recesses. Besides, I don't need your help. We've been fine on our own."

"You have. I can't say I ever doubted it. You never needed me, Nell. You've got more steel in you than the Brooklyn Bridge. But just maybe Chloe might like to have a father around. I would think it's an important role in some way."

She studied him, the shivers making it hard to think. She had come to a crossroad and had to make a decision about which way to go. Chloe was pushing her in the direction Jack wanted, but her reservations were making it difficult to take the first step.

"What about Eloise? I'm still not okaying a test. She could make Chloe's life miserable and I won't allow it."

Sudden anger lit his eyes, the stormy grey darkening.

"Neither will I."

Dropping her gaze to the marble floor beneath her feet, she admitted, "Chloe's begun to ask questions about you. I think it might be time to rethink the arrangement. But I'm not there yet."

His expression changed to reflect hope.

"Could you try to hurry it up?"

"Have you discussed it with Eloise? Shit will hit the proverbial fan when she finds out you're going against her edict."

"Her edict is almost twelve years out of date."

"I am not dealing with her attitude, and there's no way in hell I'll allow her to persecute my daughter."

"You think I will? And wasn't the sticking point our relationship? We're no longer together and she has far more important things to do with her time than give you grief."

He'd allowed Eloise liberty with their whole relationship, to insult and intimidate at will. Why would she think things had changed?

"Still living in that little bubble, aren't you? I've got to get going. I have a flight to catch and I'm going to be late."

And without giving him a chance to say another word, she was hurrying down the hall, towards the exit, and he watched her until she was out of sight.

Zelda came up to stand beside him.

"This thing between you is hard to miss. You said it was ancient history."

"What do you mean?"

"There might be ruins here, but they're still smoldering."

"Ash is ash, Zelda."

She patted his shoulder as if she felt sorry for him.

"Keep telling yourself that but I've found that sometimes a phoenix rises out of them."

He returned to his office, Zelda's words ringing in his head.

In all the time he'd been separated from Nell, he'd never found anyone to replace her.

She'd been his first love, the only woman who had brought him close to breaking the promise he'd made to his father, the one that had come after Lee Adams' death, but it was a promise just the same.

The voice from the past intruded.

Please take care of your mother.

He could still hear the cadence, the measured tone in that last call that had come while he was in class. He'd let it go to voice mail and found the chilling message only after he'd been dismissed. It still echoed in his head, over fifteen years later. His father had realized what was happening on board his flight and had called to tell Jack about the hijackers and the probable outcome.

Jack had raced to the quad to watch the unfolding drama, the re-runs of the planes hitting the Twin Towers, the plane that had cratered the Pentagon, and the plane that was taken down by the passengers, saving another landmark from being destroyed. No one would ever know which one it was. Dozens of students and faculty had milled around the television, somber expressions, angry retorts.

He was the only one who had a personal stake in the disaster and he'd run out, needing to get home, to be with his mother, to wait for the call that would confirm his worst nightmare.

He must have listened to his father's message a hundred times, wanting to remember the voice, the man who was his most important ally.

"Jack."

There was a long pause before he came back on the line, his voice muffled.

"Hijackers have taken over my flight and it doesn't look good for us. The plane is flying very low and it looks like we're not going to make it out of the city. I love you son. You were my proudest accomplishment and I will always be with you. Follow your heart, Jack in everything you do. And please, take care of your mother. She made me her world and my absence will be difficult for her. Don't ever—"

Lee had been cut off.

From the time stamp of the call, he had lost the connection when the plane slammed into the Pentagon. The voice had been calm, collected, as if he'd already made his peace, something Jack still hadn't found.

The waiting in the aftermath had been brutal. The body had to be found, identified, shipped home, waked, and buried. For six months following that 9/11 tragedy, his mother hadn't gotten out of bed. When she'd finally crawled out, distraught and disoriented, she anchored Jack with her debilitating grief. To this day, he kept the promise made, the one without words, made to a person already dead amongst the ruins of the United States military complex.

Nell might soon be back in his life again. It might be because of Chloe but it couldn't hurt his cause. They'd always been more estranged than split up. Nothing had changed about the attraction. As soon as he'd rushed into his office, there'd been a major shift in his metabolism. If it wasn't her mind ramping it up, it was her body. If he got to meet Chloe, see Nell on a regular basis, he had to figure out a way to keep his equilibrium.

His administrative assistant was on the phone when he'd returned from his conversation with Nell, and he signaled he wanted to speak with her as soon as she was done.

Taking the seat in his domain, he rifled through the memos, telephone slips, and notes mentally organizing how he'd spend the next few hours, hoping the visions of Nell didn't keep playing in his head.

When Tahlia appeared, he looked up at the fifty-two-year-old, still not believing his luck. He had arrived in Congress a greenhorn, and he'd desperately needed an experienced hand to guide him through the paces. Tahlia had worked for Representative Tomms, who'd retired the year he'd arrived, and she had been looking for a new challenge.

He'd easily supplied it.

Six years later, he led, and she managed an office that had the kind of synergy that made it a well-oiled machine. He'd been happy working for a woman with such efficiency and affability.

He smiled at the irony.

He'd forgotten she knew Nell until their greeting.

Not sure if he was angry or upset for other reasons, he asked, "Did you know about the arrangement Nell had with the field office staff?"

"Yes, why?"

"You don't usually keep things like this from me."

"I didn't realize I was. Dave said he'd handle the pro bono attorneys. He mentioned Nell once or twice, but I didn't realize it was something you'd want to know. There are a couple other attorneys who work for our constituents there as well. Should I have told you about them?"

Rubbing his hands on his face, his fingers through his hair, he knew he was going to have to reveal the reason.

"It has more to do with our past than the present. I've known her for years."

Tahlia inclined her head, prodding him to go on. She wasn't only his chief-of-staff, she had also become something of a confidant over the years. She knew just about everything going on in his life but there were pieces of his past he'd left out.

She closed the door and took a seat opposite him.

"You have a history? What kind?"

"Ancient."

"Dating? Living together?"

"A relationship, Tahlia. Lasted a couple of years."

"Hm. Didn't think you knew how to be in one of them. Haven't seen it for myself yet."

He glanced up from the envelope he was about to slit open.

"What about Hope?"

He'd been dating her for almost a year.

"If that's your idea of a relationship, I can see why someone like Nell wouldn't stick."

He stopped in mid-slice.

"What exactly does that mean?"

"It's kind of ho-hum. Nell has a bit more fire in her."

It was more like a roaring backdraft burning out of control and it had consumed him.

Defending his position even in the face of his feelings for the woman in question he replied, "Hope gets along with my mother and I don't have to take sides. And she's more than willing to do what she can for my career."

"It's your life."

He watched Tahlia stand as if to go, watched as her eyes narrowed and studied him, then widening as it dawned on her.

"Oh my God, Jack. You're...Chloe's father."

He met her stare before he spoke, her guess not much of a stretch.

"I forgot you would know about Chloe."

She dropped back down in the chair she'd just vacated.

"She was a darling little girl. Nell doted on her."

He could hear the criticism in his voice when he asked, "Even working as much as she did?" He sat back, stunned. It was his mother's voice.

Giving him no time to reflect on that, Tahlia contradicted his somewhat scathing opinion with a bit of judgmental leverage of her own.

"She left earlier than most, intent on being home to put Chloe to bed. She took a ton of work home with her, and she got it all done, so Tomms never minded. She couldn't have slept much. She was a good mother back then, Jack. I'm sure she still is. I often wondered where the father was."

She'd successfully put him in his place.

"Did Nell complain about me?"

"Nell never said one bad word about Chloe's dad, never said a word about...you, period."

Tahlia, never one to back down from being intrusive, asked, "Why, Jack? Why weren't you in her life? I'm assuming you knew about her. Keeping it from you doesn't sound like something Nell would do."

"I knew." The admission closed like a fist around his heart. "I'd change the past if I could."

She slowly shook her head as if disappointed in him. It rankled. In his defense he said, "I'm working on changing things. Nell's reticence has more to do with my mother than with anything else. Let's just say my mother and Nell never got along."

There was a knowing look that crept into her expression. One he didn't like. It said something he didn't want to think about. So did her question.

"Nell didn't get along with Eloise?"

"No. She didn't. Oil and water. She told me often enough that my mother was more of an influence than she should be."

Nell had suggested strongly that he didn't have much of a backbone. He had one, he just hadn't used it the way she'd wanted him to.

Tahlia chortled.

"Your mother can be a fly in the ointment. I can't tell you how much I appreciated that you talked to her about her incessant calls. I don't have time to move the chess pieces against someone who has no clue about how the game is played."

"She wasn't happy about it, but I promised to continue attending Friday night dinners and catch her up. I sacrificed it for the team."

"And it is still appreciated."

She rose again, took a step for the door before Jack stopped her.

"Tahlia, Chloe doesn't know, so it can't get out. I don't want her finding out that way."

"Your secret is safe with me."

"I know it is or I wouldn't have admitted it."

"Whatever was between you and Nell, Jack, it's still there. You can feel it vibrating in the air. You might want to take another look at what you want. It might not be placid, but it won't be boring, either."

CHAPTER SEVEN

Nell's flight out wasn't for a couple of hours, and she needed to escape what Jack still made her feel. After walking out of the building, she looked around, the city alive, churning out people from doorways, subway stations, museums, and monuments. Washington D.C drew visitors from around the globe, the cornerstone of democracy and freedom. It was a city that was never boring.

With each step forward, she took one back into the past, when she was new here, working for another congressman, a job she'd taken to distance herself from the emptiness of her life. Orphaned years ago, if the word meant being without parents, she'd lived with her paternal grandmother, summers and vacations. An undemonstrative woman, Adele Warren had given her a home, an education and the kind of strength that comes from standing alone. It was only when she passed away that Nell realized she'd loved the grizzled, old woman. The hundred-plus-year old brownstone she'd called home off and on since she was seven was too big for her alone, but she couldn't sell it and buy new. It was a family heirloom, generations old and was left in progeny to her father. She knew she could have remained there, but when Jack asked her to live with him, she'd accepted the invitation hoping, it would begin a new phase in her life. It had been a mistake of major proportions and it'd sent her flying out to California. Three years later, law degree in hand she returned home. Left a sizeable inheritance from her grandmother's estate, she could have set down roots anywhere in the city but there was nothing for her there. Jack was gone, her parents were still working overseas, and her friends had migrated to other parts of the country. After she bumped into one of her grandfather's friends, bringing him up to date on what she was doing as she awaited the results of the bar exam, he'd offered her an introduction to Washington politics and she'd taken him up on it, hoping the new environment would help her put her life back in perspective. She'd worked with some of the best minds in town, but was unable to achieve her dream of defending the innocent in the myopic tunnel of partisan politics or find the companionship she was looking for. She'd returned to Boston for good. Refusing to contemplate another move, she bought her condo and sent her resumes out. Joining Woodley and Fisher had been the best decision she'd ever made. There she not only made a difference, she'd made friends, created her own circle of family that she could depend on and trust. She'd settled into a routine that worked for her and Chloe, but it seemed like that was all about to change.

She ambled with a goal in mind and the five-minute walk took her to the face of the Capitol, an imposing structure, its historical exterior speaking to the influence of those that worked within its walls. Yet that influence had become more of a power grab by those in the majority, and the headlines they made were small-minded and mean.

Turning, she took in the majestic design of the Mall, in the distance the Lincoln Memorial, one of her favorite spots, the Washington Monument standing tall at the halfway point. The winter scene was breathtaking, the snow sparkling in the afternoon sun, the chill in the air cleansing and fresh. The Christmas tree sat alone in the distance, the lights waiting for dusk to shine. In the spring, the cherry blossoms would be pungent, the breezes warm.

Heading in a southerly direction, she let her mind sort through the pros and cons of telling Chloe about Jack. Didn't she have a right to know? She'd asked questions about her father over the years, questions like why didn't she have one, what did he look like, where did he live? Last week she'd been assigned the task of outlining her family tree. She'd come home in a huff, saying that she'd only get half credit if she only produced half a tree. Why couldn't she know? What was the big secret? Was he in jail? Was he alive? Why didn't he ever visit her? Why didn't he care about her?

It looked like things were coming to a head, and she was ready to give in to the pressure being exerted on her from opposing forces.

The problem with that? He'd be in her life for good then. His mother along with him.

Not an appealing picture. Yet Eloise was in a branch of her family that couldn't be denied no matter how much she wanted to.

Images of him standing in his office doorway invaded her mind.

She had once run to California and Stanford to escape him. He'd validated her decision when he let his mother pull the strings. Seeing him again set off some dormant emotions. All the feelings she'd thought had worn down to nothing had come rushing back and she had to force herself to keep from welcoming him back in. That would be a mistake. Did she want to spend her energy resisting something that was still so powerful?

She was no closer to a decision now than she'd been before her walk. It hadn't cleared her head as she'd hoped, but instead had created a quagmire of unruly thoughts. As she approached the Lincoln Memorial, she stood before the majesty of a man who'd also battled for the downtrodden. He'd withstood vitriol, betrayals, hatred to do the right thing, as he saw it.

Taking a deep breath, she let herself relax into the moment.

She heard the voice from behind her.

"I thought you had a plane to catch?"

Startled by the shimmering energy racing up her spine, she pivoted around to face him.

"I do. I just couldn't resist coming here."

She looked out over the panoramic view. It was mid-December but there were still a multitude of flags in celebration of Veteran's Day and they were rippling in the cool air. Washington was alive due to the two-week orientation of the new members of Congress but would empty out again until the two bodies convened in early January.

"I come here when I want to get away from the madness, want to think. It's peaceful no matter what time of year."

His voice reaffirmed one of the problems of letting him back in her life. It was cool yet resonant and struck a chord.

"It was my favorite spot when I was here before."

He glanced over at her, his eyebrow arched.

"Why doesn't that surprise me?"

There were so many ways they were alike, had some of the same tendencies. It was the few that were in disharmony that had driven them apart. Brushing her bangs off her face, her hidden bracelets tinkling, she returned to her original position, facing the statue.

"Seems things worked out well for you and Eloise."

He took a step closer, so he was standing beside her.

"Nell, she's my mother. You were—"

"Not good enough if I remember correctly. Totally unsuitable as the wife of a future president."

He couldn't have missed the animosity that was still humming all these years later and he responded in kind.

"According to her. And I have no plans to run for that office."

"Her opinion carried weight." And it had nearly crushed her.

"She'll always be a part of my life, Nell. I can't help how she feels and I can't control what she thinks."

Her eyes snapped at him in challenge. "But you could have—"

She stopped in mid-sentence. It didn't matter anymore how he managed her. It wasn't her problem.

His eyes filled with curiosity, his voice carried an insistent ring.

"I could have what? Tell me. What could I have done to improve the situation?"

Taking a deep breath, not wanting to hash this out again, she said more moderately, "Until you realize what kind of influence she holds over you? Nothing."

"She doesn't anymore. I'm my own person."

Examining his suit, she asked, "So you buy your own clothes now?"

His fists found their way into his pockets.

"It gives her something to do."

"Oh, the parties, the bridge club, the Daughters of the American Revolution sorority, lunch with friends doesn't keep her busy? How many boards does she serve on? I believe it was four when we were together."

"It's what she did for my father. It's what she was trained to do."

"You are not her husband. You're her son. What about that statement doesn't register?"

He waved her off, his un-ease with the topic apparent.

"You're being ridiculous. You make it sound sordid. She likes shopping. I don't."

"She also liked paying your bills. Has that changed?"

"I can't maintain any kind of lifestyle on the money I get from being in Congress. I tap into my trust fund periodically."

"Still living in the apartment attached to her house?"

He felt like he was on the stand and she was cross-examining him. Agitation was swirling in his gut, but he kept on defending himself.

"It's cheaper than getting my own place. The condo here in the city is expensive."

"You're going to have me believe you pay for it? I bet she bought it for you and it's free and clear."

He couldn't deny it, so he let silence fill the space where there should have been an answer.

"Still haven't grown up yet, Jack. She still holds the purse strings, or maybe it's the apron strings. Doesn't matter which it is: they'll strangle you one way or another."

He cringed at her assessment.

"I'm surviving just fine."

"If that's all you want out of life, then I guess it suits you. I always wanted more."

"Like all my time."

Her face flushed as her ire grew.

"I only wanted an equal share, something you had a hard time portioning out."

He noticed the exact moment she caught the escalation in her voice.

She shifted to a more subdued tone.

"This is so non-productive. We are no longer together, so what your mother does or doesn't do is no concern of mine. And I'm not looking for any of your time anymore. It's a win-win-win."

"My mother needs me, Nell. I'm all she has. I can't turn my back on her."

She spun around to face him. "Who did I have? You were supposed to love me. I didn't need to come first, but I needed to be part of the equation."

His mouth spread into a thin-lipped grimace.

"You were a big part of the equation."

She contradicted him, betraying her annoyance.

"The x factor. The solution changed every time a new variable was introduced."

Eloise would need an escort, would be sick and need tending, she'd need a ride to the doctor's, a friend's house, a dinner party, her heat was too high, she was too cold, she'd didn't like dining alone, so she would demand he eat with her. He'd cancel their plans.

"I'm sorry you feel that way, Nell. It was never my intention."

"I got over it. I moved on. I was invisible most of my life and I felt that way when we were together. I don't anymore."

"Again, that was never my intention."

"No, it was Eloise's. She won, I lost. Not something we need to go over again."

She looked him straight in the eye.

"She is one of the major concerns I have in telling Chloe the truth."

"For good or for bad, she's her grandmother and I should never have let you persuade me into giving up my rights."

"You relinquished them, Jack. When you sided with Eloise."

"All she was asking for was proof..."

"No, what she was asking for was your loyalty, your undivided attention, for you to choose her over us. You did. End of story."

"Unfortunately for you, it isn't. The end of the story. If I need to wait until Chloe's eighteen to introduce myself, I will. Then it will be on you. I'm her father. You can't change that, no matter how hard you fight."

"You're right. You are, and I can't. I guess all I can do is say thanks for all the help you gave me. Oh, wait a minute. You gave us nothing. I owe you nothing."

She spun away, but he reached her and took hold of her arm.

"Nell, please. I didn't mean for this to get so hostile."

She took a breath when he settled those eyes on her, the ones that could reach into her soul, and he did the completely unexpected. He dipped his head and his mouth touched hers, the familiar softness, the intoxicating textures prodding her to give in to it. He pulled her closer, his tongue sliding between her lips, and she exalted in how he tasted, how he felt. The fire that was always there beneath the surface ignited, creating a backdraft of intense heat that she'd only felt with him. Her hands were pressed against his chest, their bodies close within his tight embrace. Her instinctive response to him was powerful and she had to fight her way back up to reality. As she pushed him away, their eyes met and held.

"It seems some things never change."

He was right. The combustible way their bodies merged had always been...combustible. She inhaled ragged breaths: his breathing seemed labored.

"Chloe and I don't come part and parcel. This won't get you what you're asking for."

"Please, Nell. I'm asking you to release me from my promise. Let me meet her."

She hung suspended in the moment before rational thought came rushing back.

Had he kissed her to get her to agree? Would it be so bad if she did? She needed to let the sparks die down before she could answer in a more cogent way.

"I'll think about it, Jack. That's all I can offer you right now."

She was shaking as she all but ran away. She felt like Cinderella at the stroke of midnight, the threat of pumpkins and rags propelling her away from danger.

The kiss was only going to make the decision more difficult. She knew she'd never get over him or his betrayal. If she couldn't trust him, how could she entrust her daughter's heart into his care?

She was in a no-win situation and she'd have to think long and hard about giving in to his request.

And that's what she did on the flight home, the drive from the airport.

She kept coming back to Eloise.

The terms were too dear, the cost too high.

She hadn't erected the wall between them.

Eloise Emerson Adams had, and he'd done nothing to prevent it from happening.

Nell pulled into her assigned parking spot at her condo and sat in the car for a few minutes to get her bearings. She loved it here, loved the acreage, loved the greenery. So different from the kinetic energy of DC and the city.

Researching it before purchase, she'd found that the original owners were nomadic Brahmins from the Back Bay in need of a summer retreat. It had been renovated as condos in the eighties, but the developers had kept the period details and the wood-burning fireplaces and hers had an abundance of natural light and an open concept that made it feel spacious and airy. She had purchased it upon her return from DC, right after she'd gotten the job at Woodley and Fisher. It was the kind of place she'd hoped to convince Jack to move to so they could be together in their own space, with only their lives to worry about. But he'd refused to move with her, adamant that his mother still needed him close-by. For the first few months, she had imagined what it would have been like living here with him, eating breakfast in the small kitchen, watching TV together while a fire roared in the fireplace, entertaining their friends, but it had done nothing for her spirit so she'd given up the dream and focused on her real life, diving into work with a vengeance. But her home always welcomed her in and it had become a retreat from a long day, a bad loss, a choking frustration.

After climbing out of the car, she went through the front entrance to the condo and entered.

Chloe looked up as she was setting the platter down on the dining room table. A tablecloth was draped over the oval and a small vase of flowers sat as centerpiece. Jelani must have stopped to pick them up on the way here.

"Look what I made."

Chloe was talking to her again. Her heart lightened.

It looked like a meatloaf with baked potatoes and green beans and it looked professionally plated.

Jelani was placing a bottle of wine on the table, smiling at her.

"I tried to start her off easy. She could excel at this and I told her so. You're going to have to let her experiment or get her cooking lessons. I might know who you could call. She's a friend, owns a store front and sells home-cooked take-out meals."

After kicking her shoes off, Nell sat on one of the empty chairs.

"Or I could see if she can deliver a week's worth of meals that Chloe can heat up."

"Thanks for your confidence in me, Mom."

Chloe rolled her eyes for good measure. Something she was doing with more regularity lately.

"That's not what I meant. We get home late, and you wouldn't have the time to make a full meal from scratch. Maybe we can do something different on the weekends but school nights? You could warm something up for the two of us."

After Nell took a bite, she noticed Chloe tentatively studying her.

"It's delicious, Chloe. I'm duly impressed."

She got down to some serious eating.

Jelani smiled at the chef before turning her attention back to Nell.

"What did the big-wigs in Washington want?"

"Zelda has a presentation to give at one of the upcoming hearings and she wanted some input. She threw out an offer for me to become a lobbyist."

Chloe's fork was almost to her mouth when she asked, "What's that?"

"A person who gets paid to influence legislators."

"What did you say?"

"I turned it down. I'm not moving us anywhere."

"That's good cause I wouldn't have gone."

Nell let it go. She wasn't going to have an argument over something that was already decided. Instead she asked, "Any projects coming up?"

"Just the family tree for Social Studies. Remember, I'll only get half credit if it's only half-done."

"I'll talk to your teacher."

"I'd rather you tell me who my father is. I'm old enough to know, Mom."

Maybe this would give her the impetus to get it all out in the open. Prepare her for the possibility that her grandmother would close a door that had barely opened. Maybe.

"It's been a long day, Chloe. Please don't push this right now. When's the project due?"

"At the end of January. We've got to go on Ancestry.com and do an extensive search. We're also supposed to interview one of our relatives. I don't have any on your side, unless I Skype Grandma or Pops. If they're available. If they agree."

Jelani seemed pensive for a moment and Nell thought she was ready to side with Chloe about the father thing.

"Your ancestors have been here from the beginning, haven't they Nellie?"

Nell breathed a sigh of relief at the topic.

"They didn't come over on the Mayflower, but they fought in the Revolution. The Warren's have been here since the 1700's."

Jelani laughed. "Really? That must be where you get your fighting spirit."

Chloe was more serious and seemed miffed.

"Why didn't you tell me this before?"

"I guess it never came up."

"What did they do? Did they write the Constitution or anything?"

Hers hadn't but Jack's had. With Chloe's pedigree, her tree would be illustrious. Not that it mattered. Eloise didn't think the Warrens had retained the purest of roots and it was one of the reasons she didn't like her. It made the worry about Chloe meeting her more pronounced. If Nell revealed who her father was, Chloe would want to meet the grandmother she didn't know. And that could only end in heartache. Eloise didn't want her, didn't accept her, and wouldn't allow her to become part of her life.

"Do you know my Dad's story? If you just give me the names, I can look them up."

"I'm not discussing this tonight, Chloe."

"That's what you always say. What are you trying to hide?"

That he gave his daughter up for his mother's money. Didn't care enough to push back against Eloise's accusations and demands. Not enough to make her feel it would last and he'd always be there for them. Better to cut him off at the start rather than be abandoned. She knew what that felt like and she didn't want that for her daughter.

Now?

He was in a different place, successful, independent...yeah, right. He'd never become his own person, was still depending on his family's money to live his life.

"Did he even know about me? Did you ever tell him?"

"I did tell him, Chloe, but his family put stipulations on things that I couldn't live with. He didn't care enough to disregard them."

"He didn't love me."

Looking her daughter in the eye, she admitted, "No, Chloe. He didn't love me."

The words struck more of a chord than she'd wanted. The knowledge of that simple statement still had a way of messing with her heart. Hearing the words out loud put a stake through it.

Chloe's eleven-year-old angst didn't give her time to wallow in it. She stood up from the table, threw her napkin on her plate, and yelled, "You have no right to keep him from me. All you ever think about it what's right for you. It never matters what I want."

She was running up the stairs to her room before Nell could come up with something to say that might mitigate the situation.

Jelani had sat quietly while the verbal skirmish waged. Now that Chloe was gone, she took a tentative step onto the battle field.

"That went well."

The emotions that had surfaced at seeing Jack had frayed her patience. She still could have handled it differently. Better.

"What exactly am I supposed to tell her?"

"Don't take all the blame, Nellie. It's not all your fault."

"I never wanted her to think he didn't care about her."

"But he didn't. Or, like you said, he didn't care enough."

"Maybe I should have introduced them the first time he asked. She was only three. If it hadn't worked out, she wouldn't have remembered."

"If that's true, you'd still be having this discussion."

"Okay, then when we moved back here. She was six."

"Does he get the urge every three years?"

"No. After that there was nothing. Well, up until a few months ago."

She thought it might have to do with his father and his death. The call had come on the anniversary.

"You don't do anything to discourage him?"

"Of course, I discourage him. He made me a promise and I made one back. I've kept mine."

"Maybe you shouldn't have. He's getting to know her, he's curious, he's realized what he's missed out on. Can you blame him?"

"No. But I'm biased."

"You're going to have to think about it, Nellie. Better Chloe learn the truth than be imagining things. The more you resist, the more important it's going to become. He'll become larger than life. Maybe you can introduce him as a friend first. Let them get to know each other for real. See what happens. See how well he deals with his mother."

"And if things work out, tell her."

"And if things work out, you tell her."

"And if they don't?"

Jelani had no answer for her but a shrug of her shoulders.

CHAPTER EIGHT

Pushing through the glass double doors of Woodley and Fisher at a little after eight a.m. the next morning, after dropping a still not-speaking-to-her Chloe off at school, Nell went straight to her office, kicked off her heels and sank into her chair.

This was home.

This was where her friends, her family lived and breathed.

She was never invisible here.

If she lost a case, Jelani or Arianna would join her for a glass of wine and commiserate with her. If she won one, Camille and Emilia would celebrate the victory. Her opinion was sought out and valued, her company was enjoyed, her presence appreciated. She could also find support and advice when dealing with insurmountable odds.

It was what Jack represented today.

His kiss had thrown her off. She hadn't expected it, hadn't been prepared for how it would feel. She'd missed the kind of spark they made together, and she'd been reminded that she would never outdistance the emotions he evoked, no matter how far away she moved. Or how much she refused to admit it.

Maybe that was the key. Accepting it. She'd been on her own long enough to know she could depend on herself to get through whatever it was she faced. Her grandmother had taught her self-sufficiency: her parents had taught her independence. It didn't mean she wasn't looking for someone to love her. Only that it had been fleeting at best most of her life. When she'd found out she was pregnant, she'd been shocked. They'd always used protection. The shock had transmuted into happiness. She'd looked at it as if she were growing her own family. A child would fill something that had been missing since her parents left: a sense of belonging. Those first few years had been tough, but she'd not only survived, she excelled. She'd found a woman whose children were grown and gone, who was looking for something to fill her days. They'd helped each other. Millie had provided the care and love Chloe had needed while she'd attended class, studied into the night. Chloe had provided the love that Millie had lost when her kids moved away. It had been traumatic for all of them when Nell moved back. She'd thought about staying in California indefinitely, but she'd missed the seasons and the history. Her history. She wanted Chloe to grow up where her ancestral roots were. At odds, loneliness infecting her spirit, she'd found herself in DC working for a man who'd become like a grandfather. She'd learned about justice and truth, about how to make things work through collaboration and cooperation, how to manipulate the system so it helped the most vulnerable. When he'd retired, she'd moved home. She was still in touch with him and his wife, went to dinner several times a year and he was one of the few she'd counted on to help her through the Supreme Court process. He was one of the few she trusted.

The others were here.

Looking out her window, she was a witness as Boston came alive and she felt a symbiosis with the city. It was a hot bed of revolution. Had been since the early days of the republic, and she never wanted to live anywhere else. Progressive, it moved into the twenty-first century better than most. Far different from the capitol, where obstructionism had reached its zenith. The phrase *do-nothing Congress* had been coined back in the 1940s, but it had nothing on the one in session today. The election upset had been a huge shock. For the politicians and the electorate at large. The Republicans had clamored in alarm during the campaign, but now that they'd won, they'd shut down the distress signal. The repercussions would be reverberating in the Senate and House for years.

No one knew what was going to happen, but she was determined to prepare herself for the siege against the immigrants living in her city and the environs.

Unaware that Arianna was standing in her doorway, she wasn't expecting a voice to intrude on her thoughts.

"Glad you're back. I thought they might try to kidnap you or something."

With no hesitation, no invitation needed, the senior partner walked in and sat down, curiosity written all over her face.

Nell answered honestly, "I'm scheduled to attend one of the judicial hearings on constitutionality and civil rights in January. Spend a day or two as part of a forum on immigrations over the next couple of months. I also agreed to be available for consultation. Out of Jack Adams' office."

Arianna leaned in, the shock on her face making a statement.

"That's interesting."

"Like watching worms in a pail."

Arianna looked bemused.

"This could be kismet."

"Not kismet. Bad luck."

"Still have the hots for him?"

She gave her, her sourest look.

"Wouldn't matter. There is no way I'm climbing the ropes into that ring again. If I'm going to fight someone to the death, it'll have to be for a bigger prize than Jack Adams at the end."

"What happened? He kiss you or something?"

Nell picked up a pencil and began to chew the end of it, not wanting to show what the kiss had done to her. Was still doing.

"As usual, we argued about his mother. And he wants to meet Chloe. It was a two-for-one sale. I'm not sure I want to go down that primrose path."

She and Chloe were close, relied on each other. How would that change if she gave in and let them get to know each other? Thing was, changes were already taking place. Chloe had become moody, confrontational. Was it her age, the hormones beginning to do their job? Or did Chloe resent her for working so much? Or was it simply the fact that she wanted to meet her father?

Nell shook her head, trying to get the indecision to take a hike. She disliked people who couldn't make up their mind. Take a stand and go with it was her motto. If you made a mistake, you'd learn something along the way.

Camille popped her head in. She was wearing a concerned look. Shaking her hair out of her face, Nell put on a smile for her partner's benefit.

Camille asked, "Do you have some time this morning? I need your opinion on a case I'm working on."

Camille was her counter-part for immigration, her expertise in the area of asylum. They bounced things off each other when they needed a fresh look, another opinion.

"Sure, check with Hani. See when I have a free moment."

Since the outcome of the Supreme Court decision, the firm was getting an influx of calls for representation. Pro bono along with paying clients. Her schedule was now bursting at the seams. She could possibly chalk up a couple more hours a day of work, which didn't bode well for her relationship with Chloe.

"I'm going to need it ASAP. There's someone waiting underground. I'm not sure how to handle it."

"Where did this someone come from?"

"Ukraine. Journalist. You know what's happening over there."

Too many were getting killed. A lot of cases looked like suicide. The mysterious gaps and circumstances suggested otherwise.

"I do. I can give you twenty minutes now."

"Thanks."

She came fully into the room, a dossier in her hand. Arianna stood to leave.

"I'll leave you two to your work. We're going to have to talk about adding some new faces to the firm if the calls keep coming in."

Chloe's scowl came to Nell's mind.

"There are already too many for the six of us. It's only going to get worse. Set up some interviews and we'll make time."

As she walked away, Arianna grumbled good-naturedly, "I'm running out of offices to hand out. You may have to start sharing."

Camille smiled at Nell. They knew Arianna was just kidding. If they had to lease more space on one of the other floors, they'd do that. None of the partners would be willing to give up the offices they had earned through blood, sweat, and tears.

"Okay, what do you have on this journalist?"

⌐

Jack made his way into his office at the Longworth after meeting with the incoming Intelligence Committee. He was glad orientation was over and he could concentrate on his own agenda. The introductory session was held earlier than usual this time around, and it was broken up differently than when he was a freshman. When he was first seated, there was a full two-week schedule filled with briefings, hearings, breakfasts, field trips, ethics indoctrination, financials, a how-to-staff-an-office instructional and how to find your way through the labyrinth of underground tunnels beneath the Capitol. This year the schedule was as jam-packed but condensed into six days and he'd been racing from one place to another. He was part of the steering committee for the newly elected Democrats, offering guidance in how to hire a chief of staff, organizational acumen, and the legislative process. Today was the last day before the end of the year recess, Christmas less than two weeks away, and he had a lot to catch up on. At least he wasn't changing offices. He could have, as he'd gained seniority, but now it seemed a waste of time. He liked his space and there was a flow that worked. He didn't want to jinx it. It also reminded him why he was here, kept his focus on his constituent work and not his surroundings. Palatial meant power and he wasn't going to buy into that kind of hype.

There was a lottery held for the new members. It was an archaic method but fair, he supposed. Lined up in alphabetical order, each representative would pick a number for office space. The lower the number the better the pick, number one getting first choice in real estate. He'd drawn a mid-level number his first year but with each successive term, his office space improved. Representatives didn't get the kinds of digs that Senators got, but he couldn't complain. His office worked at peak efficiency, due to the organizational skills of his chief of staff. He'd made a couple of good decisions along the way and his staff worked better than most.

Peeking his head into Tahlia's office, he asked, "Anything I need to know about?"

"Ron's coming by for your call bank session."

"Please, shoot me instead."

Ron came into the office as Jack was issuing the request.

"They don't allow guns in federal buildings."

He turned toward his friend and grimaced.

"I can take off my tie and you can choke me."

"I'll do that only if you don't get moving."

"I quit."

"Sorry. You're here for at least another two years. And that doesn't even start for another month."

"This should not be where I put my time."

"I know that. You know that. The staff knows that. But until the leadership of the party changes the strategy, or Citizens United is overturned and put to sleep, it doesn't matter."

Ron picked up a portfolio and nudged Jack toward the door.

"Let's go hot-shot."

Tahlia stopped him cold when she called out, "Oh, and there's a school in Massachusetts, your district, that asked you to speak to the middle grades. Dave called in the invitation, said to talk to you personally. His daughter is in the same class as the sixth-grade teacher's. The teacher sought him out to see if it was an option. They're doing a block on Civics 101."

He didn't have to ask which school. Dave's daughter went to the same one as Chloe. His heart began to beat like a thundering horde of wild horses.

"Standish Academy. I don't care what you have to do but fit it into my schedule."

"Your reaction tells me something I surmised. Don't worry. The date they gave me works perfectly. It's the Friday before Christmas."

"Good. Thanks."

Jack's hands went into his pockets, fingers busy with the loose change.

He moved toward Ron who was watching him and Jack passed him on the way towards the entrance of the building. Hurrying to catch up, Ron reached him and asked, "Do you really think that's a good idea?"

"This opportunity dropped into my lap. I didn't go looking for it. Let's just say I'm just doing my congressional duty by meeting the needs of my constituents."

"They're a little young to be that."

"The teachers are. Besides, I think it's important for the education system to stress civics. If it was taught as a priority, maybe we wouldn't have found ourselves in the mess we're in."

"Schools like Standish don't scrimp on learning. It's the public schools you need to focus on. Are you going to go into the public middle schools in your district or only the private ones?"

"That's a good question. I'll talk to Tahlia, see if we can put out some feelers. I wouldn't be adverse to that."

"It's good to hear there are things you don't mind doing."

"There's only one thing I detest and it's the miserable business of soliciting money."

They made their way out of the Capitol building and toward a line of row houses where offices were set up as call banks by some of the lobbyists or fundraisers, with phones, partitions and very little privacy.

"Don't complain. You're participating in the only thing that has a bipartisan flavor to it."

"Oh, then, by all means, count me in."

He did well at fundraisers, but leadership was always asking for more. They needed to shore up the candidacies that weren't going well, and expected everyone to chip in to get the job done, in and out of an election cycle. If there was such a thing.

When he'd first came to the Hill, the veteran politicians told the newly minted Congress members they'd be expected to spend at least four hours a day at the job. Raising money ranked higher on the to-do list than attending hearings. If he did what the DCCC expected, fundraising would squeeze everything else out. He'd have very little time for legislative work, preparing for committee meetings, hearings, building relationships, learning about key issues. He felt that he was elected to work for the people not the party, so he'd bucked the system almost immediately. He came to DC to do a job and it wasn't to dial for dollars. The amount expected of him increased every year and would continue to go up as his influence did. His dues went up incrementally as well. Ron kept the data in his big black book before turning it in to let their computer analysts keep track of who gave, how much they gave, and how often they gave. He tried valiantly to keep from bothering anyone more than he needed to. It was a sorry way to do business.

He sprinted up the steps and found an empty room. He didn't need the *Book of Scripts*. He'd been doing it long enough now to have his routine down, all while trying to stay spontaneous.

Some people thought this was a big reason Congress didn't get things done but, most of the popular incumbents performed due diligence in their real jobs. The reason nothing got done was polarity between the parties and with the current atmosphere, it was only going to get worse.

He finished dialing the number from his personal phone book and held the receiver to his ear.

"Hello, Ms. Huntingdon. This is Jack Adams. How are you doing today?"

CHAPTER NINE

Nell kicked off her shoes as they entered the condo vestibule, scooped them up, and carried them to the foot of the stairs. Jelani had once asked her why she wore them. She didn't need them for height and she took them off whenever she could. Nell had laughed and admitted she felt like the intimidator in them. She didn't want to lose that edge.

Chloe dumped her bag just inside the kitchen.

"Why don't you take that to your room, get changed, and warm up the ziti and chicken parm. I'll join you as soon as I get out of this suit."

Footsteps followed her up to her bedroom but continued down the hall.

"Okay. And thanks. I'm having fun pretending to cook for us."

Nell had taken Jelani up on her suggestion and she'd picked up some pre-packaged meals that Chloe could cook on her own. It seemed to have improved her mood.

"On Sunday night, you'll get to go all out. I won't even try to help."

"Good to know. You could make boiling water for tea an experience."

"Love you, too."

She walked into her bedroom, a smile on her face. Friday nights were their nights. They followed the example of Lorelei and Rory, of *Gilmore Girls*, picking up a movie, bags of candy, popcorn, ice-cream, and soda. Wine for her. They'd binge-watched the show before *A Year in the Life* came out and picked up some hints on how to spend quality time together. Not that they hadn't already been doing that.

Over the last several years, she'd seen all the *High School Musicals, Legally Blonde, Freaky Friday, Star Wars* and the *Harry Potter* series. Fortunately for her, Chloe didn't mind sitting through some of her favorites as well, *Pretty in Pink, The Breakfast Club and Back to the Future.* As Chloe got older, her taste matured, and they both enjoyed the *Divergent series*, and *Hunger Games.*

Tonight, they were watching a movie that was new to the streaming service they watched, Chloe's pick. Unlike some of the kids her age, she didn't like horror movies, always seemed to lean towards romantic comedies. It was Nel's choice next week, and she was looking forward to one about a coffee shop owner. Seemed her taste ran in the same direction as Chloe, although she didn't know why. She wasn't as sentimental as her daughter and she knew a happily-ever-after ending wasn't in her future. A pizza would put a smile on her face. That used to be a Friday night staple which she'd grudgingly turned down tonight to appease Chloe's attempt at domesticity.

After throwing on some jeans and a sweater, her feet bare, she returned to the kitchen where she found Chloe setting the table with cloth napkins and the good dishes. The china belonged to her grandmother and she'd been allowed to claim it. She seldom used the elegant gold-rimmed plates, a bit ostentatious for her, but Chloe loved setting a pretty table, had since she was little, and she would always give into her request to use them.

"Dinner is served, Ma'am."

"Why, thank you, kind child. Whatever would I do without you?"

"Eat pizza."

Chloe was right. It was amazing what she'd given up for the love of this child.

After taking a seat at the table, she helped herself to some pasta, making sure there were several pieces of chicken mixed in.

"I've been thinking. Maybe we could call around see what kind of cooking classes there are out there."

Chloe had taken a seat opposite her, a broad smile blossoming on her face. "Really?"

"Really. It's too bad they don't have something like that after school, like the drama classes. It would make transportation a non-issue."

"Maybe I can ask Keileh if she wants to do it with me. Then you can car pool. Or maybe we can find a class on Saturday. That's easier for you, isn't it?"

"Either would work." She smacked her lips, the sauce perfectly seasoned, wiped her mouth with her napkin and said, "This is good, Chloe. I didn't realize there were other Italian dishes I would enjoy. You're pushing my palate to new heights."

"Mom, it's macaroni. Not a big deal. You really need to get out more."

"Maybe you're right."

Nell took another mouthful, enjoying the taste. She'd picked up a couple of packaged meals at the place Jelani suggested and the owner could cook. It was unfortunate that she didn't give lessons, but Nell's request had sparked some interest in starting them.

"Any one thing you learned today that you want to talk about?"

"When I was doing some work on the ancestry page, it gave some information about DNA testing. I think that would be cool. Even though you think you know what your racial heritage is, they say a lot of people are surprised with the breakdown. Can I do it?"

"I'm not sure. Let me think about it. I don't like the idea about your DNA floating out in the universe."

"Every time some of my skin flakes off, it's out there. What's the big deal?"

"Putting it that way, I guess I can't make that argument stick. I still want to think about it. Talk to Em and Arianna. See if the disadvantages outweigh the pros."

"What are we, anyway?"

"English, on both sides. A little Hungarian on mine."

She'd known that before Eloise made such a big deal about it. Her maternal grandmother was one of her favorite people and used to tell her stories about the country she was born in. Aliz Dobos Daschle would have taken her without question when her parents left but she'd succumbed to cancer a couple of years before. Her grandfather had followed in his wife's wake within months. She was convinced it was from a broken heart.

"I'm sure there's more. Aren't you curious?"

"Not really. It doesn't serve any purpose. It won't change the way I think of myself."

Chloe tilted her head, looked at her mother for a minute before asking, "How do you think of yourself?"

"An American. I've never been into the add-ons. But then again, my ancestors have been here for hundreds of years. The Native Americans might have a problem with that and I understand why...but I'm good with it."

She got up to clear the table, ordering in a firm voice, "Google, play eighties music." As soon as the music streamed through the room, her body began to move to the heavy metal beat of one of Boston's famous rock legends.

Chloe raised her voice to be heard above the twanging guitars. "I thought it was my turn? Movie night, music night. We made sure they were the same so we wouldn't forget."

Bent over the dishwasher as she placed the plates inside, Nell said, "I listened to your rap on the way home. Doesn't that count?"

"No. Google Home, play hip-hop."

Nell rolled her eyes in exaggerated fashion as the room filled with an insistent, recurring beat pattern. As she tried to imitate the pump kind of dance that went with it, Chloe laughed. "Don't give up your day job, Mom."

"Lucky for you, I don't plan on it."

They cleaned up the kitchen, laughing and joking as they usually did. It did a lot to help Nell relax about the oncoming freight train.

"Get the stash out. I'll get the drinks."

"Will do."

They shut the music down, Chloe running over and jumping on the couch, the remote in her hand.

"You ready?"

"As I'll ever be."

Settling beside her daughter, Nell's feet up on the coffee table, the candy spread out in front of them, she reached out to snatch a Milky Way as Chloe hit the play button.

⌒

Jack let himself in through the thick mahogany door and would have shed his jacket in the vestibule if it had been allowed. His mother required full dress at her dinner table, so he moved right through to the sitting room, where he knew Eloise would be waiting. The heavy drapes would block out any residual light the sun was willing to share as afternoon faded into night. The portraits hanging on the walls would have given guests an impressive glance into their ancestry. Jack always disliked the room with its pomp and circumstance and the only time he'd enter is if he had no choice.

Eloise was flicking the watch on her wrist.

"You're almost late, Jack. You need to be more prompt."

"Almost late means I'm on time."

"I like it better when we have time to sit and chat first. It makes for a more pleasant experience."

"Well, I had to check in at the district office and got hung up. I could have cancelled entirely but I intended to keep my promise."

"Dear, you spend much too much time there. Isn't that why you hired Dave? To handle things for you? Isn't he pulling his weight?"

For as much as his mother thought she knew about politics and what it involved, she had no idea. It was the interaction he had with the people living in his district that had propelled him into his fourth term, not his name attached to sponsored bills, most of which went nowhere. Dave was incredibly good at knowing which group he needed to talk to, kept abreast of the community chatter, expressed valued opinions of what needed to be addressed, and always kept him in the loop.

"Dave's doing a great job. I think it's important to keep a visible profile there. Let people talk to me face-to-face. It must be working because I keep getting elected. Isn't that what you wanted?"

"I wanted you to carry on our legacy. Plain and simple. Now help me up and let's go eat. I'm famished."

Eloise was only in her mid-sixties, spry and healthy, and had no trouble getting up herself, but rather than argue with her, he offered her his arm and she let him escort her into the dining room.

Once they were seated, Eloise asked, "So what's new in the capitol?"

"More of the same. Nothing."

"What's your strategy for working with the opposition?"

"There is no strategy. The ball's in their court. Or haven't you heard?"

"I think you should use your powers of persuasion, Jack, and get something moving. Just think what a feather in your cap it would be."

"Mother, I don't wear hats with feathers. I'll let the leadership deal with the vitriol."

"In my opinion..."

He didn't really want to hear her opinion on anything tonight, but he had to start paving the way for his introduction to Chloe, putting Nell back in his life.

"There is one new development."

Eloise wiped her mouth with her napkin and sat up straight, straining forward with eager anticipation.

"Oh, what?"

"Zelda's brought in a new lawyer as consultant to help us maneuver the minefields of any new immigration conflicts that come up."

"Who?"

He paused, wanting to extend the anticipation, study her face for her reaction.

"Nell Warren."

The sour look that came over her face wasn't what he'd expected. It was a surprise, as was her question.

"Why on earth would Zelda choose her?"

He sat, his knife and fork in either hand. Why the contempt?

"Maybe you've missed the news, but she was a prime story the last couple of days."

Wiping the corner of her mouth with the pointed edge of her napkin, she narrowed her eyes at him, as if he were some simpleton who didn't understand the way the world worked.

"She likes the limelight, Jack. She always did want to out-shine you."

His mother was wrong. Nell wasn't like that, hadn't gone into law to make a name for herself. Eloise never could understand why Nell worked so much, why she took such controversial cases, why she drove herself so hard. That she was good at it got under her skin more than the actual caseload.

"Anyone could have won that case."

His mother's voice was dripping with antagonism.

He cocked his head at her. Nell had predicted the disdain, something he'd scoffed at, not for the first time.

"It's a landmark case and she set precedent. If someone could have done that, they already would have."

"I see you're still defending her?"

He let the utensils fall to the table.

"I'm not defending anyone. I'm stating facts. What is the real problem here?"

Eloise fiddled with the napkin on her lap, her mouth in a tight line.

"She's a gypsy. And I never liked her. Her grandmother was from Hungary you know."

He was stunned. Yes, Eloise had admonished him for ignoring Nell's background but he didn't know it went so deep. Nothing Nell could have done would have improved the situation. Not unless she could go back in time and slice a limb off her family tree.

"That's what you based your opinion on? Her ancestors' point of origin?"

His rising temper must have sounded an alarm, because she back pedaled.

"Of course, it's not the only reason. She was always trying to influence you. Telling you how to run your life."

He sat back in his chair, giving up the pretense of eating.

"She seemed to think that job was already taken."

The sarcasm went right over her head and Eloise barreled on.

"That girl was never right for you. And you better be careful. She might try to finagle a way into your office."

He felt a smile tip his lips.

"She already works at my field offices representing the people in my district."

His mother's mottled complexion indicated how upset she was.

"What...Why?"

Her elbows were on the table, a guffaw she'd reprimand others for, her hands linked in desperate prayer.

"Jack, I think this is a grave error on your part."

"I don't see why. She's doing pro bono. How can that be a bad thing?"

"Why didn't you discuss this with me first? We always talked about important issues before you took a step. I could have pointed out the ramifications of this decision. I believe you need to...

Eloise couldn't have noticed the change on Jack's face as irritation set in. His mother's words echoed one of Nell's major complaints.

She insists you follow every one of her missives, and she wants to be in on every decision. Don't I have a say in our lives, have a stake in your future?

Nell had often been angry at the confidences he shared with Eloise, told him she felt slighted, invisible. He'd told her she was imagining things and not to be so childish.

The image of her during the news conference after her victory made him wince. Nell was a force to be reckoned with, independent and mature. His mother, on the other hand, did have the propensity to take over his life, and on many occasions, he let her. When he looked at it from that perspective, he had to ask the question, who was the one who hadn't grown up?

Wanting to rectify Nell's perception of him, he announced, "Mother, I'm buying my own clothes from now on."

He had stopped her in mid-sentence and Eloise didn't have time to shift with him.

"What?"

"I'll take care of my wardrobe from now on."

"Jack, there's no way you could put yourself together without me."

His eyebrow arched up. Did she truly believe that?

Willing to argue the point, he said, "I actually think I can. Being an adult and all. Which brings me to another change. I'll be getting my own place soon."

His mother's nervous agitation was evident, her fingers busy sliding her wedding ring up and down her knuckle.

"That's ridiculous. You can't afford to rent something in Boston that's fit for a congressman."

Drawing herself up in her chair, she gave him her imperious look.

"And you won't get a dime to waste on living expenses from me. What is going on?"

He was beginning to see Nell's point. His mother did hold the purse strings and she used them with efficiency.

"Then I'll get a roommate."

She all but blubbered.

"Like you're in college?"

"It's better than living in my mother's house at my age."

"You don't live in my house, although I don't see why that would be so bad."

"I don't pay rent, do I?"

"This is your family home, Jack. Why would I charge you rent? What's mine is yours. And why on earth would you want to spend money when you have a convenient place to live?"

"Because I'm an adult and should be paying my own way."

Eloise sat back with a flourish and said, "This is all Nell's doing, isn't it? She's back in the picture and you are making these crazy choices."

"She doesn't work for me, Mother. She has her own practice. You know, the one that earns her six figures. The one she built on her own shoulders."

"She doesn't have your pedigree. She has to work."

"She's a Warren, for Crissakes. She's got the same kind of pedigree. Her ancestor and mine sat over beers discussing revolution. Ours might have thought the deep thoughts but hers put them into action. We couldn't have won the damn war without them."

"Watch your language, Jack. Her roots have withered. The bloodline's been diluted. Her mother's mother was a gypsy. Why do you think Merry found it acceptable to traipse all over the world?"

Jack threw his napkin down on the half-eaten food and stood. He wasn't going to waste any more breath on this topic. And what was wrong with Merry following her husband around the world as part of Doctors without Borders? If they hadn't dumped Nell at her grandmother's, put her in boarding school to do it, it would have been commendable.

He stood, his hands resting on the linen tablecloth.

"Let me make one thing clear. You are to stay away from her, my offices, my staff. I'm trying to talk her into letting me meet Chloe, and I don't want you to do anything that might jeopardize that."

His mother tried to stare him down but failed. Flustered, she waved her hand at him.

"Has she finally agreed to the paternity test?"

"It's not one of my pre-requisites. That was yours and it prevented me from knowing my daughter."

"How can you be so sure—"

"I'm sure. I would think you'd want to meet her. She has our DNA, shares our heritage."

"She shares nothing of the kind. Her history is even more diluted than *Ms. Warren's*. And did you ever think she got pregnant to trick you into marrying her?"

"I asked. She turned me down. For you to assume that proves what the word implies."

She looked up at him, startled.

His voice rose, and the timbre vibrated through the room.

"She's your granddaughter. And Nell is her mother. I'm warning you. Stay away from them."

"Jack, don't be so dramatic."

Shaking his head, he left, her voice calling out to him that he hadn't finished his dinner.

All but slamming out the front door, he hurried down the steps, swung around the iron rail, and took the steps up to his place.

The apartment had been carved out of the main structure when his grandmother fell and needed tending. The hired nurse had handled the day-to-day care, but the family had checked in on her as required, or dropped by just to visit. His father would go over at night and sit with her for hours, keeping her company, taking advantage of the remaining time with her. Eloise had wanted her mother-in-law to stay with them, but the elder Adams had refused. Never wanting to become a burden, Beatrix had settled for their company, satisfied they were nearby but happy knowing she hadn't stolen their privacy. He was almost twelve when the work on the separate living space had begun, and fifteen when his grandmother passed away. The apartment hadn't changed much since then, and that was almost twenty years ago.

As he unlocked the heavy wooden door, he took a step into the vestibule. His footsteps echoed on the marble floor as he made his way into the sitting room. Throwing his suit coat on the back of the ancient chair, he sank down into the couch and worried his forehead with his fingers.

Eloise hadn't skipped a beat and it looked like she still had some fight in her.

But why?

Nell had left him, had been out of his life for years. Why was Eloise baring her claws?

Was Nell right? Did his mother's animosity have more to do with Nell herself than with the relationship? Did it extend to Chloe?

He'd tried so hard to keep the peace back then. He never wanted his mother to feel as if he'd abandoned her. He even refused to move out of the apartment when Nell had suggested it within the first week of moving in with him. She wanted a place of their own. Somewhere they wouldn't be distracted by a knock on the door or a phone call beckoning him over. Far enough away that they wouldn't be required to dine with her several times a week. A home she could put her own stamp on, an environment that spoke to who they were as a couple, not a remnant of his mother's renovations. He'd put her off, and off. Reminded her she'd be moving to California for the school year. She'd all but implied she'd bypass Stanford, attend a local college if it meant they could be together. She'd warned him that if they stayed here, his mother would eat them whole. He'd disagreed.

Their last night together, Eloise had called, insisting he meet with her financial advisor that evening. Nell had come home early, picked up dinner on the way, set the table with candles and the night had the promise of something sweet. It wasn't something she did often.

He'd asked her to give him a couple of hours. Said that the meeting wouldn't take long.

What he'd found when he got back told him he hadn't kept his promise.

The dinner table was still set, the candles out but half-spent, the wine unopened.

A note rested against the platter of cold and withered beef.

He could still remember the exact words that screamed up at him in black ink.

> *Jack,*
>
> *I hoped we could make this work, but it seems your mother is more of a priority than I am. I feel like I'm seven again and taking a back seat to my parents' sense of duty. They were so consumed with each other and their cause there was no place for anyone else, not even children. My mother lost who she was in the process and I lost my family because of it. I swore I would never find myself in the same type of situation, and yet, here I am, feeling those same feelings of insignificance. There's no room for me in the kind of arrangement you have with Eloise. She wants to run your life and is trying to chip away at who I am. She says she only wants what's best for you and I believe her. The problem is I am not on that list. Never will be.*
>
> *Wishing you a long and happy life together.*
> *Nell*

He'd torn through the apartment but all he'd found was an emptiness that was soul deep. Her closet was empty, the drawers he'd given her devoid of clothes.

He'd called her cell but got voice mail, tried over and over as the night transformed into daylight. She'd reached out once she got to Stanford, with the news that she was pregnant. If he'd just gotten on a plane and flown cross-country when she told him, it might have all worked out differently. Instead, he'd given in to his mother's threat and let Nell cut him out of her life. She'd never looked back. After law school, she'd moved to DC, working for one of the most influential men in politics. Then came home and pulled the law firm she worked for into the top ten in the country dealing with women's issues.

She certainly wasn't insignificant anymore.

Not that he'd ever seen her that way.

He glanced around the dimly lit rooms, took a fresh look at where he was, beginning to see what she had. The place was old, outdated, dark, and confining. He was disappointed in himself.

He'd chosen this instead of them.

CHAPTER TEN

Nell padded down the stairs, dressed in fitted jeans and a white-and-blue-striped button-down shirt. Saturday mornings were a continuation of Friday night, when her daughter came before work or play.

"I smell coffee."

Chloe was sitting in the corner of the couch, a book in her hand.

"I mixed your chocolate marshmallow with some chocolate glazed donut. It came out pretty well."

Nell disappeared into the kitchen. "My taste buds thank you. What are you reading?"

"It's for school. It's pretty good."

"What's it about?"

"A girl in the foster system who wants a place to belong."

Interesting. She'd have to read it, see if the girl found it. She'd spent half her life wanting the same thing. Taking a sip of the steaming brew, she returned to the family room.

"Is it part of a homework assignment that you need to finish this morning?"

"Not due until next Friday. I started it last night to get ahead, but fell asleep. I figured I'd bring it down and read until you got up. I'm almost finished. You slept in kind of late for you."

Chloe was right. It was just after eight o'clock. It wasn't that she'd gotten a full night's sleep. She'd worked into the early-morning hours, playing catch-up with the files that needed her attention. She had glanced at the clock several times this morning before finally dragging herself out of bed.

"I thought maybe you'd like to go to the Holiday Open House at the Old South Meeting House. We've never been there together, and they have some material about some of your forbearers. It might make a dent in your ancestry project."

Chloe scurried up off the couch.

"Yes. I would love that. Can we go now?"

"There's a re-enactment at mid-day so we still have some time. Why don't you get dressed and we can stop somewhere for breakfast?"

"Faneuil Hall?"

"If you want. The day is yours."

It was another reason she'd stayed up so late. She'd hoped Chloe would want to do this with her.

"Sweet. I'll be right down."

And she was true to her word, taking all of ten minutes to tuck herself into some jeans and a sweater.

They stopped at one of the bagel bakeries, sat inside where it was warm.

"Did you stop here so you could get a pizza bagel?"

"Yes, as a matter of fact, I did. I gave it up last night, didn't I?"

"Mom, you are too flipping funny."

Chloe got a more traditional breakfast, the bagels right out of the oven warm and gooey good.

Once their bellies were full, they walked the short distance to the Meeting House, where a line was already forming. Nell knew December was a significant month for the gathering spot, the church where the Sons of Liberty had rallied round Samuel Adams in 1773 and planted the seeds for revolution. Today was an important date in the history of the colonies. It was when five thousand or more patriots had met here hundreds of years ago, to debate British taxation before taking to the harbor. British cargo ships had been raided, and tea was dumped into the chilly winter swells, the event becoming known better as the Boston Tea Party. Today's re-enactment would be a time machine back into history, providing the visitors a glimpse into the past and the simmering tensions that were brewing between England and the burgeoning new nation.

After reading the guided brochure, Chloe said with disappointment, "We're too early for the tea dump."

"I'm sorry about that but I have that thing tonight. We will get to see a performance by two men, one representing the English gentry and the other a member of the Sons of Liberty."

"I've learned about them. They didn't want to pay a tax that the English put on the tea."

While tucking Chloe's hair beneath her hat, she said, "Your relatives were part of that motley crew."

Grey eyes brightened up with excitement.

"Really? Totally lit."

The doors finally opened to the gathering crowd. As they walked in, Nell breathed in the atmosphere, shivers of pride rushing through her. The historical significance never failed to impress her. Knowing some of her ancestors had sat in these box pews, listening to the rabble-rousing rhetoric of Sam Adams, John Hancock, and Joseph Warren, all willing to put their lives on the line for the cause of freedom and liberty, instilled a deep sense of patriotism. In the coming months, or years, she knew that she'd have to do her part to keep their vision alive.

"It's beautiful. The pulpit is so big. It looks twenty-feet high." Chloe's voice was hushed with awe.

"It is. It's traditional New England architecture, from that era. I think there's some Anglican influence thrown in if I remember correctly."

The walked down the short aisle and took a seat.

Nell watched Chloe crane her neck to take in the interior of the Meeting House, the tiers of seats, the chandeliers, the clock that hung from the balcony.

"It's so..."

"Austere?"

"I guess. If that means kind of formal."

"It's stark in its simplicity. We have puritanical roots, Chloe." She glanced around, light spilling in from the abundance of windows. "Ironically, this place offered a platform for free and open expressions of ideas and was the organizing point for the revolution that came after."

A hush descended over the crowd as two men strode to the front of the church, each dressed to represent oppositional forces of the time period.

Nell glanced over mid-way during the performance to find Chloe paying rapt attention. This was how kids learned about important subjects, an interactive approach to something that could be dry and boring. She knew Chloe had learned bits and pieces during elementary school, but she doubted it'd had this kind of impact.

The performance lasted close to thirty minutes before the actors faced the audience to answer questions. She was thrown off when Chloe raised her hand.

"Yes, fine lady." The faint British accent was meant to be a replica of the British subjects living here at the time.

"Could you tell me a little bit about the leaders of your group?"

The performer took a step closer to where they sat, using his arms in sweeping, dramatic expression.

"Samuel Adams is our leader. He is unable to be with us this day, probably behind closed doors as we speak, planning our next move. Dr. Warren is out exhorting other groups throughout the countryside to take up arms against this tyranny."

"Dr. Warren. Is that John Warren?"

"It is, indeed."

"Didn't he die at the Battle of Bunker Hill?"

"He did. That battle was fought at Breed's Hill, and he was one of our first fallen heroes. His voice was an important one, his dialogue drawing unprecedented numbers to our cause. His brother Joseph provided surgical care for those that were injured during the war. The family gave generously to our revolution."

Nell heard Chloe whisper in her ear, "Was he one of our ancestors?"

"He was."

"Wow. I'm impressed."

On leaving the building, Nell not wanting to end their time together quite yet, suggested they stroll through Faneuil Hall again. They moved in and out of the stalls, ordering a coffee to go before heading back, the chill in the air chasing them back to their condo sooner than she would have liked.

They spent the next few hours working on their own, Chloe busy on an ancestry website doing research for her project, Nell moving through some of the client file folders analyzing how best to defend the men and women who'd come to her for help. Nell dropped her daughter off at her friend's, where she would spend the night, before heading to the Boston Plaza.

The hug she received before she left warmed her heart.

It was early in the afternoon when Jack inserted the key and opened the door to his field office in Everett. It used to be an old tattoo parlor that he'd bought cheap and reconfigured to meet the needs of the staff. Because it was on one of the main streets of the city, the constituents could drop in during open hours and discuss concerns with his representatives, who would pass all valuable info on to him. It was designed as a place for congregating, with a sofa, a couple of chairs, a table with piles of magazines, and a coffee maker that was always brewing fresh.

His office was in the back, but he rarely used it for anything other than private meetings. He was more often out with the staff, available to those who dropped in to talk. Tahlia, charged with the overall running of the three field offices, and Dave, the district director, who saw to the everyday needs of them, had put together a great staff and group of volunteers. Everett pulled to him more than the others. It claimed thirty-three per cent of its residents as immigrants, both documented and undocumented. Most towns and cities in his district could make the same assertion. His other two offices were located in Cambridge and Randolph, both designated sanctuary cities, where immigrants were offered a modicum of protection. As congressman, he was the voice for a diverse array of citizens and non-citizens alike and made sure that the locations reflected that diversity. It was one of the reasons he'd agreed to join the Judiciary's subcommittee, Immigration and Border Patrol. He was willing to go to great lengths to get a bill written and a law passed that would protect them under federal law, not only state statute.

He spent his time on the weekends traveling between the three offices, meeting people, and attending local business conferences and festivals, and his schedule was as packed at the state level as it was on the Hill.

He didn't have any official meetings this afternoon. He'd come in to catch up. Dave and his scheduler, Michael Hardstrap, were joining him to fill in some of the holes in his day planner with a more diverse array of immigrant issues. Resigning from the Education and Workforce Committee was forcing him to shift his focus from labor to immigration, easy enough to do here. Afterwards, he was heading out to get dressed for his date tonight.

Sitting down at his field clerk's desk, he powered up the computer, thinking to fill his time while he waited for the others to show.

Clicking on the Zillow site, he began to punch in different towns in the area, getting a feel for what was on the market.

Dave strode over to him as soon as he walked in.

"What are you doing?"

Without taking his eyes from the screen he answered, "Looking for a place to live."

Bending over to see the condos up on the screen he asked, "For who?"

Jack looked over his shoulder.

"For me."

"You're moving out of your apartment?" Dave's voice echoed the surprise reflected in his eyes.

Jack's focus was back on the screen as he continued to scroll, but the price increased each time a new page came up.

"Technically, it's my mother's apartment. And yes, I'm moving out. I'm just not sure how yet."

Dave pulled a chair behind the desk and dropped down next to him.

"Whoa. What prompted this? Eloise yell at you for not using the right fork for the salad?"

Jack moved the mouse, creating new filters, like a lower selling price.

"Please. I've known since I was two which fork to use for the salad, the main meal, and dessert."

"Seriously, what prompted this?"

He sat back and glanced over to see Dave, the look of surprise genuine.

"Can't a man decide to move without eyebrows being raised?"

"Sure, but you never seemed inclined to live on your own."

Jack felt his irritation rise. It wasn't as if he lived in the main house. He was free to come and go as he pleased, think what he wanted to think.

"I live on my own."

"In an apartment attached to the house. Rent free. Is Eloise willing to fund this new adventure?"

Jack leaned forward again, scanning the column of condos for lease and sale.

They were expensive.

He rubbed his forehead with his fingers.

"No, she isn't. She said she wasn't putting out good money for something that was unnecessary."

"I don't know why this is such a shock, Jack. She's done this—since your dad's death."

He wasn't going to argue. He and Dave had been friends since high school and attended Harvard Law together and Dave had a good sense of the relationship before and after the tragedy.

"I know, Dave. And I don't know what to do about it anymore."

"Moving out might be a step in the right direction. It's not like you'll be moving cross-country."

Which was what he'd wanted to do when he'd found out about the pregnancy. She'd stopped him then with the same weapon.

"She's blaming Nell's influence." Jack dragged his eyes up to meet his college friend. "And in a way, it is."

"What do you mean?"

"Nell told me I haven't grown up."

Dave rolled the chair back, crossed his arms over his chest and whistled. "When?"

"The day she came to DC"

"And you didn't set her straight?"

"After her third degree, there was nothing left to defend."

Dave leaned forward, his fingers curled over the keyboard, entering another town that might be more affordable.

"She wasn't able to influence you when you were together. What's different now?"

"I couldn't move back then. I didn't have a job, and law school was looming ahead of me not behind. No way I could afford it."

"Nell would have found a way. She worked while she was at Yale, didn't she?"

"Yeah. Her grandmother thought it would be a good lesson in conservation. Nell was taught that money should never be wasted, and hard work never hurt anyone."

"In other words, she was on her own."

Jack looked up, met Dave's eyes.

Was there condemnation there? Dave knew as much about Nell's past as he did. Even though Dave had attended a different college, it was local, and they'd hung out together on the weekends Nell came up to visit. Dave knew about her parents, how alone in the world she was.

"In more ways than one, wouldn't you say?"

Jack could only nod. It was the truth. Another one of those things he'd downplayed.

"Your mother always paid your way. You've never had to sacrifice anything to have what you have."

Jack arched his eyebrow "How can you say that? I think I've sacrificed too much to have what I have."

He'd lost a modicum of freedom and respect. Along with his daughter and a relationship with a bright, beautiful woman.

Fingers rubbed a forehead that was beginning to pound.

"I have to find something. It's way past time."

"Do you have the cash?"

"Yeah, for a down payment. I can get a mortgage, though the monthly payments will be coming out of my fund. There's not as much in there as people think. I've got to go as inexpensive as I can. The next disbursement isn't for a couple of years."

Congressmen didn't make very much, not when you considered the travel involved, flying back and forth between home district and the capitol. Then there were the dinners out, the expensive suits, the lodging in two places. Some of his contemporaries slept in their offices, others shared apartments. He'd been approached to write a book but he'd had no desire to share his story. He might be forced to rethink the generous advance.

His ancestors had spent their time idling away the hours, spending most of the assets that were earned a century back. His father had been trying to build them back up, assuring Jack that he'd have a legacy someday, to do with what he wanted, to leave his children, invest in a service career without worrying about the financial piece. John Lee Adams had been unable to keep his promise. He'd died instead.

Dave asked, "Back Bay's out?"

"That's a definite yes."

"It should be in the district."

"I know. That means Milton, Randolph, Cambridge, Chelsea, Everett...Those I should be able to afford on my own."

Michael came through the door, yelling back to announce his presence. Jack shut the computer down and added, "I've got to think this one through. I'm not sure I'm ready to give up my trust fund for a place I don't need."

"You trust fund kids have it so rough."

"Rougher than you think. Now what's on the agenda for next weekend?"

"Several appointments here, a roundtable at the job fair at the Wyndham and a town hall meeting in Milton."

"Now that I'm no longer on the Workforce subcommittee, we'll have to substitute the job fairs with more pertinent activities."

His district schedule allowed him to have a bit more control, which meant he could be a bit more pro-active. Part of the job he loved was meeting with people, listening to their concerns, and coming up with ways to satisfy them. This issue he could sink his teeth into.

He heard Dave and Mike discussing possible events as he stood at the front window.

Snow was falling lightly. He examined the sidewalks as they accumulated a fine misty sheen. The weatherman predicted merely a dusting, which wouldn't impact the law association dinner. A multitude of legal minds would be there, lawyers from private practice, DA's, judges, the police commissioner, and high-ups on the force. He'd been invited this year as keynote speaker, the judicial branch of government gearing up for what was ahead, and they wanted him to go over the congressional agenda. Accepting was a given. Many of his supporters would be there and he'd be able to mix business with pleasure. This gathering wouldn't take much, just a high-energy sales pitch. Hope would be accompanying him, which meant he'd have to spend some of his time by her side. She was a steady influence but didn't know much about politics. Nor did she care. Anyone she talked to wouldn't get much about his vision or his goals. He'd depend on his staff for that. He'd purchased a table for the event. Ron was flying up with Tahlia and Evelyn. Meg, Terry, and Jaiden were local and would be there along with Michael and Dave.

He'd gotten a text earlier in the day asking if he would be willing to present Nell Warren's award. She was being honored for her fight for immigration rights.

His answer had been a resounding yes.

CHAPTER ELEVEN

Jack was on his way to pick up Hope. He didn't like taking her to these types of events, but he'd been roped into it. His mother had mentioned it to her at one of their weekly lunches and they both had assumed... *Someone like Nell was better suited.*

Shaking the thought out of his head, he pulled onto the long, curving driveway. The house sat a quarter mile off the road and he stopped his car in front of the elaborate entrance.

Hope still lived at home, which made him more comfortable about his own living arrangement.

He never needed to defend himself to her.

Yet he could never be part of the idle rich, nor was he expected to be.

His father had been adamant about him getting an education and, afterwards, doing something worthwhile with his life. As a member of a think tank that had offices in both Washington DC and Los Angeles, Lee Adams had satisfied his own need to work and his wife's need to cling to tradition. He'd walked the wire between the two with finesse and humility, his wife content to be the woman behind the successful man. Insisting that Jack attend Harvard and study something of value, he'd promoted a philosophy of service and they had talked about politics being one way to achieve that.

Like his ancestors.

After Lee's death, Jack had floundered and postponed the inevitable. His mother had taken up the gauntlet, insisting he throw his hat in the ring several times after law school but he'd fought against it as hard as he fought against

Eloise's need for control. He'd gotten a job at a corporate law office and found it depressing. He'd been out of his office more than he was in it. When it was pointed out by the senior partner, he'd left without a backward glance. The nagging had begun in earnest again until he capitulated when Tomms announced he was retiring.

Hope, in contrast, was living off the dwindling trust fund set up decades ago, attending all the social events of every season, contributing very little to society.

At times pretentious, at times frustrating, she nevertheless provided him with an agreeable relationship. No highs, no lows, just a level-headed partnership. She did what she needed to for his career: attend luncheons, dress appropriately, speak politely, accompany him to dinner.

There was one thing she refused to do. She would never stoop to ask for money on his behalf, thinking it vulgar and tasteless. She lacked one of the necessary credentials of a politician's wife, but she had one that redeemed her. At least in his mother's book.

Her name and lineage.

Why had he ever asked her out after his mother's introduction?

If he looked at it closely, he thought of her as a diversion. He hadn't dated seriously since Nell and thought it might be nice being part of a couple again. Hope had become a habit, a very attentive one, but with Nell back he was reminded...

What?

That he didn't really enjoy Hope's company. She was too bland, too accommodating, too passive. And nothing about her life interested him.

Nell woke up a room just by walking into it. And she'd be walking into a room at the Moakley later this evening. He was looking forward to it more than he had anything in a while.

With a smile on his face, he ran up the front steps of the mansion and rang the bell.

As he walked into the glass walled atrium, which offered a spectacular view of the harbor, Jack's eyes swept the gathering crowd, catching glimpses of both adversaries and friends. The Moakley was the seat of the Boston judiciary. It was one of the few federal courthouses that dedicated its space to public use. Every year the city's bar association held a catered event for attorneys, judges, court officials, key local officials and federal workers, many of whom had supported him through every election. It took him a while to find the trio he was looking for among the hundreds of guests milling with drinks in their hands and smiles on their faces. Nell mustn't have arrived yet. He knew she wasn't fond of small talk and would gravitate to her friends, wanting the solidarity they offered.

He mingled, Hope's hand resting gently on his arm, and felt a shudder of excitement the exact moment Nell walked in. His breath caught.

Dressed all in black, her waist cinched with a leather belt, her heels strappy, her bracelets visible on her wrist, her hair swept up and framing her face, she looked almost edible.

Witnessing Devlin Howard's peck on her cheek as she entered the lobby put him on high alert. There was something in the way the man was leaning into her that he didn't like. It seemed almost territorial.

⌒

After removing her coat, Nell handed it over to the woman standing behind the half door and put the check stub into her purse, edging into the room. Wanting to get her bearings, see who was here, she let Howie lead her over to the bar on her left. There were a lot of familiar faces. The same people attended the same events, and although she tried to curtail her involvement, there were expectations as a partner of a prestigious law firm. Networking was one of them. The bartender made his way over after serving those in line before her. With a warm smile, she gave him her order.

"Glass of Chablis, please."

It would take more than one glass of wine to get through the evening. She almost ordered something more potent but demurred.

While glancing around the room, she made eye contact with some of the men, smiled at the women she knew, gearing up to face Jack. Remaining at the end of the cuffed counter as long as she could, she sought out and found with her eyes the main attraction. He stood as if he prided himself on his bearing, a delicious example of an updated aristocrat wearing a suit that fit as if it were made for him. Which it probably was. Standing next to him was a prim and proper Hope Astor.

Licking her lips, she took Howie's arm and her wine-glass and moved over to where he stood. The air was buzzing when she arrived.

"Jack."

His eyes took her in and there was a flicker of desire in them. She glanced away quickly and turned her attention to the woman standing by his side.

"Hope. It's good to see you again."

She could feel the tension in her facial muscles when she attempted a smile.

They'd met once, at one of the non-profit luncheons held for the YWCA. Hope was willing to lend her name to many causes, but little of her time. The only reason the debutante was here tonight was to complement the congressman at her side.

Hope's lips thinned even more tightly into a grimace.

Jack reached out to shake Howie's hand with what seemed an overdone machoness.

"Howie, how is it in the DA's office? Looks like you can play nice when you need to."

Everyone here knew that Nell and Howie were adversaries in the court room. Howie worked for the state in matters of deportation and immigration law.

Howie let the intended insult roll off his back.

"Nell's an easy one to play nice with."

Wanting to get away from the open hostility, Nell took a sip of her wine and said, "I guess it's time to mingle."

Jack reached for her hand and stopped her.

The tingles were immediate, and they raced along the nerve endings in her arm. She tried to snatch it back, but Jack hung on.

"There's some people I'd like you to meet. Excuse us Hope, Howie. We'll be back."

Wanting to tamp down the flicker before it became a flame, Nell said, "I know everyone here, Jack. I work with them, remember?"

He was guiding them in the direction of a group of men who were milling and chatting on the opposite side of the room. Men she didn't like and didn't want to waste time on.

"Yeah, I remember. I thought you might want to get away from Howie. He looked like he was a little too close for comfort."

Her tone became chilly.

"We're dating. Not that it's any of your business."

"You came in alone. Why didn't you come together?"

"I had to drop Chloe off at her friend's for a sleepover."

"Doesn't he like her?"

She could feel a fluster coming on and did her best to stop it in its tracks.

"Of course he likes her. I didn't want to hold him up."

Jack was working his charm on the crowd, smiling in all the right places, even as they sparred.

He stopped by an empty food station, picked up a plate, filled it with some of the petit fours filled with cucumber and cream cheese.

"Here. Let's pretend we're having a pleasant conversation."

"I don't like cream cheese, remember?"

She folded her arms against her chest, unwilling to take the plate from his proffered hand.

In a low tone that brooked no argument, he admonished, "I have rights, Nell."

Her eyes flicked up to him. Where did that statement come from? And why here? As she looked around, making sure there were no eavesdroppers, she answered, "You had them, Jack. You agreed to give them up. You're the one changing the rules."

"Is it dating as in going out periodically or dating as in...sleeping together?"

He was going in so many different directions that she had to shift gears to keep up.

"That is so none of your business."

"How serious is it? Is Chloe going to have a step-father?"

She finally knew the real reason for this interrogation. This had everything to do with Chloe and nothing to do with her. She swallowed past the knot of regret that lodged in her throat.

"I've found that living with a man doesn't work for me."

"She should get to know her father before you introduce her to a step."

"And what do you think Hope will say about the situation? I can't see her taking on someone else's daughter, especially mine if your mother holds sway."

He glanced back, his expression changing to one of annoyance, shrugged his shoulders and said, "If I get to meet Chloe, she'll have to get used to our being together."

"If you get to meet Chloe it has nothing to do with us. I am not signing on to that war."

"I want you there the first few meetings, as a buffer. You're not going to tell me you disagree."

"All depends on what kind of battles I'll wage in the trenches to make it happen. I don't mind fighting windmills in the courts, but I'm not sure how long I'd be willing to fend off the attackers in your inner circle."

"Please, Hope doesn't have your stamina or your wily nature. I have no doubt you'll best her every time."

"Such accolades. I'm flattered."

A group of men approached the station and she plastered on a fake smile. These were the kind of men who made back door deals, the gatherings devoid of women or bipartisanship, members of the old boys' club, an institution most men denied existed. You had to be a woman to know it did. The doors were triple-locked, but the female sex was smartening up. They'd stopped pounding on the door for entry. Now they were building their own club, with their own resources. They were finding that solidarity got things done, and if they persisted, they were more powerful that they'd thought.

Bradford Garner, a step away from a judgeship, was fifty-something with hair greying at the temples, but it distinguished him rather than diminished his looks. Which was too bad because he knew it. They'd met on opposite sides of the aisle in court and she held the opinion that he was a self-centered jerk.

"To what do we owe this honor, Ms. Warren? You don't usually attend these kinds of functions. Trying to improve your networking skills? My suggestion? Go more for tact than bold."

"Tact doesn't always work with men of your stature. I find two-by-fours are much more effective."

"You won't influence many people that way."

"I don't need to. My priority is my client, not fragile egos."

She was satisfied when he gave up his diatribe.

"Are you sure there isn't a job for her in Washington, Jack? It wouldn't hurt our feelings if she was far, far away."

Nell smiled, but it wasn't a pretty one. She'd bested Garner in court more often than not and understood where the sentiment was coming from.

"You're not going to get off the hook that easily, Mr. Garner. I still have lots of fight in me and I'm doing it out of my office."

One of the judges, whom she liked, asked, grinning, "What kind of fight are you looking for, Nell?"

"I joined the resistance the day after the election. I'll be on the front lines for the next several years. If he lasts that long. It will be the judges and the courts that keep things in balance. I count on all of us to make sure we keep our democracy in check."

Disappointment coursed through her when she caught Jack glancing over to where Hope stood. She needed to staunch those feelings. He was attached to someone else, someone Eloise was fond of. She wasn't going to fight for love anymore. She'd given that up when her parents signed on for their second assignment. They'd yet to come home for good.

"I best see what's going on over there. Averell is a big donor and I can't let Hope distract him from why he's here."

She watched him walk away, releasing a breath she didn't even know she was holding.

Looking at the faces surrounding her, the lone female among the men, she said, "If you'll excuse me, I need to find Howie."

As Jack made his way to where Averell and Hope were, he glanced back to see Nell heading toward her partners. He wished she were the one he was here with tonight. There was an aura around her that sparked with life, an energy that was indistinguishable. He could never get enough of it.

His father had been dead a few short months when he met her. The death was so sudden and unexpected that it changed his life in dramatic ways, weighing him down with a burden he'd yet to remove all these years later. It had become even heavier over time.

A month after the funeral, depressed, in grief, he'd pushed himself to finish what he'd started at Harvard.

Meeting Nell had been like a breath of fresh air.

The two years they were together helped him navigate the treacherous shoals of what his life had become and had brought him a degree of happiness that he felt in his soul.

The problems had come when they moved in together, under Eloise's roof. There were certain things Eloise expected. A good marriage, grandchildren, a presidency. She didn't think Nell was good enough for any of them. Pedigree was important. To her.

As he approached Hope, he noticed a speculative gleam in her eye that made him cringe. She had the same type of agenda, an appropriate marriage, and he fit the mold. It was all about pedigree for her as well. She came from generations of the upper crust of Boston society, who intermarried to make sure they remained entrenched as part of the elite. His father had joked about them, suggesting they were nothing more than a harmless, untitled aristocracy. Lee Adams had had better things to do with his life than live that kind of limited thinking. He'd passed that wisdom on to his son. At least he had tried while he was growing up. With the elder Adams gone for so long now, it was his mother's influence bearing fruit. How had he let that happen?

He felt Hope's hand on his arm and he looked up.

"Thank goodness you're back. Averell was asking me about things I have no answers to."

She wouldn't. She didn't like flexing her brain muscles.

Howie was off doing some networking of his own when Nell rejoined her friends. Jelani wasted no time asking, "What was that about?"

"First it was Howie, then we got to his new favorite subject. Chloe."

"Ooh. Jealous?"

"Of what?"

"You with another man?"

She knew that wasn't the cause of the interaction. Chloe was the female on his mind. Casting aside the disappointment, she threw some shade and asked, "Did he think I became a hermit?"

"You have been a hermit."

Taking a gulp of her wine, unable to swallow due to the residual tingling of her hand, she insisted, "I'm not having this discussion again."

Jelani was smiling broadly now. "Nell, this is so unlike you."

Nell was always calm under pressure, animated at times, perhaps, but only when in a discussion on something she was passionate about.

And there was no denying she was passionate about one good-looking congressman.

Arianna was all but drooling again and asked, "How can you ignore what he has to offer?"

Mia pointed out, "She's already sampled it, so apparently, she couldn't."

Jelani couldn't help but add, "An eleven on a scale from one-to-ten."

The low growl echoed in Nell's throat.

"This is why I don't tell people my deep, dark secrets. Once they're out of the box, they're open for general inspection."

"But we're your family. Who'll give you a hard time if we don't?"

"If this is what family does, I'm glad mine's been absent."

Howie came back in time to sit with them at dinner and once it was over, the president of the association went to the podium and tested the mic before making the introduction.

Jack sat at his table at the center of the room, his eyes taking Nell in as she sat amongst her partners, her forehead slightly creased as if she was thinking. He had probably gone too far but he didn't like thinking of Nell with someone else, kissing her lips, touching her skin. The memory of how she felt, him tucked not so neatly inside of her, the catch of breath, the fall into cataclysmic rumbles, was cell deep.

"Congressman Adams?"

His head snapped toward the man speaking to him, realizing it wasn't the first time he'd been addressed.

"Sorry. My mind was elsewhere."

"On some of our concerns?"

"Of course. Thank you for the introduction."

Jelani elbowed Nell. "He was lost in you. I just know it."

"Shush."

But Nell had known it, too. She could tell by the look in his eyes. She'd seen it there before, just before they'd...

"Shush," she told her mind. What they had was purely physical. She had to face the truth and accept it for what it was. He was going to fight his mother for Chloe's sake, not for hers. That was a dream best kept buried.

As she watched him stride to the dais and adjust the microphone, she gulped hard. He was a sight to behold, all gorgeous flesh of him. She'd have to find a way to escape the torture before long.

"Good evening, everyone. Thank you for inviting me to speak to you tonight. I am honored to be your representative in Congress and will continue to work hard for the people who live in the district. This is one of my favorite types of events. I get to mingle with all of you, get to know what you're thinking and what you need to do your jobs better. The judiciary will play an important part in the next few years and it is up to those in this room to be alert, conscientious and diligent. The rights of every citizen and non-citizen are at stake."

He transitioned into his speech, about the improbability of fulfilling an agenda, the unclear course that the in-coming president was setting, comments about the importance of NATO, climate change, national security. It was a stump speech, like the ones he'd given over the course of the last year, promoting a more progressive and liberal strategy than the one being offered by the other side. The one he knew worked. He presented facts to support his opinions.

As soon as he wrapped up his address, he paused.

"Attorney Woodson has asked me to introduce this year's award recipient and I accepted with alacrity. I met the honoree many years ago, in college, and have found no one to match her keen mind or social consciousness. She's spent years helping those less fortunate, those huddled masses we associate with the Statue of Liberty and her fight has become one of the most important ones of the day—for the undocumented men and women who are the silent citizens of our towns and cities. Her pro bono work is legendary and her recent Supreme Court win validates her passion and fervor, an outward sign of how well she does her job. There are few among us who would be able to persuade the highest court in the land to side with them, and she is one of the few. It is my honor to present Nell Warren with the Humanitarian of the Year award. Nell, can you come join me at the podium to accept this plaque?"

She sat for a moment in stunned silence.

She turned to Jelani, and asked under her breath, "Did you know about this?"

"Why do you think Arianna forced you to come?"

"I'm going to kill you all."

Then a plastered smile was on her face as she walked slowly up to where he waited.

Smoothly, he asked, "Would you mind saying a few words?"

Her whisper to him, "You never ask a question you don't know the answer to," caused his smile to dip.

There was applause at her introduction and she waited patiently for it to end.

"Thank you, Congressman Adams. Thank you to whatever committee voted to give me this prestigious award. I believe there are many unsung heroes and heroines out there who deserve this more than I."

She perused the crowd, taking the moment in. She'd had no idea this was coming wasn't sure what she could say to show her gratitude.

"As most of you know the only place I'm comfortable is in a courtroom, so I will be brief. I am proud and honored to accept this. The work I do has always been important to me, and I am blessed that the law firm I am associated with has allowed me the freedom to choose the cases I take on, whether our client could pay or not. Without their vision for the firm and our community, I could never have achieved so many victories for the people I serve. In the coming months and years, we will need to be vigilant, to keep up the fight and to make sure no one's civil liberty is abused or diminished. Keep up those calls to your congressman. Make sure your voice is heard. It will be up to them to get a reform bill written and new legislation put in place to make the road to citizenship a less rocky one. Thank you again."

Turning her attention to Jack, she added, "Thank you, Congressman Adams. Keep those lines open. We'll be in touch."

There was general laughter among the group as she made her way back to her friends.

He couldn't keep the pride from showing as his eyes followed her.

Regaining his position in front of the open microphone, he admitted, "Sometimes it seems like we're pushing a thousand-pound rock up a steep incline, but if we can get bipartisan participation, we can do our jobs again. I'd say take the message to the streets, but the streets of Boston are already paved in good intentions. It's the rest of the country we should get on board. That's my job and I thank you for helping me continue to represent you in the fight."

He stepped down to another round of applause and he immediately looked over to where Nell was.

A slow smile took over his face and she returned it, her eyes glowing that deep amber that suggested an inner fire. He didn't like standing outside of it. He'd let himself be consumed by it once, and the temptation to breathe new life into their relationship was a strong one. If the opportunity came to pass, would he even try to escape a fiery death?

CHAPTER TWELVE

She was sitting tucked away in Jack's office in Everett when she heard the outer door open. She stopped what she was doing to listen. She'd dropped Chloe off at Jelani's for an early-morning client meeting and was putting her notes in some semblance of order, thinking she'd have the office to herself for at least another hour before Jack's field rep, Jaiden, came in, but it seemed like she was no longer alone.

Then the voice gave away the early-morning intruder. She never thought he'd keep her kind of hours.

"Who made the coffee? That's usually my job."

She smiled. It was his job when they were living together. There was a picture of her in whatever dictionary had coined the term *can't even boil water.*

She sent her voice out to the reception area, where the machine was set up.

"Won't be up to your standards but I needed a cup this morning and didn't take the time to stop."

He walked over to the door and peeked in before stepping inside.

She was sitting at his desk, her laptop in front of her, stacks of paper to either side.

Her eyebrows rose in appreciation at the sight of him.

His clothes were impeccable. She had to give Eloise her due. She knew what looked good on him and she showcased him as the thoroughbred he was.

He had a smirk on his face but there was a light shining in those grey orbs.

"You didn't totally destroy the taste."

She sat back in her chair, her fingers playing with the bangles on her brace-let.

"I've had years of practice getting it only half-bad."

He openly smiled and took a seat opposite her.

"What are you doing here so early?"

She was keenly aware of his gaze and dipped her eyes away from him to steady herself.

"One of your constituents needed representation. Dave called the other day and asked if I could meet with her. This was the only free day she had but she didn't want to be late for church, so here I sit."

"Is she already gone?"

"Yes."

"Are you going to be able to help her?"

"Not sure. Her husband responded to an interview at the immigration of-fice, was handcuffed and arrested. No criminal record, wife and children American citizens."

"I thought we didn't do things like that in Massachusetts."

"ICE can do anything they damn well please. Our local police can't detain anyone to give ICE time to step in, but they can't stop federal agencies from doing their job. Or what they've come to think of as their job."

"Do you get a lot of your clients from my district?"

"I do. Do you have a problem with that?"

"Not in the least. I asked Megan to put together a list of attorneys to call if they need help. Your law firm is top of the list from what I hear. The response to any SOS, immediate."

"Why thank you, kind sir."

She fiddled with her bracelet, hesitant to know but curious, as well.

"What are you doing here this early? I have a copy of your schedule, so I can set up my appointments around you. You weren't due in for a couple of hours." She smiled and added, "I can't believe what you cram into a day."

"Sometimes I can't either. Is there a reason you work around me?"

"Other than the one I gave you? I need the office for privacy. I don't want to displace you."

"I don't use it much so don't worry about that in the future."

He pointed to the laptop.

"Doing research?"

"Wanted to check the headlines. There are some names floating out there as possible cabinet members. It doesn't look promising. They're all big money and they seem to signify the destruction of the political infrastructure. The chosen are in direct opposition to the precepts of their intended agency. DeVello against public schools, Pitts against saving the environment. It's crazy."

"It won't stop the majority from voting them in."

She began moving papers around with nervous agitation.

"Can't talk about that."

He took a sip of coffee, as if what was happening in the capitol was rational and reasonable. "Dangerous if we stop."

He was right, but the headlines drove her crazy. She'd read the bold print and scan for some other article that wouldn't get her blood pressure soaring. She rarely found one.

She looked up and studied his face. There was barely a ripple of displeasure. He knew how to keep his cards close.

She didn't and admitted, "I can only take it in, in doses. Small, small doses."

"I'd have to argue with that. You jump right in, drowning yourself in the sordid details."

"Muddy up the waters, you mean."

"Sometimes they need muddying."

"How can you be so...placid?"

"I'm the surface of the lake, you're the underbelly. We're different in our approaches but we're striving for the same goal. It used to be a good combination."

His grey eyes were watching her intently.

Was he expecting a reaction? She hoped not, because he wasn't going to get one.

After a few moments of silence, his gaze slid to the disarray on the desk.

After taking another sip of the coffee, he asked, "Do you follow the Twitter feed?"

She didn't need confirmation about whom he was speaking.

"No. Don't have time for falsehoods. I get my daily briefs from credible news sources."

The problem with that was pure journalism was fading away. No longer the beacons of truth, the news agencies shot off sound bites, hosted aggressive amateurs, who had no problem lying outright to the audience and she clicked off within seconds of clicking on. She followed some newsworthy sources on twitter, but the president elect didn't fall into that category.

"All of those lies may be working to our advantage. We're getting a lot of constituent calls. The switchboard's been on overload."

"About time they start paying attention to what's going on in the world."

"If nothing else good comes out of it, I think the citizens have awakened."

Resting her chin on her hand, she gave him a bemused smile.

"I think the new term for it is '*woke*'."

"I just hope it can be sustained."

"I have to believe the resistance is just beginning to swell."

"Are you planning on marching?"

The Women's March the day after the inauguration was going global. The rally was being organized to protest the incoming administration. There were a lot of fears and tears the day after the election results. At least in her part of the world. Woodley and Fisher had a contingent marching in Boston, leaving only a skeleton crew behind. Joining the masses of disgruntled citizens had never been in question.

"Absolutely. It's going to be huge. Are you marching with us?"

She saw him visibly bristle.

"Hadn't planned on it."

She sat back in his chair and studied him.

"Why not?"

Meeting her eyes, he admitted, "That's not who I am."

"It might have been once. I'm almost sure you would have marched right along with me if we were still in college."

"I have to be a bit more circumspect now."

"Why? It's an important cause and there are a lot of women who live in the district. You do know there are people out there who want to wipe out Planned Parenthood, don't you?"

"It won't happen here."

"No, because we're more progressive than some. But it's already happening in other parts of the country. This is us taking a stand in solidarity."

"I work behind the scenes, always have."

"I could never do your job. Too impatient for change, too extreme for most, too undisciplined to fall in line."

"I know you don't believe it yet, but I don't fall in line either. I learned from the best."

Not knowing how to respond to that statement, Nell put them back on track. Work was safe territory for her. Pushing some of the paper on the desk aside, she said, "I've put together some facts on Immigration and Border Patrol. Shit might hit the fan soon on that front."

His elbows were resting on the desk, his coffee mug in between his hands.

"It will, no doubt. I wish it were already out on the table so that we knew what we were facing. Then we could counterattack. Now it's just guess-work."

"If people could just see some of what I do...Most don't want to be bothered with the details of individual faces. They should come to the intern-ment—" in a mocking tone, she changed to the correct term— "the detention center, with me. Maybe they'd realize there are innocent victims in the polar-izing political climate."

The fire erupted as it always did when she was passionate about some-thing. It made her more volatile than she liked sometimes.

"That might not be a bad idea."

She stared up at him for a minute, tongue-tied.

"What? To take them to meet some of the illegals."

His eyebrows shot up.

She corrected, "Their word, not mine."

"Not them, me. I should go in and talk to some of them. It might give me some ammunition to contradict our contemporaries."

He flashed his gorgeous eyes at her.

"Could you set something up?"

Catching herself from falling too deep, she said without thinking, "I could if you're serious."

"Why would you think I'd suggest it if I wasn't serious?"

"There's a lot of talk in DC that doesn't quite intersect action."

His voice had turned gruff.

"I don't work like that."

Aware that she'd insulted him, she apologized.

"Sorry. Bad assumption. I'll trust you until you prove that I can't. I can call the head of the center later today. When did you want to do it?"

"Over the weekend if possible. Maybe this Friday, early afternoon. I'll be flying back Thursday night after the last roll call but I have a speaking engagement the next morning."

She added it to the to-do list she'd already put together for today.

He surprised her when he asked, "You'll come, I hope?"

Her eyes flashed up to meet his. His gaze was cool, calm and collected. They had fallen into familiar territory. They'd often discussed things like this in the past, bounced ideas off each other. If she focused on the topic at hand, the importance of his request, she might be able to handle being in his company for such a dramatic exposé.

"If you want me there. It would give me a chance to see if there are any new clients."

"Tag Michael and see what time works. Tell him to re-arrange things if need be."

"He overlaps appointments and you're not given much time to get from one place to another. I'm not sure he can squeeze this in. To do it justice, you'll need a couple of hours."

"He somehow manages the impossible."

A blossoming smile brought an immediate softening to his features.

"I'm sure Tomms had the same kind of day."

"He did but—"

He got up from the seat and finished her sentence.

"He was a god on the Hill and I'm just...some jerk who didn't even know what he wanted to do with his life."

She could feel the blush. She'd insulted him again.

"I didn't mean it that way."

"I'm pretty sure you did, but it's okay. I'm not offended. Tomms *was* a god."

He picked up the day's agenda from her desk and scanned it.

"What else have *you* got going on?"

More at ease with this line of questioning, she stood, beginning to file her papers in the folder on the desk, her shoulders losing their tension.

"I've got some research to do on immigrant victims' rights. I'm defending a woman who was gang raped and beaten. She should be eligible for the Violence Against Women Act but is in detention, scheduled to be deported. Later this afternoon I have a meeting at your Cambridge office. Jaiden asked me if

I'd put together some tips for what to do if ICE shows up at the door. When I dropped them off, he asked if he could set up a Q and A session."

As if joking she added, "Give a member of your staff an inch, they make me walk my walk a mile. I'm hoping Chloe won't mind coming with me. She used to love tagging along, now...not so much. She says she should be able to stay by herself but I'm not comfortable with it yet. Besides, I haven't seen her much this week and it'll give me some time with her. Another iffy proposition lately."

"Did you check with Jaiden about what else was going on there today before you accepted?"

"No, why?"

He waved the schedule at her.

"I'm meeting with some of the beat police who are working hard at evading the immigration enforcement officers."

"Shit."

"You'll be in what I laughingly call my conference room, but we will be in the office together."

She saw him pause. Heard a deep intake of breath.

"It might be a good opportunity for me to meet Chloe. It wouldn't look staged, it would be on neutral territory..."

Her guard went up, her vexation evident in the tone of her voice.

"You call *your* office neutral ground?"

Showing no signs of relenting in the face of her annoyance, he explained, "There will be a lot of people here, between the people you're advocating for, the police who might want to stick around to hear your salient points, my staff. I probably won't even get to talk to her. I have a full day, with the breakfast, a meeting at the hospital about the opioid crisis, a meeting on ICE with some of the lawyers who attended last night and the meeting with the police. And just so I don't have a free night, a town hall meeting in the South End at seven. I'm busier here than I am in DC."

He turned to leave, then stopped.

"I've already told my mother to stay away from you, from Chloe. I'm the guy who should have told her that years ago. I promise I won't let her hurt Chloe in any way."

"Jack, I think your mother is deathly afraid she'll lose you. If she thinks Chloe is a threat, she will aim to kill."

He turned to face her, but she didn't get the dispute she expected.

"I will nullify her before it gets to that point."

He looked solemn, sincere and it scared her.

"Nell, the worst thing I ever did was leave you two alone. The more I get to know Chloe, the more I realize how much I've missed. I don't want to miss anything else. I promise I won't overstep my bounds if you bring her along as planned. I just want to meet her. Is that really too much to ask?"

As if knowing he wasn't going to get an answer, he looked at his watch, the same one he'd had when she'd been living with him, and turned toward the door.

"I've got to get going. I'll see you later."

She watched him leave, heard his footsteps, then the door clicking shut.

And breathed one deep long breath, before wrapping everything up and leaving. She had to pick up Chloe at her friend's house and had promised to be there by mid-morning, but she had to stop off somewhere first.

⌒

Jack was sitting in his car in the parking garage, not ready to go into the hospital for the scheduled meeting. He still had fifteen minutes before he was forced inside.

He was having a hard time keeping his mind focused. When Nell's voice had floated out from his office, it'd sent images of other times through his mind, when she'd call out from the bedroom, the shower, when she walked through the door at night. It was a warm voice, washed over him in waves of emotion, taking him back to the good-old times, when they'd sit and chat over coffee discussing their courses, Political Science, Psychology, Critical Reasoning, American Government, picking each other's brains for ideas, analysis, logic. Even the summer they lived together, when things had gotten rocky, she would tell him about her cases as a legal aid assistant. His days were filled with job searches and interviews. Which meant she'd do most of the talking. He never did find a job that summer, his mother insistent that he drive her to her various board meetings, appointments and volunteer venues for the DAR. Nell had harped about it and it had caused no shortage of arguments. In hindsight, it had served him well. He'd met a lot of influential people, networked with the higher-ups who funded the political machines, and used all those resources built and developed when he finally entered the run for Congress.

If he explained it to her, would she ever admit it wasn't the waste of time she'd thought it was or would the notion that he was at his mother's beck and call that summer win out?

He should have honestly discussed his future with her, but he'd been torn between doing what his mother wanted and trying to figure out what kind of life he wanted for himself. He should have understood Nell's need to know he had one. They had one.

It was only after he interned a couple of years after law school that he'd found what he thought was his calling. Working for a friend of his father's, one of the state senators, showed him the facets of governing that he'd come to love. Tomms' announcement that he was retiring is what he'd needed to jump into the political ring and he'd traveled throughout his district, meeting the people he wanted to serve. His mother's fundraising efforts were extraordinary, his college friends had come on board and worked as hard as he had, his volunteers had committed themselves to him in ways he could never repay.

If Nell had been with him, she would have been an asset to his career and his life.

She was as passionate about the law today as she'd been in college, her keen mind both analytical and progressive.

When he had peeked into the office, she'd even looked like the girl he remembered. She was dressed more in the style he associated her with, rather than the power suit she'd worn in DC. Her hair was casually knotted at the back of her head. She had on a black skirt, white silk blouse, black boots and a leather belt that sat low on her hips. Her bangles jangled from her wrist. Professional yet with a bohemian flair. She might have the soul of a gypsy, but she had the heart of a lion. Willing to help anyone who needed her expertise, she could draw out their vulnerability while making them feel well protected. He was sure she worked the same kind of cases, would have the same kind of stories about women beaten, raped, assaulted, harassed. She felt their pain, their fear, their burden of shame and fought for retribution on the sidelines of a court system that still tilted with male bias. Back then she'd been a legal assistant but one with a fine-tuned knowledge of the law and what kind of power it could wield. Today she was a full-fledged lawyer, with the experience to go with it.

His heart filled with the kind of pride saved for the people you valued the most.

He checked the time. He'd be late if he didn't hurry and it was an important meeting even though it wasn't his focus in Congress. The opioid crisis encompassed everything from heroin to pain pills given out like candy and it stretched from coast to coast, the worst epidemic in the country's history. The hospitals were on the front lines, the EMTs racing too many ODs through their doors. Narcan had become an ambulance staple. And with all the fine minds working on it, it seemed like they were never going to find a way to manage it. The meeting today was just a preliminary check-in that would preclude much more work down the road.

He made his call to Dave as soon as he left.

"I'm on my way to Immigration Services. I shouldn't be too long. I just need to check in with my contact, see if we have any new problems. I'll be back by two."

"Okay. We had a couple more police contact us for a seat at the table. I've got to cap it, but you'll have a full house. Or should I say office. Nell's meeting in the conference room so that's not available."

"How long has she been using the office?"

"A couple of years. Between the six partners, they can cover any contingency. Most of the cases center on immigration, deportation and civil rights. That's Nell's purview. Her appointments are so early some days we decided to give her a key to the Everett and Cambridge offices. That way neither Geena nor Jaiden have to be there before sunrise."

"Why didn't you ever tell me?"

There was a hesitation that hung heavy on the connection.

"She asked us not to, Jack."

"And you felt your loyalty was to her, not me?"

"I didn't realize we had to pick sides. I thought we were here for our constituents. She serves them better than most."

He was sure she did. What were the odds that he'd never bumped into her in all the years she'd been doing it? She must have worked damn hard to stay under the radar.

He was going to have to look at her caseload personally get to know the people she was working with. He'd always been concerned about the immigration issue, thought reform was sorely needed, but his committee work took him in different directions. Homeland Security and the TSA were his primary focus. He'd spent years working hard to cap the number of immigrants coming in from certain countries. The government fucked the 9/11 debacle up to a fare-thee-well. He'd kept track of the missteps, the mistakes, the total incompetence of those in command, before the first plane even hit the tower, information that wasn't disseminated, warnings that had come but were ignored or passed over. In the aftermath, the left hand didn't know what the right hand was doing. They might have saved at least one of those planes from disaster if they had acted. They hadn't. Now he sat on the committee that oversaw the airports, the borders and he made damn sure his voice was heard. None of the discussions he'd had with Nell when they were dating had altered his opinion and she'd debated him using all her keen observations and in-depth knowledge of the law. He still stood adamant in his position.

At his breakfast meeting, he came to understand how far apart he was from the opinions of his state's contingent. They agreed with Nell, that this country was founded on immigration, believed intensive vetting was the answer. He didn't think anything would sway him to change his mind or his vote if it came to that, so he determined he'd get out in front of it with immigration reform. Fight for sweeping naturalization for anyone who'd been in the country for a reasonable amount of time, was married to a citizen, had children born in the country, had jobs and who were productive members of society. The visit to the deportation center was means to that end. He'd become a willing advocate and voice for the undocumented, all while tightening security on the borders to inhibit the influx of foreign nationals who banged at the door.

Nell knew his position. Knew the reason behind it. Had since the day he'd told her about his father's death.

They'd only known each other a couple of months but she'd worked her magic on him and he found himself telling her his most innermost thoughts and feelings.

They had gone to one of her favorite pizza places near campus.

She'd innocently asked why he'd chosen pre-law. She already knew it wasn't his passion.

"My father died in one of the terrorist attacks on 9/11."

Her expression had changed from curious to sympathetic.

Tilting her head at him, she'd said, "I'm so sorry. Were you close?"

He took precious moments to answer unsure he wanted to go back there. He gave her a one-word answer that didn't tell her anything at all.

"Yes."

Fiddling with the charm at her wrist, she'd prompted, "I get the impression it hurts to talk about him, but I'd love to get to know him better."

He'd stared out into the distance, as if looking for an answer to an unasked question. Then his eyes flicked at her, his hands pressed against the table.

"It's still kind of raw."

Her hand had covered his and he'd clasped her fingers.

"Can you tell me what happened?"

He'd felt the pressure on her fingers tighten.

"He was on the plane that crashed into the Pentagon."

Her eyes had flashed up at him. She'd sat mute, didn't seem to know what to say which was almost humorous. She always knew what to say. It was one of the things that made him crazy.

She'd offered the one slim thread she knew about.

"That flight left from Dulles, didn't it?"

"Yeah. He was traveling to LA for a meeting. He was based in Boston, but he'd been in DC for a conference and left from there. I found out after it happened. He left a message on my cell. Said good-bye."

"I read about some of those heartbreaking calls, in the days right after the tragedy."

He could feel the pain shred at his heart, still ached at the gravity of his loss.

"I flew down to DC when flights resumed and was at the site for a couple of days. There wasn't much coming out about it, news focused on the towers, the plane downed by the passengers and I wanted to see for myself what was going on. It was like the portion of the building where the airplane had hit had turned upside down, inside out. There were steel rods jutting out. The debris was still smoldering. Hazardous material was strewn everywhere. Four-man crews were going in and out of the damaged building with body bags, coming out with body parts."

The waitress had come back to the table, depositing the food on the table, asking if there was anything else she could bring.

Nell had shaken her head and thanked her and he'd resumed the story when she walked away. Once he'd started, he couldn't stop the flow. Sharing the burden of his grief seemed a natural extension of what he felt for her.

"They worked for fifteen consecutive hours that day. It took several days to recover all the bodies. Dad was one of the last ones found. We didn't know it at the time. He hadn't been identified yet. He was a victim of catastrophic burns. I learned later that some of those remains were frozen, brittle like the bodies found in Pompeii after the volcanic eruption."

"Was he...all in one piece?"

"I wouldn't call it that. Pieces of him had chipped off, as if he were a charred piece of meat and, whenever touched, would crumble. I went home before his body was returned to us. My mother had fallen apart. I couldn't get her out of bed for months. Only for the funeral. He was her world. I almost quit school but knew my father wouldn't approve. They gave me a bye for most of my classes that semester."

What he wouldn't tell her back then was that Eloise had replaced her husband with her son. Had been so traumatically scarred that she clung to him as if he were a life preserver and she was adrift in the ocean.

Nell had been the only saving grace in his life that year, given him a new focus, made him laugh, pushed him to do better. It was as if his father had come back through her. She was a lot like him. When she'd left, he'd felt the same kind of agony, the same raw emotion, maybe worse. She was alive but had become untouchable.

CHAPTER THIRTEEN

Nell pulled up to the Hamade's house, got out of the car and went up to ring the bell.

Keileh's mom, Samira, came to the door.

"Come on in, Nell. She'll be right down."

"I can't thank you enough for keeping her last night. Our house next time."

"I'll take you up on that. I may have to go to Iran for a couple of weeks. My mother's ill. It would be good to know she has Chloe to talk to."

"Anything you need, let me know."

Samira nodded.

Nell stood in the foyer of the English Tudor home. Chloe loved the style and said it was the kind of house she wanted to live in when she grew up. She often complained that she was the only one of her friends who lived in a condo. Nell thought she'd done a better job of dissuading her of the notion they should keep up with the Joneses'.

"How was she?"

"Always a pleasure."

Chloe came running down the stairs, Keileh beside her, backpack slung over her shoulder, a satchel carrying her clothes over the other. It was one of her good days.

Samira grabbed hold of Keileh and hugged her.

"I made sure they worked on the report for a few hours last night, but it meant they had to stay up late to catch up on the social amenity piece. She might be a bit tired."

"That's part of the fun of a sleepover. Staying up way past your bedtime."

Taking a strand of Chloe's hair in her fingers, she said, "Looks like you had a good time."

"GOAT."

"And that means?"

The eye roll preceded the meaning.

"Mom, you asked that already. Greatest of all time."

"It's actually a pretty cool acronym."

"Please don't start using it."

"Wouldn't think of it. Don't want to be one of those pathetic parents who try to sound cool. Say good-bye and thank you."

"Good bye and thank you, Mrs. Hamade. It was—"

Samira joined Nell in a chorus of "GOAT."

Even the girls thought it was funny and laughed along with the mothers. As she ambled down the walkway, Nell turned and said, "Thanks again. Call me when you know the details."

"I will."

Chloe skipped down the stone steps just as Nell clicked open the locks of the car.

As she pulled out of the drive-way, Chloe asked, "So what are we doing this afternoon? You said something about shopping."

"I did. I also mentioned having a Q and A, which is set for midafternoon, so name your store of choice and we'll spend some money there, grab something to eat, and then I have to meet some people at Congressman Adams' office in Cambridge. I know you probably don't want to come with me, but I like hanging out with you."

"I still don't see why I can't stay at the condo while you're busy. It's not like you're going somewhere overnight. What will it take, a couple of hours?"

"If that. Megan will be there, and I know you like visiting with her."

Chloe looked at her and asked critically, "How come the congressman is never there when we are? I've never met him, and you've taken me along for years. And you never talk about him. How come?"

"He's in DC most of the week and I have talked about him. He's a...friend of mine. Emilia and Arianna talk about him all the time."

"Is he Mr. Gorgeous Eyes?"

Nell flashed her daughter a concerned look. That was not what she wanted Chloe to know about Jack. She was going to have to come clean soon and she didn't want Chloe to have the wrong impression. Her partners respected Jack and what he'd accomplished which had nothing to do with his looks.

"That's how they refer to him. There's a lot more to him than his eyes. He's just been elected for his fourth term and he's doing some good work."

Nell wasn't sure Chloe was even listening to her, her thumbs busy texting one of her friends. Proving she was good at multi-tasking, Chloe offered, "He's coming to talk to us at school this Friday."

"What?"

Chloe looked over in surprise.

"What, what? Problem? You just said he's a friend of yours. I thought you'd be pleased."

"No, no problem. It isn't on the calendar of upcoming events. When did this happen?"

"I don't know. Mrs. Witmer announced it in home room on Friday. Mr. Cross told us we were going to cover a block on civics next term. Maybe one has to do with the other."

Mr. Cross was Chloe's history teacher and Nell surmised, with the current political climate, he thought it was a good idea to introduce the students to the aspects of citizenship.

Chloe asked, "What is civics exactly?"

Nell glanced over to see Chloe wasn't paying attention to her.

"He didn't explain it?"

"He said theoretical political something."

Her thumbs were busy again.

"Do you really want to know or was it a rhetorical question?"

She gave her a side glance before putting her phone down as if she was gearing up for a dissemination of information, Nell style.

Nell said, "You're the one who asked."

"Sorry. I guess I do. But could you make it simple? You go on and on, sometimes."

"You want succinct. How's this? Civics is defined as how government works, what a citizen's rights and duties are as a member of our democratic society, and civil law and code."

"Why didn't they ask you to talk to us? You know all about that, don't you?"

"I do but Congressman Adams is a member of Congress and has a pretty good idea about how government works."

"I thought you said it wasn't working lately. Will he be honest with us or will he toe the party line?"

She laughed to herself. Chloe was being raised to be knowledgeable about how the world worked. They watched the news together, and Nell made sure to discuss important events that might make the headlines. She wanted her to be aware...and woke. Seemed she'd done too good a job at that. Her questions were right on target, although she leaned to the left. How could she not?

"That's a very good question. Maybe you can ask him this afternoon. He's supposed to be there."

"Cool."

With Chloe's concentration back on her phone, Nell put hers on the road, nervous agitation beginning to roil in her stomach. Chloe didn't seem overly interested in meeting Jack, but she knew that wasn't a two-way street. What would he say? Should she give him a head's-up?

She was still anxiously awaiting his impressions of Chloe when they arrived at his Cambridge office, with several bags of new clothes in the trunk. They'd hit Downtown Crossing, one of Chloe's favorite places, where there was something for both, from shoes and accessories to vintage clothes for her and current pre-teen fashion. It was one of the things they loved to do together, even in the depths of winter. They bundled up and wandered up and down Washington and Winter Street, stopping off at Café Nero for a latte and scone.

The extra caffeine hadn't done her nerves any good.

It took a while to find a parking space even though it was Sunday. It was a corner office on Mass Ave, one of the old brick buildings that was probably a historic site. The biggest space he leased, it had a conference room she used whenever Dave asked her to hold a seminar. The wind had died down, so parking farther away than she would have liked wasn't a big deal. She held the door open as Chloe went ahead of her, her head down, her thumbs busy.

"You need to watch where you're going, Chlo. People get killed texting like that."

Without lifting her head, Chloe said, "You'd never let anything happen to me."

Nell could only shake her head at the logic of that statement.

Megan was at her desk when they went in, along with several policemen mingling in the lobby.

"Hey, Nell, Chloe. How are you guys today?"

Chloe looked up. Nell knew she loved Megan. Old enough to organize a congressman's field office but young enough to come across as a cool adult.

"Hi Megan. Aren't you sick, of babysitting me yet?"

Nell was quick to point out, "She's not your babysitter. I wouldn't ask that of someone on the congressman's staff."

"I don't look at it that way, either. You usually entertain yourself."

"Thanks. Can I sign on to your Wi-Fi? Then I won't bother you too much."

"No problem."

"Cool."

Chloe took a seat on the couch, her earbuds in, her laptop open. Once Megan was finished, she told Nell, "We're waiting on one more family. FYI, Jack's just finished with his meeting and he's in his office."

She'd made it clear in the past that she wouldn't interfere with his time here. It was the excuse she used to have zero interaction with the congressman. No one had to know the sordid details.

"Actually, I'd like to talk to him."

Megan glanced up, her surprise showing in her expression. "I'm sure he won't mind if you go on in."

Nell felt butterflies, fluttering around her heart. She was going to introduce Jack to their daughter and she was all but hyperventilating.

She stood alone, just outside his office, at the doorway, not making a sound. Watching him, his jacket off, his head in his hand, his finger turning pages as he scanned another report, she was impressed again. This time with his diligence. She had never seen him at work, thought he was content being idle, and this was something she hadn't anticipated. Leaning against the threshold, she leisurely took him in and the effect was mind-tingling.

He must have felt the hum of her body, because he finally became aware of her standing there.

His expression was wary.

"I'm beginning to respect what you do here, which is not something I thought I'd ever hear myself say."

"Thanks. I appreciate it. I love what I do, for the most part and I think I'm good at it. I wish I had been more like you. Taken the step without over thinking it."

She stepped inside the office, not as well appointed as she'd expected. The furniture was worn and old but still impressive.

"What did you overthink?"

"Politics was something my dad and I talked about. For me. And to be honest, I was always drawn to. I fought it for a long time...because..."

"Your mother took over the agenda and you didn't want to give in?"

"My mother was trying to pick up where my father left off. She didn't want his death, or the reasons for it, to derail me from what they both thought was where my future lay. It took a lot of time for me to get over 9/11, to let go of the hostile attitude I had towards government, Congress specifically. I would have loved discussing it with you. Maybe you could have helped me see beyond the blame, but you thought my mother was running the show and...you would have thought I was caving again."

She straightened, stunned by his words.

"My God, Jack. I'm sorry if that's what happened. You should have been able to talk to me about anything without being concerned about my reaction." His pronouncement startled her. Had she been partially to blame for his indecision? "What made you move forward?"

"The timing was right. When Tomms announced his retirement, I decided to go for it. An opening doesn't come up that often and I didn't know when there'd be another one."

"My partners supported you from day one. I admit I didn't. Something else I never thought I'd hear myself say but Eloise was right. It was a good choice for you."

"This wasn't my mother's choice for me. It was mine."

His eyes penetrated deep into hers, as if wanting her to believe him.

"Point taken."

Leaning back in his seat, his hands behind his head, he was studying her, and it was making her uneasy.

"Look, now that we seem to be on better footing, would it be possible to discuss strategy with you on some issues? I always valued your opinion."

Her face was touched by astonishment. He stood and came around the desk, sat on the edge, his arms crossed over his chest.

"You don't believe me."

"I'm...I never felt that way."

"Not at the end, no, you wouldn't have. But in the beginning? You have to admit we discussed everything."

She gave him a brief nod.

"What do you say? I've given the 2013 Senate Immigration Bill a cursory glance, but I'd like to go through it step by step, get your take on each of the points. I have a lot of catching up to do."

"Why did you agree to this committee? I know how you feel about it."

"Judiciary is a plum assignment. You don't turn it down. Besides, most of my constituency is ethnic and I want to see if there's anything I can do to protect them on a federal level, not just with state statute. That we agree on."

"It's going to be an uphill battle."

"I can read the writing on the wall as well as you can."

"And we'll probably lose."

"We need to keep moving in the right direction no matter how steep the hill is."

That sentiment forced a smile out of her.

"I want to learn as much as I can, although there are things that disturb me about the numbers being allowed in. We've always set quotas on certain countries, depending on what was going on in the world. I need to understand the whole picture before I can give an opinion on a reform bill. I want your side of the debate before I decide."

She felt like she'd been hit with a cold bucket of water.

At least she didn't feel the itchy need to touch him again.

Taking a step back, she asked, "Are you saying you might vote for a travel ban?"

He must have noticed her retreat because he got up and took a step towards her, his hands in his pockets.

"No. I'm saying I have concerns about some of the points. Am I for naturalization? Yes. Am I for sweeping reform? Yes. Am I for a clear and consistent path to citizenship? Yes. Should we have open borders? Not so sure."

"That's who we are, as a country."

"No, it's not. Not at the beginning. It's who we've become. I think the Statue of Liberty gave the world a different view of us than we had for ourselves. I admit, we perpetuated it, but remember there have always been certain ethnic groups barred from entry. The Chinese, the Japanese, anyone who wasn't Caucasian. Now it's Muslims."

"I believe that's a result of 9/11."

"And all the other terrorist attacks going on across the globe."

"I believe it's a result of unfounded fears. More Christian whites have committed violent hate crimes than Muslims."

He pulled at his ear as if considering this.

"This is the reason I want your take. You will challenge me to see the other side, if you're willing."

She nodded, not sure where she was going to find the time to spoon-feed him the finer points of immigration reform or the unconstitutionality of a travel ban.

"I don't think I congratulated you on the award you won last night. Was that a hook to get you to attend?"

"I wasn't told about it. Arianna knew I wouldn't want it. Too many others deserve it more than I do. No hook. I attend that event every year. You don't."

"I would think you avoid it like the plague. You never liked working a room."

She almost let the smile slip out.

"Arianna gave me a middling grade on my networking skills."

"I would have been the one doing that. You could have just stood there and looked nice."

"I might have been able to look nice, but I never would have been able to just stand there. Not with my make-up."

Dave and Michael had come to the office door, Dave peeking in. "We're just about ready."

She glanced up at him and nodded, then looked at Jack, weighing her tone and her words. "I hear you're speaking at Standish on Friday. How did that happen?"

Nodding in Dave's direction, he said, "Blame him. Chloe's history teacher has a kid in the same grade as Genna. He asked, I agreed. It gave us the idea to offer the same kind of mini civics class to some of the public schools in the area. Good idea?"

"It can't hurt. I figured since you'd probably finagle an introduction...to some of the students, I brought one of them along today. A more private setting."

He was momentarily speechless. Looked at her skeptically before noticing that Michael and Dave were within earshot. Nell was vague and speaking in general terms for Michael's benefit.

He could feel his hands begin to tremble. He'd waited so long for this, but now that the moment was here, he was unsure of how to act, what to say. Chloe couldn't know what kind of momentous occasion this was, so he had to keep his mood tempered.

He moved back toward the desk, grabbed his suit coat, and shrugged into it.

Michael chuckled "Already trying to influence your future voters."

"Why not? She's only seven years away from registering. Can never start too early."

He walked toward the door, his eyes focused on Nell, her amber-colored eyes burning into him.

Trying hard not to appear nervous in front of his staff, he reached for some calm and followed Nell out to the reception area. "Chloe, I'd like to introduce you to Congressman Adams."

He stood breathless. Up close, she was the image of her mother. Shape of the face, hair, even the smile was a replica. The only contribution he seemed to have made was her eyes. They were a soft dove-grey that indelibly linked them together in a way that he never would have understood if someone explained it.

She had gotten up and stepped forward to shake his hand.

"Congressman Adams, it's a pleasure to meet you."

"Please, call me...Jack. And the pleasure is all mine."

Nell noticed the laptop open.

"What are you doing?"

"Trying to keep from being bored."

"How?"

"Looking at recipes. You wouldn't believe how many I've found that are kid friendly."

"Remind me to look into cooking classes for you this week."

"I already found a place that specializes in teaching kids but it's in Newton."

"I'll work it out somehow. Text me the phone number and I'll call tomorrow."

"Really?"

"Really. You enjoy it and it'll be good for you."

Chloe ran at her and threw her arms around her.

"Thanks, Mom."

Jack glanced in Megan's direction. "I never thought to ask. Should we be providing our younger guests with some games or activities to keep them busy while they wait?"

"That might not be a bad idea. Many of our visitors bring their children. Especially when they come in to meet Nell or Emilia."

"Take it out of petty cash if we have it. Make it a priority this week."

"Sure thing."

Jaiden came over to Nell and announced, "It looks like everyone's here. You might want to get started."

"Thanks, Jaiden."

The TV overhead began a new cycle of press conferences starring some of the House members. Before leaving the spot, Nell looked up to catch Jack standing in front of some reporters, listening to the questions being peppered among members of the Intelligence Committee, who had come out to put a spotlight on the need for an investigation into the Russian interference that took place during the election. The ranking member, a vocal component of the party, was issuing a verbal warning on the consequences that could result if ignored.

"Any foreign intervention for the express purpose of affecting an election is not only unacceptable, it sets a dangerous precedent."

One of the reporters, a member of the *Boston Globe* crew, directed his question to his state's rep.

"Congressman Adams, do you believe the reports that are coming out of the intelligence community or do you think they lack credibility?"

"Ted, being on the CIA subcommittee, I have the highest regard and confidence in their efforts to bring this to light. It is problematic in every sense if it is not taken seriously. We cannot allow the Russian government to undermine our political system and although nothing will change the outcome of the election, we need to find our way to the truth so it doesn't happen again."

"Why would they have interfered with the process?"

"I think that's easy enough to answer. The CIA have determined it was done with the express purpose of influencing the election results. It should be of concern to every American, no matter who they voted for. We need to conduct a vigorous investigation into the cyberattacks and we will be requesting hearings on this as soon as our agenda allows."

"Do you think the commitment by the majority to investigate this is real or just window dressing?"

"They've been dressing a lot of windows lately, wanting to look busy while checking for the safest place to stand. They talk a lot from behind the glass, unwilling to venture out and take a risk. Unless the verbiage is an honest representation of their opinion, which will lead to action, it's useless and will do the American people no good."

Flash bulbs popped at that statement.

It had become a sound bite that found its way to a variety of media outlets. It was a good one. And she smiled at hearing it again.

"That was one of your better remarks. I know it was retweeted hundreds of times. I retweeted it myself a few."

Dave laughed.

"I never know what he's going to come out with. Sometimes I can live with it."

Nell walked toward the side room where her audience was waiting, Dave right beside her. He was the one introducing her to the assembled crowd.

"He's not preaching the party line?"

"Nope."

She looked at Dave skeptically, so he added, "You two used to talk all the time. You know where he stands on most issues. Did anything he say ring false?"

"No. I guess I forgot what he stood for."

"Ellen and I could never understand how two people on the same side could have so many debates."

"We liked to challenge each other to think."

"I know. I think you helped him craft his eventual platform."

"I always thought it was his mother who did that."

"She never had the mental agility. She might have given him her opinion on things but there was never any real dialogue. Of course, she didn't necessarily want him to think, just obey."

Dave was right. The part of the relationship she'd valued most was the way they encouraged each other to analyze ideas, articulate thoughts, use words to defend a position. That and the relationship they'd had in the bedroom. There they communicated in a non-verbal way expressing what they felt through the senses.

There was one position that she could never win. The one about his relationship with his mother. Her points were countered, placated, or outright ignored. Eloise always had the upper hand.

She'd never won with her parents either. All the reasons she'd given as she'd begged them to take her with them to whatever foreign country they were going to, were snubbed.

She'd learned not to care about either. Or so she'd thought.

Seeing him over the last few days, she was back in the department of need. She had to get out and fast.

Dave began her introduction, explaining who she was, what she did, and why she was an expert of the subject matter. When he was done, she stepped to the make-shift podium and began going over the do's and don'ts of dealing with ICE.

CHAPTER FOURTEEN

Jack took a seat beside Chloe, his hands hanging between his legs, unsure what to say, how to start conversation. He waded in picking up on the conversation she'd had with Nell

"You want to learn how to cook?"

"Yeah. Mom's started picking up things for me to heat up for us, but I want to get more creative."

"I love cooking, myself. My signature dish is beef bourguignon. My father used to make it when I was younger. He got the recipe from his parents, so I guess it's a family tradition."

"You'll pass it down to your kids, too, then."

He gulped as he nodded, at a loss for words.

He was relieved when Chloe took over the line of questioning.

"Can I interview you?"

Jack's eyes flew up to meet ones very much like his own. He wondered if she noticed the resemblance.

"I've got a meeting soon, but yeah, sure. Are you on the school newspaper or something?"

He knew she wasn't. Knew everything she'd joined since entering middle school.

"No, but I'd like to be. If I bring in an article about you before Friday, maybe they'd add it to our newsletter."

"Then I'd be honored to help you."

Chloe set up her phone, got the video and recording set, and gave an introduction. He was impressed with her articulation and her confidence. He could see Nell's influence in the way she handled herself.

Then her first question.

"What made you go into politics?"

He leaned back in the corner of the sofa, shifted his leg over his knee.

"Not any one thing really. I went to law school but found it limiting. I didn't like the black-and- white code lawyers needed to abide by. I was more of a people person than an adversary. And my father and I used to talk about ways I could give back. Politics seemed to fit the bill on every level. I reached my decision to run as soon as Congressman Tomms announced his retirement. I ran for his seat."

Pausing the interview, Chloe put the phone down.

"My Mom worked for him. We lived there for a couple of years. She left when he retired. We go to his house for dinner a couple of times a year. I like him."

"He was one of the best at what he did. Your mom helped him write several of the bills he introduced."

She looked up at him, pride shining in her eyes and nodded, telling him she knew that.

"He's told me stories of her contribution. He respects her a lot."

Picking up where she left off, hitting the pause button to get the video rolling again, she asked, "What do you think is the most important issue today? And how will you address it?"

"It's not easy to pick just one. My three top sticking points? The interference in our election process, immigration reform, and health care. As part of the Judicial Committee, in the minority party, all I can do is ask good questions and try to persuade my colleagues that it is in the country's best interests to get to the bottom of the hacking, find out who's at fault, and imprison those who have committed conspiracy with a foreign power. We don't have the numbers to vote down any new version of health care the opposing side presents. It's a game of wait and see before we know how to counteract it. Immigration reform's been on the agenda for decades. With the proposals being offered about the wall, deportation, closing borders, we have to remain vigilant and make sure the laws are obeyed, and I'm hopeful the courts will help us with that."

"With the climate change deniers, the hate speech, racial injustice, and the bitter partisanship that exists today, what kind of country will those who govern leave to my generation?"

"Whoa. That's the kind of question I could see your mother asking when she was your age."

"Yeah, people tell me I'm just like her. Is there an answer to the question? Because we're worried."

"The only piece of advice I can give you is to get involved. Our government is predicated on the idea that the citizens need to engage. Do what you can on a local level, community and state. And vote for people who support your vision for our country."

"Do you think there should be term limits for members of Congress?"

"I could give you the standard answer for that, which is, there are. It's called voter rights. If you don't like your congressman or senator you can vote him or her out. Do I think we need fresh blood, less animosity, more bipartisan collaboration? Yes, I do. I have a feeling those days are ahead of us."

"What makes you say that?"

"People are waking up to what's going on, paying better attention, getting more involved. The Women's March is a good example of that."

"Will you be walking in it?"

He wasn't sure she'd like his answer, so he turned the question around on her.

"Will you?"

"I finally convinced Mom that it was important for me to be there. It's history in the making. We are the storm and all of that. She agreed to let me walk with her and members of her law firm."

"Do you think it's important for me to join them?"

"I do. I think it goes to showing your support for the people's rights, which is what you promised to protect when you were sworn in."

She had a better grasp of the underpinnings of democracy than most adults. He had to give Nell credit for that, along with the other lawyers at Woodley and Fisher. It's where she'd grown up, being dropped off there after school every day, bearing witness to the law and how it worked.

"Then I'll have to think about it."

"Good. If you need more by way of supporting arguments, I know a couple of women you could talk to."

He grinned at her sense of the absurd.

"I may take you up on that."

She smiled at him then, a smile that sent shafts of sunlight straight to his heart.

"What is your favorite part of being a congressman?"

"Meeting people, helping them achieve their goals."

"Giving back?"

"Yes. It's a family tradition."

"That's what Mom says. Her family goes way back."

"So does mine."

"Will you run for president someday?"

"No. That's not the kind of legacy I want to leave."

He didn't want that kind of burden on his shoulders. There was a reason all presidents went gray within a couple of years. Who needed that kind of responsibility?

"Okay, last question because I hear Mom's voice in my head telling me I've taken up too much of your time. What kind of legacy do you want to leave?"

"I want to leave the world in a better place than when I found it. I want to have made a difference in the everyday lives of working-class people. I feel I can do that better on a local level than a national one."

"He also doesn't have the kind of ego you need to run for president."

Nell had stepped into the room, obviously overhearing the last part of their conversation.

He looked at her sheepishly.

"She asked for an interview. I couldn't say no."

"She has that effect on people. Consider yourself Chloed. I came out to ask if you have time to meet the people who came in today?"

"I do. That's why I stuck around. Some of the police did, too. I hope they helped and didn't hinder your talk."

"They actually backed me. It was a good community-relations move."

Chloe stood up, looked from one to the other.

"Can I come in?"

It was Jack who answered.

"I can't see why not. This is democracy in action."

Chloe stood at the back of the room, trying to stay out of the way. She usually felt so small next to her mother, not that her mother did anything to make her feel that way. She knew she was loved, completely and unconditionally.

Had never doubted it. It was hard to be the daughter of someone so accomplished. Nell Warren seemed almost invincible. But she knew she wasn't. She'd heard her cry, seen her lose a hard-fought case and how hard it had hit her, heard stories of how lonely she'd been growing up. Not from her, but from Jelani. Her mother would never say anything to make her sad. And knowing her mom had grown up alone, without the kind of love she'd felt her whole life brought her close to tears. There's no doubt her mom would be mad if she knew Jelani had told her about her childhood, but it was the kind of things she talked about with her mother's partner and friend. She kept the truth a closely guarded secret. Like mother like daughter. Her mother could keep one, too.

The question was, why? Why wouldn't she tell her who her father was?

Who would it hurt if the truth came out?

Sometimes she thought her mother was still in love with her father. She rarely went out, worked non-stop as if to fill her time with busy work so she didn't have to think, or feel. Jelani thought so, too. Howie was a nice guy but she didn't get the feeling there was love between them. Not the kind like Jack and Rose had in the movie *Titanic*. It was one of her favorite movies and she watched it every time it was on and wished her mother could find that kind of love, but with a happy ending.

She looked around the room, the people in the audience listening to Jack now. His speech seemed scripted, like he was giving them the party line. Her mother always came across with sincerity, as if what she said came from her heart.

She glanced over to where her mother stood and straightened, taking a closer look.

Her mother was looking at Jack Adams with...something she'd never seen before. A sparkle, not only in her eyes but in the way she responded to him. And it seemed the Congressman was reciprocating. He was deferential, smiled at her a lot, his eyes clinging to her every movement.

His eyes.

They were grey, like hers.

Jack Adams? Or was it the result of an overactive imagination? Was she seeing things that didn't exist because she wanted to?

Bringing her phone up, she googled him. Scrolled down his bio on Wikipedia. Parents were J. Lee and Eloise Adams. Father died 9/11. No siblings.

Direct descendent of John and John Quincy, second and fourth president of the United States.

School: Phillips Academy, Harvard, and Harvard Law.

Occupation: Congressman seventh district elected in 2011, serving third term, re-elected for fourth.

Spouse: None

Children: None

Did Jelani know? More importantly, would she tell her? Or did she have the nerve to ask her mother outright?

The crowd was beginning to disperse with Jack and her mom shaking hands with those getting ready to depart, in sync with each other like they'd done this before. Or something similar.

Megan had come into the room, signaled Nell that she had a phone call.

It had to be someone she didn't know. Everyone who needed it had her cell phone number. Her mother excused herself and went into Jack's office to take it.

Once everyone had left the room, Jack came over and asked, "What did you think?"

"I think you proved you're in politics."

As he loosened his tie, he asked, "How did I do that?"

"You sounded like a politician."

"And what do we sound like?"

"Political. Like it's all an agenda to you. The people a means to an end."

"I hope they didn't feel like that."

"Doesn't matter. It's Mom who'll help them if they need it."

"And she sounded more...?"

"Like their lives matter to her, that she'll be there for them no matter what."

He'd taken a seat at the conference table and uncapped the water bottle Jaiden had set in front of him.

Ron took a seat opposite and Jack wondered what he was thinking. He knew about Nell, and about Chloe. When they were at Harvard Law together, he'd spilled his guts one night they'd gotten drunk after one of their exams. Ron's girlfriend had an endless supply of friends she'd wanted to set him up with and he'd kept declining the invites. Ron must have talked to her because she'd stopped. It'd taken him over a year to get back into the dating pool. And even then, it was more of a chore than a pleasure.

After meeting her when she was in DC, Ron had pulled him aside to say he understood now. Nell was unique and not easily replaced.

Ron was the one who spoke to Chloe's assessment.

"You're right Chloe. That's why we call on her so often. I think you might be sacrificing something because of it. Your mom has taken a client call, so why don't you sit down. She might be a while. Michael, the schedule."

She did as he suggested, knowing her mother would take the time she needed to for the person on the other end of the line. Her eyes took in the two members of the staff she didn't know as he made the introductions.

"This is Michael Hardstrap, my appointment secretary. He organizes my activities, my attendance at congressional hearings, press conferences, rallies, speeches, lunches, breakfasts, media interviews, town meetings, ribbon cuttings, factory tours, fundraisers. He has the key to my door, setting time parameters and locales for constituent meetings. This is Ron Rubini, my communications director. He writes the words that make me sound more...real. You probably already know Geena and Jaiden if you hang out when your mother's here."

She nodded and smiled at each of them.

Michael was standing, papers in his hand that he flipped back and forth to give Jack what he wanted.

"Let's see. Friday, Standish Academy at eleven. I set up a time with Nell for a visit to the deportation center. Midafternoon. Meeting with staff of Immigration Center in Boston Saturday morning, luncheon at the senior center in Mattapan, speaking to the DAR at two, staff holiday party here on Sunday night, after you meet Santa at the Franklin Park Zoo, and attend an immigration clinic at Boston City Hall in the afternoon. Coming up, fundraising dinner with dancing at the Wollaston with silent auction on February fourteenth, trivia night at a pizza place in Everett on the fifteenth, black tux at your mother' at the beginning of March. Oh, and she called earlier and said that she set up a meeting for you after New Year's with a potential donor, early evening. Turkish businessman from Cambridge who might be looking to back you. If he likes what you have to say, he's willing to hold a meet and greet at his house. Otherwise, just the usual. Music festival, gospel concert, a bunch of holiday activities, fairs, Logitech party to support the homeless, Chocolate Festival, and City Feast. Inauguration on the twentieth. I've blocked off the twenty-first of January in case you want to join the Women's March in Boston."

Jack noticed Nell was standing on the outskirts of the room, probably waiting for a good time to break and get Chloe. She was biting her lip when Michael mentioned his mother, but he wasn't about to defend the upcoming events. His mother had always held ticketed events that brought in an obscene amount of cash. If he balked at spending so much time on the phone begging for money, he had to make it up in other ways. If he expected Nell to give in and introduce him to Chloe, he was going to have to do battle with his mother sometime soon. Reflecting on his willingness to set his mother straight about his intentions, he wondered why it had been so difficult for him to do it when Nell was in his life. With his gaze still on her thoughtful expression, thinking her mind was on something else, he was surprised when she asked a question on topic. "Do you ever hold meet and greets at regular people's homes? I know it couldn't bring in as much as you might need it to, but you'd be mingling with people who can't afford the big-ticket events."

Dave perked up. "That's a great idea, Nell. It would alleviate some of our constituent concerns if they could talk to Jack in person."

"I'd be more than happy to hold one, any one of us would and I could probably find some other supporters willing. The number of attendees would depend on the size of the houses provided."

Jack said, as if to himself, "Grassroots has become a signature move by some politicians."

Nell went even further.

"Maybe get some of the legal immigrants to come. It would give Jack the opportunity to talk to them, get a firsthand account of some of their problems.

Dave asked, "Ramona Perez?"

"She did come to mind."

"Where does she live?"

"Somerville."

"House?"

"Yes. Three-bedroom ranch. It's got a nice backyard which would give you more space, but with the snow and cold I think we're stuck inside. Unless you want to wait until summer. I could pay to have it catered."

"Unfortunately, you can't for reasons that will become apparent in time."

Jack knew what he meant. When it was out that he was Chloe's father, Nell would be limited in what she could do for him.

She must have read between the lines, as well, because instead of arguing with him, she suggested, "Then maybe we could put together a potluck kind of fundraiser. Ethnic food, different cultures, melting pot."

Dave leaned back, thinking.

"I love it. How much for tickets?"

Jack barged into the conversation at this point. "No dollar amounts. They can donate what they can afford."

Geena suggested, "Maybe you can hold something at a hall, have people bring signature dishes, and hold an auction. Invite some organizations invested in immigration reform to come and bid for them. That way the only financial output would be for the ingredients, something they probably already have on hand."

"I like that, too."

Dave added, "We could do both. Nell's right, though, it's not going to bring in much, but it might be good for community relations."

Jack stated honestly, "That's more important to me than contributions."

Geena asked, "Should I get Jon-Christopher working on it?"

He was a college student and one of the interns working out of this office. "Yes."

Jack's face suggested he'd gotten an idea. Facing Nell, he asked, "Could you make some calls, to Ramona, anyone you think might be interested?"

"I'll call Hani, have her do some background for us."

Her personal assistant had more on her plate since the Supreme Court win and influx of calls, but she knew she'd squeeze it in.

"Great."

Looking at his watch, realizing he'd kept his staff far longer than he'd meant to, he said, "That's it for today. And thanks everyone. Great work."

As his staff disbursed, he swiveled his chair around and looked directly at Nell.

"Would you and Chloe grab some dinner with me? I haven't eaten all day and I'm starved. It'll be a way to pay you back for your contribution. I loved your ideas."

Nell was about to turn down the invite, but Chloe jumped in, coming more into the center of the room.

"That would be cool. But please, I beg you, no pizza. We have that three times a week."

Positive this was not a good idea, Nell grasped at excuses to turn down the invitation.

"Chloe, it's a school night and you must still have some homework to do."

"I finished it last night at Keileh's. Her mom is stricter than you are. Please? It would be nice to have another meal that doesn't come by way of delivery."

"Your mom likes pizza, huh?"

Nell could feel his gaze, his eyes twinkling at her. She had to keep herself from puddling.

Chloe smiled up at him.

"Yes. It's usually the kid who wants it fifty-two/seven. Not in my house."

Nell watched the interplay between father and daughter. Was she seriously considering this?

Jack asked, "Have a restaurant in mind?"

Chloe seemed determined to get her way. She had no idea what she was walking them into when she admitted, "No. I don't get out much. I'll go anywhere that doesn't serve pizza, fries, Chinese or Thai."

Nell's throat felt constricted, her nerves on edge.

"You're not giving him many options."

"Mom, there's a whole world out there. Italian, Greek, French, Mexican...I could go on."

"I'm sure you could. You always did well on your geography tests."

"You guys are all dressed up and ready to go but I'm not. We need to pick somewhere casual. Otherwise I'll bring shame upon the best female attorney in Boston and one of our upstanding representatives from Congress."

"You mustn't have noticed but I've agreed. You don't have to butter me up."

Chloe all but squealed in delight.

"Yessss."

Jack got up from his seat, grabbed his keys from his desk, and went to the doorway.

"Then let's go my lovelies."

Chloe's hand went to her hip and she admonished, "Um, that's a line from *The Wizard of Oz*. It didn't end up well for those who went."

After switching off the light, he led them to the reception area and to the front door.

"I guess you'll just have to take the chance I have nothing evil in mind, if you want a meal other than pizza, that is."

"If I have no choice. Let's go."

"I've got a couple in mind. A taqueria or a Greek place. Your choice, Chloe."

Glancing up at her mother, she thought for a minute and said, "The taqueria. Tortillas are kind of pizza-like."

Nell surprised them both.

"And I was thinking Greek. They have a lamb garnish that's delicious."

"You've been?"

"I have. And this way you'll get meat, potatoes or rice, and vegetable. A veritable garden of delight for those who disdain one of the more perfect foods."

Letting them precede him out the door, Jack said, "It's a few blocks up but it's too dark to walk. We can take my car and I'll drop you back off at yours once we're finished eating."

CHAPTER FIFTEEN

Jack opened the car door for both females, Chloe climbing in the back, Nell sliding into the passenger seat. Once Jack was behind the wheel, Nell gave an off-key whistle.

"Nice car."

"Thanks. Let's not go any further than that. Okay?"

"I was not going to ask that question. Don't have to. Know the answer."

"It's leased."

"I thought we weren't going any further. Follow your own advice."

He had pulled out of the parking spot and headed down Mass Ave.

Chloe was leaning her head on her mother's head rest.

"What are you two talking about?"

"Jack always has the best of everything."

"How do you know?"

Chloe noticed her mother incline her head in Jack's direction as if she'd been caught at something.

"Do you guys know each other?"

Chloe's question set off a hundred alarms. Trying to sound measured, casual, she answered,

"I told you. We're...friends."

"No, like know each other."

Nell snapped her head to look back at her daughter.

"What are you asking Chloe?"

"It sounds like that's an inside joke. Inside jokes are a thing between people who know each other well. Like have a history. I have them with Keileh. And some of the members on my field hockey team."

Jack looked up at her in his rear-view mirror.

"We knew each other in college."

Chloe's mind started racing. Another check mark in the pro column of Jack as father.

"You didn't go to Yale or Stanford."

"No. I didn't."

She waited but Jack wasn't giving her anything else. Why? There was something going on between them, and she was now more determined than ever to dig up the past. Their past might be indelibly linked to her own.

"So how did you meet?"

"Debate team."

"You debated my mother?"

He glanced back again, a sardonic smile on his lips.

"Foolhardy endeavor."

"Yeah, I know."

Pausing, Chloe went out on a limb, knowing the branch could snap in two.

"Did you ever date?"

She noticed the look that passed between them. Her heart began beating a bit too fast, hope surging in her chest. Having Jack as her father would be...awesome. For some reason there wasn't any anger, just a fleeting glimpse of hope at knowing her lineage.

"Well? Did you?"

Her mother's voice carried into the back seat.

"We hung out from time to time."

"That means one of you had to drive to the other and that you've known each other for...twelve, thirteen years. What happened. To make you un-friend each other?"

"Who said we're not still friends?"

"Mom, you never went to one of his fundraisers, never talked about him, thought he'd make a lousy congressman."

Her mom flashed her eyes in his direction.

"I never said that. Not out loud."

"Yeah, you did. To Arianna one afternoon she was talking to you about Jack."

Jack found a parking space not far from the restaurant and parallel parked.

"I was a lousy lawyer, so your mom probably figured I'd make a lousy rep."

"How did she know that? We'd moved by then. You couldn't have been out of law school long by the time we got to DC.

"Word gets around."

Her mother looked like she was getting flustered which was something she rarely saw. As if struggling to keep a conciliatory tone, Nell said tightly, "Chloe, I was wrong. He's very good at what he does. Now, can we put all this behind us and go eat? I'm hungry."

"Fine. I don't understand why you're getting angry about my questions. I'm just trying to put it all into perspective."

They silently got out of the car and walked the few feet to the Olympian-style eatery. It was a hole-in-the-wall that had the best Greek food in the city. Nell had been here a couple of times, picked up take-out to eat at her office, but never thought to pick it up for dinner. She would from now on. She hadn't realized Chloe was sick of pizza or Thai or any of the other kinds of places she had on speed dial. Well, maybe she had but had glossed over that fact.

As soon as they walked in, they were seated in the back, the hostess recognizing the congressman and wanting to give them some privacy.

"Come here much?"

"Off and on when I'm in the city."

Chloe opened the menu, then looked up at Jack.

"Thank you from the bottom of my heart. There's meat."

Nell explained what some of the specialty dishes were, and her mouth watered at the thought of eating moussaka. She ordered it with pilaf and salad. Jack ordered the lamb chops and Chloe the beef kabab with shrimp.

The time spent together was enjoyable once Chloe stopped asking questions about the past. That'd unnerved her. It was as if Chloe had guessed the truth and was baiting her to come clean.

She sat throughout the meal listening. Chloe and Jack chatted about everything, school, her favorite subjects, her friends, his friends, his upcoming hearings, the different committees he was on. They filled in a lot of the blanks regarding each other's life, even though Chloe didn't know what was going on.

Or maybe she did. And it was way past time.

Climbing into bed soon after she returned home, the print blurring as she read making it impossible to continue to work, Nell pushed the notes onto the small stand next to her and thought about the conversation she'd had with Jack about going into politics.

She'd never known his father was grooming him for Congress. He'd never told her that little tid-bit.

It might have cut down on the sniping. Might have given her and Eloise something in common, promoting advancement in the career he'd been working toward. But he'd never said anything. Only that he was thinking. Sorting out his options. Not sure what he wanted to put his efforts and energy into. She hadn't known back then what kind of aversion he had to those sitting in power although she would have understood the why behind it. They hadn't talked much about his father while they were together but the little he'd given away told her all she needed to know. Father and son had been close and losing him had been a traumatic event in his life. She could relate to that. She'd been close to her own father, could remember him reading her bedtime stories, kissing her good night, making her pancakes on Sunday morning with whipped cream smiles and chocolate chip eyes. The day he'd walked out on her, was one of the worst of her life. She wasn't sure she'd ever make it to the other side of the grieving process. Her father hadn't died. He'd left by choice and it had broken her heart. To blunt the pain, she'd studied hard, worked hard, filling every second of every day with something to bury the ache that still throbbed at the thought of him. There was a secret room in her heart where he still lived.

Had Jack driven away the demons, given in to his father's wishes to honor his memory? Or had he given in to Eloise like she'd thought.

She didn't want to think too deeply about that because she might come up with an answer she didn't like.

But there they were, in the past, sitting at the dining room table in Jack's apartment. The antique furniture a remnant of Beatrix Adam's home, the one she'd sold when she'd developed an enlarged heart and moved in next door to her son and daughter-in-law.

Jack had cooked his specialty and one of her favorites, beef bourguignon. They were sipping wine, discussing one of her cases at the free legal clinic where she was working. She'd asked him again what his plans were. She knew he was going to be attending Harvard in the fall although she wasn't sure why.

Her Stanford spot was in place, with a hefty deposit but the rest of the tuition was up to her. She could attend or not.

He'd looked at her, his eyes a stormy grey, a stark representation of his disturbed state of mind, and admitted he might want to run for office.

What kind of expression had she been wearing?

Had she been thrown off guard by his admission? Or certain that he was giving in and disappointed in his lack of integrity?

The expressions were in shadow and she couldn't give them the clarity she was looking for.

She leaned over to shut off the light and slid down under the duvet, her mind dwelling on the mother-son relationship.

He gave into Eloise on so many things, big and small, that she wouldn't have known to look deeper beneath the surface.

Maybe if he had talked to her, instead of his mother, about life, what he wanted, she might have had something to go on. Maybe if she hadn't complained so loudly and often about Eloise's intrusiveness, he would have. Maybe they were never meant to be.

They'd wanted different things.

He'd wanted to stay close to a doting mother. She'd felt as if she were being strangled by the clenched fist Eloise had around Jack's heart.

The other reason?

She'd refused to compete for anyone's love again. It didn't get her anywhere, only hurt.

Rolling to her side, she pulled at the pillow, trying to get comfortable, her thoughts now a jumble.

What if she had jumped on his bandwagon, given in a little?

Eloise would have shoved her off.

There was no room in his life for her, just like there'd been no room in her parents'.

She'd tried to explain it in the note she left, the night she moved out.

Nothing had changed and she was not going to take a seat on the bus again. Better to be traveling her own road, her own way than to be pushed off.

The niggling fear that simmered, the one she didn't want to acknowledge, was that she'd become her mother. She might have wanted to be with him so badly, she'd have given up who she was to see it done. Gone along. Gotten swept up. Given up her life.

The life she had worked for, created, loved.

There would have been resentment at some point, a reckoning that would have pitted them against each other.

It was better this way.

When she looked back at the picture of them at the table, there was an empty chair, the one she'd vacated.

What surprised her was the look on his face.

It was one of sad consternation.

⌒

Chloe was in a text marathon with Keileh when the clock struck midnight. She wanted to run her theory by her friend, to see if she was barking up the wrong family tree or if her premise held merit.

Could Jack be her father?

Keileh told her to ask her mother outright. She didn't have the courage to do that. Maybe she didn't want to force her mother into lying to her.

After Keileh had texted good night, she lay on her bed, thinking about the first time she'd asked her mom about her father.

She'd been maybe four or five, noticing for the first time that dads sometimes picked up their kids at her pre-school. They were on the way home, Nell asking her to name one thing she'd learned that day, a question that had become a ritual for the two. Nell still asked it. Chloe had learned over time she didn't necessarily mean academics but about life in general.

"I met Tracey's Dad today. I learned some kids have one."

"All kids have them Chloe. You know that."

"Where's mine?"

Her mother had gotten flustered that day. One of the first times she'd seen it. She'd fumbled with an answer, explained that her dad hadn't been ready for fatherhood, was unable to commit to them. When she was older, able to articulate more of what she was feeling, she'd asked her mother if the inability to commit would be forever, or if he might want to meet her. She'd promised there'd be no expectations. She was just curious.

Nell had refused, so sure she'd be hurt. Promised if she still wanted to meet him when she was older, she wouldn't deny her that right. That was three years ago. When would she be old enough?

Eleven? Fifteen? Eighteen? She didn't want to wait that long.

She wanted to go to the father-daughter night with someone. This year, like all other years, she'd stayed home. It had initiated a deep-seated need to know who the man was who'd contributed to her DNA. She'd been asking non-stop since. Her mother had yet to give in.

She slid her legs out of bed and placed them flat on the floor.

Her mom got just as unsettled talking about her father as she did talking about Jack.

Were the two related? She was going to make it her life's mission to find out.

After creeping down the hall, still unable to sleep, Chloe knocked on her mother's door.

"Come in."

The voice gave away Nell had been half-asleep.

When she pushed open the door, her mother squinted her eyes at the illumination cast by the hall light.

"Why aren't you asleep?"

"I couldn't. Can I sleep with you tonight?"

Patting the space on the bed next to her, Chloe had the invitation she wanted and scurried over to slip in beside her.

Nell kissed her forehead and tucked her in the crook of her arm like she had when she was younger.

"What's the matter?"

"I think you know."

"I think I do, too. You're not going to let this go, are you?"

"No, Mom. I think I'm old enough to know."

"I'm beginning to think you're right. I'm afraid that you will be disappointed, or worse, hurt. I am willing to protect you from that with every breath I have in me."

"I know. Even if it means I don't like you much."

"Even if it means that."

"But I love you, no matter what you decide."

Fiddling with her hair, her mother finally said, "Let me contact your father, see what we can work out. Can you give me a couple of days to arrange it?"

Disappointment flooded through her. She'd been sure it was Jack Adams, already liked him a lot. What her mother was telling her was that it was someone else. Someone she had to contact to set up a meeting. Now she began to worry. What if she didn't like the man who'd fathered her? What if they didn't get along? What if he still didn't want to make a commitment to her or fatherhood?

What if her mother was right and she was too young to face all those things?

She snuggled closer, burrowing deep into the love her mother wrapped her in, knowing she'd survive it.

CHAPTER SIXTEEN

Nell dropped Chloe off at school, promising again she'd do what she could to introduce her to her father over the up-coming weekend.

"He's around?"

"He works out of town a lot but he's usually around week-ends."

"Okay."

After kissing her mother good-bye, she climbed out and waved until she was out of sight.

Nell could see her in the rear-view mirror. She looked so young standing there. And fear began to niggle again at what she was asking for. Unwilling to hesitate and lose her nerve, she thumbed through her contacts, until she found the number she was looking for and punched it in. She could hear the ringing through her Blue-tooth and held her breath until he picked up.

"Good morning."

"Can you meet me for breakfast?"

"You never did like small talk. You always got right to the point."

"Only when I have tunnel vision."

"Yes. I'd love to. Where and when."

"How about KJ's in about an hour."

It was a small café on Tremont Street. It was their go-to place for an early-morning meal when she came up to Boston to visit during college.

"I'll see you then."

After she hung up, she checked in to the office, wanted to make sure there were no fires to put out and to ask Hani to re-schedule her first appointment.

"Everything okay, boss?"

"Everything's fine. Something came up that I need to attend to. All I need is an hour."

"Okay. See you then."

She rarely took time off. It was even rarer for her to re-schedule or cancel an appointment. Hani was probably letting all her partners know she was going to be in late.

She smiled when she got a call from Jelani. It took less time than she'd anticipated.

"Yes?"

"What's going on?"

"Meeting Jack."

"Because..."

"Chloe and I had dinner with him last night and it went pretty well. Chloe came crawling into my room around midnight nagging me about the same old thing. I'm feeling some pressure here that I don't want to feel but...it might be time."

"When she stayed home from the father-daughter night, I had a feeling she was going to be relentless in the pursuit of knowledge."

"Yeah, but what if that's not the kind of relationship he wants? It would provide the kind of scandal that politicians stay away from. What if he only wants part-time perks? What do I do then?"

"Then we slice him into little bitty pieces and bury him in the wilds of New Hampshire."

"I love you."

"I love you, too. Stay strong. This is good, Nell. I'm proud of you."

"I'll let you know how it goes when I get back."

"I'll be waiting for you. I'll be the one with the shoulder to cry on or the shovel we'll need for burial."

She got off the highway and made her way into the city. The traffic was congested, as usual this time of the day, and she inched her way toward her destination. She couldn't believe her luck when she found a parking spot out front, or that Jack was already here.

He looked up from the menu when she walked in, then stood up, helped her out of her coat and held her chair until she was seated.

The waitress came right over, with a coffee cup and carafe.

It was a familiar setting and it seemed strange to be sitting across from him after such a long sabbatical.

He took the utensils out of the napkin and placed it on his lap, peered up at her.

"Do you still come here often?"

"No. There's a place close to the office I go to. I never have time for breakfast, so I just pick up a muffin and coffee."

He glanced around the interior before admitting, "I haven't been here since the last time with you."

It had been only a few days before she left.

"Did you only come here because I liked it?"

"No. I...It didn't seem right, somehow."

She shifted in her seat, wishing she knew what to say to that.

The waitress came over to take their order, and when they were left alone again, Jack took her hand, played with her fingers. Her body began to hum.

"Last night was nice, Nell. Thank you for agreeing to it. I like her. A lot."

She took a deep breath to calm her nerves. It didn't work.

"Chloe's been haranguing me about meeting her father...you. She's using all her powers of persuasion and I've finally given in. I know you'll be leaving sometime this afternoon for DC, but I thought maybe this week-end if you have some free time, we could get this over with."

There was no pause but an instant response.

"I'll make time."

She masked her inner turmoil with a deceptive calm. Her voice was firm and insistent.

"I'd just as soon she remained clueless until after you speak at her school. It would confuse her, and I'm not sure what she would tell her friends. I was thinking Sunday morning. You could come to the condo. We could tell her together."

It wasn't great timing. The day before Christmas was always busy but she didn't want to wait until after the holiday.

"I know I have a couple of things planned. Sunday at the Franklin Zoo with Santa is one of them. Maybe we could work it around that. I could take her with me if it goes well."

"You do realize if suddenly you have an eleven-year-old daughter, eyebrows will be raised."

"Let them be raised. I think I've proven my worth by now. I'm not a freshman congressman anymore."

The more they talked about this the more surreal it became. She had agreed to this after promising herself she'd never give in.

"My names been in the news a lot over the last week. I think that's a disadvantage. It would be easier if we could keep it quiet for a little bit longer." Her voice wavered.

He stiffened, releasing her hand as he did.

"Are you suggesting we keep it a big, dark secret?"

After scrubbing her face with her hands, she brushed her hair off her face.

"I don't know what I'm suggesting. Little's going to change for me. I know I'll have to share her but...it's her I care most about. There's so many things here that could hurt her."

"I want to be a part of her life, not mess it up. I'll do whatever I have to, to keep that from happening."

She took a sip of coffee as the food was brought over, held high on a round tray. Her scone was put in front of her, Jack's English muffin sandwich in front of him. He flicked his eyes up as he thanked the waitress, who hovered for more time than was necessary before she backed away.

There was a sexual magnetism about him that every female found appealing. It had always worried her. She'd never really known what she meant to him, was unsure about her place in his world. What she had known is she couldn't afford another loss. If he had ever walked away, he would have taken a piece of her with him. Sensing the writing on the wall, his mother's role in his life undisputable, and being an expert in self-survival, she'd walked away. It was better than the alternative of being left behind. It didn't mean she'd stopped loving him.

It was becoming hard to remain coherent with him sitting so close. It was also hard knowing that there might more of these meals in the future.

As he took a bite of his sandwich, she asked, "When did this become a priority?"

He leaned back in his chair, wiped his mouth with a napkin before answering her.

"I never wanted to play it your way, but I had to suck it up if I wanted law school. You set those conditions. I should never have agreed to them."

Her back went up, not for the first time.

"I was not the one who set the conditions and I resent that you keep telling yourself that." Her finger was poking the table to stress her point

He nodded his head, averted his eyes.

"You're right. You didn't. I'm finally beginning to see it from your perspective."

Deflating a bit, she asked, "When did that happen?"

"The first time you sent me one of her pictures. She was mine. I could tell."

He leaned forward, put his hand on her arm. "I always knew. That's not what I'm saying."

He studied her, as if to make sure she hadn't taken it wrong.

"It's an intense moment, when you see this child, your child. It's a feeling you can't describe. Love. I'd given it up without much of a fight. It made me feel guilty, regretful. Made me think about every detail of the phone marathon we ran after you told me. I wanted to know what I could have done differently."

"And you were able to see it from my point of view?"

"I still don't understand why we couldn't have worked things out here. I know my mother was an adversary, but I would have done what I could to soften the blows. Moving for me was an impossibility. I'm horrified to say I never had to work hard at anything. And the situation facing me was daunting. I didn't have the courage to risk my inheritance. I thought...after college, after law school, when I had something to give you, we could go back. Of course, it was too late by then."

It seemed he still didn't understand completely, was still defending his actions and his mother's demands. Her frustration spilled out in a heavy sigh.

"Softening the blows would not have been enough. I wanted them to stop completely. The only way that would have happened is if you stood up for me. You never did that. It was what gave *me* the courage to leave."

She'd never had anyone to protect her. Her father had left when she was just a child, and she had to learn to fight the monsters under her bed on her own, learn to stand up for herself.

She felt his hand reach out for hers, his fingers stroking her palm. It sent shivers down her spine and her heartbeat quickened.

His eyes were on her, the pupils dark, the grey streaked with silver.

"I'm sorry, Nell. I'm sorry I wasn't there for you. I wanted to come after you when I finished law school, but I still didn't know what the hell I was going to do. You were so successful, so self-directed, getting ready to move to DC..."

"How did you know that?"

"Tomms was a friend of my father. My mother asked him to sit down with me, try to talk me into politics. He told me you were joining his staff."

"I remember now. He spoke very highly of your father."

"My father was a good man. I wish Chloe could have gotten to meet him. You'd approve of that relationship."

"He would have had to be extremely patient, that's for sure."

The thought that anyone who put up with Eloise would have to be sprinted through her mind. When she met Jack's gaze, she tried to shake the unruly thoughts off. There was sadness in his eyes, a frown on his face.

"My mother wasn't always like she is, Nell. She fell apart when he died, and I felt a deep-seated need to take care of her. When you and I were dating, the feelings got all mixed up. My relationship with her became challenging, to say the least. I couldn't turn my back on her, and that's what I thought you were asking me to do."

"I know what abandonment feels like, Jack. I would never do that to another person."

"I know that. I should have been more supportive of your feelings. I'm sorry I slighted them."

"Thank you for the apology."

Even if it was years too late, it sounded sincere.

"I always hoped you'd call, tell me what we had, what you named her, how you were doing."

She sat back against the hard backrest of the booth, fiddling with one of the charms on her bracelet and drew a bolstering breath.

"I couldn't. I learned that if you continue to ask, beg, plead, you continue hurting. Only when you shut all feeling down, shut off all communication can you stop the pain, begin to live again."

He brought her hand up and kissed it. The bangles on her bracelet played an old, familiar tune.

"You learned that from your parents, didn't you?"

She nodded.

"I'm sorry I was just another in a long line of people who disappointed you."

She could feel tears fill her eyes and she was shocked. She never cried but he was bringing up memories she didn't want to surface, memories that had a way of spooking her. Anger was a better way for her to mask the hurt. Tears showed she was still too vulnerable.

"As long as you don't disappoint Chloe, I'll be fine."

She scraped her chair back, needing to go, needing to get back to work. She needed to fill her mind with something other than what it felt like to be with him.

She hadn't finished her scone and asked for it to be wrapped to go. Standing, she reached into her pocketbook for some money, which he waved away.

"My treat."

Fingering her bag over her shoulder, she tucked her hair behind her ear.

"Text me Sunday. Let me know what time you'll be over."

He was standing now, peeling off bills and laying them on the table.

"As early as you let me."

They walked out together, each getting into their own car and driving away.

She drove off, not wanting to give him any idea how upset she was by the conversation they'd just had, snuck peeks at his car in her rearview mirror until it became a speck in the distance.

Now that the deed was on its way to being done, she'd thought she'd feel lighter, less stress, but the nervous energy coursing through her told her she'd been wrong. How would the meeting go? Would Chloe be upset that it was Jack? Impressed? At eleven she couldn't know the gossip that would surround it for months, if not longer. And what would Eloise do once the family had been re-connected? There were too many questions she didn't have answers to and the only way she'd forget about them was to work. Heading towards her office, where there was more work than she could fit in a twelve-hour day, she put all her feelings on hold.

She found Jelani in the conference room poring over a file, looking disturbed, the papers scattered all over the table.

"Room for one more?"

"Of course. I need help. I was going to ask Em, but she picked up Teddy."

Teddy was the son of one of Emilia's friends, Nick Katsaros. He'd been one of the beat cops who'd attended Jack's meeting yesterday and he had an inconsistent rotation. Em would sometimes pick up the four-year old to ease the childcare problems.

"Where's Saban?"

Saban was Teddy's mother, Nick's wife. Em didn't like her much, but her loyalty ran deep with her college friend, the man Em was in love with. Nick had chosen Saban over Em and she'd learned to live with it.

Nell didn't know how.

"She got an emergency call from Child Services and had to go pick up a little girl left behind after an immigration raid."

"Shit."

"Yeah. Em should have taken the call but because she was picking Teddy up, Arianna had to go to the detention center. You weren't here for her to hand it off, so she had to do our grunt work."

Nell took a seat, pushed some of the paperwork to the side, to make space for herself. "Is it me or does it seem like things are accelerating?"

"It's not just you. Mia added two more cases to my already over-load. How do you juggle it all?"

Nell took on more than anyone else at the firm and never seemed to bat an eye with all the work.

"I don't go out remember."

"This is what I have to do to be you? Give up my life?"

Nell was startled and asked soberly, "Why would you want to be me?"

Jelani clasped her hands together as if in prayer and gave her an exaggerated, adoring look.

"Because you're my idol."

The laughter rippled out to the hallway and the agitation Nell was feeling fell away. She was home, safe and warm within the circle of friendship. It was then, that she told Jelani about the meeting with Jack, and Jelani offered to put the shovel away for another day.

⌒

Jack left for the airport as soon as he watched Nell drive away. He felt hollow and he couldn't believe it still hurt. When he used to leave New Haven after being with her for the weekend, he would wave until she was out of sight. It was as if he left part of himself with her, the best part, and the time always dragged until he saw her again.

He'd had a test run without her. He'd invited her to dinner at the beginning of the relationship. At his mother's. He'd wanted them to meet, get to know each other. It hadn't gone well, and Nell had refused a repeat performance. She thought they did better without Eloise's company. He'd been angry that she hadn't tried harder.

"I can't be with someone who doesn't get along with her."

"Then we might as well give it up now."

And they had.

For six weeks, he didn't see her. Six long weeks without her face, her voice, her body. Missing her so much he'd driven down to New Haven, talked her into getting back together. The stipulation: he wouldn't force the issue with his mother. It had held until they moved in together.

After that, it had all crumbled into nothing.

He'd spent over a decade without her, functioning well, working hard, but he was beginning to realize he'd just been going through the motions. He hadn't been living at all. Like a robot that had been programmed, he'd gone through the motions, gotten the grades, and studied for a test that would award him his jurisprudence license. His mother had intruded with her expectations. She'd dragged him to meetings, dinners, luncheons, introducing him to donors, to advocates, the cream of society. He was unknowingly taking the steps toward the political stage, one smile, one handshake at a time. Now that Nell was back in his life, he'd woken up, and was no longer sleepwalking through life.

When he'd seen her walk into KJ's, his breath caught, like it always did. With her hair up and the high-collar blouse that peeked out from her long, red wool coat, she looked more like a Gibson girl that a gypsy. It was as if his heartbeat returned to normal. It'd thrummed with electric impulse. He knew he was walking along a fine line, that he should just be grateful she'd changed her mind and was willing to let him into Chloe's life. She'd told him up-front; he wouldn't get access to hers. But each time they were together, it became clear that he wanted more than she was willing to give. He wanted it all.

As he parked in his reserved spot at the airport, the monthly fee less than what he'd spend on a car and driver or weekly rates, he geared up for another week of in-fighting. The upcoming holiday recess would be welcome. The problem was, it would be worse when they picked up for the new Congress in January. Then the acrimony would begin to burst into flames. He still hadn't decided if he was going to the inauguration. There were members of the state contingent that had opted out and he was still straddling the fence.

Then there was the Women's March. Did he join the forces in outward rebellion? Or did he stay behind the scenes working on a solution? As he got out of the car, Michael was pulling into his space, a couple of rows over. Michael had the lucky chore of following him everywhere he went. He'd started out as an intern his first year out of college, graduating with a degree in communications, and had become so invaluable Jack asked him to stay on as his scheduler. Able to keep everything running smoothly, Michael seamlessly squeezed in events, hearings, meetings, that were important in DC and his district. He was going to have to tell him about Sunday. He'd promised never to fill an empty slot without letting him know. He'd made the mistake of agreeing to an impromptu meeting and was caught in a time vise, unable to attend to either meeting with thorough efficiency.

He'd have to tell everyone on his staff if Nell agreed to make it public.

"Hey, boss. Ready for another round?"

"You bet. The opposing party doesn't realize yet what they've unleashed. What's on for tonight? I would have preferred taking a later flight."

"I know but you've got some final interviews for your LD and then there's a dinner for the Veterans of Foreign Wars being held at the Westin."

"That's right. I agreed to say a few words, didn't I?"

"You did. Ron's been working on it. We're meeting with him later this afternoon."

"Could you schedule a staff meeting for the same time? I need about fifteen minutes with everyone before I take off for the night."

"Done."

As one of the first passengers on, he greeted the crew before taking his seat at the front of coach. He thought it an absurd waste of money going first-class.

He pulled out the resumes Tahlia had sent him home with. He hadn't even looked at them yet, too caught up with Nell and Chloe to do any work over the last forty-eight hours. Flipping through the one on the top, he scanned the education, the experience and came to the references. A name shouted out at him and he pulled out his phone and searched for the contact he was looking for. They were still boarding the plane, so he had time before he had to power it off.

The voice that answered was resonant and it rippled through him.

"Hello, Jack."

"Hey, I'm sorry to bother you but I have an applicant for the legislative director's job that put you down as a reference. Thought I'd call to see what you can give me about her."

"That's right. I forgot Lauren was going to apply for that."

"She told you?"

"She asked if she could use my name, yes."

"Well?"

"I actually think she'd be a good fit. She's a workaholic, social, gets along well with others and can probably put up with the stink down there."

"How do you know her?"

"We sit on the parole board together. Her five-year term is coming to an end and I know she wasn't planning on reupping."

His eyes went back to the resume to ascertain Nell's statement.

"You're on the parole board?"

"Got roped into that when Arianna had dinner one night with the governor. He asked if there was anyone from her firm she could recommend. My name came up, he pressured me into joining and I'm into my third year. I won't be renewing my term, either."

"She's got the legal chops for this?"

"And then some. She'd do good work for you, Jack."

"Okay. Thanks for the run-down. Have you set up the meeting at the jail for Friday?"

"I've got a call in, but I have to go over there personally to set it up. They have very strict rules in place and I can only apply for visitation at the South Bay Jail after three p.m. Once the app is made, it needs to be approved. As I'm using your name, it shouldn't take long."

"I guess I'll see you then."

"Text me if you want to go over together or separately."

"Together. That way you can give me some background."

"And you can tell me how the talk at Standish went."

She must have hit the end call button because she was no longer on the line. He kept Lauren Boyd's vitae on top. With Nell's reference, she'd put herself ahead of the pack.

CHAPTER SEVENTEEN

Nell felt as if the week flew by. It was Friday before she knew it.

Between depositions, immigration hearings, court appearances, and working with Jelani with one of her cases, she'd been going non-stop. She'd sliced out some one-on-one time to meet with Gita Prajapati, an attorney who'd just joined the firm as associate. Every time the firm hired a new lawyer, one of the partners was assigned as mentor, and Gita would be working closely with her for the three-month probationary period. The meeting had gone well, and she was impressed, once again, at her grasp of the law and how she planned on using it to protect others. They discussed the country's history of immigration law through the decades, deportation delays that could range from three to six years, illegal vs. legal status, asylum, discrimination, violent offenders, and border crossings and they hadn't even scratched the surface. The debates were lively, the arguments heated. She'd enjoy the time spent working with the recent law-school grad.

The clock seemed to have stalled this morning. She couldn't help herself from glancing up at it every half hour or so, measuring where Jack was and what he was doing. He'd be at the school by now.

How was it going?

Chloe had been excited about the congressman's visit. She chirped away, telling her all about her interview with Jack being accepted for the newsletter and the editor asking if she'd do a follow-up once the talk was over. It didn't sit well on an already upset stomach. She'd done her best to keep her mind off this coming Sunday, but she was having a difficult time. And the slow-moving minute hand was doing nothing to quiet it. With Chloe so gung-ho about the politician, she almost regretted the upcoming introduction. What if Chloe liked him better? What if she wanted to spend all her free time with him? What if his low-key personality was a soothing balm after living with her type-A personality mother?

And what if Friday night dinners became Chloe's new norm? What would happen to their con-fabs. Was she about to lose her daughter to Jack?

Jittery from the coffee she'd been drinking all morning, she was almost relieved when the receptionist buzzed that Jack was at her desk. There'd be no more waiting.

He was picking her up. He wanted background on the building, the procedures and some back stories of detainees Nell had worked with

She had plenty.

As a volunteer attorney, she was called on at various times, to give counsel, attend court dates and deal with the harsher aspects of detainment. Her date with the Supreme Court case had been processed while Ramona was in the facility, and she'd represented dozens of women who had nowhere else to turn.

She grabbed her coat, bag, and brief case and stepped out to find Jack chatting with Heather as if he'd known her forever. That was the kind of easy, open charm that had gotten him elected.

His smile when he noticed her standing and watching him warmed her from across the room. Her whole being filled with wanting. She knew that was dangerous, especially considering a more intimate connection just around the corner.

"Are you ready?"

She wasn't sure she'd ever be ready to spend time with him, not with the fatal attraction she felt. She'd waded through all the hurt he'd caused and thought she'd gotten to the other side of it. She was staring that lie right in the face.

Not sure she could speak, she nodded and made for the door.

There was silent expectancy as they rode the elevator down and out onto the street where his car was parked. As she slid into the front seat, he closed the door, went around the back, and took his seat behind the wheel. It would take less than fifteen minutes to get to their destination.

"How did it go this morning?" she asked, her voice giving her nervousness away.

"Well, I think. They were polite, respectful, asked some interesting questions. I thoroughly enjoyed myself."

"And?"

"And Chloe asked if she could do a follow-up to our conversation last weekend. I didn't have a lot of time to give her, but I think she walked away feeling satisfied."

"I can't even begin to imagine how she's going to feel when we tell her."

"I'm glad we had this pre-trial. I like her and I think she likes me. I'm hoping she doesn't freak out too much."

"I have to be honest. I'm the one doing the freaking."

"You haven't changed your mind, have you?"

"I couldn't if I wanted to. I told her she'd be meeting you on Sunday and I can't walk back that promise now. She'd hate me."

"How about if we concentrate on the reason we're meeting today? That has to be more in your comfort zone. Give me some background."

"On...?"

"Whatever you think pertinent. About where we're going."

Nell stared out the window, processing the question before turning to him and answering it.

"Suffolk County Jail. Otherwise known as Suffolk Country House of Corrections. Built 1990's, houses nineteen hundred detainees, approximately two hundred and fifty in the removal process awaiting deportation. Everyone detained in Massachusetts passes through it at some point. Some stay, some are transferred, some deported. Most detainees are from Central or Latin America and the Caribbean. They're classified according to the seriousness of their criminal history. For eighty-nine percent, it's the first center entered, which leaves eleven percent transferred from someplace else. Sixty-eight percent of those deported had no criminal record and were picked up due to minor offenses like traffic violations. Only one judge assigned to all immigration cases, detainees appear via tele-video link at the immigrations court at the JFK building. Time frame anywhere from three weeks to see the judge, close to three months for the casework to be completed. New ICE office built in Burlington where most administrative work takes place."

"Impressive regurgitation of data."

She looked over to see his profile as he made his way through the city. Intense concentration with a small tic at the corner of his mouth.

"Isn't that what you wanted?"

"Not exactly. I could have Googled that. I was hoping for more personal background."

She picked at the small charm bracelet around her wrist. When she hesitated, he asked in a casually, jesting way, "Can't believe you're not as well versed on that side of it, so give me what you have."

Shaking her hair, pushing her bangs off her face, she gave him what he wanted.

"I'm on call as a pro bono attorney, usually called by the family rather than the detainee. Those picked up do have the right to representation, but they are not provided with it automatically. They must seek it out and pay compensation. My job is to determine whether they have a legal standing to be here, and to advocate for them if they do. Removals occur quickly for approximately four out of ten immigrants, usually within a couple of days. Several of my clients have been deported for nothing more than lacking that piece of paper that proves naturalization. They have no criminal record and have given everything they have to this country, pay taxes, work hard, go to school, join the military, probably love it more than native-born, appreciate what it offers in the form of freedom, but they live in the shadows, in constant fear. Ironically, the ones who do have grounds for redress are locked up for longer periods of time, a year or longer, until their case is heard by the court. The backlog is causing longer and longer waiting times."

"What can I expect to hear?"

"The director is supposed to pick out some half a dozen detainees to give you a sense of who is incarcerated. You'll get their personal stories."

"What's he like? The director?"

"Good guy, doing a tough job."

With limited on-street parking, they had to circle the block a few times to find a space. Protestors lined the street, signs reading, "STOP THE RAIDS AND DEPORTATIONS AMNESTY NOW," raised high in the air.

"Are there always activists out here?"

"More so now than before. The increase in deportations over the last couple of years riled a lot of people. Now no one knows what's going to happen and the protests have ramped up. I was part of an activist group that formed a human chain at the entrance back in 2014, a few months after a prisoner hunger strike."

"What was the objective?"

"We were protesting the indefinite time frame of detention, demanding action to end the suffering. It's not bad here in Boston, but some of the other centers are known for their brutality"

"Were you arrested? Have a record?"

"Arrested? Yes and no. I was handcuffed but not charged. They released me after Arianna got done with them so no record to speak of."

"I'll have to thank her. I'd hate to think of you in jail."

"I was prepared. Figured it would give me a better understanding of what they go through."

"Don't think you need it. You take good care of them."

"There are some members of ICE letting the new-found power go to their heads. I think whoever named the agency got it right. Cold bastards. Someone has to give a shit."

She noticed him look up and her gaze followed his.

Cardboard covered some of the windows with the words FREE US written across them.

"These people are here for civil offenses, not criminal ones, is that correct?"

"For the most part. There are some undocumented who have committed violent crimes but it's a small percentage of the overall population."

"They need bars on the window?"

"No more than they need barbed wire on the chain-link fence."

He fell silent as the wind whipped in gust force and as they made their way to the front entrance, where the director was waiting for them.

Shaking the extended hand, Director Knowles greeted them warmly.

"Welcome Congressman Adams. I appreciate you're coming in. Nell, it's always a pleasure."

"Same here, Dan."

Jack watched the interaction, the traded smiles. According to his file on Ms. Warren, she'd spent endless hours here giving advice, representing men and women who had no money to pay, donating her time, attention and passion to their cause. Daniel Knowles knew and appeared to respect her.

One for his side.

"I appreciate your timely response to our request. With my assignment to the Judiciary Committee, I want to get immersed as quickly as I can. This facility isn't owned by ICE, is it?"

"No, sir. They pay for each bed, whether it's filled or not."

"That doesn't seem like a very efficient use of tax dollars."

"We have to keep the bed available, so they pay to hold the spot. We haven't had many empty ones over the last few years, so we haven't wasted federal dollars, and the state makes a decent income from the arrangement."

Allowing Nell to go ahead of him, he followed in their footsteps, taking in the four-story facility, the cells, the inmates walking in single file along the inner walls.

He could read the hopelessness on their faces, their expressions somber and serious.

"What do they do with their free time?"

The director didn't slow his pace to answer the question directed at him.

"Not much. We can't allow books to be brought in, they can't work outside the walls, there's only so much time we can let them outside during the winter. They stay in their cells most of the day. We are better equipped than some other places, good food, health care services, exercise. And the culture here is not as hostile."

Nell interjected, "It might be a good idea for you to see some of the other facilities in the southwestern part of the country. It's like night and day."

"Maybe somewhere down the road. Today, I'm here."

The last stop was a conference room where he would meet with some of the detainees that the warden had selected for interviews.

"We'll bring them in one at a time. The first one is on his way now. I'll see you again on your way out."

"Thanks, Dan."

As soon as he left them alone, Jack put himself at risk by asking, "What are your thoughts?"

"This center will give you one small part of a very large picture. It's one of the better ones. There are private prisons out there that are abysmal. No health services, no exercise, color-coded clothes, hard-assed jailers. I visited one in the southwest and was ashamed that could happen in America. POWs get more humane treatment."

A sad smile reached those gorgeous eyes.

She got caught in his spell and it was broken only when the first person was brought in.

Carlos Cordova was a twenty-one-year-old young man from Honduras, who told them about the conditions in his home country, a country with the highest murder rate in the world. Rival gangs were running rampant and he was sent away by his father after his brother was gunned down. Raul Cordova thought Carlos would be safe in America. He was afraid to go back, thought he'd be a prime target for retaliation, claiming deportation would mean certain death.

The next was a mother whose husband was stabbed to death by a local gang in Central America. When the members continued to threaten the family, she'd taken her children and escaped to the United States. She'd been afraid for their lives. Her lawyer had applied for asylum, but the government was dragging its feet. Jack was startled into an awareness that those in authority refused to follow the asylum protocols in place, which meant this woman would continue to languish in an immigration jail.

Muneeba Shah was a business woman, undocumented, living and working in a community for twenty years who'd been picked up at one of the protests. A Pakistani who had converted from one religion to another, she'd traveled here to avoid the death threats that resulted from her conversion. Another woman, Pearl Aguilar, who'd fled the violence in the Caribbean, opened her door in Roxbury to a gaggle of federal immigration agents who handcuffed her and led her off as her children watched. The children were led away soon after to become part of the foster care system. As she cried during the telling, Nell sat beside her, comforting her, and finally asked, "Do you have representation? A lawyer?"

"I can't afford this. Please, help me."

"I promise. I will. I am going to make a call when we leave, and I will set up an appointment to see you as soon as possible."

The woman squeezed the hand that held hers, sobbed, "I just want to know that my children are okay. Can you do that?"

"I'll make sure they are safe."

Nell jotted down the information she'd need to set up a meeting.

"Thenk yuh. You are an angel."

Jack could tell that Nell was angry, although she was able to tamp it down as they went through the next round of interviews. Jack conferred with a dishwasher from Guatemala who was facing constant death threats from his countrymen. He was picked up in Dorchester after failing to notify the Department of Justice of a move even though he had given the Immigration and Customs Enforcement his new address. Another, a mechanic who'd left Mexico decades ago, his children citizens, was awaiting a hearing, which was possibly more than a year away.

The last was a female college student who'd been in the country since she was ten.

She came in with attitude, her hostility apparent. Her story was like so many others, but her reaction wasn't. Facing Jack, her eyes blazing, she said, "I was detained, stripped, shackled, interrogated like I was a criminal. They're still trying to break my spirit, but they have yet to do so." She faked a spit. "ICE is a good name for those animals. They have no heart."

Glydas Mendoza's chin was jutting out in defiance. "They do all they can to force me to leave, make it more appealing than staying, but I will outlast them."

He listened to her litany of obstacles they'd put in her way and wondered what he could do to help her. It came down to the law and that was Nell's sphere of influence. He'd have to count on the courts to do their jobs.

As Glydas was escorted out, one of the mayors from a surrounding town came in to the room. Jack knew him, had talked to him at a forum given by the governmental agencies in his district. The mayor was plainly annoyed, his tone defiant, as he discussed what was going on. Jack had a feeling Nell had arranged this as well, wanting him to get a local politician's perspective.

After some small talk, the mayor got right to the point.

"Most of the people in my community are immigrants and the government better not mess with any of them. We're biding our time and if ICE comes in, they'll be in the fight of their lives. We take care of our own. These people lack a piece of paper and that's the extent of their crimes. Some have come on a visa but found they lacked the money or connections to immigrate legally. We gave them no choice. They are members in good standing, work hard, love their families, add to the harmony of the whole. What ICE is doing, the Congress is doing, the justice system is doing is wrong. You need to find a way out of this mess."

Nell concurred, "That's why he's here, Mayor Stearns. Congressman Adams intends to get something done. He just has to find a way to do it."

Jack was completely unnerved by what he had seen and heard, and he was doubly committed to finding a way to citizenship for these people.

As they walked out, he heard Nell on the line with Emilia, the angry quiver in her voice as she added, "Her name is Pearl Aguilar. Her children are in the system and she just wants to know that they're okay."

Em must have assured her she'd find them because she clicked off.

Standing outside in the raw, chilly air, he waited for her to say something, but she stood there, looking almost defeated.

Her voice sounded small. "I should be used to this by now."

Pulling her into an embrace, he swept his hand down her hair as he kissed her forehead.

"You take them all personally, don't you?"

He felt the nod in his shoulder, wishing he could wave a magic wand and make this all go away.

She could feel his breath in her ear when he asked, "How many cases have you lost?"

It felt good to be held. She'd gotten used to standing alone, had put aside the disappointment of having no one in her corner. Even when she was with Jack, she'd had to count on herself. There were too many instances when he'd been absent, busy making plans without her. This was something new and she let his concern fill her.

In a muffled voice, she answered, "Too many."

"I have a feeling one would be too many."

"It's such a mess."

"I know."

"We have to find a safety net for them."

"We will."

"We've been waiting a long time. I don't expect it's around the corner."

"With you working on it, I have a feeling it is."

Her face tilted up and her eyes took him in.

A warm glow filled her with the intensity of his gaze.

"I want to believe that."

He brushed her hair back, letting the strands slide though his fingers. Then his thumbs came up to caress her cheeks. She thought he was going to kiss her and she quivered inside as the anticipation of his lips on hers kept building.

He didn't, just paused there long enough to tease her.

"I wish I could take you to dinner, so we could discuss strategy, but I have a standing commitment for Friday nights and I'm running a bit late."

Knowing exactly who that standing commitment was with, she stepped back and away. It didn't matter that they were no longer together, that Eloise had a right to have dinner with her son, she would love to have a shoulder to lean on.

She should know by now it would never be his.

When he dropped her off at her office, after fifteen minutes of silence, he thanked her for the afternoon.

"I'm sorry..."

With her back to him, she opened her door and slid out. Why did she keep thinking things could change? It was not possible to wrangle your way into someone's heart if they didn't make room for you.

"No need. I'll see you on Sunday."

She didn't hear him drive away, the throb of blood pumping through her veins causing her head to pound.

She wished she could fall apart but she knew Chloe would be waiting to tell her all about the morning.

CHAPTER EIGHTEEN

He entered the vestibule to his mother's angry voice.

"You are late, Jack. Dinner was scheduled to be served thirty minutes ago."

He hurried in to see not only his mother, but also Hope sitting there as well. He stopped short, irritation setting in.

His mother gave him a stilted smile.

"I invited Hope because it seems you've been ignoring her this week."

His glance slid from his mother to the woman sitting docile and quiet, her hands prim in her lap.

"I haven't been ignoring her Mother. I've been busy and we never communicate during the week."

"I don't see why not. You have time for other diversions."

He felt like he was being cornered and didn't like it. His mother was not going to tell him how to spend his time.

He snickered to himself.

He was here, wasn't he, so he'd already missed that boat.

Without missing a beat, Eloise admonished, "Let's not argue. Escort us in, please."

He stood for a moment in resistance, then acceded to her wishes, walking them into the dining room, pulling a chair out for both before taking his seat at the head of the table.

Flicking the napkin into her lap, Eloise asked, "What kept you?"

He busied himself in the same way, as the maid came out with the soup.

"Work."

"What exactly?"

Waiting for Mags to finish serving, knowing he was wading into a muddy swamp, he stated truthfully, "I was at the detention center in Boston."

"What on earth for?"

"I'm on that committee now, remember? I thought it important to see for myself what the conditions are like, meet some of the detainees."

"They're illegals and should be in jail. They're breaking the law."

"The children who've grown up here think of this as their country. They don't know anything else."

"The sins of the parents always descend on the children."

"It's a sin to want a better life, a safer one? Some of these people left persecution and possible death."

"You're being dramatic, Jack. They broke the law. If they wanted to become citizens, they should have followed the rules."

He wasn't about to explain to her that the rules changed every few years, that those in waiting, had no real pathway other than going back to their place of origin and coming in again. The problem was, there were quotas, stigmas, and they wouldn't be guaranteed re-entry.

"You're being heartless. I don't remember you being that when I was growing up."

She flashed angry grey eyes at him.

"Immigrants are—"

"People. Just like you and me." He lashed stormier eyes back.

After taking several sips of her soup, she put down her spoon and pushed the bowl away.

"The new reform bill has to attend to getting them out."

He put his spoon down without taking a bite.

"I think we'd best leave this conversation for something less argumentative."

Hope was the one to ask, "Did you go alone?"

His eyes narrowed.

Was her intention to cause more conflict?

Did she somehow know?

"I went with one of my associates."

"Who?"

He sat back and studied her for a moment before asking, "When did you start questioning my whereabouts?"

The look was more like a wily fox than a demure debutante.

"I'm only trying to make conversation."

Like hell she was. For the first time, he noticed what Nell had pointed out. It wasn't just his mother pushing an agenda that wasn't his.

"Nell. She set it up. She's worked with many of the detainees and knows the system."

It was his mother who took up the challenge, something he somehow knew Hope counted on. His irritation grew. He could have been dining with Nell, discussing an issue that was becoming more important to him by the day. Instead, he'd been railroaded into a dinner that had him on the defensive.

Mags came back and cleared the dishes before serving the main course of veal and potatoes in some, kind of sauce. It was French cuisine, heavy. He preferred eating light this time of day. He played with his fork, thinking, until his mother stated, "You are wasting your time there."

Glancing up, he noticed pinched lips.

"Where? At the detention facility or with Nell?"

"Both. I would have thought you learned your lesson with that girl. She left you, if you remember."

"She did, but we both know why. I don't know why you're against my spending time with her. Afraid of something, Mom?"

"She would have taken over all your time if you'd let her. And it seems she's now keeping you from spending time with your fiancé."

His shoulders tensed; his eyes widened.

"My what?"

His mother was cutting her meat into pieces with unflustered movements.

"For all intents and purposes, you're engaged. You've been exclusive for over a year."

"Exclusive does not translate to engaged."

He looked up to see a sour look on Hope's face, as if there was an aftertaste in her mouth she didn't like. There was a collusion going on between the two, something he should have seen coming.

Another bubble burst and he blinked as it did.

He shook his thoughts out, initiating different topics that he thought might interest them, the parties being thrown in the capitol, gossip he'd picked up in the hallowed halls of Congress, but they failed to capture any interest.

When Eloise steered the conversation back to her original premise, he asked wearily, "What do you want from me Mother?"

"I want your success. Isn't that what I've always told you?"

"I have it. My staff is one of the best."

"My advice is that you don't make Nell Warren part of it. You should keep your distance."

"Very soon, that's not going to be an option. Should we tell Hope all about Chloe?"

His mother sat ramrod straight in her chair and he was convinced it would crack in two.

"That's dirty laundry that doesn't need to be aired. You might want to consider what that will mean for you if it all comes to light."

There was a subliminal message there, but he was too tired of the discussion to dwell on it.

"I'll deal."

"It may have to be without the kind of backing you've had to this point."

He looked up, incredulous at what she was suggesting.

"Are you threatening me, Mother?"

"Just reminding you that there are donors out there who might not be amused."

He went back to eating in stunned silence and left before Hope did, needing to get away from the constriction around his heart. He was going to break it off with her as soon as possible. The minute he closed the door to his apartment, he reached for his phone.

⌒

Chloe spent the whole time she was cooking them dinner regaling her about the morning, putting into detail every word and action of the Massachusetts congressman. Not that she had started at home. The minute she'd stepped into her office, Chloe had jumped up and given her a play-by-play. Jack had explained the three branches of government, described how a bill was written, told them what kinds of hearings he sat in on, what the cafeteria food was like. He'd asked questions and answered them.

"And he was funny, Mom. He told some jokes about his first week on the job and how much he had to learn. He didn't treat us like kids, either. All the kids were way impressed."

"Way, huh?"

She had thrown on some sweats and an oversized sweatshirt and was sitting at the kitchen table, a glass of wine in her hand, listening to the glowing reviews. It was making her more nervous by the minute. What was Chloe going to think when she introduced the perfect man as her father? She was wishing he was a bit more anonymous. There would have been some shyness, hesitation. Now, she'd probably throw herself in his arms, fall at his feet.

Chloe talked on as she stuffed kale into the food processor, along with lightly sautéed pine nuts, salt, pepper and pulsed. As she was adding the olive oil, she looked up and smiled.

That smile lightened Nell's world and love bubbled up, sending every other emotion out.

"I hope you like this. I got the recipe on-line and we had all the ingredients. When did you start buying pine nuts?"

She shrugged her shoulders, honestly not knowing what would have prompted her to buy something she didn't even know how to use.

"Jelani must have been with me."

The pasta water had begun to boil, and Chloe added the elbow macaroni.

"Jelani said to use this kind, so the pesto has something to cling to. You know, the bends and curls. And it cooks quicker than spaghetti."

"I'm glad we enrolled you for lessons. You enjoy this, don't you?"

She'd called the number Chloe had given her, talked to the head chef. The classes ran through the school year and there was a new session starting in January. Chloe would get to meet other kids her age, doing something that made her happy. It was a late-afternoon class on Mondays and she'd already talked to her partners at the firm. They'd cover for her if she got hung up in court or in an appointment, so she didn't have to worry about transportation.

"I'm excited. I think Keileh might enroll with me. She's talking to her mother about it."

The buzzer for the pasta went off and Chloe was busy straining it, getting the garlic bread out of the oven, and spooning the pesto mixture into the pan.

When she brought everything to the table, Nell could see the pride bloom through her smile.

"Well done. I can't wait to taste it."

It was as good as advertised. Everything in one bowl, protein, vegetable, carbs, and lots of good taste, just like she liked it. She'd sprinkled some hot pepper flakes on it, adding the spice she needed to make her taste buds happy. She cleaned up, thinking it only fair, and when she was done, the dishwasher humming, she went into the family room to see that Chloe had gotten every-thing ready for their movie night.

"I've heard about this movie."

She'd scrolled through one of the streaming services and come up with one that jolted her into the past.

"This came out when I was your age. I saw it at the theater with my mother."

Chloe snapped to attention; the Milk Duds stalled in her hand.

"I thought she was away, and you were in boarding school."

"I was. But this one Saturday, she came out to pick me up. I hadn't seen her in over a year and it was a surprise."

Chloe pulled her legs up and under her, resting her upper body on the arm-rest of the couch.

"What happened when she got there?"

"I was pretty happy to see her."

"And she took you to see *Ferris Bueller*?"

"She did. We went to this pizza place first, shared one with everything on it, and then she took me to the theater where Bueller was playing. She bought me popcorn and a soda and held my hand throughout the whole movie. It was a day I'll always remember."

"Is that why you like pizza so much?"

"Maybe. In a way. I also like the way it tastes. And it's all right there in one serving. You don't have to go back and forth between meat, potatoes, and veggie. The flavors are in harmony."

She thought Chloe would see the humor there, but instead she looked se-rious.

"I'm sorry you were alone so much when you were younger. One of these days, can you tell me about how it felt?"

Taking a seat beside her, Nell leaned back, put her feet up on the coffee table.

"I made friends, Chloe. I learned to depend on myself. I spent summers at my grandmother's summer house in Nahant. It wasn't all bad."

"Tell me another good memory."

She let the past click through her mind like slides in a projector. Warm feel-ings came to the surface with one person in particular.

"Summers were full of good memories. My grandmother hired a nanny to accompany us to the beach. Her name was Dominga Sousa. She was Ecuadorian and had a daughter Pilar, who was my age. We would spend all day out on the beach, playing. She'd tuck me into bed, give me a kiss goodnight. She nannied every summer I was in grammar school. I missed her when she left us."

"Why didn't they keep her on?"

"I'm not sure. She talked to my mother, long-distance, on the last day of my last summer with her. I didn't see her again. I have a feeling it had to do with her immigrant status."

"Did you still go to the beach during the summer?"

"Yeah, but it was never the same. There was a different nanny every year. When I got to high school, I took a friend. Helen Stelzer. Her parents were diplomats and away as much as mine were. I never went back once I graduated."

"Is the house still in the family?"

"It is. It's been rented out for the last fifteen years."

"Can we live there some summer?"

"We could. I'll call the management company and take it off the rental market. I'll have to get your grandparents' approval, but as long as the money is coming in, I don't think they'd mind if it was us renting it."

"They'd make you pay rent?"

"It wouldn't matter. I'd pay it anyway."

"But we're family."

"It never really felt that way, Chloe. I'd feel better if I didn't ask them for a free ride."

They settled in to watch the movie. Nell was glad she'd opted for more of a straight comedy than a rom-com. She didn't want to watch any happy-ever-after ending today, knowing what she did, knowing where Jack was. They just weren't possible for some.

Chloe would glance over from time to time, as if measuring her mood. She was glad she hadn't told Chloe anymore about her childhood, that the visits with her mother happened very infrequently, only once every couple of years. Her father rarely came to see her, and when he did, the air was heavier, his dark mood pervasive. When it was just her and Merry, she almost believed her mother loved her, that she wished things were different, that she would have preferred to be at home rather than traveling around the world, helping her husband outrun his ghosts.

CHAPTER NINETEEN

Jack had pulled up beside the duplex. He liked the curb appeal and the fact that it was in Charlestown, one of the towns in his district. He'd already looked at a couple other places, but in his price range, he was looking at maybe six hundred square feet in living space. If part of the reason for the purchase and move was to get overnights with Chloe, he wanted it to be big enough for the two of them. His agent had given him the run-down on this one and it was twice the size of the others he'd seen. He was hopeful.

Gil Palmer, sitting next to him, gave him more information on the condo they were about to see.

"The owner just finished the renovation and it isn't going on the market until Monday. I know you wanted something ASAP and this would be available for move-in as soon as you secure financing."

"Reputable builder?"

"One of the best in the area. He's been doing high-ends in Belmont and Wellesley."

"Why did he take this on?"

"He bought it to renovate and give his daughter, but she got a job offer in Michigan. He wants to flip this so he can secure her a good place out there."

"If it was for his daughter, he would have done it right."

It wasn't a question, more of an observation, and Gil left it as that. After getting out of the car, he followed Gil up the stone steps, a paver patio outside each unit.

"As you can see, you have a bit of outdoor space."

As soon as he was inside, he was sold. High ceilings made the place airy and the windows let in plenty of light. There was a designer kitchen, original pine-hardwood floors, two bedrooms, a walk-in closet and custom en-suite. It was exactly what he'd been looking for. This was the kind of place Nell had talked about getting, all clean lines and open concept. So different than his apartment. He should have listened to her back then.

"Do I have to wait to put the offer in or can I do it today?"

"I could take it to the owner, but you'd be looking at paying full price."

"This is the best one I've seen, and I like the neighborhood. I don't have a problem with that. The only downside is there's no air conditioning, but I have a few months before I have to worry about it. I can add it before summer. It has the right ductwork."

As he pulled his check book out of the inside pocket of his overcoat, he asked, "How long does the financing usually take?"

"Anywhere from a few days to a few weeks. It depends on who you know, your credit rating and how much you have to put down."

"And if I buy it outright?"

"As soon as the check clears and the deed's recorded."

"I could close at the end of the week and move in over the weekend?"

"I think the owner would agree to those terms in a New York minute."

"Do you think he'd let me buy the furniture along with it?"

"I don't know who did the staging but everything's negotiable. I'll put it in the offer, but he might counter with a higher number."

"Let's get the offer on the table and see what he says."

"My pleasure Congressman Adams."

Once the paperwork was completed, Jack dropped Gil off at his office so he could get the offer approved and the closing date set.

As Jack drove to his Randolph field office, his mind raced with all the things he had yet to do. He'd contact his banker; see how quickly they could get a mortgage in place. If he had to, he'd close on the sale with money from his trust fund and replace the outlay when the loan was approved. He had to get a change of address, hire a moving van, if only for his personal affects. He wouldn't be taking anything else with him. He'd have to call for electric and gas hook-ups and tell his mother.

His fingers massaged the throbbing pulse in his forehead.

Was he jumping the gun? Would Nell consent to letting Chloe stay with him now and then?

There was a better chance of it happening if he wasn't living at his mother's, so he'd just have to hope it wasn't an unnecessary step.

Then the events from last night flashed. He'd made the decision to move as soon as his mother had cornered him with Hope. He had to end that relationship and soon. He had one thing on his mind right now and Hope would only make it more difficult to achieve his goal.

His Blue-tooth announced his real estate agent's call.

"Yeah, Gil."

"The owner accepted the offer as is. He's happy to let the staging go because he won't have any carrying costs if you're willing to close so soon."

"Excellent. Thanks, Gil. I know I sprung this on you last night, but I appreciate the work you put in. You found me a great place."

"Any time, Congressman Adams. Don't be shy about referring me to your friends."

Jack laughed.

"I won't. You'll be the first call."

His fingers were tapping the steering wheel as he sat at a red light. He felt good. Kind of powerful.

When he entered the office, Michael was waiting for him. He walked along at the brisk pace Jack set on his way to his office.

"And what did you do this morning that I didn't know about?"

"I let you know I'd be out of range for a couple of hours."

"You did. Your mother called looking for you and I didn't know what to tell her."

"I have a bunch of missed calls. I'll get back to her later. I bought a place this morning."

Dave came out the conference room, a shit-eating grin on his face.

"You did it? We're so proud. What's the new address?'

"It's in Charlestown. Priced right, great space, safe neighborhood, in district. What more could you ask for?"

"I have to admit I never thought you'd do it."

Dave joined them both in the private domain, which was rarely private.

Jack was leafing through mail, sorting through what he might need to tackle immediately.

"Michael, can you give us a minute? I'll fill you in as soon as we're done here."

"Sure, boss. Everyone's here as you requested. Just let us know when you want to start the meeting. There's nothing pressing but that for the next hour, then we have an appointment at one of the local retirement homes."

As soon as the door was closed, Jack sat behind his desk.

"We're telling Chloe tomorrow."

Dave dropped into a chair opposite.

"Holy shit. When did Nell change her mind?"

"We've been in serious negotiations for over a week. Last Sunday was a pre-cursor. Chloe's been pushing it as much as I have."

"That's why she was here with Nell. I wondered what was going on."

Jack scrubbed his face with both hands before addressing his friend.

"I'm scared shitless. What if she doesn't want it to be me?"

"I think the more important question here is, how are your constituents going to feel about a love child that you've never honored."

"You fucking cut right to the chase, don't you?"

"My job. As your friend and field director."

"I've been trying to figure out a way to do this gracefully. I haven't come up with anything yet."

"Well, you better get to it. Tomorrow will be here sooner than you think. We need to have a strategy in place, or the newspapers will be all over it. And not in a good way."

"I've waited too long for this and I don't care about the reporters as much as you'd like me to."

"Does Ron know?"

"Yes. He's flying in to meet with us, to discuss options."

Dave was up and pacing, his hands on his hips, deep in thought.

"Any chance Nell would agree to 'date' you? Then Chloe's presence would be a given."

Jack leaned back in his chair. He liked the idea. For more than what Dave was implying. If they pretended to date, then he'd have the time and opportunity to talk her into going back. Maybe they could finally take it to the next level. He was better armed now than he'd been back in college.

"I doubt it. But that doesn't mean I won't talk to her about it. If Chloe's well-being is important to Nell, then maybe she'll agree. I'm sure she doesn't want Chloe to be victimized by our past any more than when I asked before."

"She's always put Chloe's interest ahead of her own."

"And you would know this how?'

"Ellen."

"And how does Ellen know?"

"They've stayed friends over the years. Good friends. Nell's the one who convinced us Standish was a good school. It's why Amy and Parker are enrolled there."

"Good thing Ellen is in Human Resources at a Forbes 500 company. The tuition is too steep for men like us."

"If it wasn't for her, I'd have had to choose another field to excel in. Politics wouldn't have been on the long list, never mind on the short one."

"Our women did well."

"*Our women?*"

"I can't help but think of her that way. It's one thing that hasn't changed much over the years."

"Any pretension on her part to play girlfriend wouldn't be a stretch for you."

"It would be a long-standing wish come true."

"You do know you're stepping into a pile of shit."

"Knee-deep and skunk-smelling. I've got to tell the staff. Could you send them in, so I can get it over with?"

"Will you be telling everyone that works for you?"

"Tahlia already knows. I want everyone here to know, just in case it gets out before we're ready."

No one seemed overly concerned about his youthful indiscretion. Some even seemed delighted that Chloe was related to him. They all seemed to like her. The only question Michael asked, once he knew the particulars, was how it fit in his schedule.

As soon as he left his office, Jack picked up his cell phone.

↪

Nell was in her office going over notes for her opening statement. There was a trial starting Monday that should be an open and shut case, but she had to set the stage to keep it that way. Chloe was doing homework at her table, the laptop open to the ancestry website. Chloe had filled in most of her matriarchal family tree and kept going back to dig into the backgrounds of the women more than the men. It made her proud.

Her cell vibrated across the table and when she picked it up, saw the incoming caller's name, she hesitated. She glanced over to Chloe's back as she swiped.

"Hi."

"I've been talking to Dave, among others, about the public repercussions that might come with our announcement."

"Who said we were going to announce it?"

"People are going to know, Nell. If I start showing up places with her, questions will be raised."

"Who said I'd allow that to happen?"

"We're just going to tell her and then drop it?"

Getting out of her seat, she faced the window, looked out over the city.

"I've been going over and over it, in many different ways, and I haven't come to any conclusions other than this might be a big mistake."

"No, it's not. Please listen. Dave came up with a strategy that might work. If you're willing. It will give Chloe some shade."

"If I'm willing to do what?"

There was a long pause and she felt her lungs constricting.

"If we pretend, we're dating…"

"Are you out of your mind?"

Her voice had gone up, so she quickly glanced back to find Chloe staring at her. Tamping down her extreme anxiety over the suggestion, she tried for a more moderate approach.

"I can't see how that would be beneficial to either side."

"She's sitting right there, isn't she?"

"That's right."

"I should have known. Can you go into a conference room or something? We need to talk this through."

"Nothing to talk about. I think it would create more problems than it would solve. What happens when…we are no longer exercising that option? What happens if hopes run too high for the third party in question. You do know that might happen."

"We let her know right from the start. Explain it's the only way we can ease her into the spotlight without any fallout."

"That doesn't mitigate the expectancy factor."

"I want to be a father to her Nell. I want to get to know her, and I want her to get to know me. I want visitation, overnights—"

"Absolutely not going to happen."

"I bought a place of my own this morning. She won't be anywhere near my mother."

Now the long pause was on her side. He'd gone out on a very shaky limb. She'd never thought he'd leave the old family home. Another thought snapped into place. He'd done it for Chloe where he'd never considered it for her.

"Please. Just think about it. You can let me know how you want to handle it when I see you tomorrow."

And with that, he clicked off.

She studied the phone in her hand, as if it were an oracle and would tell her what to do. What the future would hold. What if she did as suggested? There were logistics here that had to be handled. What would Howie say? Did she care? How about Hope?

What would Eloise say or do?

That one was a critical mass that could tilt this into very dangerous territory.

"What was that all about?"

She gave Chloe a watered-down smile.

"Food for thought."

"You are the only one I know who can chop up anger and make it into food for thought."

"It's my logical side trying to gain leverage. The emotional one is simmering."

"I'm sure you'll work it out. I love you, Mom."

"Love you, too Chloe."

So much that I might take a hit for you. In the gut, the heart and the soul.

CHAPTER TWENTY

Nell spent most of the night on the phone, getting opinions, weighing options. Jelani warned her against it. Em and Camille thought it might be a way out of her dilemma. Arianna told her to go for it and Mia, being a mother, knew the why behind the consideration. They went over the consequences of Chloe getting her hopes up for a reconciliation, what steps she could take to avoid it, and what boundaries to put in place to protect her own heart. She didn't climb into bed until the wee hours of the morning. When the sun peeked out over the horizon, she gave up the pretense of sleep, got up, took a shower and sat over her coffee longer than was prudent or necessary. Her nerves were humming.

Chloe wasn't far behind her, chattering on about nothing specific. It proved she wasn't the only one nervous about the upcoming introduction.

She'd almost told her before Jack got there. Figured Chloe would know the truth as soon as he pulled up into the parking lot. And she couldn't help but see it, stationed on the chair looking out for close to an hour.

"Mom, someone's here."

She jumped up, scurried around in circles.

"I'm afraid to look. Is it him? Is he here? Who is he, Mom? What's his name?"

When the doorbell rang, Nell wiped her hands on her jeans, and walked toward the door.

"You know him, honey. You like him, too. It's going to be all right."

"What do you mean I know him?" The answering voice was tinny.

When Nell opened the door, Chloe's mouth dropped open.

"It *is* you."

Jack had stepped into the vestibule, his hands in his pockets, his expression showing his concern. Or was it fear?

Nell's eyes sought out Chloe when she realized what she'd just said.

"What do you mean, it is you?"

"I...asked Keileh if I was crazy to think it might be him. He has grey eyes, and yeah, I know thousands of people have grey eyes, but you knew each other, back when you were younger, around the right time, and...and you get flustered every time he's with us. It's not like you. I thought maybe it was because...you know...it was him."

He cleared his throat, but it didn't remove the gruffness.

"Are you okay with it?"

Nell closed the door, taking a step away from him.

"I've already advised you to never ask a question you don't know the answer to. Besides, it's not like she has a choice."

"I'm...I'm okay with it being you, yes."

She dipped her head down, looked up through her lashes. "I had a lot of questions during my hypothetical discussion about it."

"What kind?"

Nell saw the gulp before Chloe asked, "Will this hurt you, you know, politically?"

"I'm not sure."

He answered her honestly and Nell gave him a couple of extra points for how he was handling this. After a strained awkward moment, she stuttered, "Jack, don't just stand there. Come in. Take off your coat. I assume you're going to stay awhile."

He shrugged out of it, never taking his eyes off Chloe. She rushed over to take it and placed it neatly over the arm of a chair.

Nell was already on her way into the kitchen when she asked, "Coffee? Chloe made it so it's up to your standards."

"Sure. That would be great. Thanks."

Father and daughter were still staring at each other, until Chloe stepped forward. He took the steps required to meet her and they embraced in a tentative hug. With a surge of feeling, he tightened his hold, breathed in the simple joy of this moment. It was like nothing he'd ever felt before. Pure, innocent, all-encompassing. He was a mess, wanting to tell her things it was too early for, like he'd loved her the minute he saw her picture, like he was sorry for all the wasted time. That he wanted to get to know her, hang out with her, walk her down the aisle when she got married.

Chloe asked, tentatively, "So, how's this going to play out? You've got an illegitimate kid who no one knew about."

Nell noticed a shimmer in his grey depths. The only other time she'd seen him cry was when he talked about his father.

"I don't want you to talk about yourself that way. This is on me, so don't worry about my career. Let me do that."

"We don't have to tell anyone. We can just keep it between us."

Nell gave him more credit when he said, "That wouldn't be enough for me. I want everyone to know you're my daughter. I'm very proud of you."

Chloe's eyes were fixed on him as if she was having trouble believing it.

"Jack floated an idea that might work for the interim, until we can figure out what to do."

She was standing in the archway between vestibule and kitchen, watching his reaction. His head snapped up; his eyes boring into hers as if he couldn't believe she was going to agree to his suggestion.

"Why don't we sit down. I'll throw some bagels in the toaster oven and we can discuss it over breakfast."

Quickly moving past her, Chloe scooted into the kitchen and right to the bread drawer.

"I'll throw the bagels in. You'd only burn them. You can get the peanut butter, cream cheese and jelly." Her movements were hurried as if she was trying to stay busy, too restless to stay still.

Jack moved to a seat at the table. Nell poured him a cup of coffee before getting to her assigned tasks and asked, "Is anyone else feeling awkward?"

Jack glanced up at her and held her gaze, a pensive shimmer in the shadow of his eyes.

Chloe, busy multi-tasking, admitted, "A little. Meeting him the other day helped. It even got me asking myself if he was...you know, who he is."

She placed the plate of toasted bagels on the table and sat down between them.

No one moved, and an uncomfortable silence sat with them. Chloe looked from one to the other and forced a dialogue.

"What's the idea?"

Nell fiddled with her napkin, and Jack waited.

"Guys come on. Tell me. You said Jack had an idea."

It was Jack who answered her.

"We thought if your mother and I...pretended to be dating, you could accompany us to some of my events. If we were seen having dinner, or if I picked you up at school, or if we just wanted to hang out here, no one would question my relationship with you."

Her mother added, "The focus would be on me. But you must understand Chloe, it would be just what Jack said. It would not be real."

Her mother seemed flustered again. As she was never one to hold back or mince words, there was nothing familiar about her behavior and it was almost scaring her. With her mind in overdrive, she got the distinct impression her mother felt something for Jack. It showed every time they were in the same room together. If Jack was the one to come up with this idea, maybe he felt something, too. Could she bring them together again? Or were there too many obstacles in the way?

"What about Howie? What will you tell him?"

"The truth."

"And he'd be all right with that?"

"I don't know yet."

"And if he's not, then what?"

"Jack's going out with someone, too. This isn't just about me and Howie."

Jack threw her a grenade. At least that's what it looked like from the expression on her mother's face.

"I called it off with Hope, this morning."

More flustered than ever, Nell stuttered, "You what?"

Her mother's leg began bouncing up and down like a ping-pong ball, and she looked more than flustered. She'd turned a shade of pasty grey and her breath was coming in short gasps.

"I was going there anyway. I figured the timing was right."

"Jack, your mother is going to have a field day..."

"It's none of her business."

"But she could cancel your fundraisers."

"Then I'll have to find alternate funding for the next campaign. Maybe you could help with that? You know almost as many people as she does."

"Their pockets aren't nearly as deep."

"I made a bad choice once. It's not going to happen again, Nell." Bitterness filled his voice, his tone caustic.

He sat back, his shoulders losing their tension. There was an air of quiet confidence in the way he was sitting.

"Can you pass me the plate, Chloe? I think I got my appetite back."

She watched as he buttered an onion bagel, and took a bite, before helping herself to the other half, chatting with him while she spread a thick layer of cream cheese on it.

Before she knew it, they were talking like they'd known each other forever, the easy conversation flowing back and forth about her school play, his judicial hearings, the incoming administration, her friends.

Nell noticed it, too. This wasn't what she'd expected, and a niggling worry began to dig deep into her gut. What if Chloe wanted to spend all his free time together? What would that mean for them? Would she give up their Friday nights? Would she refuse to come into the office with her on the weekends? What kind of relationship was he looking for? Was she going to lose her daughter to a man who hadn't initially wanted her? How fair was that? She'd worked her ass off making a good life for them both, stayed up past midnight to spend quality time with Chloe whenever she could. She'd taught her everything she knew about life, taught her good manners, how to deal with bullies, given her study tips, rehearsed with her, read the books she liked so they could talk about them. Jack just walked in, when most of the hard work had been done. To what? Take their daughter away from her?

She was scared. Not an emotion she was familiar with. But then again, abandonment was completely within her spiral of experience. She'd managed to create a safe environment for herself, where she let only those people she could trust into her inner circle.

She knew she couldn't trust Jack.

And she didn't know what she was going to do if any of her fears became reality.

Chloe made her more vulnerable than she'd ever been and if she lost her? She wasn't sure she could withstand that kind of pain.

"Mom, how is this going to work?"

Chloe had broken into her thoughts and she was grateful. Going down that road was not a wise choice. She had to trust that what they'd forged over the last eleven years would be strong enough to withstand anything.

"I'm not exactly sure."

She glanced over to Jack. "Any more suggestions?"

"I've got an appearance to make this afternoon at the Franklin Zoo, a speech at the DAR, and a clinic at Immigration Solutions. Tomorrow's Christmas and I have all kinds of things scheduled during my congressional recess. I was hoping that we might be able to do something next weekend. I plan on moving into my new place on Saturday but it's just a load of clothes and some valuables. It shouldn't take long. I'll check with Michael, see if there's anything we can go to as a...together."

Mixed feelings rushed through her.

"You're moving in that soon?"

"I am. Don't you think it's long overdue? Oh, wait. I don't have to ask that question. You're the one who pointed it out to me."

"I have to assume you paid for it yourself. I can't see your mother paying for something that took you away from her."

His lips thinned, but for the first time ever, she didn't think the expression had to do with her.

"Your assumption is correct. And I bought the furniture that was there for staging, so I won't be taking anything with me but the clothes on my back."

Her hand flew to her cover her heart.

"You won't miss the embroidered sofa?"

"Please. That thing was more uncomfortable than a bale of hay. Wait. Wasn't that your description of it?"

"It was."

They had attempted to make love on it one night but ended up on the floor. The heat that suffused her cheeks at the memory had her changing the subject.

"Where is it? The place you bought, not the sofa."

"Charlestown."

"By the water. I bet it has a nice view."

"It's one-half of a duplex. More spacious than some I looked at. I actually like it a lot."

Chloe asked, "Will I get to see it?"

"As soon as I move in."

Before she knew what was happening, and before she could stop it, Chloe was inviting him to share their sacred time together.

"We have family night every Friday. Dinner, movie, popcorn, candy, all the junk food you can eat. Maybe you can—"

"Chloe, if I remember correctly, Friday night's he has dinner with his mother. Don't ask for an invitation. That meeting isn't going to happen for a while."

"I told you, Nell, I'm making different choices. I'd love to come over for family night."

Squeezing her eyes closed, the momentary panic of that momentous decision jarring her nerves, she said weakly, "She is never going to go along with this."

"She has no say in this. At all."

The panic morphed into fright that alternately mixed with pleasure. She was coming out ahead of Eloise for once and although it was Chloe tilting the scale, she couldn't help basking in the spoils of war.

"If she shows up at my office..."

"I've already warned her. She won't."

Chloe asked, her voice thick with concern "Why is this such a problem?"

"His mother doesn't like me. Never has and, if I have to make a guess, never will."

"Why?"

"Not sure, gave up trying to figure it out a long time ago."

Chloe turned her attention toward her other parent.

"Jack?"

"I don't know either, Chloe."

"Haven't you ever asked her?"

"She's given me reasons..."

Nell jumped up to clear off the table, her movements somewhat jerky.

"They just don't pass the smell test. My mother's mother has some Hungarian blood. I worked too much, won too many cases, wanted to outshine her golden boy."

"If you're looking for me to defend her? Those days are over."

She studied him, needing to know if he was sincere or just trying to fulfill his agenda. What she saw in his expression made her uneasy. It wasn't what she expected.

"Mom said you didn't come to California with us because you had nothing to offer. Was it about the money?"

"I'm sorry to say it was. I wasn't going to inherit my trust fund until I turned twenty-three, so up until then, my mother handled the finances. She wasn't willing to pay for any other law school but Harvard. I thought I had no alternative than to stay in Boston. Your mother refused to move back."

"Long-distance relationship was out?"

"Once I pushed for a paternity test it was."

"You thought Mom would have tried to trick you?"

"No. I knew you were mine."

Tapping her fingers on the table, Chloe looked like she was deep in thought. "Your mother again?"

He simply nodded. Anyone else listening to this conversation would have thought him a wimp of the highest order.

"And you forgot all about us?"

He'd gotten through school without calling, without asking, without rocking his boat so in a way she'd stumbled on the million-dollar question.

"No. You were always there, hidden away. When I graduated, I still didn't know what I was going to do. I still didn't have anything to offer you. Your mother ended up in DC. I knew she'd do well. I'd made her a promise to stay out of your lives and I tried to keep it."

"But..."

"I got her to agree to send me updates, pictures, let me have as much of a connection as she thought appropriate. It didn't satisfy the need I had to know you, only increased my curiosity."

"Mom, what made you finally agree to this?"

"You. None of the pressure he put on me would have changed my mind. It was your growing need to know who he was, is, that made me give in."

"Then, thank you. I'll try not to be angry that you made me wait so long." Looking at Jack, she said, "I don't want to meet your mother. Not until she can accept mine. I can't respect anyone who could manipulate people like that."

"How about people who allow themselves to be manipulated?"

There was a critical tone to his voice when he asked, and she knew who he meant.

"It makes trust an issue."

"I can understand that, Chloe. I know I need to earn that. From both of you."

He peered at Nell intently. He wanted her to read the sincerity in his eyes. He knew he had a long road to travel to get to where he wanted, but she was well worth the journey. Her returning gaze gave him hope.

Chloe must have sensed that a silent communication was passing between them because she turned to leave.

"Okay. I'll let you guys figure it all out. Mom, can I go to Keileh's for a few hours? She invited me over so I can talk about all of this."

Glancing back at Jack, Nell assured him, "She promised not to tell anyone. I trust her."

He nodded. He knew she'd need a confidant and who better than her friend.

Nell looked back over at Chloe.

"I'll drop you off and then go shopping. I still have a few things to pick up."

Chloe powered her phone back up. Texting Keileh, she got a response immediately.

"Mom, can Keileh stay overnight, come with us tomorrow?"

"Her Mom won't mind?"

She knew Keileh's family celebrated the holiday in less commercial ways but they did get a tree, and gifts from Santa were deposited under the branches, although the girls no longer believed in the jolly old elf. Samira loved the holiday, explained that she saw nothing but beauty in the love and peace it symbolized. The family read the story of the birth of Jesus in the Quran, fasting as they always did on high holy days. She might want her oldest daughter there with them.

Nell watched the thumbs in action, waiting.

"She said yes. She thinks it will give Keileh an insight into how Christians celebrate."

Putting her phone in the back pocket of her jeans, Chloe went to stand by Jack.

"I'm glad you've decided to be in my life, and I know we're going to fudge it for a while. I have an ancestry project due after the Christmas break. I was really hoping after meeting you today, I could fill in the other side of my family tree. Your position complicates things. I'll leave it blank for now."

"Fill it in. We have a few weeks before making any final decisions."

"I may have questions."

"Text them and I'll get back to you as soon as I can."

"Thanks."

She leaned in to kiss his cheek and ran off to her bedroom to get her notes. She wanted to show Keileh what she'd found so far about her ancestors.

He got up, gathered up his coat, and stepped toward the door.

Nell was right behind him.

"I can't believe she's so casual about all of this."

"Not as much as you might think. Keileh's her sounding board. I'm sure all her misgivings will come out with her."

"What kind of misgivings?"

"We've thrown a lot at her. The pretense of dating, your mother's antagonism, not being able to tell her how this will play out."

"I've made such a mess of this. I'm sorry, Nell."

"We'll figure a way out of it."

He lingered, as if he didn't want to leave.

"What are you guys doing for Christmas?"

It had crept up on her and she couldn't believe it was tomorrow. She was glad that one thing hadn't changed.

"Jelani's. We've been going to her house to celebrate every year since we all started at WF. Camille might not be able to make it this year. It has to do with one of her cases. But the rest of us will be there. You at your mother's?"

"No. We spend it at my Aunt Jane's. It's more festive. My cousins and their families are there. It was far too lonely for a few years until I forced the issue. We've been going ever since."

"I met her, your Aunt Jane, didn't I? The summer we lived together."

"Yes. She liked you. I talk to her every now and then. I guess you could say she's my Keileh."

"We all need one of them."

"Do you guys get home late?"

"Usually around eight or nine. Why?"

"I thought maybe I could stop by, wish you both a merry Christmas."

"I don't know, Jack."

"Please. I've missed so many up to now."

Another request she couldn't turn down. His grey eyes brimming with hope.

"I'll text you when we're leaving Jelani's. You can meet us back here for some egg nog."

"Thanks."

He dipped his eyes to the floor but when he looked back up, he all but kissed her with his smile.

"What are you doing New Year's Eve?"

"First Night. It's tradition"

"Can I tag along? It might be a good way to ring in our new resolution."

"And that would be what exactly?"

"Giving Chloe some shade."

She knew there'd be interaction, but a night out with him? She wasn't sure.

"Let me think about it. I'll let you know tomorrow night."

"Good."

She opened the door, hoping he'd take the hint.

His eyes sparkled. When he bent down to kiss her good-bye, she didn't fight it.

And when she shut the door behind him, she touched her tingling lips, aching for something more.

CHAPTER TWENTY-ONE

"Good morning, sleepyhead. Late night?"

Chloe looked up at her guiltily, rubbed her eyes.

"Yeah. We kind of talked about everything. She made me feel a little less crazy."

Nell knew that Keileh was a gentle soul, soft-spoken and calm. She had a feeling she gave Chloe wise council. That she was Muslim was never an issue for them. The family had assimilated well into American culture, Keileh's dad having immigrated here when he was ten, right after the Iranian revolution. He was a citizen and married Samira her last year of internship at the hospital they both worked at, Siraj as an anesthesiologist. A problem they might be facing soon: Samira was still waiting to be naturalized.

"I'm glad one of your friends knows what's going on."

Chloe opened the refrigerator and got out the orange juice, poured a glass of it and took a sip.

"Do any of your friends know?"

Sitting at the table, coffee and newspaper in front of her, Nell said, "All the partners know about Jack. You won't have to watch what you say at Jelani's."

"Really? How come Jelani didn't tell me?"

"Um, because I would have had to kill her. The women I work with can keep a secret, you know. There's lots of stuff we can't talk about."

"Confidentiality. I get it."

"Why don't you and Keileh get ready. We've still got to open presents and pack the car and we're already running behind schedule. I let you guys sleep in way too long."

~

They were one of the last to arrive. Nell was loaded down with a box of wrapped presents, Chloe had the gift bags, and Keileh trailed behind with the dessert Chloe had made before meeting Jack yesterday morning. The laughter that welcomed them felt good. The hugs filled a need she hadn't known she had. Arianna was already pouring the wine although it wasn't noon yet, the aromas coming from the kitchen promised good things to come.

This had become a yearly event, every year seeing an influx of revelers. It was one of the reasons she surmised Jelani had bought the house. It was great for entertaining and there was a domestic side that Jelani kept buried like a treasure until times like this. For all the dating her friend did, she knew underneath it all there was a driving need to embrace a husband and family. She just hadn't found the right fit yet. Wading through the throng that was gathered in the family room,

Nell cornered Emilia by the tree as she deposited the box beneath it.

"Camille isn't coming, is she?"

It was the first year one of them opted out of the gathering and it felt wrong.

"No. I still can't believe she chose him over us. There is something going on there she refuses to talk about."

Nell knew there was from their last conversation. She just hoped Cami didn't get more involved than she should. The verdict was still out on who the Russian was or what he wanted.

Em shook her head and added, "He's hidden somewhere underground. He's says he's a wanted man and she's doing her best to keep him alive, at least for the time being. Do the Russians forget to kill you if you disappear?"

"Not unless they were the ones who made it happen."

"I think she's emotionally involved." Em looked up at her, a worried look on her face. "I've never seen her so consumed by a case."

"Seemed that way to me, as well. I've been helping her research some of the other journalist's deaths. The Russians are going down like dominoes. Latest one from a suicide. But the facts surrounding it, suggest otherwise."

"Maybe you can talk some sense into her. I've tried and haven't gotten anywhere."

She had promised Cami she'd talk to Jack about Maxim Skolikovsky, see if there was a Russian scheduled to appear at one of the intelligence hearings. She hadn't had the chance yet and wasn't sure she would have shared the information with anyone else, not even Em. When Arianna came over with two glasses of wine, she was saved from having to continue the discussion.

"No business today. We are here to enjoy each other's company and nothing more. Whatever you're talking about will have to wait until tomorrow."

Handing the drinks over, she stared until they promised to do as instructed.

But Nell tucked it away. She'd talk to Jack when he came to the condo later. It would give her something to talk about that wouldn't get her into trouble.

As conversation flowed around her, Nell found herself getting caught up in it.

She winked at Chloe, who, along with Keileh, announced she was taking the younger children into another room, giving the adults time to drink and be merry.

Nell did more observing than participating. She was always interested in the way people responded to each other, the psychology of group dynamics. People watching was her favorite pastime and this afternoon she immersed herself in it.

Nick had dropped by with Teddy and Saban. None of the group liked Nick's wife but they accepted her as part of Em's small family. She was surer than ever that Saban liked to torture Em in small ways, ways that were hard to read. Little sarcastic remarks, kissing Nick as soon as Em got close, crowing about how much Teddy looked like him. She'd never understand why the man had chosen Saban over Em. Whiney bitch vs woman warrior. There was no contest in her mind.

Jelani's latest conquest had arrived in time for dessert. He was too flamboyant for her taste and she didn't think the relationship would last much longer than the end of the year. He bragged about his job as male stripper until Mia told him to shut it. He did have the build for it and Nell knew exactly why Jelani had stuck it out for so long.

Arianna's brother Baird, and his husband, James were there, Baird trying to convince Arianna to run for governor. Barker had been appointed to the new president's cabinet and there'd be a special election coming up soon. It didn't give them much time to get a campaign going but he thought she'd make an excellent politician. He was polling the members of her staff to see what their thoughts were. He was a political analyst by trade, and Nell had to admit he'd run one hell of a campaign.

"I'd have no life. I see what kind of hours they keep."

"Like you have one now?"

"Look around. It's here."

Pulling out of her own world, Baird asked, "Nell, what do you think? You were in DC for a couple of years."

"I think we wouldn't be who we are if your sister gave us up for something better."

"It's the season for women. She'd already have a solid base to start with. You'd vote for her, wouldn't you?"

"Of course not. She might win."

He threw his hands up.

"You guys are no help at all. I can't believe you'd let Evan Cox have a clear field."

"What?"

Arianna's ears perked up. The partners closed ranks.

"He has the audacity to run for governor?"

"He does, and it looks like there's no one out there willing to go head-to-head with him."

"No way I'm letting him win without a good fight. I'll help you find an opponent. We'll begin first thing Tuesday morning. Be in my office no later than eight."

Looking around the room, she said, "If anyone has a name for me, let me know. Otherwise I might have to put...Nate's name on the ballot. Or his friend there. What's your name?"

Mia's husband, Nathaniel Fisher, an intelligence analyst for the FBI in Boston, was a good sport to put up with so many women every year. He was usually odd man out, so Mia had suggested he bring a friend along and he'd taken her up on it. Alec Cleland worked at the bureau with him, was single, and pretty good looking. He was scruffy enough that Arianna might have made a move, even though he was a bit younger than she was.

Alec cocked an eyebrow at her and announced, "Alec Cleland and I'm not interested."

"Someone will have to be."

Nell thought she saw some sparks fly between him and Jelani, but it could have been her imagination. They'd argued about everything since he'd gotten there.

Nate put his two cents in, giving Baird what he was looking for.

"I, for one, think Arianna is a great choice. I also think my wife will kill me for voicing my opinion."

Mia laughed. "You are so right. I don't want to be running the place by myself. Our kids would never see either of us."

Arianna introduced a topic they'd been discussing since Mia's kids were born.

"I think it's time we move on the day care center we talked about. We've just hired a couple of married lawyers. They'll be having kids and I think it's a great perk."

Mia agreed and joked, "And maybe someday the rest of you will break down and walk down the aisle."

"Yeah, right. Like any of the women here will take the time for that. If you ask me, you're all a little too single-minded to remain anything but single."

The women, in unison, stared at Saban, who had put that out on the table.

Baird was the one to point out, "That happens when you're a warrior and not a princess. Men tend to be intimidated."

"Some men do like the helpless type. Don't understand why." Arianna's tone dripped with antagonism as she looked at Nick.

Nell shook her head. She didn't understand why Em had invited the Katsaros' or why Nick always agreed to come. She was glad the evening was winding down. It was time to go home.

After getting up, she called to Chloe. She still had to drop Keileh off at home before texting Jack. That would take an hour all told and she didn't want this to be a late night. Giving hugs all around, she corralled the girls into the car and drove north a few miles before circling back south.

Jack was already in the parking lot when they got back home. Chloe noticed him right away and jumped out of the car to greet him.

He unpacked some wrapped packages from the trunk and followed them inside.

"You got us presents?"

Chloe had thrown her coat on a chair and took the packages out of his arms, squealing in delight.

"I didn't really know what to get. Until I know what you have and what you need, it's going to be guess work. I apologize beforehand if you don't like what I bought."

"Are you kidding? I got Christmas presents from my father this year. This is lit."

Nell was watching the exchange with trepidation. For as many gifts as Chloe got this morning, she hadn't shown this much excitement. Would she feel the same way if her own father showed up bearing gifts? Closing her eyes, knowing it would never happen, she reluctantly answered yes to her own question.

"Here, Mom. There's one for you."

She looked up startled.

"Jack, you shouldn't have."

"I saw it and thought of you."

It was a small square box, wrapped with a simple red bow. Before she could say anything, Chloe was displaying the cookbooks he'd given her.

"This is awesome. Look, Mom. They're for beginners, like me. I can't wait to look through them. Thank you soooo much, Jack."

"You're welcome, Chloe. Glad you like them."

She was already ripping the paper off the second box. When she took out the pizza stone she laughed. "I think this one's for you, Mom."

Nell smiled. "Are you suggesting I make the pizza?"

"God, no. But now you'll have an excuse for *me* to make it."

The next gift was in an envelope. She carefully slit it open and pulled out a few sheets of paper. Nell watched as she tried to figure out what they were. And then it dawned.

"Mom, these are tickets to Blue Man Group. There are four of them. For next month."

"I thought you might want to invite Keileh. You two seem joined at the hip. Do you think her Mom will let her go?"

"I'm going to go call her now."

Before she left the room, she was flinging herself into his arms.

"Thank you. So much. I love everything."

He hugged her, for a few seconds longer than necessary, and it made Nell's heart soften.

So much so that when Chloe left the room, she wanted to copy Chloe's movements and recklessly steal the same kind of hug.

Why hadn't she thought of getting Chloe tickets to a show? Chloe loved movies, drama, and, it seemed, acting. It should have been a no-brainer.

"I hope you'll come with us. I got the tickets for a Saturday night. Didn't want to mess with your Fridays."

Jack's thoughtfulness was beginning to fray at her nerves. He remembered everything. Maybe it was easy to do if you weren't involved in the day-to-day craziness of parenthood. Having someone's life in your hands everyday was exhausting.

"Nell, you'll come with us, won't you?"

"Of course. It was a thoughtful gift. Especially seeing that you included Keileh."

He took a step closer to her, and in a low, seductive voice said, "Now your turn."

An oddly primitive beat sounded in the region of her heart.

"Jack, I didn't get anything for you. I'm—"

"Don't. You gave me the gift of my daughter. Nothing could have pleased me more."

She bit her lip as she untied the ribbon. She opened the white box to find a sixteen-row chain set, each row intricately designed.

"Jack, this is beautiful."

"It looked like something you'd wear."

"You would have had to go into a jewelry store to see this."

When had he done the shopping? Yesterday? Before that?

"I did. I thought about getting Chloe a bracelet, went into a store on Newbury Street. I hesitated because I haven't seen her wear one, so I wasn't sure it was her thing. This had your name all over it."

He knew her well. Still. She caught herself from falling into the dizzying sensation.

"She used to wear mine all the time when she was little. Played dress-up with my shoes, jewelry, make-up."

"I know. You sent me one of the pictures you took. It's one of my favorites."

She was working the clasp but her shaking fingers were making it difficult. He came over and took the chain from her, wrapping it around her wrist and securing it. She shook it and watched as it settled on her hand. Loose and comfortable. Just the way she liked them.

Not trusting herself to look at him, she walked towards the kitchen.

"Come on. I'll get you that eggnog I promised."

He followed her without another word.

When they were both sitting at the table, she fussed with the fine strands of metal as she asked, "How was your day?"

He slumped down to get more comfortable in the chair, the tumbler of eggnog in his hand.

"Good. It went without a hitch. It's easy being there. I don't get how different sisters can be."

"Different lives, I guess."

"I guess. How about yours?"

Her mouth curved up at the corners, her eyes filled with pleasure.

"It's always fun when the group of us get together."

"It must be what it feels like for me to be with Ron and Dave. Histories, trust, respect."

"Exactly. There aren't too many people you can feel that way about. Especially today. Do you still talk to Grady?"

He was another one of Jack's friends she'd met in college.

"Yeah. I wanted him with me, too, but he couldn't afford to take the job I offered. Working on a congressman's staff isn't exactly something to aspire to. Not if you want to eat."

"Giving back sometimes means you have to sacrifice something."

"He's doing okay. He's building a real estate empire. He donates to great causes, like my campaign."

"I suppose you had to leave some friends in the private sector."

She started suddenly when she remembered her promise.

"Camille is working with someone who says he's a Russian journalist. We're worried she's involved, that he might be on a hit list. It's one of her FBI cases. Have you heard anything about him?"

"Aren't they giving her any information?"

"Not as much as usual."

He was quiet for a minute and her concern grew. It might be confidential, something he wouldn't be able to share with her. She sat waiting, as patiently as she could.

He finally admitted, "A Russian hacker who uses the name Matrixiator is scheduled to appear before the committee sometime in January. It's a closed meeting so it's probably highly confidential but they haven't classified it yet. I don't have to tell you to keep it to yourself.

Could it be him?"

"A hacker makes sense. She mentioned it being a possibility."

They both looked up as Chloe came out to join them, dressed in her flannel pj's. It ended the conversation, but she had something to give Camille that might be of merit.

"Keileh can come with us. Her mom might be gone by then. Is it okay if she stays over that night?"

"You know as long as you ask ahead of time it's usually fine with me."

"Good. I'm going to bed. I'm wicked tired."

She leaned in to give Nell a hug and kiss goodnight. Then did the same to Jack.

"This is the best present you guys. I'm so happy."

She turned to leave but stopped, swiveled toward Jack.

"Can I call you Dad? Or is it too soon?"

A pang of anxiety erupted in Nell's chest. This was going so fast her head was spinning. Jack's answer didn't do anything to mitigate the fear.

"Chloe, it's eleven years overdue. I was going to ask you to call me that, but I thought it might be too weird."

"It's more weird calling you Jack. You're on recess, aren't you? Will I see you again before you go back?"

"I don't know. It depends on your mom."

Nell wanted to be fair. This introduction had taken a long time but the worry about Chloe's heart still niggled. There was such a hopeful look on her daughter's face she couldn't deny her the time she wanted to spend with Jack.

"I've got to work all week. No semester break for me. You guys can work something out. Just let me know so I can accommodate it."

"I have to talk to Michael, see what he has for me. I know I have a couple of town hall meetings but I'm not sure what else. I'll call with some possible times. He usually gives me an index card listing the day's events, but I don't get it until the start of the day."

"'Kay. Goodnight."

As soon as Chloe was safely ensconced behind her bedroom door, Nell got up, cleared away the glasses, and said, "My bedtime, too. I've got a full day tomorrow."

He stayed in his seat, but she could feel his eyes following her around the room as she rinsed out the glasses and put them in the dishwasher.

"Where does Chloe stay while you're at the office?"

As she wiped down the counters, her back to him, she answered, "Keileh's mom is off Wednesday so she'll stay over there tomorrow night, then I'm taking Friday off, so we'll reverse shifts."

"You can do that?"

"Take Friday? Yeah. I plan well in advance."

"No court date?"

After placing the sponge in a tray, she turned around to face him.

"Not this week. It's always quiet around the holidays. I'll spend the day working here."

Jack took out his phone and began to text. Whoever he was texting answered immediately and it wasn't long before he looked up and said, "I have a couple of things on the agenda for tomorrow but if Chloe's up for it, I can take her with me."

"Like what?"

"I'm meeting with the leadership of the Salvation Army mid-morning, then I go to Rosie's Place to serve lunch and get a tour. Michael left some time open for me to be in the field offices, so I can pretty much set my own schedule."

"I think it's a great idea, especially Rosie's Place."

Rosie's Place was the first women's shelter opened in the United Sates. They distributed food out of a pantry, provided health, educational and housing services, and advocated for women's rights in the court system.

"Do you do legal work for them?"

"It's Arianna's domain. I am one of their donors."

"I can drop her by your office or Keileh's afterwards or keep her for the rest of the day."

"I'm not sure it's a good idea. You being with her. Not until we've set some groundwork."

"Then come with us."

"Jack, I have a full schedule tomorrow. I can't just leave my desk on a whim."

"Is that what you think this is? A whim?"

"No, I didn't mean it like that. But I can't come and go as I please. I've got to plan around things like this."

"It'd be an hour. And it would get it out and over with. You do stop for lunch, don't you?"

"I eat at my desk unless I have an outside appointment."

"Of course, you do. Nothing's changed, has it? You still drive yourself to do as much as you can. Do you ever just stop and smell the roses?"

She did on occasion but not as much as her partners. Arianna stressed that they had to be well-rounded. Play had to take up some of their time. If not, they'd burn out and wouldn't do her, the firm, or their clients any good. Mentally calculating what she had going on tomorrow, she looked up at Jack. He was scrutinizing her with a somber expression.

"Not as much as I should."

"Come with us. You can bring Chloe with you and then I can keep her for the rest of the afternoon, drop her at Keileh's if you want. That will save you time and you can catch up."

He was right. If she didn't have to drive Chloe out to Newton, she could make up the time lost, prepping for trial.

"That will help."

No matter how much she was unwilling to admit it, the guilt of working so many hours did get to her. This might mitigate it just a bit.

He was getting his coat on, gearing up to leave.

In one fluid motion, he was standing in front of her. She stood frozen, not sure whether to stay or flee. When his arms pulled her into an embrace, she had her answer. It always felt like home.

His voice was low and smooth, his words chilling.

"Nell, I have to be honest. I want to stay, stake a claim. But I know I can't do that yet. I just want you to know that's my intention. I'll take it slow, build some trust."

Not wanting to reflect on what that meant, she used humor as a counterbalance.

"Stake a claim? We're not some gold mine in the Wild West."

Wistfulness stole into his expression.

"You're right, it's not the Wild West and I'm no gunslinger. But you are a gold mine. I didn't take care of my rights."

She could feel the flush suffuse her face, but she remained silent, afraid of what would come out of her mouth.

He looked down, his eyes a smoky grey, and paused, his lips hovering over hers. His hands moved underneath her sweater, his thumbs stroking, his fingers petting. She moved closer on contact, her arms winding around his neck.

He whispered into her ear, "Why does this feel so instinctive? Why are we still so drawn to each other?"

"I don't know. I only know how good it feels."

He kissed her then, deepening it, and she wanted more than a taste. She wanted to feast. Memories of them entwined, satiated, so clear in her mind it was difficult not to take it further.

He knew as well as she did that was not happening tonight. Not with Chloe in the next room.

He kissed her forehead, his breathing labored.

"I'll meet you there?"

After her brief nod, he slipped out the door.

CHAPTER TWENTY-TWO

Nell explained the plan for the day to Chloe before they left for her office. Instead of arguing with her about hanging around in the office, Chloe was more than eager to get going.

"What time will we be meeting him?"

They went through the double doors, the office already buzzing with activity.

"Noon. Did you bring something to do?"

"I have a book and my laptop."

"Okay, why don't you go into my office. I want to check in with Hani, see if anything's come up that I need to attend to."

"Just so you know I'm not hanging around here much this week. We need to talk about my staying home."

"Nope, but I will try to find things for you to do."

Mia and Arianna had their heads together in the conference room, Baird sitting between them.

"What's going on?"

"Going over some names for the governor's race."

"Boy, you weren't kidding when you said you'd be on it first thing."

"There is no way that man will be running unopposed. I will enter the race if I have to."

Chloe chirped in, "Can I work on your campaign?"

"Absolutely."

Nell said out loud what everyone already knew.

"But you don't want the job. That's not fair to anyone."

Arianna sat back with a thud.

"There is that."

Em came in, peeked over Nell's shoulder.

"I got a commitment for one of those socials we talked about. The ones for Jack."

"Who?"

"Jasmine Vargas. She's undocumented, so we can't let the newspapers anywhere near it."

Jelani shouted down the hall, "I got my sister to agree and she loves the spotlight."

Chloe stood just outside the door, listening intently to what was going on.

"Dad will be psyched. Can I do some of the planning?"

Everyone there looked at Chloe with stunned faces.

"What?"

Jelani was the one who asked, "You're calling him Dad already?"

"Well, he is. My dad. Although one of you guys should have told me."

Jelani scrunched her face at Chloe.

"Not. We're sort of like the Sisterhood of the Suits. We keep each other's secrets."

"Whatever."

"Will Keileh spill yours?"

"No. I can trust her with...Oh, I get it. Like that."

"Like that. Now shoo, fly. Go do kid things and let us earn our pay."

Noticing the new bracelet on Nell's wrist, Jelani said, "Nice bangle. Where'd you get that? Howie?"

Em added, "He's too practical to buy her something like that."

Tightening the strap of her briefcase over her shoulder, Nell backed out of the room, muttering, "Not Howie. We broke up."

She couldn't get away fast enough, although Jelani followed her into her office and said, "Spill it."

"Fine. Jack came back last night and gave us presents. That's when Chloe asked if she could call him Dad. He said yes, left, and I need to get to work."

She was moving forward, forcing Jelani back and out.

"He knows you well if he bought you that."

"We spent two years together. He should."

"He also should have taken better care of your heart."

"Or I should have. Either way, I have to get to work. I'm taking Chloe to Rosie's Place for lunch."

"Did Arianna ask you to take one of the cases?"

"No."

"So why?"

"Can't I take my daughter to a women's shelter, show her around, let her see a downside to life?"

"Yes, but today? You have a full schedule."

"I'm working around it."

"Why?"

Chloe couldn't have timed her re-entry to her office better, or her ill-fated question. "So where am I going with Dad after that place we're going to?"

Jelani gave her a head jerk and stared.

"I guess that answers my question. And I can't say I'm disturbed by it. If he can get you out of the office when no one else can, I'm all for this."

"This? This is nothing more than my meeting him to drop Chloe off."

"He couldn't have picked her up?"

"How would he explain why Chloe is with him?"

"You're not telling the world?"

"Not yet. We want to make it an easy transition."

Chloe was sitting in one of the chairs, a book in her hand, a smile on her face.

"They're going to pretend to date so I can hang with him. Isn't she cute when she gets flustered?"

Nell's eyes narrowed, telling Chloe she'd better stop while she was ahead.

Jelani whistled a happy tune on her way out.

The rest of the day went without a hitch.

⌒

Jack was restless, waiting by his car, checking his watch every five minutes. He finally relaxed when he saw them pull in.

"I was beginning to think you weren't going to show."

"A call went longer than I expected, and traffic was tough."

"I know you have a phone. You could have texted or called."

"We're not late, Jack. What is the problem?"

There wasn't one. He was just anxious to be with them again and he didn't like waiting.

Without another word, he escorted them in, the director ready to meet him.

"Nell, what a nice surprise."

"Hello Clara. This is my daughter, Chloe. I hope you don't mind if she tags along. I'd like her to see what a great job you do."

Chloe shook hands with the woman in charge.

"Not at all. Maybe someday she can do some volunteer work for us."

The tour was a revelation and Jack was impressed with what the staff and volunteers were accomplishing for the women in the community. Chloe was shy at first, something he hadn't seen before, and he was reminded again how little he knew her. He wanted to learn, so he observed mother-daughter interactions as closely as the inner workings of the shelter. Nell seemed to be her safety net, and Chloe hovered close until she felt comfortable with their surroundings. It was only then that she became the talkative young girl he'd come to appreciate. She was both introvert and extrovert, depending on the circumstances and it was the same type of dichotomy that had drawn him to Nell. He was unsure as to whether Chloe would want to stay with him when Nell's time allotment was up, but she surprised him by tagging along to his office in Everett, where they sat and chatted about his history, in between his meetings with some of his constituents.

As they spoke, Chloe jotted down names she could add to her family tree and had taken notes about what her ancestors had done with their lives. She repeated out loud some of the names he'd given her.

"Gosh, I can't believe where I come from. Presidents, other kinds of politicians, statesmen, an ambassador, Secretary of Navy, a historian." Chloe commented dryly, "Your mother's side was less active in politics."

"Her ancestors were industrialists and there was no shortage of thievery with their robber baron tendencies. Rich, yes, but money came before everything. Family, community, and country. Not the kind of legacy I want to leave at all. My parent's marriage was a strange mix of pedigree. Her parents were not pleased when she chose my father over other men more financially secure. Intermarriage among the exclusive group of Boston gentry was commonplace, even in the 1970's and 80's. They did come to respect him over the years, so the relationship was less caustic."

"Why did she marry your father?"

"She fell in love with him. Devoted her life to his. She fell apart when he died."

"What was she like when you were younger?"

"Fair, even-tempered, busy. She lived through him and when he was gone, she didn't know who she was anymore. She changed."

Some days he thought his memories had to be wrong. She'd been loving, warm, and kind. She never would have manipulated lives. Had true empathy for those less fortunate. It seemed she'd lost her sense of humanity with Lee's death, reverted to the teachings of her youth when she learned to be hostile to immigrants, judgmental of others, part of the revered group whose destiny it was to guide the American experiment. It was that that had been the driving force behind her mission to get him elected to public office. It wasn't to serve, it was to guide and influence, as his birthright dictated.

"Did money run in the family?"

"She was left a small fortune in her grandfather's will. Her father might not have appreciated her marrying into the Adams' family, but old Ebenezer Emerson looked at it with a sense of pride. She was left another windfall when her father died, so he must have gotten over his snit. She was the one with the money in the family although it never bothered my father. He did what he could to bring himself up to speed, wrote a couple of highly praised books that sold well, managed her portfolio. It was doing well in his hands."

"You don't have any money of your own, right? Otherwise you wouldn't have stayed behind to go to school."

"I have a trust fund left to me by my grandfather. He structured the will so that I receive graduated amounts as I get older. The first disbursement was made when I was twenty-three, the second will be when I turn thirty-five, the third when I hit fifty. I was only twenty-two when I went to law school, so, no, I had no money to speak of."

"Could you have waited until then to go to law school?"

"I could have but his will stipulated that I go to Harvard. I was on the losing side no matter which way I turned."

"I'm not sure I like your family. Grandma and Grandpa Warren at least let Mom live her own life."

"Yeah, but how do you think that felt when she was your age?"

"I can't imagine it. Mom's always been there. If I had to go to a boarding school so she could work in another country? I'd be asking why she had me."

"I'm sure she wondered the same thing."

"Jelani's told me some stories and I get sad when she does. Mom was so alone growing up."

"She was always so mature and accomplished, I tended to forget she had no one to help her. That she became that all on her own."

He still did. And it was a bitter pill to swallow knowing he perpetuated it.

When the afternoon came to a close, he dropped Chloe off at Keileh's, meeting her father, who was home for the day.

"Come in, Congressman Adams. Please. I have coffee brewed. Could I get you a cup?"

"Please, call me Jack."

With no plans until later in the evening, he accepted the offer and spent an hour discussing the opioid crisis and what might be done to alleviate it. With the discussion fresh in his mind, he went to his town hall meeting in Roxbury able to better answer some of the questions there with a more cogent understanding of the problems this community faced.

～

After she got home from the office, Nell made several calls before pouring herself a glass of wine. The morning's events had gone better than she'd expected but her emotions were in turmoil. There had been some speculation at the shelter. Jack's deference to her and Chloe had to be arousing curiosity. He'd kissed her good-bye in the parking lot and anyone looking out a window would have seen the gesture. Chloe had looked on with a sad kind of smile on her face. Like she wished it were for real.

Why had she offered to go with Jack's plan? The pretending part of dating didn't mean it would go smoothly or without some backlash. They'd have to seem interested in each other, attend some of his events together and she knew he had plenty. Could she play the role of lover and stay detached from what her heart wanted?

Confused, she wandered restlessly around the family room.

Jelani had cornered her about the break-up with Howie. When she'd told her there had been no choice when he said those three little words she couldn't reciprocate, Jelani said she'd known they didn't have a future from day one. It was a good thing it was over.

She had to agree. He was a great guy but there was no spark between them. It's why she'd stayed in the relationship. It was safe. It just hadn't been fair.

Now?

When the doorbell rang, she glanced at the clock. It was late. Who the hell could be here? Jelani had offered to come over, but she really needed to be alone. To try to figure out how she was going to achieve the impossible. If Jelani was here, she'd have to admit the whole thing was unsettling her. And where it could lead.

At the door, she peeked out to find Jack standing there, his hands in his pockets. This was not what she needed. Her thoughts had been full of him all day, and seeing him here, like this, wasn't going to do her any good.

Taking a deep breath, she opened it. He was still dressed in his suit, and he looked...good.

He studied her for a minute, his eyes taking her in from head to toe, then smiled and asked, "Do you remember the time I came to New Haven for our first date?"

"I do. You were dressed in a suit. I had on jeans."

She opened the door wider, giving him access, and he stepped in.

"You offered to change. I told you, you looked great and not to bother."

"You took off your suit coat, undid your tie, rolled up your sleeves, trying to go for casual."

"And we went to that pizza place you loved."

"And talked until closing."

"You still look great in jeans."

His eyes clung to hers, analyzing her reaction to his compliment.

The ones she had on were worn, the sweater a white cashmere. She always did like mixing old with new.

"What are you doing here?"

"I knew I wouldn't be able to sleep. I thought you might have a hard time as well."

She closed her eyes, needing to regain her equilibrium. He'd taken her back to that first night they were together. It had been an unexpected treasure. Never thinking he'd call, she was surprised when he had. Never thinking it would amount to anything, she was shocked to find she liked him. Nothing had changed.

"Come in. Can I get you a glass of wine?"

He shrugged out of his overcoat, giving her his answer.

Padding into the kitchen, her bare feet making soft falls on the hardwood, she felt his presence behind her. He didn't give her time to get another glass out. Instead, he turned her around to face him, lingered there for a precious moment before leaning in and brushing her lips with his.

The heat was immediate.

His hands threaded through her hair, molding to her head as he pulled her closer, taking the kiss deeper, his tongue mating with hers, and she gave in without hesitation.

Her heart was hammering against her ribs. The love she'd been so careful to withhold came rushing back, making her a prisoner, his prisoner. She'd never be free of him or what she felt.

"I've missed you, Nell. Missed this."

She could feel his uneven breathing against her cheek, felt the tiny kisses on her neck, behind her ear, tingling at his touch. Her arms found their way under his jacket and around his back, pulling him closer, letting him know she felt the same.

His hands roamed her back, down to her bottom, and he snuggled her body against his. She fit as she always had, perfectly. Tilting her head up, she found his lips again, and his mouth crushed hers with a familiar hunger. There was no way she was turning back; no way was she turning this down. She'd never felt this kind of sexual fire with anyone else and she wanted to feed it.

She tugged off his jacket, and let it fall to the floor. Standing mute, she watched him unbutton his shirt, his fingers moving slowly, the anticipation mounting as he moved his way down the column, his eyes never leaving hers. She licked her lips, knowing what lay beneath. He was muscular from his days of playing squash, his body textured with fine hair on rugged skin that felt like heaven against her own. Unable to withstand the torture, she reached out eagerly, drawing the shirt off and letting it fall to their feet. She traced his collar bone with her fingers, the temptation to explore all of him growing more powerful by the second. She guided her hands over the contours of his biceps, down his chest to the waistband of his pants. When she heard his intake of breath, it emboldened her. But he stopped her, his eyes probing to her very soul, and she fell into them as he lifted the hem of her sweater and pulled it over her head in one swift movement. Unclasping her bra, she spilled into his ready hands, the touch of his thumbs on her nipples creating a spiral of need. A tremor quickened through her; a moan slipped through her parted lips.

His let his gaze slide from her extended nubs to her face, and the grey ash of their past smoldered in his eyes. Groaning, he asked, his voice filled with passion, "Do you know how often I've thought about this, about you, us?"

This wasn't real. It wasn't permanent, so there was no need to trust him. She would never place her heart in his hands again, but she could enjoy his body.

"I can't think about that Jack or I'll have to..."

He didn't give her time to finish her thought. His mouth fastened on her breast, suckling, arousing, drawing her in deeply. She gasped as the jolt screamed through her body from nipple to womb, in one hot-white streak of lightning.

Small convulsions began to thrum inside, and she knew she was on the verge of a powerful surge and climax.

She whimpered when his mouth began an assault on her other breast, wanting the torment to end, yet wishing it could go on forever.

He released her, the peaks of her nipples moist and glistening and brought her to the floor. Sliding his hands to her pants, he worked the snap and zipper, freeing her flesh so he could feast on another part of her. Writhing beneath him, her body arched like a bow as she felt the stirrings of orgasm build."

His tongue found her secret spot, flicking gently, leading her to a place where only he could take her and she let herself go, free-falling into ecstasy. The spasms continued, and she tried to squeeze her legs together to get the pulsing to stop. Before she could, he had stripped off his pants and was easing his way in. He must have been able to feel the paroxysms, because he surged forward, her grip on him now secure. She wasn't letting him go. It was a familiar intimacy, pain mixing with pleasure. It didn't take long for him to stiffen, to plunder into her depths, and become fused with her.

They stayed wrapped in each other's arms, savoring the age-old feelings, the close connection they'd shared, once upon a time.

The aroma of fresh-brewed coffee greeted her. He was standing just inside the door, coffee mug in hand. They had made it to the bed at some point and she'd spent the night swathed in his embrace. She had slept soundly, never felt him leave her.

"If I know you as well as I think I do, you're running behind schedule."

She glanced at the clock and jerked up and up of bed.

"I am going to be so late."

She sprinted to the bathroom, grabbing his coffee out of his hand on her way.

"Thanks. I needed this."

"That was mine."

He chuckled as she disappeared from view.

"I made a full pot. I'll just get me a cup. I'll be here when you get out."

He wasn't sure she heard him as the water pounded against the glass shower door.

After returning to the kitchen, he checked his phone, not wanting to contemplate what had happened last tonight. If he thought too hard about it, it might evaporate out of existence.

He found it impossible not to dwell on how she felt in his arms, how sweet her kisses were, and what a fool he'd been to let things go the way they had. He wanted another chance and he was hoping that this thing with Chloe would give him that.

Chloe.

She was an amazing girl. Bright, but with the humility that she must have inherited from her mother. He couldn't wait to get to know her better, show her that she could trust him to have their backs from now on. He knew he was going to have to battle his mother, but it was a battle he was more than willing to wage.

Nell emerged, her hair still slightly damp, shoes in her hand, dressed in a deep purple suit with a black and white silk blouse, tied at the neck.

"You always did know how to dress for success."

"I don't have my clothes made for me like someone I know. I buy off rack. My problem is finding the time to shop."

She drained the last dregs of coffee and went to pour another cup.

"I'm not wasting any of this deliciousness. I don't know why I can't make it this good. Isn't it just dumping coffee into the filter and adding water?"

"Not exactly. You need to measure. For someone so detail-oriented, you'd think you'd know that. What time's your first appointment?"

"I have to be in court in an hour. Jury selection."

"I'm sure you're as ready as anyone could be. What kind of case is it?"

"Rape. Not one of my favorites. What I want to do is pummel the kid, wipe the arrogant smirk off his face. His parents have money, he thinks he was entitled."

They had him dead to right, his DNA a match for the semen left behind. If it wasn't for male bias in cases like this, it wouldn't take long to convict.

"Who's the defense attorney?"

"Parker Lobell. I want to wipe the smirk off his face, as well."

She anticipated the jerk would present the case that the defendant's life would be radically harmed if sentenced.

"I have a feeling you will. In spades."

"If I could use the spade as a shovel, and bury them both, it would work for me."

It wasn't her case. She was going in as part of the team for the selection process. Arianna always asked her to be there, thought she had some kind of intuitive magic that helped empanel the best jury for their client.

Staring at her, he asked, "Have a minute, or do you have to run?"

"I have to run. What time's your first appointment?"

"Early afternoon. I'm going to go back to the apartment and get some stuff packed. I picked up some boxes yesterday after dropping Chloe off at Keileh's. I'm not taking much, so it shouldn't take long."

She was leaning against the counter, examining the cup in her hand.

When she looked up, she wore an expression he didn't recognize.

"You told me that you didn't want to be involved with government. What changed?"

He remembered the exact minute it had all changed for him. He'd gone into the main house to raid his father's library. Lee Adams had hundreds of books collected over the years. Jack was making his way through them, reading the scribbles in the margins more studiously than the texts.

"My father used to write notes to me while he was on the road. He kept it up until the day he died. I'd gone into his library to pick up another book, noticed one on the desk I hadn't seen before. I thought it might be the last one he'd been reading when...he died. His bookmark was a slip of paper filled with his scrawl, thoughts he'd jotted down. I assumed they were for me."

He took a sip of his coffee.

"It was dated late August. The thoughts resonated. I could clearly hear his voice in my head. He said that I'd always be part of the problem if I didn't make a conscious effort to be part of the solution. Those words spurred me to rethink my position and I decided I couldn't complain if I wasn't willing to get in the trenches and fight."

"Wise man."

Jack gave her a sad smile.

"He was."

There was a moment of intimate connection and she felt the heat of his gaze, the tremors that started to pulse through her. She couldn't allow it to continue.

"I've got to get going, climb into my own trench, fight the good fight."

She turned, placed her cup in the sink, hurried to the desk in the family room, picked up her briefcase which was stuffed to overflowing, and headed for the door.

He walked to the parking lot with her, his overcoat over his arm, her winter coat buttoned up, her scarf wound around her neck.

Standing by her car as she clicked the locks open, he asked, "Will I see you again this week or do I have to wait for Friday?"

"Text Chloe. See what she wants to do. I'll be in court for the next couple of days."

"Maybe I can keep her occupied for you."

"I know *she'd* like that. I wouldn't hate it, either."

"Maybe we could cook dinner for you tomorrow night. I'll teach her how to make beef bourguignon."

She was already climbing in behind the wheel of her car. After starting the engine, she said, "That's too good a proposition to pass up. Talk to her. See if she's willing. Gotta go. Bye."

He got out his phone and texted Michael.

I'm on my way in.

>   Appointment here in an hour.

What else?

>   Lunch with members of the business community at Chamber of Commerce, afternoon meeting with a workforce collaborative, and last, regional planning experts to talk about need for affordable housing.

Am I free tonight?

>   Town Hall meeting in Milton at seven. Y?

Fill in block of time from four to seven. I'll be with Chloe.

>   Will do. SUS.

He texted Chloe next to see if she wanted him to pick her up at Keileh's to go grocery shopping, or right before dinner.

Grocery shopping. Are U cooking?

>   I'm passing on one of my ancestral recipes.

Mom OK?

>   I went with her favorite.

OMG It was U who cooked for her.

>   She told U?

Yeah. What time?

Three thirty. I have a meeting tonight so we'll have to eat early.
I'll be ready.

He very rarely used emojis, but he texted back a smiley face.
It matched his own.

CHAPTER TWENTY-THREE

Arriving at the courthouse a bit more unnerved than she liked, Nell couldn't help but smile at the memories last night held.

"Well, look at you. You're almost glowing, and that smile. Did we score an eleven?"

Her head snapped up to see Arianna standing outside the courtroom door with a shit-eating grin on her face.

"What?"

"You haven't look that satisfied...ever. You're even walking different." She made the pretense of studying her. "It's like you're walking on air."

"Arianna, please. What kind of kooky juice did you have with breakfast this morning?"

"I know my children. Anything you want to cop to?"

"Fine. Jack came over last night."

"And? I want to hear about the juicy bits, the part about the glow- stick."

"Oh my God, Arianna. You didn't just compare his penis to a glow stick, did you?"

"If he's an eleven, I think it's a good correlation."

She felt her cheeks pinken. "FYI, it still works quite well."

"I knew it. Are you getting back together?"

"Slow down. We had sex we didn't commit to a future. And I won't any time soon. I still have major trust issues with the man."

"It's a step in the right direction."

"I'm of a differing opinion. I think it's a major step in the wrong direction."

The smile gave away the truth. Nell wasn't sorry at all.

"Come on, I have the list of jury pool. I want to go over it before the judge and Naomi arrive."

Naomi was the co-ed who'd made the mistake of going to a frat party, drinking too much, and being cornered by a friend of the fraternity brothers. One of the them had stepped forward as a witness for the plaintiff and helped set the stage for jail time for the defendant.

"I still can't believe how you got him to cave."

"I have a way about me. You know that."

The two women sat down at the table and began to formulate a strategy for the voir dire, the questioning phase of jury selection.

"Are you going out with lover boy again any time soon?"

"He's going to pick Chloe up and make dinner tonight."

"Light saber, meet glow stick."

"Don't think so. He has a town hall meeting and I am so not doing anything with Chloe around. That would really get her hopes up and getting back together is not on the menu."

"Oh. Why do you keep disappointing me?"

"Because it would be dangerous for me to keep doing this. I like my world to be a safe place."

Gita walked toward them, briskly. She was working second chair for the case, getting her feet wet in her desired field. It was the kind of case she wanted to sink her teeth into. The partners had concentrated their hiring efforts in the direction of women's rights rather than immigration. They didn't want to lose the foothold or reputation they'd built in that area with the increased publicity around their success in detainment and deportation cases.

"Wasn't Molly going to sit in?"

She was another new hire, recently graduated from University of Chicago. With New England roots, she'd come home. The firm had been able to add another potential star to their roster.

"Emilia's mentoring her, and she needs her to second chair the case she's working on."

"How's the thing with Nick going?"

"I wish she'd dump him as a friend. He takes advantage of her feelings."

"He doesn't know her feelings. We do."

"I don't like it and I don't like Saban."

"We're all on that bandwagon but there's nothing we can do about it. It's Em's decision."

She nodded in agreement, a frown on her face. Within minutes she'd brightened up.

"Take off early. Go play. You don't do enough of that."

"We'll see how it goes."

The question lingered far too long for her peace of mind and by the end of the day she'd decided she just might need to borrow that glow stick.

When she got home, she kicked her shoes off, the sounds of happy voices competing with the aromas wafting out for her attention. There was nothing better in her opinion.

They didn't need to tell her where they were, but when Jack called out to her, the sound was so welcoming, she padded in stocking feet into the kitchen.

She stood watching the pair, father and daughter bent over the open oven door, stirring the contents of the pot.

"We could have cooked it longer, but I didn't have the time to devote to it that I usually do. The longer it roasts, the more tender the meat, but I think you'll get the full taste as it is."

Chloe looked up at her, her face pink from the heat, her smile taking up her whole face.

"Dad made it from scratch. Bacon, meat, wine, carrots, onions, garlic, tomato paste, some herbs. And he had me complete every one of the steps. It was totally lit."

Dad.

Nell winced for some reason. The connection seemed to have strengthened in such a short time it was scaring her. Sure, she and Chloe had their own bonding experiences but nothing like this. They shopped, watched movies, ate take-out, or more recently ate what Chloe had heated up for her. She provided transportation, a shoulder to cry on, feminine advice on hygiene and bodily functions, and they talked. About everything. But they'd never participated in a collaborative effort like this. From start to finish. Were her fears going to be realized? Would Chloe prefer his company to hers? And if so, what was she going to do about it?

Jack had the bottle of wine raised as if in salute. "I picked up a nice red burgundy. Want a glass?"

She felt her temper rising. With a dose of petulance. This was ridiculous. She wouldn't lose Chloe's love. She had to relax, be happy with the fact that Chloe was experiencing something she'd looked forward to for years.

Forcing a smile on her face, she said, "Yes, please. I'm going to change. Can I have it to go?"

He poured a generous splash into the wineglass and handed it over.

She sipped at it as she changed into more casual attire, letting the smooth fruity taste mellow her mood. She was okay. Chloe was okay. The dynamics might have changed but their relationship was solid. She couldn't worry about the rest.

The meal was delicious, just as she remembered but it felt surreal. She was sitting across from Jack, like she had once before. She was itching for a touch, a taste, something she was still trying to resist. The operative word being trying. Chloe's chatter was a welcome distraction.

"Can we do this again?"

"Sure. I'm moving into my new place on Saturday. Maybe you and your mom can come over for dinner, help me figure out what to do with it."

"Can I help you cook?"

"Of course. Do you have any favorites we could learn together?"

"How about beef stroganoff?"

"That's one of your favorites?"

"I don't know. I've never had it, but the recipe is in one of the cookbooks you bought me."

"Let me take a look at the ingredients and I'll pick them up. I've never made it, so it'll be a first for me, too."

"Cool."

When Jack announced he had to leave for the meeting, he got a big hug and kiss from Chloe, before she asked, "We'll see you Friday, right?"

"You will. Anything I need to bring?"

"No, we have it covered."

Nell glanced up and added, "Bring your sweet tooth. This girl loves her sugar."

"That I can do."

His eyes held hers, a sensual gleam in them.

"I wish I didn't have to go."

She wished he didn't, too.

But when he came back and rapped at the door close to midnight, she let him in. All her promises about not inviting trouble with Chloe in the house going up in flames.

Jack snuck out of Nell's early so Chloe didn't find them together.

After returning to the condo he'd be leaving soon, he was unable to fall back to sleep. Not without her in his arms. Or in this bed. They'd spent months making love here. It's where Chloe was conceived. Where it all went wrong. Having known that kind of love, it was hard to be satisfied with anything less. He'd never found the sweet spot he'd had with her.

He couldn't wait to move out hoping it would be a new beginning. For all of them.

Sitting up against the headboard, he thought back to the first time they'd made love.

She'd come up to Boston, close to six months into their relationship, willing to stay over. He'd taken her to a hip burger place where they'd sipped local brewed beer and munched sweet potato fries while solving the world's problems. She'd excited him, imbued her passion into every topic they covered. It hadn't ended over dinner. They'd toppled into this bed when they got home, and together they'd found a tempo that bound their bodies together. The first coupling was like nothing he'd ever experienced. Her fire had ignited his soul. It still did.

It shouldn't have surprised him that they'd created a tangible expression of their love.

How had he turned his back on it?

Throwing off the covers, now aggravated with himself all over again, he climbed out of bed and got ready for his day, plans for what lay ahead rippling in his heart. He desperately needed her touch, her kiss, her heat. And he was prepared to do anything to get them back.

He dressed carefully, knowing she'd be at his Randolph office. Taking the day off tomorrow, to be with Chloe and Keileh, Nell had re-arranged her schedule, putting his constituents on the agenda for today instead. He was making a stop at his attorney's office before-hand, to sign the papers on the condo in Charlestown. He wanted that done so that he could concentrate his time tomorrow on packing. He didn't want to be late for movie night. He had so little time left with them. His congressional recess would end on Sunday at midnight and he'd have to be back in the capitol for the opening of the new Congress bright and early Monday morning. He'd be gone for a full week, which didn't happen often. Gone were the days when the members of Congress stayed in Washington. Now, all work was conducted between Tuesday and Thursday, giving the representatives time in their districts. Not so much for constituent work as fundraising. He skipped that part of the drill. He liked getting into the thick of local issues, loved talking to people about what he could do to improve their lives. Like his father in that, he'd rather spend time in a think tank than at a dress-up event.

Taking a few boxes into his bedroom, he placed them on the bed. Before he could get more than a few cursory things packed away, the doorbell rang.

Cursing under his breath, he had a feeling he knew who was at his door. He'd given Michael a few days off before the flurry of activity started in earnest, and no one else would need to stop by.

He opened it up to his mother who was standing on the front stoop. He probably should have given her a head's-up about the move, but he didn't want to ford that stream until he got to it. It seemed as if it was time to wade in. When she gave him one of her imperious looks, he became more resolved.

"I think there's some things we need to discuss." There was a tinge of a whine in her voice.

Without even waiting for an invitation, Eloise invaded his home, seeing herself into the living room and taking a seat.

He shook his head, and followed her, knowing it was now or never to begin the siege.

"I had some things to do before I came over. I was going to tell you I'm moving out."

"What do you mean moving out? I was hoping you've seen how egregious it would be to my sensibilities."

"I'm closing on a place this morning. I'll be packing up some things and moving on Saturday."

Fear, stark and vivid, shone in her eyes.

"Jack, you can't do this. I've come to depend on you being close at hand."

"Too much so, I'm afraid. I've enabled you to use me for your own selfish purposes and it's going to stop. This weekend."

"How can you say that?"

"Quite easily. Men my age are married, with families, not still living next door to their mother. You brought me up to be independent, to think for myself. Since Dad died, you've done nothing to encourage that."

"I would have been lost without you."

"No, you would have learned to take care of yourself. You're intelligent, resourceful, and financially solvent. You would have been fine."

"This has to do with Nell, doesn't it?"

"It has more to do with Chloe. I want to be able to invite her over for dinner, to have her stay over some nights. I know it won't happen if I'm living here. Besides, I will not have her involved in any of your manipulations. That stunt you pulled last Friday night finalized the decision for me."

"What stunt? I don't know what you're talking about."

Her expression became petulant.

"I broke it off with Hope, as you probably well know, and I won't have you moving around your chess pieces to affect a different outcome."

"I don't see why. The two of you are perfect for each other."

"For you maybe. Not for me. I've been willing to give up some of my freedom to attend to you, but I will not give up my choice of life partner."

"You can't be speaking of Nell again, can you?"

"Nell wouldn't trust me to tie her shoe. We've both seen to that."

"Well, that's a relief. I was so worried..."

He was angry. That was a new feeling. Usually he only felt sympathy for her. He tamped it down.

"No need. Is that all you wanted to discuss?"

He took a step toward the door, his subtle hint that she leave, falling on deaf ears. She stayed seated, tears collecting in her eyes, her look one of capitulation.

"I feel like I'm losing you. You're all I have."

Coming back to where she sat, her look one of pure desolation, he took a seat opposite, and grasped her hand. With more patience than he felt, he reminded her, "No, Mom. I'm not. You have your sister, your friends, a full life and the money to fulfill every desire."

She squeezed his hand, looked out into the distance, as if in a trance, and told him something she'd never confided before.

"I felt cheated when your father died. We won't get to grow old together." Her eyes came back to meet his. "I still miss him Jack and you are the only one who can take away the loneliness of life without him."

"Do you know what kind of a burden that is, Mom? It gets heavier every year. I'm not your husband. I'm your son and you've got to let me live my life."

He'd used the same words as Nell had the other day. As soon as he'd said them, he understood what Nell had been trying to say.

"I just want what's best for you and to see you happy."

"I'm beginning to think you want what's best for you and it's suffocating. Nell is the mother of my daughter. She was the woman I loved but you made the situation difficult for both of us. Does that really sound like someone who wants my happiness?"

She looked as if he'd struck her. Her face was mottled, her eyes boring into him.

"Nell was as much a part of the problem as I was. She wasn't willing to defer to you in anything. She was driven, and she refused to take a back seat to your future."

He got up and began to pace, trying to rein in his irritation. His mother wasn't hearing what he was trying to say. Raising his voice, the exercise in patience not working, he said, "I'd yet to decide on a future. I shared my doubts about Congress with her and she was not willing to push me into something I didn't want. It didn't help that you were. It made her think you had too much control over my life."

"If she couldn't see what was best for you—"

"She thought I might be able to figure that out all by myself. Novel concept, don't you think?"

"Your father wanted this for you."

"He did. And I wish he'd been there for me to talk to. But it was his death and the government's mishandling of the attack that made me rethink it."

"He asked you to take care of me, Jack. Have you forgotten that?"

"I will always do my duty to you Mom. But I think we both forgot he also told me to be happy and to live the life I wanted. That life includes Chloe. I've met her. She knows I'm her father. And I couldn't be happier."

Startled, she raised her hands to cup her face.

"When did this happen?"

"Last Sunday."

"I didn't know you were talking to Nell about it. What are you going to tell everyone? This will hurt your career."

"If it hurts my career, then I'll find a new one."

"You're being impulsive."

"I've been asking Nell if I could meet Chloe since she was six. I'd hardly call that impulsive."

She got up, and began to pace, her fingers clasped tightly together.

"Why didn't you tell me?"

"Because I knew you would try to fight me on it. I'm not going to let anyone keep me from knowing my daughter. If you don't want to meet her, that's your loss."

She was flustered and took a step toward the vestibule.

"We can discuss this further tomorrow night, at dinner."

Thrusting his hands in his pockets, he said, "I'm sorry but I won't be attending any more Friday night dinners. We'll have to pick another day, maybe Sunday brunch. I can arrange my schedule around that."

"This is all happening too fast, Jack. You can't change our whole life in one week."

"Our lives changed in a second when Dad's plane hit the Pentagon. So yes, we can."

She was wringing her hands again and her brow was furrowed as if in deep thought.

What was she planning now?

"Invite Chloe for brunch on Sunday. Dress as usual. I can have Mags make eggs benedict, or asparagus and swiss quiche."

"I'm not ready to introduce you two yet. I don't want your feelings about Nell to rub off on Chloe. You could never keep your opinions to yourself. Nell's her mother and I won't have her slandered. She's done a great job raising our daughter. Alone, thanks, in part, to you."

She stared, long and hard, a myriad of expressions crossing her face.

"If I'm willing to accept this granddaughter and behave accordingly, can I meet her?"

"In time. I need to build a foundation with her first. She doesn't trust me any more than her mother does."

"Has Nell poisoned her mind against you, us?"

The caustic tone was back.

"No, Mom. I did that all by myself when I walked away from them. It's not going to happen again. I love her every bit as much as you love me. Maybe more. All I want is for her to be happy."

Heaving a sigh, she accepted defeat.

"You'll come on Sunday?"

"I will. Is eleven o'clock acceptable?"

"It is."

She came to where he stood and hugged him.

"I do love you, son. And if Chloe is the way I can keep you in my life, and if a relationship with her makes you happy, then I want to meet her. And I promise I won't say one bad word about her mother."

"I'm still going to take my time with this. I can't afford to make another mistake."

Eloise nodded and turned to leave.

He dropped down on the couch when he heard the front door click shut.

That had gone better than he'd expected. It was as if he'd finally gotten through to her. He just wished it wasn't eleven years overdue.

As he entered the field site, he saw Nell standing at the door to his office talking to Terry, the volunteer who manned this location. The dress Nell wore was more her style than the power suits she'd been wearing. This was the Nell he remembered, feminine, the muted colors of lavender and ivory with a jacket and heels to match, her hair down, softening her features, the bracelet he'd given her adorning her wrist.

When she turned, her eyes burned right through him, the honey color dark like nectar. It took him a couple of minutes to get his brain to work before he could offer a greeting.

"Good morning."

She returned the smile, never taking her eyes from his.

He held up his key ring. "I am the proud new owner of a condo. Signed, sealed and delivered."

"Congratulations. May you be very happy there."

He didn't want to be happy there unless she was there with him but that would have to wait for a more propitious time to tell her.

"You still planning on coming over on Saturday?"

"It's all Chloe talks about. With you so willing to share your kitchen, I'm afraid she's going to want to move in."

He couldn't tell if she was joking or there was fear lurking in her eyes.

Chloe popped out of the small room to his left, Keileh right behind her.

"I'd never leave you, Mom. You're stuck with me."

There was a small bell above the door that tinkled, announcing a visitor. He turned to see a small woman, her hands clasped tightly together, walking slowly toward the reception desk.

"I'm here to see Attorney Nell Warren."

Nell came forward and grasped her hand.

"Hello. You must be Martine. Please call me Nell."

"Thank you for seeing me."

"It's my pleasure. Come into the office and we can go over what kind of representation you need."

Chloe was watching the exchange when she said, "Hi...Jack."

He re-assured her. "Everyone knows, Chloe. This is our safe space."

"Even when there are other people here?"

Her eyes were on the woman who'd just arrived.

"I don't think anyone in need of your mother's services is going to concern themselves with my bio. I fade into the woodwork when she's here."

"Don't we all?"

He looked at her in a thoughtful way before asking, "Does that bother you? I know she didn't like feeling invisible when she was younger. She wouldn't like it if you felt that way."

"She never makes me feel that way. I'm front and center in her world even if she gives most of her time to others. I sometimes envy her, though. She kind of blows people away."

Keileh standing right beside Chloe, laughed. "And you're just like her. You just don't realize it. Everyone's in your shadow when you're around."

Putting her hands on her hips, a frown on her face, Chloe looked at her friend.

"That's not true. I am so not a spotlight seeker."

Curious, Jack asked, "You think your mother is?"

Chloe shook her head, the frown deepening.

"No. She just can't help drawing it to her."

Keileh piped up, "Neither can you, Ms. Eleanor Roosevelt."

"Hey, I didn't know it would be the best part. My mom thinks she's GOAT. After learning about her, I do too."

There was a trace of laughter in his voice when he asked, "Would you guys want to go to a music festival tonight? I have to make an appearance but maybe we can grab something to eat before or after."

Chloe looked over at him, hesitated before saying, "You better run that by Mom. I don't know what kind of plans she has."

She checked in with Keileh who gave a slight nod, and said, "It's okay by us."

"Will do."

He picked up the newspaper and sat in the outer area waiting for Nell to finish up with her client.

CHAPTER TWENTY-FOUR

Nell was relieved.

Martine Del Gallego was from the Philippines, had come into the country through a sponsorship by her brother, but her visa was about to expire. This would be an easy fix. After filling out the appropriate paperwork, she explained the process and sent her on her way. The appointment hadn't even taken an hour. It was much easier when the applicant didn't try to circumvent the law, sought counsel before the deadline and was willing to follow the protocol set by Immigration Services. The odds were good that Martine would be able to extend her stay, giving herself time to apply for naturalization. To be sent back would mean another long waiting game to re-enter the country, there being a twenty-year backlog.

She fingered the bag she'd brought in with her. She'd meant to eat what was inside for breakfast but she'd yet to touch it. Taking her muffin out, Nell set it on the flattened bag and pinched some of the blueberry goodness and popped it into her mouth. It was luscious and filling, just as her taste buds had anticipated.

When Jack stuck his head in, she felt tiny pinpricks of pleasure.

"How'd it go?"

"Better than most. What are you still doing here? Don't you have a veteran's lunch?"

"I forgot you know my schedule better than I do." His eyes lit up when he asked, "Is that a Perfect Taste muffin?"

She laughed, pinched another portion and licked it off her finger.

"Both figuratively and literally."

"Next time you go, can you pick something up for me? I'll reimburse. The cost will hurt less than staring and salivating at yours."

"I'm sorry. I didn't even think—"

"Don't. It's just a request. Not a guilt trip."

"Registered."

"I wanted to know if you and the girls want to come with me tonight. I'm doing an interview with the public broadcasting network. They have a Celtic group performing that I thought you might enjoy. We can stay in the mood by eating at the Irish Pub we used to go to."

"Is this all part of giving Chloe shade?"

"If you need it to be. For my part, I like your company. Chloe's, too."

"Sure. We don't have any other plans. But you go right home afterwards. I already broke rule number one. I'm not breaking another."

"Okay. Suit yourself. You'll be sorry though. Rules are meant to be broken."

He leaned in across the desk, sliding her hair behind her ear, caressing it like a kiss in the process. The heat was palpable and she felt her blood rush through her system like a river on fire. Her eyes closed, the sensation nothing short of heart-stopping.

Indulging herself in his touch, she was caught unawares as he broke the muffin in half and popped it into his mouth.

"Hey, that's mine."

"I love it when you pout. You're so damn cute. You should have eaten it then, and not left it out as a temptation."

She grabbed the other half before he could steal the rest. He stepped through the doorway, chuckling.

"I'll pick you up around six."

"Dress up?"

"No ripped jeans but anything else is fine."

She stared at the open doorway.

She could tell he was gone. The electricity in the air had amped down.

She pinched another piece of the muffin, placed it on her tongue, smiling at the way he'd stolen part of it. It was as if they were back together, the connection an intimate one where they shared everything. Tonight, would be a replica of what they'd done when they were dating. Music festivals, foreign movies, museums, gospel concerts. All spur-of-the-moment, based on how much homework they had, when her shift at the restaurant would end. They'd had to steal time for each other. His mother intruding in his life, work intruding on her hers. Her grandmother had paid all her tuition bills, lodging expenses but everything else had fallen to her: books, meals, clothes, car. She'd worked as a waitress for the first few years, taking the busiest shifts, which meant Fridays and Saturdays weren't her own. It was an upscale restaurant and the tips were good, but the patrons took pleasure in their food and drink and stayed until closing. If he was waiting when she got home, the exhaustion melted away, and she lost herself in the fire of his love. It was good back then. And she'd thought it would last forever. So sure, she'd begun to make mental changes to her plans, researching other colleges in the area that could provide her a law degree. Her mother had assured her that her grandmother had left the funds for her tuition and it didn't matter to them where she went. Nothing mattered to her parents as long as she was out of the way.

It didn't take much longer than that to realize his mother didn't want her around, either.

Nothing she did was good enough. She worked too many hours, she earned too little, she dressed too artsy, thought too liberally, didn't cook, and couldn't manage a household and as the weeks wore on, she'd stopped trying to win Eloise over. Working more had become her solution. It had given his mother the opportunity to fill those empty hours, using every took in her toolbox to get him to drive her everywhere, meet a variety of people. She could tell he enjoyed it by the stories he told, and it had probably given him a strong foothold to base his future campaign on. Looking back, it was time well spent. It might have been good for his career, but at the time it was destroying their relationship.

She tried talking him into moving but he refused.

"I don't want you supporting me."

"You let your mother."

"It's different."

"How?"

"It's family money."

"So, my money's mine? That implies you don't consider me family."

"That's not what it implies."

"Then explain the difference."

His voice had risen an octave and he'd yelled in frustration, "I can't."

And she couldn't live with things as they were. He was talking to his mother more than with her, he was cancelling plans, going to parties, staying away from home, all while telling her it wasn't what he wanted.

She'd been so confused.

The last straw had been the night she'd left. Wanting to tell him about the pregnancy, needing to know how he felt about it, she'd picked up a nice dinner, set the atmosphere for an intimate evening. When he'd gotten called away, when her requests for him to stay with her had fallen on deaf ears, she'd known she had to go away. She wouldn't continue to compete for his affections. She'd done that once before and it only made her feel more invisible, less confident.

Now?

She'd forgotten how good it could be when he was present. In tune. His mind was as facile as ever, his work inspiring, his integrity more pronounced. Until she knew he was his own man, who could stand on his own two feet, and he could include her in his family circle with full rights and privileges, she couldn't give in to the deep-seated desire he evoked.

And even then, she wasn't sure she wanted to spend the rest of her life pitted against a rival who wouldn't give up the fight.

⌒

Eloise Adams walked into the dimly lit restaurant, the rich mahogany panels creating a warm ambience. It was one of her favorites, and she came for lunch more often than dinner but she didn't want to waste another day without talking to her sister. When she'd left Jack's, she was numb. He was no longer threatening to move; he was doing it. What was she going to do without him next door? What was she going to do if she'd driven him away?

The day he'd come home with the news of Lee's death, she cried like a baby in his arms. He'd stepped in to fill the void and the empty space at the head of their table. He'd helped her meet the challenges of living alone. Now?

She didn't know if she could live through another loss.

Her sister was the only one who could help her. Jane had been there for her in the aftermath of the tragedy, helped her plan the funeral, insisted she clean out Lee's closet. She'd sat with her nights that Jack was gone, when he visited New Haven and the girl who had drawn him like a bee to honey. She'd resented Nell then, and she resented her now.

The maître-d' walked over to her and smiled.

"Mrs. McKendrick is already waiting for you, ma'am. Please, follow me."

Eloise weaved through the tables covered with fine white linen tablecloths, sterling silverware and china dinnerware. It had elegance and an old-world charm. Her sister would never have chosen this for herself. Jane was more modern, less resistant to a change of status. Married to the owner of an insurance firm, she was well-off but without any pretentiousness.

Her chair was pulled out for her and she descended into it gracefully.

"Good evening, Jane."

"Hello, El. It's good to see you although I don't know why it was so important to meet tonight."

"Did you have other plans? I'm sorry I pulled you away from Richard."

"Richard's fine. He had his poker game tonight. I was hoping for some quiet reading time but... you sounded depressed."

The waiter came over and asked, "Would you like a drink before ordering, Mrs. Adams?"

"Yes, a glass of burgundy please. The house brand is fine."

"I'll bring it right over."

She waited until the wine goblet was placed back to the left above the knife before giving her sister the reason for the call.

"I needed to talk to someone, and you seemed the most logical. You've been telling me for years to let go of my dependence on Jack and it seems now I'll have to. I'm not sure I'm ready."

"Of course, you're ready, El. He's a grown man, and one to be proud of. It's time you released him from being your caretaker."

"I am proud of him. And I did everything in my power to get him there."

Jane arched her eyebrow at her, like she did when they were children. Seven years older, Jane took on the role of mother at times and the gesture brought back memories.

"This isn't about you, Eloise. So please don't try to make it so."

Her embarrassment showed. Crowing was in bad taste. The intention to insinuate herself into her son's life made it necessary to point out how much he needed her.

After taking a gulp of the wine, Eloise winced.

"He's met his daughter."

Jane leaned forward, placing her hand on her sister's arm.

"Oh, that's wonderful. Her name is Chloe? Right?"

Unaware that she was taking another swipe at Nell, she whined, "How could Nell have named her that? It's kind of...well, it's Bohemian. There were so many more traditional names from history to choose."

Taking back her hand, Jane shook her head.

"I think it's lovely. Different. A breath of fresh air. I wasn't exactly fond of the name Amanda picked out for my granddaughter, but we have to keep with the times."

"What you're saying is that you like the name Maisie Imogen?"

"It suits her."

"Maybe I'm just stuck in the past."

"I don't have to say it. We both know you are."

"What am I going to do?"

"What you would have done when you were younger. Before your husband died. You were never this much of a clinger. You gave Lee a run for his money when you were dating. I never imagined you could change so much." A shadow of annoyance hovered in Jane's eyes and her tone was almost snippy. It made her feel like a chastised child.

"Becoming a widow changes everything."

"Not for everyone, El. I know plenty of people who have gone through it and transitioned just fine. The memories will always be there, and some of the pain, but it happened a long time ago and you should have passed that threshold by now."

"You'll never know what that did to me."

"I do know. I was there. You leaned on me as heavily as you did on Jack. I was just smart enough to step away."

"Are you saying I'm a burden to my son?"

"Yes. You are. I think it's time you give him some breathing room. What you want from him isn't healthy."

"If I do, he might end up marrying that...that woman."

"That woman is accomplished, intelligent, and poised. You knew her grandmother. Wasn't she one of Mother's friends once upon a long time ago?"

"It doesn't mean they're right for each other."

"Eloise, what is the real underlying reason you won't accept her?"

"I've already told you."

"And I think it's more than what you've implied."

"You don't know anything..."

"I know when Lee died, you dug a hole and dragged Jack in it right alongside you. You didn't think you could survive another loss. And I couldn't blame you. Then."

Eloise had miscarried several times before she finally had Jack. One in her last trimester. It had taken a toll on her. She'd managed to submerge it while Lee was alive but once he was gone, she'd put all her attention into the one left to her.

She felt her eyes fill with tears. Not the crocodile ones she used on occasion to guilt Jack into doing what she wanted.

"I loved Lee so much."

"I know you did, Eloise. And no one was sorrier about his death than me. Did you ever think that maybe that's the kind of love Jack felt for Nell? You took that away from him. Just like the terrorists took Lee away from you."

It was such a scandalous suggestion Eloise sucked in a breath.

"Don't be ridiculous."

The waiter came over before Jane could say any more.

"Are you ready to order?"

"Yes. I'll have the sea bass. Jane?"

"I'll have the filet mignon please, medium."

"No appetizers for you tonight?"

"No, thank you. But another glass of burgundy would be lovely and another of what my sister is having served with dinner."

"As you wish."

He discreetly left them alone to continue their conversation.

Jane said what she'd said before, but it had always fallen short of its mark.

"I always got the sense he was crazy about her."

"He thought so."

"And who the hell are you, Eloise to tell him what he felt?"

"I know what's good for him."

"And you being primary female in his life is on that list?"

"There was Hope."

"Hope couldn't have kept up with him. She has the mental agility of a carp."

Eloise knew her sister was right, but Hope was safe. As if trying to convince Jane of something she'd been unable to convince herself, she said, "He just needed a woman at his side."

"You certainly don't know your son all that well if you think that would have satisfied him."

Eloise swallowed hard. Through gritted teeth, she managed to say, "Nell would have taken him away from me. And he would have followed anywhere she went. Blindly. I would have been left alone, with no one."

"If you hadn't chased her away, you might have had another chance at a family. No one would have replaced Lee, but there was the opportunity for you to fill the void. Your granddaughter could have given you a new lease on life, Eloise. Instead you shut them all out."

Jane was right, and she wondered if it wasn't already too late to rewrite the script.

"I'm scared Jane. Jack won't even let me meet Chloe. He says he doesn't trust me not to hurt her."

"He's just going on your track record. You chased away the woman he loved. Why wouldn't you do the same to his daughter?"

"Because she's his daughter."

"Nell's daughter, too."

Once the meal arrived, Eloise sat in silence, eating in small bites, her stomach unsettled. Her sister was right, of course. It's what she'd needed to hear. She'd made all the wrong choices, afraid that Jack would leave her. Involved him in her financial decisions, her board meetings, dragging him with her to all her events, insisting on dinners. All a husband's duty. Not a son's. She had to face the fact that she'd robbed him of something precious. And begin to make amends. If that meant finding common ground with Nell, then she'd best get to it. Her best chance of that was through Chloe. And if she were honest, she was dying to meet her.

CHAPTER TWENTY-FIVE

When he rang the bell on Friday, Jack was carrying a pizza box. One Nell recognized. It was from her favorite pizza place and when she let him in, she was already salivating.

"I know you said not to bring anything but if Chloe gets her sugar fix, I thought it only fair you get a fix as well."

Grabbing the box out of his hands, she opened the lid, inhaled the aroma and lifted a slice out. It was half-eaten by the time she got it to the kitchen.

Chloe was staring at them.

"Can you remind me why you two broke up? You're like kids when you're together." Giving Jack a glance, she shrugged. "I don't know about you, but Mom sure smiles more."

"We *were* kids when we were together before. Seems we've taken a time machine back. We loved going to the movies. And we always got pizza before the show."

"Why doesn't that surprise me? What else did you guys do for fun?"

"Your mom worked most weekends, so I didn't get to see her until after her shifts. I'd hang out with her roommate, Noreen, or her boyfriend until she got back. She usually wanted to study when she got home but sometimes, I could convince her to go out."

"She doesn't play much."

As Nell listened, she had to admit Jack was the only one, besides Chloe, who could get her out into the world, get her to put aside her work or study.

He was doing it again and she was letting him. She hadn't realized how much she'd missed it.

Chloe poured the bags of candy into a bowl, mixing them up so she'd have a variety of choices, and carried it into the family room. Nell got a plate and filled it with the pizza and followed her in, taking a seat on the couch. She placed her wine on the end table and asked, "So what are we watching tonight?"

Chloe picked up the remote and kept flicking until she came to the movie of choice.

It was about friends of a bride who wanted to break up the wedding couple before the vows. True love was waiting around the corner for one of them.

Her pizza was half-way to her mouth when Nell paused to ask, "Why this one?"

"I don't know. I thought it looked interesting."

Announcing to Jack, who'd taken a seat next to Chloe, she said, "She's queen of the rom-com. Doesn't like thrillers or anything scary."

"I like happy endings. What's so bad about that?"

"Nothing, baby, but sometimes life doesn't co-operate like you want it to."

"Just eat your pizza, Mom."

"This is my happy ending."

The threesome quieted down. The action began right away without music or a montage of what was to come. It didn't mean that there wasn't some talking during the feature, but Chloe kept it all to a minimum, entranced with the action.

When she clasped her hands together as the credits disappeared into a corner of the screen, Nell smiled.

"You liked it."

Almost mooning, Chloe replied, "Yeah."

"What did you like best?"

"The guy got the girl."

Jack popped a handful of jellybeans into his mouth. After he was finished chewing, he disagreed with Chloe's assessment.

"I'd say the *girl* got the *guy*. Feminism at its finest."

"Kick-ass women. Just like Mom and her peeps."

Nell shook her head, off-kilter with the way Jack was smiling. This kind of togetherness could be addictive.

Jack picked up Chloe the next morning so Nell could put the finishing touches on her opening statement for the trial set to begin on the following Tuesday. She had given her input on Arianna's rape trial and her duties there were done. Now she was moving on to a case of her own. She promised Chloe they'd go to First Night together and she wanted nothing on her mind except her daughter.

Jelani was there when she arrived, and she poked her head in into her friend's office before heading to her own.

"What are you doing here? No late, date night?"

"No. I'm swearing off men after Micky completely embarrassed me on Christmas. He might have great abs, but he also has too big an ego."

"Does it have anything to do with Alec?"

"Hah. No. He's another walking gallon of testosterone."

"You seemed...shall we say interested."

"He's a jerk and he's sent in his resume for a job as supervisor of special agents for Homeland. I don't go out with people like that. He has to have a heart of ice."

"Is that what you were sparring about?"

"I just gave him my opinion on ICE agents."

"He doesn't have the job yet."

"Doesn't matter. He applied. 'Nuff said."

Nell laughed at the absurdity. Jelani didn't usually care about what a man did for a living if he was buff, scruffy, and built. Alec was all three.

"Who are you and where did you put my friend?"

"I'm getting a bit more discerning. Okay?"

"Okay. I'm going. I only have a couple of hours until I'm expected for dinner."

"Where?"

"Jack's new place. He's helping Chloe cook beef stroganoff."

"She finally has a teacher. She'll love that."

She felt a slight frown curl her lips.

"You are pouting. I've never seen you do that."

More serious than she meant, Nell asked, "Chloe and I are solid, aren't we?"

"Of course. You don't even need to ask."

"I...don't do stuff like that with her. I don't really do anything with her."

Jelani got up and walked to the other side of her desk and leaned back against it, her arms folded across her chest.

"I didn't know your memory was failing. Either you don't remember all the things you've done with that girl or else you don't think they rate. Friday nights, sleep-overs, shopping sprees, tourist attractions, book discussions are what you give her."

"Do I give her enough of my time?"

"You give her every single second you're not working. More time than you give yourself."

"I'm afraid, Jelani. I'm afraid she'll want to be with him. He's fun, has a great sense of humor, loves sports, cooking, reading. All the things that she loves."

"You've given her security. She knows she can count on you no matter what. That's not something to be scoffed at."

"I guess."

She turned to leave, the heaviness settling in around her heart.

Work took her mind off her fears, as it always did, and she finished the draft she'd use for her opening statement. Camille had handed it over to her, and once she read the brief, there was no turning back. Hanley Castro, three years old, and his mother Renata had been detained in a state out west, their case languishing in the court system for over a year. Fleeing certain death in Honduras after the surge a few years ago, the Castro's were caught up in the controversial policy of jailing asylum-seeking mothers. By becoming Hanley's court appointed advocate, Nell intended to get a green card for both mother and son. Instead of transferring the small family to a secure and licensed facility, as required by law, they were transferred to Boston. She couldn't wait to get them out of prison, seeing no significant advantage of any child inhumanely detained for so much of his young life.

These were the types of cases she lived for.

Justice, with a little bit of sanity, thrown in.

She finished right about the time she had to leave for Charlestown.

⌒

Father and daughter stood outside Jack's condo, Chloe fiddling with her hands, signaling her excitement. As he turned the key and opened the door, inviting her in, he assured, "We've got to get right to it. Your mom's going to be here in a little while."

When he flipped the light switch, the place was illuminated by the cans overhead. He looked around and smiled. This was home. His mother's apartment had never given him this kind of contentment. It was a collection of antiques, discards, all tasteful but all Eloise's. There had been nothing of him inside the walls. When Nell had asked him to move out, he'd declined. Not only with words but his actions had spoken loud and clear. He hadn't been willing to budge. He should have made a home with her. Maybe she would have stayed.

Chloe seemed impatient and grumbled, "Let's go in already."

She was looking around. There was no entryway, so she was already standing in the family room.

"This is a nice place. What made you pick this one?"

"It felt like home."

"That sounds like something Mom would say."

Jack laughed.

"Kind of girlie, right?"

"Not really. Is this like the kind of house you grew up in?"

"God no. That's more like an updated mausoleum. I felt comfortable here. I liked its personality."

He hefted the bag in his arms and walked toward the kitchen.

"While I was looking at places, the one thing I noticed as soon as I walked in was how it felt. I never really thought about that before, that there are different styles, different types. The apartment I lived in didn't tell my story, it told my mother's. I had no investment in it. This one, I want to make mine."

He placed the newly purchased recycled bags on the counter. Chloe had been aghast that he was going to have the clerk pack the food in plastic.

"I'm hoping you'll come to feel comfortable here. I want you to feel like it's home. Well, a second home anyway."

Her hands were running over the granite counters.

"This has great work prep space. I like it."

He smiled at her. He thought so, too. It was one of the reasons he'd bought the unit. And the thought of Chloe cooking with him made it even more important.

"This is all new. If you have any suggestions as to where to put things, I'm open to them."

He pulled out the package of sirloin, butter, sour cream, parsley, and mushrooms and placed them in the nearly empty refrigerator. He'd picked up some essentials this morning, like coffee, milk, half and half, juice, and eggs but they looked almost lost in the cavernous space. With the bag of flour, noodles, bottle of olive oil and beef broth in his hands, he did a 360-degree turn.

"Where do you think these should go?"

"Pantry."

"What?"

Chloe pulled the knob of the large closet across from the counter.

"This is called a pantry. It's where you store food or dishes. But you have so many cupboards you'll never run out of room. Let me have them."

She placed the dry goods and oil on different shelves, added the beef broth and ketchup. Then she opened a few of the cabinets, trying to figure out what should go where. Satisfied she'd picked the most efficient one, she deposited the salt and pepper on one of the shelves.

"Garlic can't be refrigerated and shouldn't be closed up. You'll have to get one of those hanging baskets or a bin to keep in it.

"I know. I used to leave it on the counter in my old place in a plastic container. Without the lid on, of course."

"There's so much more you have to get. Do you have dishes for eating?"

"I took some from the apartment I was living in I'm planning on buying new ones, but they'll have to do for now."

He hoped they didn't turn Nell off. She was a master of detail and he knew she'd recognize them.

Once everything was put away, Jack asked, "Want to see the rest of the place?"

"I'd love to."

They walked down the short hall to his bedroom, the walk-in closet and full bath, another perk in such tight quarters.

"I haven't exactly unpacked yet. Sorry about the mess."

There was a box of books and an open suitcase lying on the floor in the closet.

She glanced around and nodded. "Nice."

"Your bedroom will be downstairs. Come on, let me show you."

She followed him into an open area where a daybed was pushed against a wall. A bureau lined another. The window made it feel airy even though it was below ground.

"You can do anything you want to it."

"You won't be here often, will you?"

"Just weekends."

"And you'll be at our house on Friday nights?"

"If I get invited."

"Then I don't see when I'd stay but I like that you asked. What do you say we get going?"

"After you."

They busied themselves, following the directions of the cookbook Chloe had brought along.

Once the meat was sliced, Jack let Chloe brown it in the hot oil, making sure she didn't get too close to the flame. After taking it out of the pan, she sautéed the onions, mushrooms, and garlic, then deglazed it with the broth and wine.

She set her eyes on him and asked, "Do you have any music? Mom and I usually fight over the station when we're doing stuff, but I'd be willing to listen to whatever you like."

"I don't. My iPod is all I use but I never got a dock for it."

She pulled out her iPhone.

"What kind do you like?"

"I don't know. I don't listen much. Soft rock, I guess. Your mom used to love the eighties. Prince, Jackson, Bon Jovi, Fleetwood Mac. Has her taste matured?"

"Nope. That's still who calls to her."

She had the music programmed and playing before he could ask how she did it.

Prince's guitars pierced the air and she began to move to the beat. It was so reminiscent of Nell he could do nothing but laugh.

"You, acorn, didn't fall too far from the tree."

She chopped at the parsley, her knife matching the tempo of the music. He was watching, her movements precise. Should he be letting her use such a sharp instrument? His heart was in his stomach.

After scraping it off the cutting board and into the pan, she added the ketchup and Worcester sauce, giving it a stir.

"Would you fill the noodle pan with water, please?"

He'd relaxed a bit now that the knife was safely soaking in the sink.

"At your service, ma'am."

He turned on the faucet, let it run until there was enough water to boil the macaroni comfortably.

Placing it on the stove, he turned on the gas burner beneath it.

A different artist's voice filled the room, another he recognized.

Chloe looked up from what she was doing and said, "This was one of Mom's favorites. I wonder now if it reminded her of you."

He listened for a moment until he could make out the words.

"That we should have held on to what we had?"

She paused to study him.

"You had each other. Wasn't that enough for you?"

He was leaning against the counter, his legs extended in front of him, his arms braced on the edge.

"It should have been."

"You mustn't have loved her as much as she loved you."

"If truth be told, I loved her more than she thought I did. I let things get in the way."

He told her the story about how his father had died and what it had done to the family dynamics, the promise he'd made to a man already gone.

"If I had met her at a different time, maybe... No, that's not right. Your mother saved me from crashing and burning. She helped me study, play, live. Without her I wouldn't have finished what I started at Harvard."

"Did you ever tell your mother that?"

He glanced up, surprised at the question.

"No. I never did. I guess I was too busy pretending that everything was fine."

Noticing the water boiling, she put the noodles into the pan just as the doorbell rang.

He went to answer it just as another familiar voice penetrated the air.

He opened the door, Steve Perry's words an invitation.

He wished he could open his arms, have her in his embrace again. Living without her had been hard although he didn't realize how hard until she was back in it.

How had he lived without her fire? It was as if his heart had turned to ice, frozen in time, waiting for her warmth to melt it.

"Are you going to invite me in?"

"Sorry. Just thinking."

"About?"

"Missing you."

She ignored his statement, took a step inside, looked around.

"It's nice. You did good."

CHAPTER TWENTY-SIX

Chloe came out from the kitchen. "Dinner is almost ready. Why don't you show her around while I set the table? You are missing a lot, Dad. No salt and pepper shakers, no napkins."

"I've never stocked a kitchen before. Make me a list. I'll try to get what's on it before you come back."

"Okay."

He couldn't help smiling at her.

"She's so grown up."

"And bossy."

"She gets that from you."

"I'm not bossy. I'm confident in my point of view. It's always on target. I don't wait around for people to come to that conclusion."

"You give them a shove in the right direction."

"Whatever it takes."

"As you can see, this is the living room. There's the kitchen."

He was pointing in the direction where Chloe disappeared.

Nell kicked her shoes off and followed him down the hall.

"This is my bedroom. It's kind of a mess. I haven't had time to get organized."

Nell was drawn to the box of books, the one on top a history textbook about the media. She picked it up and flipped through it. There was writing in the margins, highlighted passages. The one underneath was an anthology of slave stories.

She looked up at him quizzically.

"That two years while I was trying to decide what I was going to do? I got a master's in History. Figured I could teach if nothing else. My mother wasn't too happy about it although it kept me in the city. That she liked."

"Why am I not surprised?"

"You knew I loved the subject."

"Everything you ever read outside of the curriculum was history based. I often wondered why you didn't major in it."

"But never said anything?"

"I'm not bossy that way. I would never have told you what to do with your life."

"Sometimes, I wished you had."

She placed the books back where they had been before taking a step to the bureau where he had two pictures, in frames. One was of Chloe a few years ago. The other one, of them. Dave had taken it one weekend she was in Boston. They'd gone ice skating at Faneuil Hall. It had been cold and she'd lost feeling in several parts of her body. He had her wrapped in a bear hug trying to warm her up.

"I never did like sports."

"Why'd you agree to go?"

"I guess it never mattered what we were doing, as long as we were together."

There was a sensual spark when she added, "I liked indoor activities better."

He'd walked over to her, took her face in his hands and was ready to lean in for a kiss when Chloe announced, "Come on, you two. It's time to eat."

He needed to let Nell know what she meant to him, how much he loved her, how much he wished he could change the past.

He yelled back, "We'll be there in a minute."

His mouth covered hers hungrily, all thoughts of food lost for the moment, and he hoped she'd understand what he was trying to say.

Chloe had fallen asleep on the couch and to give her some privacy and quiet, Jack refilled Nell's glass of wine and suggested they go down to Chloe's room. There was only one place to sit, the daybed, and they sank together in the middle.

His fingers sought out the bracelet that adorned her wrist today.

It was gold, with charms that hung from it, evenly spaced.

Inspecting them one by one, he thumbed a teddy bear, a heart, a Christmas tree, a disk engraved with a small amethyst stone, a child, a book, a question mark, and a record player.

When he was done, his eyes penetrated hers.

She answered his unspoken question.

"My parents gave me a bracelet when I was a year old and added to it every birthday and Christmas. I'd forgotten all about it until I was packing up my grandmother's house and found it. My wrist having thickened in the intervening years, I went out and replaced the gold chain with a bigger one and added the old charms."

"And they each stand for something?"

"They do."

Pointing to two of them, she said, "I used to love reading and listening to music when I was younger."

"What does the question mark signify?"

"I was always asking questions. My mom said that I didn't use a declarative sentence until I was in first grade."

He could believe it. Her curiosity about life, people, the law drove her passion.

"There aren't that many."

"The presents stopped when my parents left, so my personal history for them ends at age seven. They don't know I have a passion for pizza, love yoga, joined the debate club, fell in and out of love, wear bangles of some kind every day."

He was storing this in his Nell drawer. He wanted to add to it. A slice of pizza, a yoga mat, a diploma, a heart, a bracelet for the bracelet? What could he buy that would signify her latest win?

"Do they know you won a Supreme Court case?"

"Not unless they have daily newspapers in the small villages on the Ivory Coast. And it wouldn't be something to call them about. They would think it's inconsequential compared to what their patients face every day. There wouldn't be the pride that one might expect. Like with your mother."

"Is that where they are now? The Ivory Coast?"

"Yes, until the term runs out next year. I'm still afraid they'll be sent to Aleppo. They've got the experience and the commitment. I've been lucky so far. I've had a couple of scares over the years but that would be a daily worry."

His gaze became one of searing heat. How could she consider herself lucky when her family history ended almost twenty-five years ago?

She really didn't have anyone to praise or comfort her. He had been no better than they were.

His expression shifted when he caught the drift of her meaning.

"What kind of scares?"

"Once, when they were in Darfur, they were caught in some bombings. I heard about it on the news, called their contact person. He didn't know if they were dead or alive and I didn't find out for sure until the next day. It was a tough night."

"When did that happen?"

Was she eight, thirteen, twenty?

"When I was at Yale."

He'd never heard about it. "Before we met."

Her eyes dipped to the glass of wine. She took a sip, licked her lips.

"No. I was a senior."

He shifted, turning so he could look at her.

"Where the hell was I? Why didn't you ever tell me?"

"You were supposed to come down for the weekend. I figured I'd tell you when you got there but you...had to do something for your mother and couldn't make it."

"And you knew about it when I called you to cancel?"

"I found out right around dinner time, so yes."

"And you didn't tell me to get my ass down there because you needed me?"

"I'd stopped competing by then."

Her eyes held a vulnerability he hadn't seen before. How could he have missed it?

He felt a storm of emotion sweep through him.

"Nell, there would have been no competition. I would have come. I swear I would have."

He was hoping he was telling her the truth. He couldn't know for sure what had kept him in Boston that weekend. How important his mother would have made his presence seem.

Biting her lip, she looked away.

"I guess I wasn't feeling very brave that night. If you hadn't, I would have had to face a very painful decision. Not knowing, I could put it off a bit longer."

"You should have been able to count on me. At least for things like that. I...I don't know what to say."

"It's okay. It's over. No more guessing, hoping, being disappointed. You're free to do what you need to without any guilt or arguments. Noreen stayed with me that night. Ellen drove down. They threw me a pity party."

"You never told me, even later."

"It was anticlimactic by then. They were safe. We were still together."

He all but ground the words past his clenched teeth.

"What good was that if I wasn't there when you needed me?"

He watched the play of emotions cross her face before she answered. He was sure pain was one of them. Her answer was innocent in its simplicity, which cut him to the core.

"I loved you. When you were there with me, it was so good that I forgot all about the nasty parts."

His arm went around her, pulling her close. Her head rested against his collarbone. It was such a familiar gesture, one he'd missed. He took a moment to just be with it before diving in again.

"The night you left. You came home early, brought dinner. You knew about Chloe, didn't you?"

"I was planning on telling you, yes."

"Why didn't you insist I stick around?"

She lifted her head, her eyes meeting his.

"I thought I did. You told me you wouldn't be long. I waited. And waited. I knew I couldn't live like that anymore. I needed to stop hoping for something that wasn't going to happen. I'd spent most of my life doing that and I felt it was time to stop. I wanted to share my life with someone, not be a footnote."

He reached out, ran his fingers across her cheek, sorry he had let his mother control so much of their lives.

"Mom?"

Nell jumped up off the daybed, and scurried to where Chloe stood, disoriented and still half asleep.

"What are you doing down here?"

"We were just talking."

There was an apology in her eyes.

"I can go back upstairs."

Looking at her watch, Nell said, "Actually, it's time to go home."

They bundled themselves up and got ready to go.

He saw them out, waited until they were out of sight before closing the door, shutting down the lights. He wished they were still here, wished Chloe was sleeping down in her room, Nell was ensconced in his arms.

His head was pounding.

She'd been alone when she needed him. He had chosen his mother over her, time and time again. No wonder she'd left him.

He hadn't deserved her.

Still didn't.

But he needed her more than she'd ever know.

$\sim$

Nell got Chloe to bed, and crawled under her covers, her thoughts a mass of confusion. They were talking, about critical issues, something they avoided like the plague back when it would have mattered.

He'd apologized. He'd moved out of his mother's. He'd taken their daughter into his heart.

The sex was still an eleven, maybe had inched up to a twelve. Either that or she'd just gone without great sex for far too long.

And the pretense was working. They'd already gotten some attention during the interview he gave at the radio station. They asked him outright if he was dating anyone seriously. He'd glanced up at her and nodded his head. "A very special woman."

When asked what happened to Hope, he'd given them the answer they'd worked out. He'd bumped into an old college friend at the law association dinner and it had prompted him to end it with his long-time girlfriend. He added that he was happy and getting to know Nell's daughter.

First Night would be their first outing out in public with Chloe, and she was nervous about where it might lead. Chloe was hopeful. She could read it in her speculative looks, in her questions, her eyes. She didn't want her daughter hurt, but it was becoming more difficult to stay detached. It would help that he'd be leaving on Monday. Distance always worked in her favor. He forgot about them when they were out of sight, and the first week of the new Congress would take all his focus.

When her phone buzzed, she picked it up and checked the number.

Snuggling down, pulling the covers up, she swiped and answered, "Hi."

"I was just lying in bed thinking."

"About?"

"I haven't gotten to the good part yet, where I'm thinking about you, here, in my new bed, my new place. Which I will before I fall asleep, but for now, I have a favor."

"Okay...what is it?"

"Can Chloe come to my swearing in? I'd like her to be part of this and I think she might like it as well."

"She's going back to school on Tuesday."

"You wouldn't consider letting her skip a day or two? You could look at it as a continuation of her civics block, Civics 102."

Her hesitation gave him the opening he needed to keep up the harangue.

"Families are there, Nell. Kids get to see their parents take the oath. She'd be part of the history, my history. I could show her my office, take her on a tour of the Capitol. She'd get to see the chamber where laws are written, and votes are cast. And you could come with her. I'd like you there with me as well."

"Can I think about it, talk to her? If she's excited about the prospect, then chances are I will agree. Although I don't see the point of me—"

"You'd have to, Nell. I couldn't explain why she was there if you weren't. Unless we hand the story to the press."

"Not for this. There'd be a field day with it. She couldn't enjoy herself."

"Right. So, you'd have to come."

"I would, wouldn't I? I think the manipulation gene got handed down. I'm not sure I like knowing that Chloe may have inherited it."

"I'm really not trying to do that. It's an honest request. One I hope you'll honor but I'll understand if I didn't earn it yet."

"Point taken. We'll talk about it tomorrow."

Her voice faded to a hush.

"How have we spent the last eight out of ten days together? I did not see that coming or even realize it was happening."

He answered, his tone husky, "I'm just lucky, I guess. I'll go back to thinking. Only this time I'll think those other good thoughts. You know, you, me, together, in bed. Goodnight, Nell."

"Good night, Jack."

She held the phone to her chest, her heart beating like a hummingbird's.

He'd taken her back again, to when they were dating and he'd call during the week to catch up, tell her how much he missed her, explaining in detail what they'd do when they were together again. She closed her eyes and let the memory seduce her to sleep.

CHAPTER TWENTY-SEVEN

"I talked to Jack last night and he asked if you wanted to go to DC for his swearing in. We'd fly down with him, stay overnight, and come back on Wednesday. I'd have to get the okay from school but it's a great supplement to the class you're taking."

"That would be lit. I couldn't let anyone know...that he's my father. Right?"

"I'm sorry, not this year. You don't have to go if you don't want to."

"I want to. I think it will make a memory I want to keep. Will I get to see his office?"

"That and the House chamber. I don't know if you remember her, but Tahlia is his chief of staff. She held the same job for Congressman Tomms when we were there."

"I kind of do. She was nice. She let me play dolls in the conference room on the few occasions I was there. Does he have the same office?"

"No. Jack's in a different building. By the time I worked for Tomms, he had seniority and had one of the best offices on Capitol grounds. Jack isn't there yet."

"Can I ask Keileh to come with me?"

"Mmhm. That might be a good idea. It will give you someone to talk to when there's downtime. I'll call her mother, but Samira might not want to keep her out of school the day after Christmas break. Don't be disappointed if she can't."

"I'm kind of excited either way."

"I'll book the flight once I know about Keileh, get us a room at a hotel."

"We won't be staying at Dad's?"

"I won't. I guess you could if you wanted. I'll have to ask."

"I don't want to unless you do."

"Chloe, I told you, this is not going to turn out the way you might want it to."

"I know. But if there's no chance of you guys getting back together, what's the big deal?"

Chloe asked a very good question, one that had no answer. At least none that she was going to give.

"I told Jack that you could text, call or whatever. I'll let you decide what you want to do. I'm staying at a hotel. I'll book two rooms, just in case you decide to stay with me."

Chloe was already on her phone. Nell didn't know how she could move her thumbs so quickly. Practice did make perfect.

She called Samira's cell and left a message, then got back to work.

It was a few hours later that she heard back from Samira. Yes, Keileh could go. The students wouldn't be working on anything important the first day back from vacation and she thought it would be a good experience, seeing the process up close and personal. Nell also heard from Jack. He tried to talk her into staying with him but to no avail. She'd booked the same flight as him and then booked the hotel. She was determined to stay in control of what could be an out-of-control natural phenomenon, glow stick be damned.

Nell was zipping up her carry-on, taking a last look around her room to make sure she wasn't forgetting anything. After lifting it, she carried it out to the kitchen and put it down near the door. She claimed the last cup of coffee, cleaned out the pot, and left it drying on the sideboard before stepping to the bay window. The snow had melted with the unusual weather pattern that had hit yesterday, so there was no white adorning the trees or walk-way. First Night had been perfect. The weather chilly but manageable, the walking around holding Jack's hand priceless.

They were going to be a family for the next twenty-four hours, or at least a pretend one. Would people notice the similarities between Jack and Chloe? The grey eyes? The nose? The same quick smile? In her experience, people only looked at what mattered to them. She doubted anyone in that environment would care.

She could hear Chloe and Keileh laughing in the other room and the pre-teen chatter made her smile. Keileh had stayed over last night. She thought it would be easier if they were all in one place for the early-morning flight. She'd paid through the teeth for the three tickets, but she wanted the same non-stop from Boston to Dulles that Jack was on and she was just lucky the seats were available. It would put them in Washington before nine thirty, which gave Jack plenty of time to get settled in before the gavel banged the old session out and the new one in.

"Time to get moving, girls."

"Okay, were coming."

They were laughing as they came out from the bedroom, each carrying a backpack, phones in hand. She'd insisted Chloe dress appropriately. Even though no one knew she was Jack's daughter, she thought it important to dress as if they did. She was wearing one of the new dresses they'd just bought her with her knee-high boots. She looked so grown up, her hair in a French braid that Keileh had managed for her, lip gloss pink and shiny. Her heart blossomed with love and pride.

Did Jack feel the same kinds of emotion when he looked at her? Or did it come from years of watching her grow and mature? If he did, she couldn't blame him for wanting to be in Chloe's life. Hadn't she punished him long enough?

Where had that thought come from? Was her stubborn refusal to introduce them a cover for what was below the surface? A need to penalize him for choosing his mother over her.

She honestly hoped not. She didn't want to think she was that vindictive.

They arrived at the gate to find Jack already waiting, Chloe foregoing the hug but bestowing on him a beatific smile.

He came over to where they stood.

"I can't believe my luck traveling with three such beautiful females."

His eyes held a fatherly appreciation when he returned Chloe's smile.

Nell couldn't miss how Chloe stood taller at his compliment.

She bit her lip, guilt gnawing at the edges of her heart. Chloe had been missing a piece of her identity. She should have introduced them sooner. A girl needed this. It was a father's perception that told her she was a woman, reaffirmed she was pretty, laid the foundation for her sense of self. Her own father had left too soon to build that stage and when he was gone? She'd doubted herself, wondered why he'd found it necessary to stay away so long.

For a few years she'd played the pick me, pick me game until she'd realized no one noticed. When she'd shut the door on the pain, knowing she would never gain the approval she craved, she'd began to work hard. The recognition came from other sources, for her achievements, her friendships, her skills. And she was still doing it. Maybe it was time to take stock of where she was. She'd driven herself hard over the last few years, her success hard-won but at what cost?

She glanced up to see Jack staring at her, the familiar tingle shooting through her body. It wanted more than just a glance. It wanted an in-depth immersion in his touch.

"You look lovely, Nell. And thank you again for coming."

He was mouth-watering in his suit, his hair neatly coiffed, his manners impeccable.

Her mind issued a warning. They weren't where they needed to be for her to let her fear go. It was still far too risky. Too many unknowns still lay ahead.

The tingles didn't abate. Sitting beside Jack on the plane only made them more pronounced. His hand holding hers, his aftershave a tantalizing scent of man and heat. Keileh and Chloe were in the seats in front, their heads bent, the chatter exhausting from take-off to touch down. It gave her the time to enjoy the man and the easy conversation.

She was almost sorry when the plane landed, and they began to disembark. She thought that would be the end of the connection, but he told her otherwise when he reclaimed her hand with his. Keeping both girls in sight, they wove their way through the concourse out to the taxi stand. She hadn't been this content in a long time.

They arrived at the Longworth Building and proceeded through security, the girls now serious as they watched the people in front of them. After being frisked and deemed harmless, the girls walked along the marble-floored hallways, sufficiently reverent.

"Wow, Mom. I don't remember it looking like this."

"You weren't even four at the time, Chloe, so it's not surprising."

There were dozens of people rushing around, looking busy, in pairs, talking to each other, individual men and women reading file folders, talking on their cells, or stopped in small groups for a mini meeting. Keeping close tabs on the girls, Nell shepherded them through the maze until they reached the door they were looking for.

"This is it. My office."

Chloe stopped to read the plaque outside the door, a broad smile on her face. She was duly impressed.

"Can we just go in?"

"You've got a standing appointment, so whether I'm with you or not, the answer is yes."

Nell was amused as she watched Chloe examine every inch of the outer office, the reception area, where phones buzzed constantly, the waiting area, where several men sat on a sofa reading the morning paper. The dialogue exchanges between offices was non-stop, a rapid fire of directives, questions, and assessments.

"This is so different than your office in Cambridge."

"This is where it all happens."

Nell noticed Lauren come out from Tahlia's office, a couple of accordion folders in her arms. When she looked up and saw who was standing there, she came right over.

"Nell, I haven't had a chance to thank you for the reference. It swung the verdict to my side, and I know I'm going to love working here. The office runs like a well-oiled clock and I've never worked with a more knowledgeable staff. They do love their boss."

It was one of the things Nell had noticed, had her re-evaluating Jack's success. Loyalty was not easily won.

"I didn't realize you'd started already. What are you going to do with the last year of the parole board?"

"I'll fly up whenever I have to until the term expires. They needed someone asap and I didn't want to turn it down. They were more than gracious about letting me finish it out."

Tahlia came out soon after. Her eyes widened when she took the girls in, her expression almost comical.

"My God, Nell. She's so grown up."

"She is, isn't she? This is her friend, Keileh Hamade. Girls this is Tahlia Stone, Jack's chief of staff."

For some reason, Chloe turned shy, inched closer to her, a tentative smile on her face.

"Hello, Ms. Stone."

"Please, call me Tahlia. Everyone else does. She looks just like you, Nell. And she's tall for her age, isn't she?"

She had to have a couple of inches on Keileh, which made it hard to miss, as Keileh pointed out.

"My being short, helps that illusion, Ms. Stone."

Tahlia beamed at both before turning her attention to her boss.

"Hello, Jack. Are you ready for the upcoming circus?"

"As I'll ever be. At least this year I'll be providing some of the entertainment."

"I can't see Chloe running rampant up and the down the hallways."

"No, but I'll be getting Chloe selfies with some of our more prestigious officials."

Chloe's eyes lit up.

"Like who?"

"The out-going vice-president for one. Is there anyone you'd like to meet?"

"Senator Corbett. She's on the news all the time and her tweets were awesome during the campaign. She has a way of making the guy elected go nuts."

"She is one of our more vocal advocates but she's in the Senate, not the House."

Glancing over at Tahlia, he asked, "Can you give her office a call, see if she has five minutes for us today?"

Chloe's eyes glowed. "Sweet."

Tahlia nodded and got right to the task.

Jack's attention was back on Chloe.

"Anyone else? The Speaker?"

Chloe had a sour look on her face that was almost comical.

"Um, no thank you. I don't like him or his politics. I can do without that introduction."

He laughed.

"Seems you've been listening to your mother."

"No. I've been reading his Twitter feeds."

Jack looked surprised.

"I didn't know you followed what was going on so closely."

"Do you really think Mom would let me remain ignorant while history was being made? We were all bummed the female candidate didn't break the glass ceiling. Someday there'll be a woman in the White House."

He was impressed, although not surprised. Nell had claimed her part in the resistance, and it seemed she was raising their daughter to understand the why behind it.

Tahlia came out with a document and handed him a pen. He scanned it before scribbling his name. He repeated with another brief before she said, "Senator Corbett would love to meet Chloe. She said you could bring her by the open house the Massachusetts contingent is having this afternoon. She'll make herself available."

"Thanks, Tahlia."

He turned his attention back to Chloe. "I have to be in chamber pretty soon. Do you want to wait here or come over with me? It could get boring."

"We came to experience this. We have our phones. We'll stay busy."

"Okay then. You ready?"

Nell asked, "Street or tunnel?"

"I thought they might want to experience the tunnels."

He noticed Chloe take a step towards her mother before asking, "There are tunnels? Underground? Um, I don't think so."

Keileh seemed more excited about the prospect of exploring the subterranean carved out crevices.

Nell knew why Chloe was not thrilled with the idea. She experienced claustrophobia. Didn't like elevators but used them if she had to.

"It's not what you're imagining. The pedestrian walkways are wide, well-lit by way of skylights, and there isn't a spider web in sight. You won't feel cramped, I promise."

Jack had put his arm around her, spoke low in her ear.

"And I'll be with you. I know the maze like the back of my hand, although that took years of trial and error."

Keileh urged, "Come on, Chloe. It'll be something we can tell the class about when we go back. How many of them will have walked under the Capitol Building?"

Chloe finally acquiesced although she walked close by Nell's side until they got to the passage. The number of people striding through, newspapers and phones in hand, gave her a bit more courage because soon she was side-by-side with Keileh, her fears completely gone.

It put Nell next to Jack, following just behind. When he linked his hand with hers, she felt a jolt, along with a promise of something she shouldn't want.

"I figure we should get the ball rolling on this dating thing. Let loose lips talk."

"We're where no one can see us, and those who do, don't care."

"Okay, fine. I just like the feel of your hand in mine. Deal."

She couldn't argue with that. It felt good, solid. Like it used to at the beginning. He'd always reach for her hand wherever they were, walking across his campus towards the library, walking down Newbury Street the times she'd visit him in Boston, during the midnight showings of some cult film or show at the Yale Repertory Theater, while they sat in Ellen's apartment, where she stayed in the city, talking with friends. She hadn't gotten up to Boston often. Work had taken up a good portion of her weekend, study the other lion's share but they'd eked as much time together as they could. Treated every minute they were together as if it was the precious commodity it was. He'd convinced her he was in love, wanted her with him. He was acting the same way now. But once burned, she couldn't fall into his arms again. Especially now, with Chloe's heart at stake.

They reached the Rayburn Building, the more recent build to accommodate government officials. "Girls stay with us. It's easy to get lost here."

He must have glanced up to make sure they were in front of him every five seconds, taking a head count, one, two. These feelings were new, and he wasn't sure what was rational concern and irrational worry.

"I feel like I have the crown jewels in my possession. I can't relax."

She gave him a gentle laugh.

"Paranoia does strike deep from time to time. They'll be fine. Chloe isn't exactly the rebellious type. She won't try to run away."

"What if someone comes up to her and kidnaps her?"

"Jack, why would they do that?"

"Because she's young and beautiful."

"It's going to be like that, is it?"

"Like what?"

"It should have been a gradual process. They grow, you watch, they gain some independence, you learn how to let go. You haven't had that graduated learning curve."

"I know too much. About what's out there. What can hurt her."

"I'm sure you do. Talk to her. Let her know how important it is not to talk to strangers and to stay in her seat. My warning? Don't treat her like a child.

She won't like it. You'll get further discussing it in a more mature manner. She'll be more willing to co-operate."

"These tried-and-true suggestions?"

"Yes. It'll save you years of cluelessness."

They stood just outside the House chamber, jostled by others who were heading in. Little kids, all dressed up in suits and ties, fancy dresses, and patent leather shoes were everywhere. Both the new and re-elected members of Congress brought family, kids, grandkids, and friends to the event and it was badly orchestrated chaos and would be throughout the day. The chamber would be stuffed to capacity and bedlam would ensue. Politicians would be glad-handing, working the room even though they'd already been voted in. It was the natural order of things.

When Jack finally led them in, everyone holding hands in order to stay together, Chloe stilled.

"Wow. This is amazing."

"Come on, let's get you seated. It fills up quickly and I want to make sure you're in the front row. This place eventually becomes a playground and I want you safe in your seat before that happens."

"Will you be sitting with us?"

"Some of the time. When I'm sworn in, you can come with me. I'm hoping you will."

"I'd like that."

He led them down the aisle and deposited them in the second row of seats. They'd have to sit longer than he'd like, but he wanted to guarantee they got to see the historic ritual that would be performed today. The House was not a continuing body. They had to officially end one two-year term before beginning a new one.

He turned to Nell. "You'll come, too, won't you?"

"I'm here to give Chloe some cover, so won't I have to?"

"I want you to come for me, not for Chloe."

His nearness was overwhelming, and the tangible bond between them was vibrating with emotion. So proud of who he'd become. So happy to be here for this moment with him. The heart-wrenching tenderness of his gaze completely undid her.

And she felt herself surrender to the undertow.

CHAPTER TWENTY-EIGHT

The call to order came at twelve o'clock sharp.

Jack was back with them for the first two pieces of business, once the clerk had called Congress in session. He wanted to be with Chloe when he cast his vote for Speaker of the House, which was third on the agenda. Now that he knew Chloe's feelings about the current one, he squeezed her hand when the Clerk called on him and his voice rang out clearly with the name Pellacio. He felt Chloe squeeze back. They both knew it was impossible for her to be selected, the majority running the show, but it gave the impression that he was on the right side of things. His last name put him at the first of almost everything and soon he was called down to be sworn in. He'd asked Zelda to do the honors, and with his hand on a copy of a Bible borrowed from one of his state's contingent, he swore to support and defend the Constitution, bear allegiance, and discharge his duties. Once he repeated the oath, Zelda hugged him and studied the picture the four of them represented. He could tell by her expression she knew Chloe's parentage.

"Jack, will you do the honors and introduce me?"

"Zelda, you know Nell. This is her daughter, Chloe and a friend of hers, Keileh Hamade."

"It's good to see you again Nell. I have to admit I'm surprised."

"I thought Chloe would benefit from seeing government in action."

"It is a special day for all of you. I'm glad you asked me to do the honors. I might have missed this auspicious occasion."

Nell explained, "Chloe, this is the woman I came down to talk to. She's the ranking member of the Border Security committee for Judicial."

"Please work extra hard to make sure the travel ban isn't put in place. Keileh's Mom is from Iran and it would make it hard for her to go back and forth to see her mother."

"I will work very hard for that. Jack's on the committee with me and I'm hoping he brings his strengths to bear as well."

Both Nell and Zelda gave him a speculative look. The women knew where Jack stood on borders and immigrant crossings.

Jack glanced at Keileh, who was staring at him. She was expecting some assurance that he would be one of their champions.

"You know how I feel about the immigrants already here. I'm as much for reform as anyone."

Chloe looked up at him startled. "But...Jack, a travel ban is unconstitutional. You can't be for that, can you?"

"I'm certainly not for Samira being banned from the country."

"You think it should be studied case by case?"

"It's a lot more complicated than that, Chloe."

Nell sensed Chloe's growing unease with her father's stand, and this was the wrong time and place for an in-depth discussion on the merits of the travel ban. They'd have lots of time for that later.

"I bet Zelda would pose for a picture with you. Would you like that?"

Chloe narrowed her eyes, as if knowing what Nell was doing. Pausing for a moment, she put on a smile and said, "Yes. I'd like that. Jack, will you be in it, too?"

He put his arm around Nell's waist and brought her close before tucking Chloe and Keileh in front of him. Zelda stood on his other side.

"Everyone in the picture. I'll have a copy made for each of us. It'll be a memento we can look back on."

He snapped the photo with his phone, thanked Zelda again and was about to escort the group toward a man leaning against one of the railings, just chilling when the senior congresswomen called out, "Jack, give me five minutes tomorrow. I'd love to talk to you about a phoenix rising."

He shrugged his shoulders before smiling. "It hasn't risen yet."

Nell asked, "What was that about?"

"Just an inside joke. It has to do with the committee."

Trying to erase Zelda's smirk from his mind, Jack turned to Chloe and said, "I don't know if you want to hang around here or go back to my office. It's going to be a very long afternoon. We have to adopt the rules and Peters is going to announce the floor practices. I hear he's coming down hard on recording on the floor. Our punishment for the sit-in we staged before the election. Then they'll assign committee leaders and whips, and the rest of us to our committees."

Nell had the same sour look at the mention of the Speaker.

"I for one don't want to listen to anything the Speaker has to say but if the girls want to stay and watch the whole thing, I'll suffer through it."

"I would, Mom."

"When he's speaking, maybe we can take a break and go to the open house, introduce you to Senator Corbett."

"That's a good idea."

Chloe was over the moon at meeting the senior senator from Massachusetts. And Patricia spent a good fifteen minutes talking to the girls about what they expected to come in the first ninety days. None of it was promising.

When they re-entered the chamber, the whole place was abuzz. Ron came running over to them and announced, "You won't believe this, but the R's are trying to ram something through this afternoon."

Nell was the one who asked, "What?"

"There was a closed-door secret ballot to gut the Ethics Office."

Nell all but laughed in the face of it.

"There'll be such a backlash their heads will spin. They haven't figured out yet that a new day has dawned."

"I think you're right. It's already been leaked, and the switchboards are lighting up. Even other R's think it's a very bad idea."

"Not a great way to start your majority rule."

"Who ever said they were smart? I still don't understand how they get people to vote in their own worst interests. It's puzzling, to say the least."

"We just don't get our message out well. We have the programs; we just can't seem to translate it well to the working class."

They'd been miscommunicating for years.

The upcoming slashes in health care, taxes, environmental protection, women's rights might tilt the scale for the next time around. The Democrats needed to come up with a candidate who sparked a fire and offered something other than platitudes. New blood.

Shaking away the morbid thoughts, Jack said, "Make sure we have enough phone coverage. We won't get as many calls as some on the other side, but our constituents like to have their say."

"I'm going back to the office now. I'll let them know to be ready."

Turning back to Nell, he smiled. "There goes their agenda. I know they were going to begin to take the steps to repeal the ACA. They just got in their own way. Maybe we won't have to do anything to block them. We can just sit back and watch them go bust."

He led them back to find some vacated seats so Chloe could watch the rest of the procedure. And when the night finally ended, they went out to one of the finer restaurants to celebrate.

They were still dissecting the day when they returned to Jack's condo for the night. He'd been able to talk Nell into staying as soon as Chloe had voiced her preference. There were enough bedrooms to go around although he knew she'd be scoffing at the opulence the whole time she was there. Silently, but he'd be able to read those thoughts.

Once the girls were asleep in one of the bedrooms, he poured Nell a brandy and brought it over to where she stood by the wall of windows. She'd already changed out of her dress and had put on some well-worn jeans and a long-sleeve tee shirt. Very few got to see her dressed down. She was even sexier, more human, less intimidating. She became soft and vulnerable, which was something she tried to hide about herself.

It was a side he loved more than any other, and there were many facets of her to admire.

As he handed over the tumbler, their fingers touched, and sparks flew. There was a sensuous light that passed between them before she turned her face away from him.

"I have to admit it's got a beautiful view."

"I do a lot of my thinking here. The lights have a way of making everything clear."

"I do the same thing in my office. The view of Boston is almost as spectacular as this."

"What made you join Woodley and Fisher? I'm sure you had options after DC, and they didn't even have a rating yet."

"I liked Arianna and Mia. I liked that they dealt with women's issues and I thought it would take me less time to make partner than if I joined one steeped in experience."

"Did they mind when you stepped into philanthropy?"

"I have a few causes I donate to, but not extreme amounts of money. I don't donate to many causes, so I think that's the wrong word for what I do."

"In your business, time is money. How many billable hours don't you bill?"

"Without Arianna's blessing, I couldn't have taken on so many pro bono cases."

"You never did like taking credit for your accomplishments. Why is that?"

Brushing her bangs off her face, her bangle somehow glinting in the muted light, she pressed her lips together and finally admitted, "I think it's important to stay humble. That way you always stay on the right track. I've seen too many people get caught up in their success, and it diminishes the quality of their work."

"You've consciously made the choice. It's not part of your make-up."

"It might be a bit of that. I was always pretty much in the background when I was growing up. Maybe it became a part of who I am."

"I can't see you in the background. You have what Chloe implied. A presence."

"I told you I felt invisible growing up. That changed when I became more confident in myself. Maybe I just stopped trying to please people."

"Who did you have to try to please?"

"My parents, before they left, my grandmother, your mother."

The look she gave him was a contemplative one. Her eyes were shining with emotion.

Then she explained, "When I was younger, I didn't really exist for my parents. My grandmother didn't really want the responsibility of raising another child. My attempts at being perfect failed miserably."

She gave him a feeble smile. She walked away from the window, and took a seat on one of the overstuffed, white brocade sofas. He followed, taking a seat beside her.

"I thought you were close with your grandmother."

"That came over time. It only happened when I became a grown woman."

She took a sip of the brandy and closed her eyes as it burned its way down.

"Right before my parents left, I overheard my grandmother tell my parents that she was too old for another child. My mother told me to be a good girl, so I tried to stay out of the way, tried not to interfere with her life. It was when someone from school called my parents that they realized Adele hadn't been joking. I'd lost a lot of weight, wasn't eating so stressed by the arrangement that my mother came back, enrolled me in boarding school. She knew I'd at least eat and might have an easier time if I was with other kids."

"Did you? Have an easier time?"

"I couldn't wait for summer, when I'd be back home. I liked the security of it, of family. I at least felt connected to something. When I got to college my grandmother seemed to close the distance between us, called me once a week, wanted me home for the holidays. That's what you saw. She was eighty by then, so maybe she just didn't want to be alone. Maybe she'd come to like me. I don't know. We never talked about it."

Jack's heart ached. He'd never known this, never asked her about her childhood. By the time he'd entered her life, she seemed close to old Adele Warren. Why would he think there'd been years of isolation?

She was in boarding school. That would have implied plenty. Why didn't you pursue it?

"Why didn't you ever tell me?"

"What was I supposed to say? Oh, Jack, by the way I was kind of ignored as a child? Wha, wha, wha...I learned it never helped to whine."

"That wouldn't have been whining. That would have given me insight into who you are."

"It was hard for me to talk about."

"We lived together, Nell. We talked about everything, or so I thought. I'm beginning to realize we skipped over some of the important things."

"When we lived together Jack, you began to shut me out. I thought your mother had convinced you we weren't right for each other. There didn't seem to be much commitment to the relationship on your part."

"Because I spent so much time with her?"

"There was that. It was as if you didn't give much thought to what she asked. You just acted on it. You never seemed to take me into consideration. I'd come home, you'd announce you were taking her somewhere. You never asked if I needed something or had other plans. You were in sync with her, not me. At the end, I didn't know where I fit in your life. I didn't think you'd even miss me if I was gone."

"I missed you, Nell."

"I never knew that. You never told me."

Thinking back to their last conversations, about the pregnancy, the mandate his mother had put in place, he realized he'd never told her he wanted to be with her. And when he'd stayed in Boston, he was telling her he didn't miss her. Not enough to give up his comfort.

"I can't believe I never told you. That you didn't know how I felt."

"I envied your relationship. I dreamed she'd come to love me, too. That I could be part of a family again."

He shuddered at the emotion crammed into that admission and cursed himself for a fool for not being there for her. She never had anyone in her corner and the thought of her so lonely was crushing him. Hundreds of questions were racing through his mind, but there was one that took precedence.

"Why did your parents leave you?"

There was a pregnant pause as if she was thinking about whether to tell him or not.

Then she focused her eyes on him as if she were trying to read what was in his.

Slowly, she parted with some truth.

"I had a brother. His name was James. He died when he was nine. My parents left six months later."

He couldn't speak he was so shocked.

"You weren't an only child."

"No."

"How old were you...when it happened?"

"Six."

There were tears in her eyes as if the grief was fresh and just below the surface.

He grabbed her hand, he squeezed.

"I'm so sorry. How did it happen?"

"He developed an inoperable brain tumor. It was bad at the end. He was in so much pain."

"Your father's a surgeon, isn't he?"

"Yes. He was devastated that he couldn't do anything to help Jamie. He stopped working for months and then he got the offer to go to Ethiopia and he took it. My mother naturally went with him."

Anger shot through him.

"Did they forget they had another child at home?"

"I think my father couldn't get beyond the grief to see anything else. My mother felt it was her job to help ease his suffering."

"God dammit, Nell..."

"Grief is a funny thing. It drove my parents away from everything familiar. It had the opposite effect on your mother. She pulled you closer. Each person deals with it in a different way."

"How did you deal with it?"

"It was hard. I cried a lot. I missed him so much, especially after my parents left."

"Did you tell them how you felt?"

"In the beginning. More than patience allowed. My mother used to get upset. She flew home a couple of times to reassure herself I was okay. But she never stayed more than a few days. Once I was enrolled in the school, her visits were few and far between. I learned to accept it for what it was. I stopped asking when they were coming home, stopped expecting things to go back to normal."

How could they have done that to her? How could he have followed the same path?

"Is that why you couldn't tell me when you needed me?"

"You were always busy."

Just like her parents, he'd put someone else's need above hers. She'd stopped asking for love, attention, affection, caring. She deserved it more than anyone he knew.

He rose from the couch, took her hand, and led her to his bedroom. He was surprised when she let him.

When he took her hand, she couldn't fight. The memories of her brother always made her sad. He'd been her hero when she was younger. He'd been smart and kind, an older brother in every sense of the word. He'd taken care of her. Her father had worked a lot of hours, one of the premier surgeons in the area who was called in whenever a tough case presented itself. She'd learned to take on pro bono from him, many of his surgeries performed on people who couldn't pay. One of his mantras was "no one should pay with their life."

Jamie had been the heir apparent. Tall and good-looking he was being groomed for big things. When he'd fallen ill, it was a nightmare. He'd complained of headaches at first, and it had taken several doctors to find the root of the problem. The MRI showcased a tumor so embedded in his brain that surgery was a waste of time. She would sit and hold his hand, never wanting to leave him alone. She would tell him funny stories, trying to make him laugh, trying to take away his pain. Her father began his downward spiral in

Jamie's last days. Unable to do anything to alleviate his suffering, to fix the problem, he'd grown more and more despondent. When death had finally come to claim Jamie, her father had buried himself in grief and booze. Only when the call came from Doctors Without Borders had he rallied. Needing to get away from the site of his failure, he'd taken on the job of saving others. Merry had taken her in hand on one of her visits home and tried to explain the move, told her that her father's sanity was at stake. It would only be until he recuperated, and then they would be home.

"Be a brave girl. Do as you're told. And we'll be home before you know it."

All her pleading to go with them had been denied.

She'd never told them she didn't want to live without Jamie either. That her pain was so big her six-year-old heart hadn't known what to do with it. She couldn't have. She hadn't had the words. Instead, she'd stopped eating. Hadn't had the energy or the hunger it required. Lost in her own grief, from her brother's death and her parents' abandonment, she'd lost interest in the world.

Spending all her time in her room, outside the time spent in her new elementary school where she had no friends, she sat at the window, waiting for her parents to come back to her.

It was one of her teachers who had called. Not her grandmother, but her mother. Told Merry that her daughter was wasting away to nothing.

Merry had returned, for a few days, to enroll her in the boarding school, making sure she had everything she'd need for the transition.

And then she was gone again, only visiting every few years to check in. They were the brightest days of her life.

Until Jack. And then once he was lost to her, Chloe.

Now Jack was back. She was going to treat it in the same light as she had her mother's temporary presence. Enjoy it for what it was and plan for the devastation that would come when it was over.

When he led her into his room and kissed her, it was like spiraling back in time, when it had been good between them. In his arms she felt safe, as if nothing could hurt her. She'd learned it was an illusory cocoon but tonight she was going to pretend it was forever. Like she'd done when her mother returned for a visit.

Her body tingled, her breath held as he whispered kisses along her neck, her cheek, taking her lips hungrily in his own. She let herself get swept up in the passion that had once been theirs, his tongue probing, his hands roaming her body, every one of her cells alive and on fire.

He was touchingly tender, almost restrained as his body consumed hers, after their clothes were shed, and they were skin to skin. She writhed beneath him, straining to reach a climax, moving against him until the world careened off its axis. She clutched his back, gasping in sweet ecstasy, the tremors drawing him deeper, until she felt his body explode inside her. Their bodies were always in such exquisite harmony, each coupling better than the one before.

His head was buried in her shoulder, his groan telling her he felt the same. She wrapped herself around him, surrendering to the love she felt for him, knowing it was too good to last.

CHAPTER TWENTY-NINE

The next morning, Nell was back to routine. They'd taken an early flight home, and an hour after she dropped Chloe and Keileh off at school, she was knee deep in depositions. By late afternoon, Chloe back at her office with her, she dropped into her chair, exhausted from the mind-numbing process of questioning those who she was representing. Interpreters were on call, and she knew every one of them by name. This case involved a married man who had made the mistake of getting behind the wheel after a couple of drinks at a family barbeque. Stopped by the police, he'd been arrested and taken to the Suffolk jail. Today she heard from the wife, another undocumented immigrant who'd sat and cried over the accumulating debt. Without her husband's income, she was doing her best to get by on her eight-dollar-an-hour job at an IHOP. Transportation, rent, phone calls, filing fees that were going toward the crime of moral turpitude were piling up. Committing an act that was not in the best interests of the community was the cause of many deportations. It meant the undocumented had to stay underground or live perfect lives. Who could do that?

Malik Kelembar was behind bars, awaiting the decision that would send him back to his country of origin or re-unite him with his family. Judges were overwhelmed with staggering numbers of immigrants who faced a hearing. Time constraints forced ten-minute decisions in these life-and- death stakes. She had taken the case on with the intention of getting his file re-opened and would need every resource she had to get the judge to agree with her assessment: Malik was one of the good guys who'd made a mistake, fear and bad luck compounding the error in judgment.

"Mom."

She was looking out over the vista that was Boston and answered absently, "Yes, honey."

"Dad texted. Asked if we were on for Friday night?"

She swiveled her chair around so she could see Chloe's expression. It was compelling her to think long and hard whether to say yes or not.

"Is this something you two talked about? Making it an-every-week affair?"

She winced at the word. An affair was not on her agenda and she had to scrub it out of her vocabulary.

"Kind of. Is that a problem for you?"

"I thought we'd both get a weekend night, you know separately. Me, Fridays as usual, you and Jack on Saturdays or Sundays."

They'd yet to discuss visitation but she didn't expect this.

"Why?"

"Because we are not really together, Chloe. Remember, this is pretend?"

"But we had a good time last week, didn't we? And neither one of you is with someone else. I don't see the problem."

Nell knew she'd never see it. Ever. It would mean sharing feelings that were inappropriate. Chloe didn't have to know she'd never stopped loving Jack or that his betrayal was a hurt too big to heal.

"I thought you'd want to spend some alone time together. Without me."

"I like being with you. I think he does, too. Again, what's the problem? Do you still love him?"

Chloe's question hit a nerve. She couldn't lie outright. It wasn't in her nature, so she had to skirt around the issue.

"Love has nothing to do with it, Chloe. We didn't work back then. We wouldn't work today."

"Why?"

Nell closed her eyes, waves of regret washing over her.

"We both bring too much baggage to the relationship. I want to share my life with someone. That spot's already taken by his mother."

"Maybe she'd make room for us? He says she wants to meet me."

Nell jumped up from her seat, frustrated by Chloe's incessant chatter, and began to pace the empty space around her desk. Her mind scrambled as she tried to come up with a way to keep that from happening. Could she really forbid it? It would make Chloe even more interested in meeting her grandmother, if only to see for herself what the woman was like.

Fiddling with the charms on her bracelet, Nell continued to pace, her movements more frenetic.

"That would be up to the three of you. I won't pick a side on that issue."

"You don't want me to."

Nell stopped and looked at her daughter.

"Hypothetical situation. There's someone who doesn't like you. I decide I'm going to hang out with her out of curiosity, see for myself what she's like. I like her despite how she feels about you and continue to have interaction. How would you feel?"

"Not good. But this isn't a friend; she's family. Mine anyway. Isn't that different? Are you asking *me* to take a side?"

Hadn't she already? Didn't she tell Jack she didn't want to meet Eloise because of the conflict?

Trying to shift her perspective, to encompass Chloe's change of heart, she faltered.

"Like I said, it's up to the three of you. I won't interfere."

"You'd never come with us."

"Never."

She'd come too far to go backwards. She didn't understand Eloise's hostility. Never went out of her way to be disrespectful, never returned the insinuations about her character. Maybe she should have. If their break-up was going to happen anyway, she wished she'd spoken her mind. She'd told Jack keeping quiet hadn't earned her any points. He'd asked if it was a competition.

There was a winner and a loser, so she'd have to answer yes to that question.

It hurt that she was the one who had lost. Again.

Chloe must have sensed she was adamant, and it was not worth arguing about, so she dropped that subject to ask again, "About Friday? Are we good?"

"I tell you what. You can have your Dad over and I'll find someplace else to go."

There was a hint of petulance when Chloe said, "Fine. I'll tell him no."

With that pronouncement, she got up and left the office, her backpack hanging from her shoulder.

Nell turned back to the window, took a deep breath, wanting to cry. She was losing Chloe. Or rather she was losing one of their routines, when it was just the two of them. Jack had successfully infiltrated their movie night. If she stuck with the no, he'd still be there, his absence more pronounced than his presence would be.

What the hell was she going to do?

Jack hated putting them on the plane. Hated being away from them for what he knew would be an interminable week of loneliness.

Spending the night with her in his arms reminded him just how much he loved her, needed her in his life. He was going to be living for the weekends, just like he had when they were in college, in separate cities with miles between them. Fridays would become family night with Sundays devoted to his mother. He'd have to strive for a balance between the two and, putting as much effort into his time with Nell as he could. It might be easier than he'd anticipated. His mother had lightened up about Nell. Now her attention was on Chloe, wanting to meet her, make her part of their Sunday brunch. He was still stalling. Still unsure it was a good idea. He never knew what his mother was planning and even though she seemed sincere, he wasn't sure he trusted her to do as promised.

Swiping his phone on, he dialed her number.

"Hello, Jack. How was your swearing in?"

It was the first time Eloise hadn't been invited and she was taking it better than he'd hoped.

"It went well. I think Chloe got a sense of the historical context. I wanted to ask about something."

"What?"

"Do you remember anything about Jamie Warren's death?"

"Oh God. Yes. It was horrible. That poor woman losing her child like that."

He was taken aback. Eloise had very few good things to say about Merry.

"You felt bad for her?"

"Of course, I did. You're not supposed to bury your children."

"Did you know that's why the Warrens left?"

"There were rumors James was almost suicidal. He began drinking, stopped working. Then they were gone. One of the men in our circle of friends was a doctor on staff with him. He said it got bad, that Merry insisted they leave the area, contacted Doctors Without Borders and got him into the rotation."

Thinking out loud, this shifting the kaleidoscope crystals into a new pattern, he said, "She chose to save her husband by leaving her daughter alone."

"I believe you know how little I think of Merry Warren."

"I thought you felt bad for her."

"I did. It doesn't mean I still don't have a problem with the way she lived her life."

"Are you saying this was the reason that you disliked her?"

"What kind of mother traipses around the world with her husband, letting her daughter fend for herself? The girl was just a child."

"You treated Nell badly because of her mother's actions?"

"What kind of role model would Nell have had? I believed she'd make a terrible mother for your children."

The truth. Finally uncovered. It was more than her lineage. It's what Nell's mother had done. He took a deep breath before he went on the defensive. Again.

"You were wrong, Mom. She made an excellent mother because of it. She'd never think of putting Chloe in a boarding school. Nell was alone most of her life. She was alone when Chloe was born, grappled with a newborn, school, work. And never once thought of abandoning her."

"Maybe so. I would have to meet this girl if I am to agree with your assessment."

"Putting stipulations on whether you could love Chloe or not will get you nowhere."

"I said meeting her could alter my opinion on what kind of mother Nell is, not whether I could love the child."

"We were the ones who walked away, Mom. We played the role of Merry in this story."

There was a long pause.

Had she hung up on him?

"Mom, are you still there?"

"I am. And although I don't want to admit it, you might be right. I might have made a gross miscalculation."

"One we're still paying for."

Before hanging up, his voice filled with regret, he said, "You know what she told me, Mom? That she'd hoped to finally have a family with us. With you. She knew how much you loved me, and she hoped that you could find it in your heart to love her, too. That you couldn't, hurt us all."

Not giving her time to respond, he ended the call. Let her think about the damage they'd done. He couldn't let himself off that hook. He'd let his mother's opinion color his decision, let his fear of the unknown determine his course. He should have spent his time and energy trying to bring the two women he loved together. Instead he'd made it into a competition. He'd never made it clear where Nell fit in his life. She hadn't been the loser. He had.

The next two weeks flew by. He'd gotten back into his work routine, playing squash every morning with Ron, getting to the office to read the newspapers, checking Twitter for any new updates, meeting with his staff to discuss the day's committee hearings and votes, and caucuses. He belonged to a few and it was one of the only places where there was a possibility for bipartisan agreement on some key issues. There were ongoing discussions about the impact of ACA repeal before members from his party drafted a memo to the Speaker, outlining their opinion. He greeted constituents who dropped by for a tour, attended meetings on Syria and the Russian hacking debacle, made it to the floor in time to vote on several bills that were supposed to provide more transparency and accountability. That wasn't their underlying agenda. There would be rollbacks on common sense regulations that the Republicans thought overburdened business. What happened to representing the people? Wasn't that their job? Allowing factory owners to release refuse, with less oversight, less regulation, would result in the pollution of rivers and streams. Didn't people have the right to clean drinking water? Hadn't Flint taught them anything?

His days were filled with hearings, fighting cuts, and cabinet nominations. His days didn't end until late at night, with him eating dinner on the fly or at some scheduled event.

Friday nights became his focus, his prize for getting through the week of bitter partisanship. He loved watching mother and daughter together, the closeness, the love that emanated between them. At times, he felt like an outsider.

Was this what Nell had felt when he was with his mother?

There was a difference. Nell and Chloe didn't go out of their way to make him feel it. It was the result of missing so much of their lives.

Another recess interrupted his workflow in DC, but he made the shift back to his district with a renewed sense of energy. His calendar was filled with more local concerns, homelessness, violence in the workplace, against women, environmental issues, immigration, VA hospitals, and family aid. He spent most of his down time with Chloe, building memories, giving Nell the opportunity to work without guilt. He opted to skip the inauguration, walked in the Women's March with them.

With so much togetherness, the whispers started in earnest about his relationship with Chloe.

They decided it was time to make it public. There wouldn't be a formal announcement, but Chloe would be able to call him Dad without worrying who was listening. They were even talking about adding his last name to hers.

"I kind of like it. Chloe Adele Warren-Adams. It's kind of like Em's name. I always thought it sounded so international."

Jack laughed.

"Yours is far from international. You are so home-grown American your roots have roots."

He was cooking with Chloe every free night he had, and at the mid-way point in his recess, they were at his place, trying out a new recipe she'd found on Pinterest. This had become one of their favorite pastimes.

"Mom's going to love that we're making her pizza."

"I'm not sure this particular kind will satisfy her pizza tooth."

"She liked the Alfredo sauce we made last week."

Chloe was spreading the sauce on the shell with a brush. The shrimp, parsley, and spinach were ready to add, the oven already set to four hundred degrees. They were making one to eat here and one for Chloe to take home. Nell had only been over once during the recess.

He'd been hoping she'd feel more comfortable as time went on. Was it the press keeping her away? Once the lid had been lifted on Chloe's paternity, Nell was questioned about their past relationship and she didn't like the attention it was drawing. She also told him, now that the information was out there, there was no longer any reason for the pretense of being together. He'd accepted her withdrawal with little discussion. He was going to have to change that.

"What are we going to do this weekend?"

He glanced up from his laptop. He was working on the speech Ron had sent for the Veteran Affairs dinner he was attending tomorrow night.

"There's Chocolate Festival I thought might be fun."

"Um, yeah. Anything having to do with chocolate is always a good choice."

As she spread the shrimp on the pizza, he asked, "Do you want to invite Keileh to come with us?"

"I don't know. With her mom in Iran, her Dad has been a little protective. He's worried about what's coming and doesn't let her out much."

He didn't want to admit it, but he was, too. There was a shoe hanging somewhere, he could feel it, but he had no idea when it was going to drop. It could be sooner than Samira's return. It was unsettling all of them.

"Do you want me to call her Dad? See if there's anything we can do for them?"

"You're in Congress. You should be able to do something."

She placed the pizza pan on the bottom shelf of the oven, closed the door and set the timer.

"I'm in the minority. Remember?"

Taking a seat opposite him, her leg tucked under her body she said, "That shouldn't pre-determine the outcome."

"I know. But it's come to that."

She'd started drawing a pattern on the tablecloth with her finger.

"Do you think Mom will come with us?"

"I don't know. We can ask."

He had a sneaking suspicion she was going to give what had become her standard reply.

CHAPTER THIRTY

Jelani stuck her head in.

"Hey, you. How you holding up?"

Nell put her pen down. She'd been trying to go over one of her files, but she found her mind constantly wandering to Chloe, where she was, and what she was doing.

"I've been better. He's got her all the time lately. I have to make an appointment to see her."

"Don't they invite you along?"

"Yes, but we're not a family. I think someone has to remember that."

Jelani came in and sat down across the desk from Nell.

"They're just trying to play catch-up."

"That's what I keep telling myself, but they seem to have so much fun together. I'm not the fun one."

"You're the one who's taken care of her all her life. She won't forget that, Nell."

She sat back, the swivel chair moving slightly to the left. She righted it with her foot.

"You should see the meals she's bringing home for me. That's what they do every day. Cook. How can I compete with that?"

"Has it become a competition?" It would seem she was doing it again. "Why do I do that?"

It shouldn't be a rivalry. They were co-parenting. But didn't that mean equal time?

She was acting like a kid fighting for her parents' attention, Jack as their stand-in.

"Do you want to go for a drink before you head home? Talk about it?"

"No, but thanks. I've got to go over some of my notes for the deportation hearing tomorrow."

"You know, Nell, you could give it a rest one of these nights. You don't have to work so hard."

"That's what Jack used to say to me when we were in college. He was one of the few who could get me to put work aside. Chloe was the other. Now? I can't go with them, and I don't want to curtail her activities when he's in town. There's a reason I work."

"To forget?"

"To focus on the things I can change, not the ones I can't."

"You wouldn't consider easing back into the relationship?"

"Why? The reason he's back in my life is because of Chloe. It has nothing to do with me."

"Are you sure?"

She hadn't been when they were sleeping together. With Chloe at his place so much, those nights were gone. And he hadn't given her any indication he wanted them back. Her natural inclination was to step back, and he'd let her

Then why does he invite you to go everywhere, with them?

They had dropped the pretense of dating as more and more people realized the truth. It hadn't hurt his career in the least. In fact, it was making him even more popular.

"I'm only sure about one thing. I lost something the day I introduced them."

"I think you lost your heart a decade ago. I'd think you'd want to reclaim it."

Her cell rang and when she picked it up, she smiled.

"Hi, honey. What are you doing?"

"Making you a pizza."

Her heart swelled.

"Want to come over and eat with us or do you want me to wrap it up and take it home?"

She glanced up to see Jelani studying her.

"I was going to leave soon to pick you up. I guess I can eat with you before we go home."

"Cool. We'll keep it warm."

"I should be there in fifteen minutes."

"I love you."

"Love you, too, Chloe."

Swiping to end the call, she looked up.

Jelani seemed happy with her decision.

"You need to see if this will work, Nell. You've never gotten over him. It seems he wants into your life again. Nothing is getting in the way. Go for it."

"I'll think about it."

"I think you've already done that. You *are* joining them for supper."

"It's pizza. You think I want to wait until I get home to have some? I'd have to smell it all the way there."

Jelani got up when Nell did. After packing up her briefcase, buttoning her coat, she headed out the door, flicking off the lights as she did.

"See you tomorrow."

"You will. And Nell, give them both a big kiss. Let them know you're glad to see them."

When she arrived, she gave Chloe a big kiss. All she could manage with Jack was a smile. He looked too good and one small kiss wouldn't satisfy the deep need for something more. He didn't dress in jeans that often, but when he did, they were always pressed and neat. Tonight, he was looking more disheveled than usual, his long sleeve Henley a change from his button-down shirts.

"What?"

Jack was looking at her expression.

"I've never seen you...un-ironed."

"Yeah, well I don't have live-in help anymore. I don't own an iron and wouldn't know what to do with it if I did. Do they look bad?"

"I kind of like the look. You seem more human, less...perfect."

He leaned against the counter and gave her a sparkling smile.

"You thought I was perfect?"

She took her coat off and hung it on one of the chairs in the kitchen.

"Didn't say that."

"Then what are you saying?"

"You were always dressed to impress. I never knew what was real and what wasn't."

The smile faded. His expression became serious.

"It didn't help that I never told you."

"No, it didn't."

Chloe had been listening and asked, "Why don't you both sit down. I've got this covered. Unless you want to get the drinks, Dad."

He moved to the refrigerator, pulled out a bottle of wine and a water.

Opening one of the cabinets, he collected two wines glasses and poured.

"You seem to have stocked up."

Last time she was here for dinner he had just moved in and all his cabinets were empty.

"This week helped. I spent a lot of time shopping around, checking things off the list that Chloe made of things I needed."

Chloe let him in on a secret.

"I made up the list by looking in our cabinets. Mom might not cook but we always have everything on hand as if she did."

He handed her the wine and said, "Cheers."

"To what?"

"Your being here. I wasn't sure you'd ever accept another invitation."

"There's no point anymore. Chloe's out of the closet."

His brow furrowed.

"Is that all it was?"

Concentrating on remaining detached, she took a sip of her wine and said coolly, "I thought that's what we agreed to." She raised her eyes to find him watching her and the quakes started just along her spine. How did he still do that to her?

"Enjoying my company was all a pretense?"

"No...that was real."

"All of it?"

She knew what he was asking. With Chloe here, he couldn't come out and say it.

It seemed he didn't need to because Chloe seemed flustered and refused to look up at either one of them as she set the table.

"Can you guys stop with the coded talk. I can't even."

I can't even? Nell and Jack mouthed the words at the same time.

"You two are so lame. It's an expression that means..." She rolled her eyes. "Never mind. Time to eat."

Nell dropped into the chair and bent her head to sniff. Then picked up a piece and took a bite. She brightened up. Chloe had suggested this might not be her thing. It was very much her thing.

"This is good."

After chewing, her expression almost looking bliss-like, it fell when Chloe said, "We're going to a Chocolate Festival on Saturday. Will you come with us?"

"You don't want time alone with…"

"We get lots of time alone. I want to spend the day with the two of you. I'm not asking if you'd *like* to come with us, I'm straight out asking you to come with us."

Throwing caution to the wind, the pure pleasure of being with them both too much to turn down, she said, "I would love to."

As soon as they got home from her Dad's, Chloe kissed her mother good-night and went into her room. After climbing into her pajamas, she scooted under the covers with her phone and dialed her friend. Things were tense at the Hamade house and Keileh was scared with her mother out of the country. She was watching the news, following Twitter feeds about the possibility of a travel ban, and venting all her fears to her friend.

When Keileh answered, Chloe asked, "Have you heard anything?"

"Yes, she's booked to come back in a week."

"That's great. Then you can stop worrying."

"I won't stop worrying until she's home. Have you heard anything?"

"No. Mom's set to move if anything goes down. She's been tapped to write a request for an execution of a stay. She's already met with a couple of other lawyers on the language."

"And your Dad?"

Chloe still didn't know where he stood on the issue, but she had some doubts about his willingness to help. It was the only thing preventing her from trusting him full out. She wouldn't be able to get beyond his problem with open borders.

"He keeps saying his party is in the minority and there might not be anything he can do. It'll have to be at the local level."

"I think we're too young to know this much about what's going on."

"I think you're right."

"What's your news?"

"My mother is being so stubborn. She finally agreed to come with us to the festival but she's not co-operating at all. I practically had to beg her. I don't know what more to do to get them back together."

"Are you sure you should be doing that?"

"You've seen them together. They are so fricking cute. And I know they still love each other. They don't say it, but the way they look at each other, it's crazy."

"If they want to be together, Chloe you should let them get there on their own."

"It'll never happen if I leave it to my mother. She so doesn't trust him. I think it's time she did."

"I don't think that's up to you. Is it?"

"No. But, Keileh, I want this so badly. I love them both so much and I want to be a family."

"I know you do, Chloe, but you wanted to know who your Dad was. You got that. Why are you pushing for something more?"

"I thought knowing would be enough. Until I saw them together. My mom needs someone to love her. She's been all alone most of her life."

"I know that makes you sad but it's her life Chloe. You should let her live it."

"I'll give it one more week. If I can't get anywhere, I'll give it up."

"I hope the week goes like we want it to."

"Me, too. I'll see you tomorrow."

"Good-night."

Chloe ended the call and lay in bed thinking of different things she could do over the next week to guarantee the success of her plan.

⌒

Jack stood in his kitchen, wiping down the counters. Chloe had cleaned like a pro, so he didn't really need to put any energy to it, but he needed to stay busy. He felt the emptiness creeping into the condo one small inch at a time. His females had left about a half hour ago and he was still trying to figure out how to get Nell to give them another chance. Dinner had been nice. They'd talked about everything and it looked like she was poised to be one of the agents of change if a travel ban was put in place. It didn't surprise him. She had the experience with the courts, she had the trust of the immigrant community, and she knew some of the judges who would decide the case. He was impressed time and again with her legal mind. It was Chloe's expectations that had him unsettled. She was counting on him to be in their corner if it all came to a head, but he was still on the fence. Getting to know Keileh had put a face on it. His opinion wasn't as clear as it used to be. Samira Hamade was a surgeon. She was an upstanding member of the community. If they put a ban in place, the country would lose some its best health advocates. Did it really matter where she was born? What her religion was? Why would it be fair for Keileh to lose her mother when neither had done anything wrong? Samira was a green card holder, was on the list for naturalization, had two children born American citizens, was married to one.

He knew he couldn't pick and choose who crossed borders on an individual basis.

His hand stilled at his task.

Wasn't that what they were already doing? Isn't that what the vetting process was all about? The government's failure to keep his father safe wasn't open borders, it was not vetting who it let in.

Big difference.

He was going to have to pick a side soon. Not only for Chloe's sake but for the sake of his constituency.

And Nell.

He wouldn't stand a chance with her if he fought her attempts to get a stay.

Talk about being on opposite sides of the aisle.

He also couldn't ignore his conscience.

Or maybe it was his anger still rearing its ugly head.

He'd have to wait and see what happened. His decision might have to wait until they were, in the midst of the emergency. Until then, he was concentrating his time and energy on the woman who he wanted back. She consumed him in a fire that was unremitting. He felt it spark every time she walked in a room, and it was getting harder and harder to see her walk away.

CHAPTER THIRTY-ONE

Chloe's week was almost up, and she hadn't gotten as far as she would have liked. They'd gone to the Chocolate Festival together, and it seemed as if her parents had enjoyed the day as much as she did, but since then, her mother had gone all detached again. Tonight, would be her last attempt to get them to re-unite. Her father was coming over for their Friday movie night. Her mother was in a particularly prickly mood even though she'd offered to have pizza for dinner.

"Whatever you want is fine."

"I called Dad. He's picking up your favorite."

"Good for him."

"Mom come on. Can't you just enjoy it?"

Nell had stopped what she was doing and glared at her.

"No. I can't. Why do you keep insisting we share this night? It used to be our time Chloe. Don't you have enough time with him to give me this?"

She hadn't expected this kind of reaction. Her mother rarely got mad at her, but she was feeling angry herself. Her mother was being so selfish.

"I...I think of this as family night."

Using a carefully, controlled tone, Nell said, "We are not a family. What part of that don't you understand?"

Chloe marched right into her mother's personal space and yelled, "We could be if you weren't so stubborn."

Her mother laughed. It wasn't a pretty laugh it was an angry laugh and it scared her. Maybe she'd gone too far. Maybe she should have given her mother equal time, maybe she shouldn't have kept inviting Jack over or insisting she be with him.

When the doorbell rang, she scrambled to answer it, unsure what to do or say to explain the way her mother was reacting.

Jack walked in, the pizza in hand, the smile quickly losing some of its warmth when he noticed Nell. She was getting her coat on, grabbing her pocketbook.

"I'm done with this. You win. Again. Keep Chloe with you this weekend. I'm going to be unavailable. I'll pick her up on Sunday night."

And with that, she slammed out of the condo without looking back.

Chloe raced out after her. "Mom, I'm sorry. Please come back."

Her mother never answered her. She proceeded to her car and pulled out of the parking lot with minimum care.

Jack was standing beside her, outside the complex, his arm around her shoulder.

"What just happened?"

"I screwed up."

"How?"

She started to sob. It finally dawned on her she'd been ignoring her mother and her feelings. Nell had never walked out on her like this before. She'd never let her anger come between them.

"I was trying to get you two back together."

"By forcing things with your mother?"

She was nodding, the tears sliding down her cheeks.

"I shouldn't have done that. I don't want her to be mad at me."

"She'll get over it, Chloe. She loves you too much to stay angry."

Glancing over to him, his features set in stone, she began to cry again. She'd come to love him, but he wasn't Nell. She wanted her mother. She was afraid she'd lost the only one she could count on to be there.

He drew her back into the condo, but the movie night was put on hold. Neither was in the mood for a light-hearted romance.

Jack was more than upset. He couldn't believe that Nell had just dumped Chloe with him. She didn't do things like that. She was not like her mother. This had to be his fault somehow, but for the life of him he didn't understand how.

"What were you two talking about when I got there?"

"She wanted our Fridays back."

He glanced over at her, the tears streaming down her face making him more than uncomfortable, but he had to ask, "Is this the first time she told you?"

"No."

He glanced over again to find her looking at him.

"You've been ignoring how she feels?"

Her face crumpled.

"Yes."

People had been doing that since she was six. He shook his head, knowing how much Chloe's actions must have hurt her.

"I wish you had told me."

"I do, too."

"She deserves her Friday nights with you."

Sniffling, Chloe agreed.

"Your mother's strong and smart and independent. We take that for granted. We forget sometimes that she has needs just like we do."

He handed her the box of tissues and she blew her nose, held on to the sodden mass. Her chin was trembling when she wailed, "I want my mom."

He was patting her leg, not knowing what to say to make this better. He was way out of his element here.

"I know. I'm sure she'll call you. Never doubt she loves you."

"I don't but she must be doubting I love her. I don't want her to feel like that."

She hiccupped a long sob.

Uneasy worry filled him. Did Nell feel she was in another competition? This time Chloe's affections the prize instead of his? He was the common denominator in each case, so there was something he was doing wrong, and he thought he might know what it was. He'd been going along with Chloe, knowing it wasn't the best way to handle the situation. He wanted the same thing. Problem was, neither one of them was giving any consideration to what Nell wanted. Every time Chloe put something in place that would bring them together, he took advantage of it, no questions asked. Just like he had last time, hoping it would all fall into place, denying there was even an obstacle to overcome. Ignorance wasn't bliss, it was just insensitivity in different clothing. He'd never told her the important things, how he felt about her, that they had a future, that he'd figure it all out if she was with him.

He was repeating the same pattern.

What was he waiting for? For her to declare herself? What was he expecting her to say? Come break my heart again? Without thinking, he'd done exactly that. She thought he'd taken Chloe away from her. Something he'd promised he'd never do. Did she think that was the reason he spent so much time with their daughter? That she didn't fit into the equation? It's how she'd felt before. How he'd made her feel.

Herding Chloe into the car, he set the intention he would tell her everything that was in his heart. She was going to know that he loved her, body and soul. What she did with the information was anybody's guess.

Once he'd opened the door to his place, Chloe was running downstairs to her bedroom before he had a chance to say anything.

He tried calling Nell as soon as Chloe had disappeared, but he was unable to get through. Leaving a voice mail, he asked that she get back to him, said that Chloe was a mess and needed to speak to her and that he did, too. He wanted to tell her all the things he'd forgotten to say: that he'd known since the day she opened her dorm door the night of their first date that they belonged together, that he wanted to be the one to hold her, dry her tears when she lost a case, that he was tired of circling the rotary of regret.

At midnight, he still hadn't heard back.

⌒

Nell called Em as soon as she left the condo. She was the one she felt might be home on a Friday night. There wasn't a chance in hell Jelani would be.

"Hi. What's up?"

The tears that had all but choked her as she ran out came flooding out.

"Can I come over?"

"Of course. What's going on?"

"Chloe... I've ...She's with Jack."

"I'm here waiting for you. Hagen Das or something more lethal?"

"More lethal."

"I have some Skoli."

"On ice. I'll be there soon."

With every passing day this week, she'd begun to feel smaller and smaller. It was how invisibility worked. You became less and less of yourself, detached from the pain, crawled inward like a turtle in its shell. Chloe wanted Jack over her and the ache that came with that realization throbbed mercilessly. What was she going to do? Give in and let it happen, or fight as if it was the battle of her life? She wasn't giving up this time, wasn't walking away. She'd give up some of her cases, spend more quality time with her, learn to cook if she had to. She'd done more difficult things than that before to keep it together. She would not let Jack win this round. She'd beaten him before, and she knew she could do it again.

And as soon as she got to Em's, she fell into her arms, sobbing for another love lost.

After a restless night, she sat on the couch waiting for it to be late enough to call Chloe.

Em had loaned her a pair of leggings and a long-sleeved tee, which she guessed belonged to her friend Nick. It was too big to be hers. Sipping her coffee, the black pungent taste helping her conquer the queasy stomach from too much Skoli, she flicked on the tv and every cell and organ sobered up.

He'd signed the travel ban into effect as of late yesterday afternoon.

Rifling through her things to find her phone, she powered it up to find over a dozen missed calls and several voice messages. Most from either Chloe or Jack. Then she found the one she was looking for.

Finding the contact number, her fingers fumbling as they hit send, she waited for him to pick up.

"Siraj. I'm sorry. I..."

She didn't want to go into a lengthy explanation why she'd shut her phone off. It had been the first time since she joined the firm and she swore she'd never do it again.

"I was unavailable last night."

"She is sitting on the plane, still. They will not let anyone debark yet. They are trying to find a place for them to sit and wait. What if they send her back?"

"They won't. Not if I can help it. I'm heading home to change, and I'll be at the airport as soon as I can get there. I'll find her, Siraj. I won't let them send her back."

"Thank you, Nell. I know if there is anyone who can stop this foolishness, it's you."

Ending the call, she called out, "Em, shit's hit the fan. I have to go."

With a quick thrust of her head out the bathroom shower, Em asked, "What's happened?"

"Travel ban's in place. Airlines aren't allowed to let their passengers off. I'm going home to change and head over there."

"I'll be right behind you. Want me to call the others?"

"I'll reach out in the car. See you there."

Gravel spit in every direction as she pulled into her parking space. Scanning the area before she got out of the car, making sure that Jack hadn't kept Chloe here, she raced inside to change and was back out in record time. She'd already reached out to all her partners, and a couple of the lawyers she'd be filing paperwork with for a stay. Gunning the car, she headed to the airport.

Chloe's phone rang but it took her a couple of minutes to wake up and fumble for it. Looking at the time, she couldn't believe she'd slept in so late. Of course, she waited most of the night for her mom to get back to her. The call had never come.

With a groggy voice, she skipped Keileh's hello and got right to, "My Mom still hasn't called."

Keileh sounded frantic. "She's on her way to the airport."

Chloe bolted up, fear racing through her system. Was her mother leaving her?

"Why?"

As Keileh talked, part of Chloe relaxed. The other part let the fear run rampart for her friend's sake.

Her mother was still around, but Keileh's?

"If anyone can stop it, my mom can."

She felt the tears creeping back. She had let her mother down, something Nell had never done to her.

Never.

"Keep me in the loop. I want to see what my Dad's going to do."

"Okay."

Jumping out of bed, Chloe called out, "Dad, Dad did you hear?"

"I did."

He was watching the news, the chaos and confusion evident at the airports being covered by reporters.

"Mom's there."

He looked up at her, a somber expression on his face.

"How do you know?"

"Keileh's mom was on one of the planes that landed this morning. Passengers aren't allowed to get off. Some people have already been sent back. Can you do anything, like call someone at the airport? You're on the TSA committee, aren't you?"

"I am, Chloe, but I can't do that for one person."

"Why not? People get special treatment all the time."

"Chloe, I can't. Your mother—"

An angry snarl curled her lip.

"Yeah, Mom to the rescue again. And you're going to do nothing, right? Do you know not one of the countries where the hijackers were from are on the list? Why don't you do something about that if this is so important to you?"

The doorbell rang but he hesitated to answer it. He didn't need his mother to hear the fight they were having. It would reflect badly on Nell.

When it rang again, he had no choice but to open the door to see Eloise standing there.

"I came as soon as you called."

"Thanks. I didn't know who else to leave her with."

"It's my pleasure. I'll finally get to meet her although I would have preferred it be under different circumstances."

Chloe stood and gaped.

"What are you doing here?"

Jack was the one who answered, "I have to go to one of my offices. There's panic in the immigrant communities in my district and I should be a face for them. I couldn't leave you alone, and most of your mother's firm will be at the center of this crisis."

"You're leaving me with her?"

He snapped at her, fatigue and fear becoming a lethal mix.

"Chloe, show some respect."

Turning on her heel, she raced down the stairs. "I'm going to Mom. I want to be with her."

He stood at the top of the stairs and yelled down, "I can't let you do that."

"You just try to stop me."

Turning to his mother, he said, "Look, I'm sorry. She's not usually this rude. Her friend's mother is being detained at the airport, she expects me to wave a magic wand to release Samira due to my connections at the TSA, and she...did something that drove her mother away. She's not in the best head space, at the moment."

His mother asked, "What are you going to do about it?"

"I can't do anything except put out some fires and assign the best people to petition the court. I've already spoken to a couple of other congressmen

this morning. We've got a memo coming out in the next few days condemn-
ing the act."

"You're going to sign it?"

"Absolutely. He didn't run it by anyone in DOJ or Homeland Security. It
runs against the constitutionality and non-discriminatory grain of the country. If he didn't outline it as religious prohibition, then he'd be in less trouble
with the courts and my decision would be harder to make."

Chloe was running up the stairs, her backpack over her shoulder.

"I called Uber. I'm leaving as soon as the driver gets here."

He grabbed her by the arm as she raced by him.

"There is no way I am letting you go off alone with an Uber driver. Your
mother would have my head."

"I'm not staying here."

There was defiant gleam in her eye he'd never seen before.

When she tried to yank her arm out of his grip, he increased the hold.

"You can come with me, then."

"Why? So, I can sit around and watch you do nothing? I'd rather be with
my mother."

After releasing her, he began to pace, at wit's end, not knowing how to
handle this. He rubbed his temples, wondering if Nell went through this on
a regular basis. What would she do in this situation?

While he was trying to decide the best course of action, his mother offered,
"I'll take her, Jack. I don't think you're going to persuade her otherwise."

Chloe stopped and stared. At least she'd stopped threatening to leave on
her own.

"Why would you do that? I thought you didn't like my mother."

"Your actions remind me of my own, once upon a time. Passion can be all-
consuming, and it can cause us to have tunnel vision."

Jack looked at her, dumbfounded.

"I've never known you to be rebellious."

She met his eyes with her own, a small smile on her face.

"When my parents told me that I couldn't marry your father, I told them
to go to hell and went off anyway. I never regretted my decision."

What went unsaid between them was he could have done the same but
hadn't.

He wasn't making that mistake again and she knew it.

"You go to the office. I'll take her to the airport. Is there any way we can get through to her to let her know we're coming?"

"She's still not answering her phone, but I'll keep trying her and Jelani."

Eloise clasped her hands in front of her.

"Chloe, I don't think we've been formally introduced. I am your grandmother and I am very happy to meet you. Now let's go. I have a feeling we're going to be seeing history in the making."

Jack watched them drive away, his heart in his throat. He had no idea how this was going to go. He'd gotten his mother involved. It might be the last straw for Nell. Was there a chance in hell she'd consider a life with him now?

Chloe was surprised by her grandmother's outward appearance. She didn't look like an ogre. She looked young for her age, well-put together, and her foot was heavy like her mother's. It wouldn't take them long to get to where they were going.

After using a tissue to wipe her nose, her tears having abated now that she was on her way, she announced, "My mother's a very nice person."

Paying attention to the traffic as she entered the on-ramp to the highway, Eloise said, "I've heard that. What did you do that you feel guilty about?"

Chloe looked out the window, not sure she could share this with Jack's mother, one of Nell's adversaries.

"I've been trying to get them together and my mother thought I was pushing her away."

Eloise glanced over, a questioning look, on her face.

"I don't understand how one would be related to the other."

"I made her give up my Fridays with her, included Jack in everything hoping...they'd..."

Her eyes filled up again. "I wanted to be a family."

In an all-knowing tone Eloise pointed out, "It backfired on you."

"Yeah. It did."

As if thinking, Eloise took a moment before admitting, "When I tried to manipulate them, it backfired on me, too."

"How?"

"I missed a whole lifetime with you."

Chloe swallowed hard. She didn't know what her mom was going to say when she saw Eloise with her. She hadn't thought this through well enough. Her main goal was to get to her mother, let her know she loved her and that she was sorry. Then she'd go wherever her mother wanted her to go. She watched the snarled traffic as Eloise wove the car through it, inwardly grateful that she didn't have to take the Uber. She was afraid of getting in the car with a stranger, but she wasn't going to let it deter her. When they pulled into the airport, Eloise parked in the overnight parking garage and they walked in together. The place was bedlam, voices raised, people trying to get through security, signs that protesters were already waving in displeasure.

"Chloe, wait. Why don't you try to get through one more time? I don't know where she is and it's not safe to roam aimlessly."

Chloe did what she asked. When she didn't get her mother, she tried Jelani. She answered on the first ring.

"Chloe, what do you want?"

Jelani didn't sound happy to hear from her. It stung.

"I'm here. At the airport. I want to see my mom."

"You're here? This is foolishness. Whatever possessed you?"

"She's not answering my calls. I need to talk to her, Jelani."

"I'll get her and have her call you. Stay where you are until you hear from her."

"I will."

Not five minutes later, her phone chirped.

Skipping hello, Chloe got right to her point.

"Mom, I'm so sorry. I don't want you mad at me."

"Jelani said you were here. Why the hell did Jack let you talk him into this?"

"He didn't. I called Uber."

"He let you get into a car with a stranger?"

There was a high-pitched squeal attached to the question.

"No. He wouldn't let me so...so...Grandma brought me."

"Grandma? As in Eloise?"

"Yeah, he'd called her to watch me. He had to go to his office, and he didn't want me there or alone."

"Where are you?"

Chloe scanned the area.

"I'm near the baggage claim. Grandma wouldn't let me go any farther until I heard from you."

"At least there is one smart Adams in the family. I'll be right there."

"Have you talked to Mrs. Hamade?"

"I have. We're close to getting her released. Your timing isn't exactly ideal."

"I'm sorry. If you'd just have called me back..."

Now there was impatience in her tone.

"I've been a little busy. I thought you'd understand."

"I need to talk to you. I love you, Mom."

"I love you, too. You know that. Don't you?"

"Yes, but I want you to know I love you back. All the way."

"I'll be there as soon as I can."

"Okay. I'll be here."

She waited what seemed like forever. Eloise waited patiently beside her, keeping an eye on anyone who got too close.

Then Chloe saw a familiar face amongst the crowd. She ran, throwing herself in Nell's arms.

Nell's heart was in her throat. Not wanting to breathe until she saw that Chloe was safe, she hadn't expected to be bowled over. She hadn't expected the tears or contrition either.

"I'm sorry."

Nell held her close, her hand running down the back of her head, trying to comfort and protect.

"I know baby. It's okay. It was my fault for running out like that. I was going to call you this morning but then this happened. After I got the call from Mr. Hamade, I didn't want to take the time to do anything but get here."

"I'm glad you're helping them. I knew you would. Jack's not doing anything."

She moved Chloe back to look in her eyes.

"Jack? What happened to Dad? Did you fight with him, too?"

"I asked him to call someone at the TSA. He said he couldn't."

Cupping her face, she said, "He was right. He can't. This is something that needs to go through the courts. Helping one person doesn't help the rest."

"But he doesn't care."

"Of course, he cares. His hands are tied right along with the rest of us."

It was then that she noticed Eloise standing to the side. Prepared for a disgruntled remark about Chloe's stubborn streak, she met it head on. What she got surprised her. It was a smile.

"Jack wouldn't let her come by her own means and I couldn't stand seeing her so upset."

"Thank you. I appreciate your making sure she was safe."

"She's my granddaughter." Nell noticed her puff up with pride. "She's got my eyes."

When Nell looked back at Chloe, she frowned.

"She's never been this recalcitrant before."

"She was afraid you were still mad at her."

"I didn't exactly handle last night that well. You know how it feels when you think you're losing someone that you can't afford to lose?"

"I do. I didn't handle that well, either."

There was a meeting of the minds and the tension that had settled over them disappeared as if in a stream of smoke.

Chloe tried to explain.

"I just wanted us to be a family, Mom. I never had that before. I thought you...and Dad...got along so well, and I kind of forced him to do things so you'd have to...be with us. I never meant to push you away or make you feel invisible."

Invisible?

"Who have you been talking to?"

In an attempt to get her mother to smile she said, "There are several sources but I'm protecting their identities."

"I don't have time to sweat the truth out of you, but don't think I'm letting this go."

Nell couldn't miss Jack as he barreled through the revolving doors, striding towards them with an expression she'd never seen before. It looked like panic.

"Nell. Mom. Is everything all right?"

Startled with his appearance, she was struck mute. It was Eloise who answered him.

"We're fine, Jack. But we have to get going so Nell can do her job."

Giving her attention to Nell, she asked, "Can I bring Chloe home with me? One of you can pick her up when you're done working."

She studied Eloise. Had they reached a truce of sorts? Had Chloe given them a reason to reach middle ground? All she knew for sure was she was happy Chloe would have somewhere to go.

"That would be great. I'm not sure how long I'll be. As soon as I get Samira released, I'm joining a couple of other lawyers to file the paperwork needed for a stay."

"She can stay as long as you need her to."

Jack told her, "I'll be done late this afternoon. I'm meeting with a couple of the state contingent to get the wording down for our letter to the president."

Nell couldn't take many more surprises this morning.

"You're what?"

"How he went about this was wrong. And I'm no longer on the fence about this. Chloe made a rational presentation to me this morning and I've taken her opinion to heart. I'm for extreme vetting but open borders."

"Well, will wonders never cease."

"I've got to let go of the past. I can't continue to blame everyone for what a few radical extremists wrought."

Nell hugged Chloe good-bye but before she turned to go, Jack went over and took her hand. "I know you've been pushing me away lately, but I think it's because you still don't know where you fit in my life. I should have told you this before, years before."

Nell licked her lips. Should she let him know that's exactly why she'd been pushing him away?

But before she could say anything, he kissed her. With her face in his hands, his eyes burning into hers, he said, "You *are* my life, Nell. Have been since the day I met you. Now go kick some Republican butt."

She backed away slowly, letting his words sink in, a smile blossoming on her face.

"I'll be back as soon as I can."

"I'll be waiting no matter how long it takes."

She left the three of them there, her step lighter than it had been in a long time.

And she did just what Jack had told her to do.

CHAPTER THIRTY-TWO

It took late into the night to get the paperwork filed with the federal court. A couple of other states were doing the same. Hopefully, a judge somewhere would stop this craziness. She'd achieved her main goal by getting Samira released and she was probably safe at home by now. It had been a long night and she was finally on her way to the condo, her bed and sleep uppermost in her mind. Jack's words were still reverberating in her heart and the nerve endings in her spine. He loved her if she was translating correctly. Wasn't that what *you are my life* meant?

He was hers, too, if she was honest. She loved him more than she'd thought possible. More now than before. He was gainfully employed in something that spoke to him. No more indecisiveness, no more ad nauseum discussions on what he should do. He was doing it.

And Eloise?

She was almost friendly when all Nell had hoped for was civil. Had she redeemed herself in some way? She still worked too much, still embraced her passion in ways that had turned Eloise against her. Now?

She was too tired to think it through. It would have to wait for tomorrow.

Once the door was opened, she stepped through, kicking her shoes off and leaving them. She couldn't be bothered with expending any energy that she didn't have to. She stopped dead in her tracks when she saw Jack standing at the edge of the kitchen.

"What...?"

"I thought you might be hungry when you got back. I made a couple of sandwiches while I waited."

He was like a mirage in the desert. Her thirst parching her throat.

"Where's Chloe?"

"At my mother's. They seem to be getting along, and my mother is extremely grateful you let her keep her." He was quick to add, "For the night, anyway."

"I'm grateful Chloe had somewhere to go. Eloise might not like me, but she seems fond of her granddaughter."

"I think she's had a change of opinion."

"Why? Is it something I've done?"

If so, she would have done it much sooner if it meant being with Jack.

"You stuck."

"What?"

"With Chloe. She thought you'd end up like your mother. The long hours, the independent streak, the stubborn refusal to change. For anyone."

"What did she think I was going to do?"

"Leave, put her in a boarding school, ignore her."

She saw his expression and read what it said.

"My mother taught me what not to do. I would never have left Chloe like that. I know what it felt like."

"I know. I should have been on the offensive. Instead, I just kept defending you to Mom, Mom to you, trying to keep the peace."

He took a step closer to where she was standing.

"I never told you that you were important to me. More important than my mother. I know it didn't always feel that way."

There were tears in her eyes and she brushed them away.

She was tired, emotional, wired.

He reached out and pulled her to him. She settled in and breathed.

"I meant what I said earlier, Nell. You are my life. I can't go back to before. Not now. Not after having spent so much time with you. I want us to get married, have more children, grow old together."

Her eyes fluttered closed. She wanted that, too.

"I know you're wiped out. Why don't you have one of the sandwiches, then you can sleep."

"I'm too tired to eat."

He scooped her up and into his arms and headed toward the bedroom. Once there, he began to undress her, first her suit jacket and then one button at a time.

His fingers moved slowly, and she felt the stirrings of that fatal attraction traveling down her body, electrifying every cell with each brush of his fingertips.

"You know I've loved you from the first minute you opened your mouth at that debate. I haven't stopped, not ever."

He was so close his breath tickled her face. The kisses were heaven, her heart beating thunderously in her chest.

"You were so much a part of who I was for so long I didn't realize how difficult it would be to go back to a time without you."

He slowly fingered her blouse off and let it fall to the floor before they moved to the zipper on the skirt.

"I shouldn't have let Chloe force you into being with me, but I wanted it as much as she did. No, that's not right. I wanted it more. Part of the reason I was so fixated on meeting her was to get you back in my life."

He had moved the skirt down over her hips and it puddled on the floor. Pantyhose were next and then she was standing in front of him in her bra and panties, his fingers never idle, now moving across her bare skin and she shivered from the touch.

"You need to sleep. But I'm sleeping with you. I never want to be alone in a bed without you. I know I'll have to grin and bear it while I'm in DC. But I'll picture you in our bed in our home. I'll call to say good morning and goodnight. I want you to be the first one I talk to in the morning and the last one I talk to before shutting off my light. I need you. I need you so much."

He had pulled her close in his embrace, and she knew she had to say something. Between the exhaustion of the day and the way he was driving her crazy with his words, his body, and his mouth, she couldn't think straight. Couldn't put words into a cohesive sentence.

Could she trust him? Could she trust herself?

Did it matter?

"I love you, Jack. I was afraid to want it. Afraid you wouldn't want me, that I was meant to be alone."

"Nell, I want you. You'll never doubt it again."

His head dipped and he took her lips in his. It was the lightest of touches and not enough, so she deepened the kiss, tasting him again without reservation. It was like those first few months when it was new, exciting, satisfying.

He carried her to the bed, insisting that they wait but she was too ready to consummate this new commitment. He took her slowly; with such intensity she was afraid she was going to shatter into a million pieces and when she did it was the closest to heaven she'd ever come. They spent the night making plans, making promises, making love.

They next morning, they stood out on the stoop of Eloise's house. Too nervous to talk, Nell chewed her lip, still worrying over brunch and how it would go. The invitation had been extended early this morning when Jack had taken a minute from her arms to call and see how Chloe was doing.

Eloise had asked if they'd join them for Sunday brunch. She was hoping they could start a new tradition, a family-honored one. And she told them to "come as you are." The dress-up routine would no longer be a part of it.

When the door opened and Jack escorted her in, his jeans as wrinkled as ever, she held her breath, hoping Eloise wouldn't hold it against her. She'd chosen a better pair of pants, with a silk blouse. When Chloe came running towards her, wearing her ripped jeans and an oversized tee, she all but blanched. Until she saw Eloise.

There was a smile on her face and a twinkle in her clear grey eyes.

And she was dressed no differently than Chloe.

"Do you like the new me?"

She twirled in a circle.

"Chloe took me shopping yesterday and insisted I stop looking like a matron. I have to admit that these clothes are much more comfortable than my other ones."

Nell shook her head, not believing what she was seeing. Or hearing. Sun was streaming through the windows, the dark drapes drawn open, the atmosphere no longer a tomb.

Was this the same woman who'd made her life unbearable? Jack didn't seem as surprised.

"This is the mother I remember. I'm glad you're back."

"It's good to be back. Let's eat."

Brunch was wonderful. They talked about the upcoming fight for their democracy, Chloe's family tree project that was just about finished, where they might spend Nell's birthday, which was coming up.

It was the family that Nell had always wanted. One with a strong connection, with a shared past and present, and love. Eloise might not love her yet,
but she had a feeling that one more grandchild could do it.

And she was more than willing to take some time off to get the job done.
Jack had a way of pulling her out of herself, persuading her take time off to
laugh and have fun. No longer would work take priority. She didn't need accomplishments to make these people care about her and she no longer had to
bury herself, so she didn't feel the ache of loneliness. Growing old together
sounded like a good plan. One she looked forward to with relish.

Acknowledgments

This series *Fire and Ice* has become a labor of love. It's also become a release for some of my concerns. Research for the four books has brought me a better understanding of what it is to be a citizen and I'd like to thank the authors for their contribution to my "woke" perspective.

Women have made great strides recently and I want to thank all those who have stepped forward with courage to address harassment, inequality, and those who have shown the world a more compassionate way to act towards others.

As always, I'd like to thank my friend and reading guru, Bunny, for her patience and persistence. All my drafts are placed in her hands, and she never fails to give me sound advice and grounded encouragement.

I'd like to thank my editor, Amy from Blue Otter Editing, for her expertise. She has become a valued partner in my writing life and I don't know what I'd do without her.

Jaycee DeLorenzo from Sweet 'N' Spicy Designs has done it again. I want to thank her for her great work and the amazing covers she created for all four books of the series.

I'd also like to thank Joan Frantschuk, from Woven Red Author Services, who not only formats my work for eBook and print but who has become a valued resource.

And of course, I'd like to say thanks to my family. Jeff, Kait, Juan, Justin, Kathryn, Jaiden, Jakob, Jon-Christopher, Dominic and Liam. They surround me with the kind of love necessary for creating novels that touch the heart.

And to all who read my books, I thank you for taking time out of your life, to journey with me.

ABOUT FAITH

Faith O'Shea is a contemporary women's literature writer who loves writing about strong women and the friendships they build. She throws in a little magic, a little romance, and develops unique personalities, and what you get are characters who come alive on the page. She's found that strong women need more than a happily ever after.

Faith lives in a small town in Massachusetts with her husband Jeff, dogs Cooper and Molly, and Isis, the Egyptian feline queen. Her children live close and are a big part of her life. In her spare time, she reads, walks Coop, dabbles in all kinds of cooking, and takes time to play with her grandchildren.

You can visit her on Facebook and Twitter or find her through her website at www.faithoshea.com.

SKOLI ON ICE

Camille Bissonnette was an expert at filing asylum applications. It's why the FBI kept handing her high-profile emigres but the last time out, it turned ugly. She'd promised herself she wouldn't accept another but when the special agent in charge called her, she agreed to take the case. Did his being Russian have anything to do with it? Or was it because she hadn't learned anything, like how to say no?

Maxim Skolikovsky wasn't willing to give anything away, not even his real name. Where he came from, you didn't trust anyone. It could mean the difference between life and death and he'd seen that up close and personal. When the attorney assigned to him by the FBI came knocking on his door, he opened up to a lot more than he'd bargained for.

When Camille becomes his fighter, Maks begins to relax his guard but as she uncovers things that only a few people know, he begins to doubt he can trust her after all. With his life in the balance can he afford to cut her loose and if he does, can he afford to live without her?

CHAPTER ONE

November

He slid the plastic key into the slot and pushed open the door.

After calling out and hearing only the silence that enveloped the room, he took tentative steps across the threadbare carpet, into the darkness. The heavy drapes were covering the windows and the early-morning sun was being denied entry. Nina didn't like the light. It's where her monsters lived.

He felt his way to the bed, the smell arousing an unspoken fear. It was strong enough to cut through the thick, stale cigarette smoke. His fingers sought her form. When he found it, he groped, trying to distinguish where she lay. He snatched them back, the body he'd found wet and slick. Flipping on the lamp by the bed, he all but gagged at the picture illuminated in the shadows. Bile rose in his throat and he swallowed the foul taste down.

Nina lay on her back, the cut across her throat, deep and wide. Her head was barely hanging on to her torso. Blood was everywhere; on the walls, the body, the bed linens, the comforter, the rug. With shaking limbs, knowing there was nothing he could do for her, he searched the room. Everything was gone. Her computer, phone, satchel, purse, and the notebook she'd been writing in before he left. Unwilling to be found with a corpse, he hurried out, the door slamming shut behind him. There would be too many questions if he was found here, and it would give her murderers a shot at the mark they'd missed. If Nina hadn't sent him out on an errand, he could very well be lying in the same pool of blood. Shoving his hands in his pockets, the red substance evidence of where he'd been, he pushed the elevator button with his jacket and stepped in as soon as it swished open.

Leaning against the wall, as the rumbling cage made its way down to the lobby, he breathed in, trying to relax his nerves. It had the opposite effect and he started to hyperventilate. He squeezed his pocketed hands into fists, knowing they could be after him. And they would be if they knew he had most of her notes. If they knew what else he had, he'd be a marked man for sure. Once the doors opened, he was more in control and strode out as if he had nothing to hide.

Checking what was around him from every angle, he hurried out of the hotel and onto the busy street. As he tried to blend into the throng of pedestrians, he continued to glance behind him. There didn't seem to be anyone following him, but he couldn't be sure. There were eyes and ears everywhere.

He stopped in at a restaurant, one he'd never been in before, and made his way to the men's room at the back. He needed to clean himself up, wash the blood away, maybe get himself a stiff drink. He lathered up his hands, washed away the evidence, but no matter how much soap he used, he couldn't get rid of the stench. Yanking at the towel, he dried off as best he could, a sliver of red still beneath his fingernails. He washed again and again, feeling like he'd never come clean. Stealthily, he opened the pockmarked door, surveyed the area, and stepped out.

His hands were still trembling when he sat at the bar and ordered a vodka. He had to think. He had to figure out where to go from here. He looked around, paranoia settling in and he saw the enemy in every face his glance fell upon.

After shooting the clear liquid down in one gulp, he ordered another.

That's all the time he'd allow to calm his nerves.

Back on the street, he hailed a cab to take him the short distance to his apartment. He had to chance the stop, needing to collect the valuable material stored there. Then he'd head to the train station, hoping his luck would last, and leave the city. Death was everywhere, a war of terror being fought by those in control. And they were cunning. They rarely chose the most obvious dissidents, which kept everyone guessing, who would be next. Through the chaotic noise in his head, a picture of where he could go emerged. He knew what his next step would be.

Nina's editor would help him, he was sure of it.

After the stop, another cab.

Entering the clean and well-lit space, he walked the terminals, waiting for service to St. Petersburg. Train tracks dissected the area. He could hear doors as they slid open and closed, passengers getting on and off in the interim, talking loudly, announcements being made over the intercom, the outside traffic competing with whistles and engines, wind whistling through the doors as they were whipped open and slammed shut. He squashed his cigarette under his boot, the concrete littered with used butts, a garbage can nearby over flowing, with cans, paper wrappers, and Styrofoam. He pulled his coat more securely around him, the air thick with frost. He paced until the blare of the horn and the clacking train on the tracks alerted him that he would soon be aboard. As the engine screeched to a halt and opened its doors, he scrambled in and fell into the first available seat.

He was almost safe.

www.ingramcontent.com/pod-product-compliance
Lightning Source LLC
Chambersburg PA
CBHW061933170626
46813CB00006B/2381